WALTON'S CREEK

WALTON'S CREEK
Land of Our Fathers

by

RICKIE ZAYNE ASHBY

P.O. Box 238
Morley, MO 63767
(573) 472-9800
www.acclaimpress.com

Book & Cover Design: Frene Melton

ISBN: 978-1-956027-71-6 | 1-956027-71-8
Library of Congress Control Number: 2023946775

First Printing: 2024
Printed in the United States of America
10 9 8 7 6 5 4 3 2 1

This publication was produced using available information.
The publisher regrets it cannot assume responsibility for errors or omissions.

CONTENTS

DEDICATION

This book is dedicated to the memory of my maternal and paternal grandparents—Melvin D. Ashby and Eva Tichenor Ashby and Charles L. Fielden and Annie Myrtle Williams Fielden—and to my father, Alfred F. Ashby, and my mother, Lenora B. Fielden Ashby. My personal legacy of Walton's Creek was their gift. This book is also dedicated to my late brother, Lyndal B. Ashby, whose early years were inextricably woven into the fabric of the community.

ACKNOWLEDGMENTS

Book cover images by John Ward.

Drawings by Eric Lindgren and Joe Vick.

Author photo by Pat Vincent.

Leon Vincent and Tom Foster, Illustration Advisors.

Professor Charmaine Mosby, literary consultant.

AUTHOR'S NOTE

Dialect has played a vital role in human history, and vocabulary and grammar, then and now, differed from one community or region to another. The range of dialect is as diverse as the disparate geographical, nationalistic, ethnic, and racial components represented in a society. American immigrant groups struggling to adopt English developed a peculiar version of their new language that was commensurate with their cultural and linguistic background. The loss of dialect depletes our understanding of the culture that nurtured it.

The dialogue in this simple story of the Atlees and the Caughills is as close to authentic as I knew how to write it. By using genuine dialect, I hope to present the reader with fully faceted characters molded by the richness and complexity that common speech provides. Jesse Stuart scholar Mary Washington Clarke said it best when she wrote that the language of pastoral people was born from the land. Henry David Thoreau was more prophetic when he wrote "...those who have not learned the ancient classics in the language in which they were written must have a very imperfect knowledge of the history of the human race."

Many of the characters in this work are based upon members of my own family. I trust that readers will appreciate my attempt to honestly depict the most important people in my life.

A PROMISED LAND

We gaze across the valley
The sun slowly rising
On a calm uncloudy day
Is this where we are supposed to be?

Many acres along a creek
The sparkling water tickles our tired feet
The trees in exalted splendor stand
Is this where we are supposed to be?

Old ox drawn carts squeaked for many weeks
Our belongings stacked to the sky
The dogs' tails wagging
Is this where we are supposed to be?

A land in a wee valley
Hidden by a dark and bloody ground
And God said for all times,
"This is where you are supposed to be."

—R.Z. Ashby

Where It All Began

WHERE IT ALL BEGAN

THE YEAR WAS 1807 when wooden carts pulled by teams of oxen topped a small hill near the tiny stream called Walton's Creek.

Jake Atlee and his large family surveyed a landscape of 1,000 acres in a small valley that had been purchased from surveyor Matthew Walton.

The pristine area was what Jake called their Promised Land. It had been a long journey from Virginia, but the Atlees had finally found the land of their dreams and home for them and their descendants for over two centuries.

Jake declared that the Walton's Creek community is where God wanted them to always live. The book of Isaiah was prominent in the minds of the Atlee clan. The 1000-acre survey was indeed their land of milk and honey.

Jake Atlee knew well the words in Genesis: "... to your descendants I have given this land." The Atlees would still call Walton's Creek home well into the 21st Century. If they did not live in the area, sons and daughters would carry the idyllic homeplace in their hearts forever.

Jake helped establish a church and school with portions of his survey. A community would bind around these institutions.

After 200 years, Jake's descendant, Mickey Atlee, preserved in his memory many generations of family oral traditions. A nostalgic return to Walton's Creek during a Memorial Day weekend unleashed a flood of those memories about Walton's Creek. Mickey recalled that his own father had echoed their ancestor's charge about always residing in Walton's Creek. He concluded that it was still a Promised Land, and it would live in his heart forever.

Book One

A WONDROUS REQUIEM

Where the Creek Still Flows (2008)

WHERE THE CREEK STILL FLOWS
(2008)

MICKEY TURNED HIS green Toyota Tacoma off the highway and drove slowly along the narrow gravel Carter Ferry Road. The country lane caressed one end of the Walton's Creek Cemetery for about a hundred yards. The graveyard had been recently mowed, with fresh flowers on about half the graves and American flags on nearly a dozen burial sites. The ancient sandstone markers of some Ohio County, Kentucky's, earliest settlers looked forlorn with very few decorated for Memorial Day. Mickey recalled visiting the graveyard as a youngster when many of the graves still sported roses, peonies, and other heirloom flowers planted there by family members. In recent years this tradition had faded in favor of artificial flowers. Younger generations showed less time or inclination to follow time-honored customs, but Mickey made this pilgrimage once a year and knew he would do so as long as his health permitted.

The front of the Walton's Creek Baptist Church greeted Mickey as he eased his truck onto the long driveway that approached the small building erected soon after he was born. Walton's Creek Church was established in 1814 on land purchased from Mickey's paternal ancestor. Throughout the 19th Century, houses of worship and schools were modest log structures. The current building glistened with new vinyl siding and green carpeting on the steps leading to the front door. The church looked so new that a stranger could scarcely guess its age or its long history. The original congregation consisted of some of the county's first citizens and mentored numerous other churches in the area.

The tombstones in the cemetery faced the church with silent reverence, while the backs of the headstones disregarded the traffic on the road in deference to the symbol of life's perpetual promise; the church stood as a gatekeeper to eternity. The marriage of church and cemetery is a custom across the rural Southern landscape but rarely seen in towns and cities.

The truck's front bumper came to rest a couple of feet from a shade tree at the edge of the cemetery. Cars and trucks belonging to Mickey's family had been seeking the shade and comfort of the old tree for decades. Mickey turned off the engine, glanced in the rearview mirror, and swatted casually at a couple of strands of gray hair. The face staring back at him was starting to show the wear of nearly sixty years of life.

"Lostie, you forgot to remind me to get this ol' mop of hair cut yesterday."

The little Border Collie curled up in the seat beside him, tail thumping as she tilted her head to one side in an attempt to understand what he was saying. Mickey's father had always said that was the sign of an intelligent dog since "... a dumb dog don't care what yere sayin'."

"You had better get out and pee, Lostie."

The small stock dog bolted from the truck and squatted immediately in the gravel. Mickey exited the vehicle after the dog but in a more calculated manner. He was favoring one knee slightly, and his back was stiff from the long ride.

"OOOH, my aching bones. Pooch, why didn't ye make me stop on the way over here?"

The dog was not interested in anything her owner had to say. She was running from tombstone to tombstone sniffing intently. Mickey shook his head and laughed.

"That's it, go ahead and ignore me, you worthless pot licker—should have left you on the side of the road where I found you."

Mickey pulled a blue WalMart bag from the back of the truck. The sack contained one small wreath and a tiny American flag. He suddenly felt a pang of guilt as he remembered he should have brought flowers for more family members. His maternal grandfather, Jes Caughill, would probably growl about "... store-bought flowers ... damn money makin' racket." The thought of facing his grandmother, Myrtle Caughill, with such a meager offering was daunting. Myrtle had viewed the care of family members' graves as a sacred trust and would not be bashful about reminding her grandson of his failed responsibility. Mickey made himself a solemn promise to bring flowers for all family members next time.

Mickey removed the faded flowers from Ralph and Anna Atlee's graves and replaced them with the new wreath. For many years his father had rested in the gravesite alone. Today, after a separation of nearly fifty years, his mother now lay beside the man she had loved so dearly, in a community close to both their hearts.

Ralph Atlee had never been able to leave the Western Kentucky community of Walton's Creek for long periods of time. After all, it had been home to his family since before the War of 1812, and he never expected to live anywhere else. With her husband's death, Anna had been forced to move to town and start a new life, but home was always Walton's Creek. She often exclaimed that the twenty-three years she was married to Ralph Atlee were the hardest but the happiest of her life.

Marvin and Elizabeth Atlee were buried close by. Mickey's paternal grandparents had died many years before his birth, and a lifetime of family stories served as a substitute for memory; but Mickey always regretted that he had not known them. Uncle Tim and Aunt Kittie died when he was only five, and he had only a vague recollection of them. Uncle Al, a World War II veteran, and Aunt Polly resided a few yards away, their headstone highlighted by a small American flag provided by the American Legion. Near the edge of the Atlee section were the graves of Uncle Ray and Aunt Sally. Aunt Sally Marie, Ralph Atlee's only sister, was one of the kindest persons Mickey had ever known.

In the distance the remains of the old Atlee homeplace were barely visible as it rested a mile away on a hillside. Today, the canopy of trees hid any trace of the once beautiful old Queen Anne style farmhouse. Mickey wondered if the rugged old structure had finally met its demise. He decided to ask the present-day owners for permission to visit the site, realizing seeing the old home in ruins would be unbearable.

The grass was soft and thick as Mickey made his way across the graveyard. He stopped for a few moments at the grave of Uncle Jesse 'Blade' Caughill. His mother's brother was an avid outdoorsman who would never have been happy living in town. Mickey remembered his uncle frequently handing him a sack of firecrackers when he was a youngster, and after issuing a warning to not blow his fingers off, old "Blade" would stroll away. Uncle Jesse could be a devilish character but was often awkward in social situations.

Jes and Myrtle Caughill's grave was on the outer edge of the cemetery, about 150 feet from the highway. As a child Mickey was taught by his grandmother about not stepping on the graves of the departed and showing respect for the dead. Myrtle Caughill's visits to the graveyards were always long and tedious, as she strove to show the utmost respect for the dead. Mickey felt a renewal of his guilt for not bringing flowers to the grave of a lady who looked upon the final resting place of family members as sacred ground—he knew she deserved better.

The nearly forty-year-old headstone belonging to his cousin Jay Caughill looked almost out of place. Several years Mickey's senior, Jay was still listed as MIA in Viet Nam. There was no death date on the grave marker, and Mickey doubted one would ever be added. Jay had not shared his younger cousin's attachment to their rural heritage. For Jay, the better life was always somewhere else, and the Marine Corps was a way for a country boy to see the world and seek adventure. As he looked at Jay's grave, Mickey could still see the young man smartly attired in his dress uniform. He could not envision Jay as an old man since he had disappeared so young. Mickey wished his relationship with Jay had more closely resembled the paradigm posed by poet Robert Browning: "Grow old with me! The best is yet to be." If Jay could have grown old along with his cousin, he might have developed a closer bond to the community they both called home. Age had given Mickey a stronger appreciation for his rural heritage, and he often wondered if the same would not have been true of Jay. In more ways than one, time had stood still for Jay Caughill, as had the memory of him held for so many decades by family and friends.

When he remembered Jay, Mickey wondered if his cousin had been listening intently as he had been when the adults in their family had repeatedly shared their stories and memories; and he wished Jay had taken more fully to heart the lessons their mothers and grandmother had tried to teach them. Mickey realized that though he had not always fully appreciated these narratives, he understood the fragile nature of oral traditions. They could disappear with the passage of a single generation.

Mickey would never place flowers on Jay Caughill's grave until he was certain his cousin was dead. He shook his head sadly and walked away.

Mickey had held a lifelong admiration for his mother and grandmother's steadfast belief in honesty and integrity. They had told him that in dealing with people it is all about the "Big Eye and Little You." He could still hear his grandmother telling him that those who tell falsehoods or run people down are trying to make themselves appear more important than other folks. "Young man," she said, "it ain't hard knowin' that lots of folks act that way. The hard part is to not be that way yereself." Although Mickey never knew the origin of the philosophy, he learned this was indeed one of man's greatest weaknesses.

Mickey was a grown man before he recognized that much of the social and moral conscience he learned from his mother and grandmother was a direct result of the simple life lessons instilled in many generations of rural children by the *McGuffey Readers,* which instructed these youngsters from an early age that "Meddlesome Matties" were people who could not resist things that did not involve them. The lesson of perseverance was taught by "... if at first you don't succeed, try, try again." The men in Mickey's life had taught him much about what it was like to be a man in rural America. The women, however, had instructed him in the philosophy of life.

Mickey's father, Ralph Atlee, and his grandfather, Jes Caughill, were forever welded to his heart and soul. Jes, whose life was often painful and tortured, stood out as a determined patriarch committed and proud of a lifetime of hard work. Ralph, a quiet and sensitive man, was content to live on the land like his father and grandfather before him, despite growing evidence that his beloved way of life was slipping away. A line, often paraphrased from Shakespeare's *Hamlet,* best described Ralph: "... he is a man, remember him for you shall not see his kind again."

For most of his life, like his paternal grandfather Marvin Atlee, Mickey had pursued what can be learned in books. Marvin Atlee had loved knowledge as much as he loved the land. Over the years Mickey had come to realize that respect for the land is the greatest knowledge, and it provided him with an affinity for the grandfather he never knew.

Mickey circled the graveyard, stopping for a few seconds to place a flag on his great grandfather's grave. A Civil War veteran, his name was now only faintly visible on the tiny marker. Mickey looked across Carter Ferry Road to the location of the last one-room school at Walton's Creek. Until the 20th Century the school was on the same side of the road as the church. In 1904 the last school building was built at a new location. Unfortunately, the building was destined to spend much of its life empty. In later years it had been used as a tobacco stripping room, and eventually it succumbed to the elements and collapsed. Today the field was under cultivation, and no trace of the school could be seen.

Uncle Tim Atlee had carried a petition in a desperate attempt to save the school. In the name of progress—Tim explained—the school board was about to rip the heart out of the community. The countryside had experienced better roads, thanks to the New Deal's WPA highway projects; and coupled with the purchase of school buses, the consolidation of the tiny country schools with those in town was underway. Tim Atlee had fought a losing battle.

The last school at Walton's Creek had been a simple wood frame building. The school had two outdoor privies, one for boys and another for girls. The older boys carried water from a well on a nearby farm and in winter fired the stove that sat in the middle of the room. A bell housed in a tower on the roof summoned children to class. The boys and girls occupied opposite sides of the room. A recitation bench commanded a prominent place in front of the teacher's desk. A blackboard behind the teacher rounded out the school's meager resources.

Tim Atlee had also led the effort to build the present church building after the old church burned on Christmas Day 1949. He was concerned that Walton's Creek, which had already lost the school, was in danger of losing the church as well. He donated his own timber for the lumber and furnished labor to finish the structure. The rush to build the new church had forced the use of unseasoned wood, and the building would suffer structural problems over the years, but the church was saved.

The Atlees felt a special tie to Walton's Creek. In 1807 Matthew Walton, an early Kentucky landowner and surveyor, had sold 1,000 acres of land on Rough River to Mickey's paternal ancestor, Jake Atlee. The land for the church, cemetery and school was purchased from Jake and his descendants during the early decades of the 19th Century. For Mickey, this was a great source of pride.

Three years after the Lewis and Clark expedition to plot the opening of another frontier across the Mississippi River, Jake Atlee had moved his family to Walton's Creek, a sparsely populated area of the Kentucky frontier. For many generations the Atlees and their neighbors had lived an agrarian existence in relative isolation. Their tenacity to live a Spartan existence in a new land is what Mickey admired most about his ancestors.

Mickey spent a few minutes surveying the landscape of Walton's Creek. A few houses and some farming still existed, but most of the small farms and dwellings of his early childhood were gone. He saw hundreds of acres of reclaimed strip-mine land that remained in possession of the coal company and might never again be owned by individuals for farming or homes. This practice of separating the people from their land by those seeking coal and timber had often blighted the history of Kentucky. Today the land lay largely idle with only the cry of a crow echoing across the treeless terrain. In the future, land and industrial developers would be able to profit from the property, absent the annoyance of first removing the people.

Mickey headed back to his truck, started the engine, and sat quietly looking out at the cemetery, the church, and community that had meant so much to his family for nearly 200 years. His mother, Anna Atlee, was the last family member to return home. Mickey thought back to her final moments. After many months of being unable to speak, she greeted him that morning with a smile and a voice that was strong and precise: ". . . before you go to work, I want you to bring me fifty or so quart fruit jars in from the meat house, fill the wash kettle, and drag up enough wood for a big ol' fire. Mother's comin' up today to help me can apples." She closed her eyes, smiled, and quietly slipped away.

The truck engine was humming softly as it awaited Mickey's next command. His mind wandered for a few moments as he contemplated his family in the afterlife. Perhaps heaven for them was much like their lives on earth, except without the pain and suffering. In his mind he could see a newly plowed field on a bright summer day. A large, snow-white plow horse was lumbering across the field, pulling a walking plow. The man behind the plow was his father, but much younger and healthier than Mickey remembered. The horse was headed toward a group of people waiting at the end of the row: Uncle Tim, Aunt Sally, and Uncle Al.

Uncle Tim called out to his brother. "RALPH, get a move on. Ye been plowin' that little strip of ground since sunup."

"The women is up at the house a takin' up the bread right now . . . shake a leg. LORD help, I wish ye would look at the way ye laid off that furrie," laughed Uncle Al.

Aunt Sally Marie stood quietly with her arms around her brothers. Her broad infectious smile said all she needed to say. Mickey's father always said, ". . . that woman can say more by sayin' nothin' more than anybody I knowed in my born days." Down the road Mickey could see his grandparents, Jes and Myrtle Caughill, walking toward the group.

Myrtle was carrying an enameled white dishpan filled with green onions and radishes. Jes was balancing another container in his left hand filled with rhubarb pie. Jes's eyes were shielded from the sun with a hat as he used his right hand to pull out a pocket watch. Jes cleared his throat,

"You'll got dinner ready?"

"GOTTA bring yere own buttermilk, ol' man ... ain't got a drop," Uncle Al responded without looking in Jes's direction. To Mickey, the dinner table was so real that he could smell the food. His mother, Aunt Polly, and Aunt Kittie were busy filling it up with fried chicken, fresh garden green beans, corn, potatoes, cantaloupe, tomatoes, and cucumbers. The smell of fresh air and two large pitchers of iced tea highlighted a country feast. Unlike meals anywhere else, this dining experience was all homegrown.

The family took their seats around the table, and a fellowship that consisted of laughter, teasing, and even serious moments of conversation ensued. One place at the table was empty, and Mickey knew they were holding it for him—he could think of no better way to enter infinity.

Perhaps eternity was just as he had imagined. Maybe his father would teach him to plow with that beautiful plow horse, and they could go fishing with cane poles or stuff their mouths full of green sassafras leaves and, armed with some water buckets, head for the blackberry patch. To breathe air that always smelled fresh from a spring rain and to enjoy the fellowship of family and friends who never grow old or die—this was worth more than all the earth's treasures. Mickey had been fortunate to experience a snippet of this lifestyle in his youth. The memory of those days was a treasured heirloom that meant more to him than anything else in his life.

The image left Mickey as quickly as it had come. His foot was on the brake, and his hand poised to shift the truck into reverse. Lostie was standing on the seat whining and staring at him, with her tail wagging. Mickey had no idea how long he had been frozen in thought, but by Lostie's manner it must have been a long time.

"OK, girl, we'll go now ... I ain't crazy ... lay back down."

Mickey smiled at Lostie and rubbed her ears for a few moments. The dog had been a terrific companion since he found her half drowned on the side of the road.

After Lostie had curled up on the seat, Mickey shifted the truck into reverse. He drove slowly down the driveway as he took one last opportunity to reflect. He had no words to convey his feelings. He remembered reading that God cares little for medals or college degrees; he prefers scars. The occupants of Walton's Creek Cemetery, including the Atlees and Caughills, had scars in abundance. Their greatest accomplishment was in strength of character nurtured by a lifetime of hard work and adversity. The love they shared with other members of the community stretched from the cradle to the grave. The women were there to help deliver a new life, and the men were present to dig the grave when time on earth had ended.

Mickey pulled off the Carter Ferry Road and drove slowly down the highway about 300 yards. His right turn indicator was still blinking when the truck's front wheels made contact with the loose gravel of a narrow lane. A white farmhouse loomed a short distance away on top of a small hill. After visiting briefly with the owner of the farm, Mickey left his truck and Lostie by the barn and trudged along the barely discernible road leading to Grandfather and Grandmother Atlee's hilltop home.

The old barn behind the house had long since collapsed, but the once beautiful two-story Queen Anne style frame farmhouse was still holding off the effects of time. The house was probably built in the 1880s when Marvin Atlee was a teenager and had withstood over fifty years of neglect. The metal roof was starting to rust away and the back porch had collapsed, but the structure was only a few years past the time when it could have been restored to its past glory.

Mickey made his way with some difficulty to the front of the house. Large portions of several trees had fallen around the home, but none had dared touch this icon of a nearly forgotten era. The front porch was in poor condition, and the etched window glass that once adorned the front door was gone. Mickey was relieved that the glass had probably been removed since there was no broken glass in sight. He peered through several windows and was amazed to see that the interior was dry, and the floors still looked solid. The grate fireplace in the front parlor looked as if it could accommodate a fire.

The front and backyards still contained daffodils that may have been blooming on the property for well over a century. There was no evidence of any other flowers or shrubs among the weeds and broken tree limbs. The field leading from the front of the house was green with a cover crop and helped accent a beautiful view from the old homeplace to the highway and beyond. The Walton's Creek Church and Cemetery sparkled in the distance as the old residence continued to hold court over the once proud farm community.

Mickey could only imagine what life was like for the Atlee family when his father was a youngster. Marvin had maintained a large orchard of apples, plums, cherries, peaches, pears, and grapes that provided a bounty every year for his large family. Liz and Marvin Atlee were not wealthy, but they had a nice farm, a spacious home, and a way of life that to them was worth more than gold.

When Mickey returned to the rear of the house, he could see in his mind the scene by the porch when the family gathered to watch the High Sheriff take Marvin Atlee to the state mental institution. His mind raced back fifty years in his own life when his father, stricken by a cerebral hemorrhage, lay writhing in agony by the tractor. Those memorable events in the Atlee family had taken place less than a mile apart.

Mickey stopped halfway down the old road and looked back at the house. The old homeplace refused to die. The aging structure seemed to be waiting for the family to return so life could be as it had once been. Goose bumps popped up on his arms, and he resisted the temptation to look back again, as he sensed the house was calling after him. To see the old Atlee place again was thrilling, but he knew this was probably his last trip. To see the home faltering was one thing, but to see it reduced to a pile of rubble was quite another.

Lostie was watching for her master through the open truck door. She leaped from the cab and raced to meet him, her tail wagging with delight.

"Sorry you couldn't go, girl, but you would be a tangled mess of cockleburs. Hop back in the truck. We gotta make tracks."

Mickey pulled back on the highway and drove a few yards before making a right turn onto the Chandle Loop. He slowed down briefly to survey the remains of the Atlee Brothers slaughterhouse. His father and uncles had made a lot of country sausage in the tiny red building, but before it was torn away it had not been used for butchering since the early 1970s.

On either side, trees formed a thick canopy that allowed little sunlight to penetrate, blanketing the first 200 yards of the Chandle Loop. Near the end of the tree marquee Mickey eased the truck across a small bridge over Walton's Creek. The little stream was nearly obscured by trees and brush on both its banks.

28

The tiny branch known as Walton's Creek had its headwaters just above where Jes Caughill's place had been located ran, through the Atlee farm, and eventually emptied into Rough River a few miles away. The tiny creek that had seen the faces of Indians and pioneers had its origins seriously altered by strip mining but had survived it all. The creek had never been a major source of fresh water or fish and had not spawned a major town along its banks. It provided some natural drainage, but its major contribution was in lending a name to a community.

A few yards past the bridge Mickey came to the entrance of what had been the Billy Goat Road. The road currently served as a driveway for a brick home situated on the corner of the Chandle Loop and the old public road. A berm had been constructed just past the house and where another bridge had crossed the creek in Mickey's youth. The old Caughill and Atlee homeplaces could no longer be accessed from the Billy Goat Road.

Mickey put the truck into park as he contemplated how the road looked in his youth, when he walked it each day to and from the school bus. Twenty years before he had driven down a coal haul road that circled behind Grandfather Atlee's place, Jes Caughill's home, and his own homeplace. Locating a narrow steep drive that left the haul road down to the decrepit remains of the old Billy Goat Road, that day he had exited his car and tried to locate the remains of Jes and Myrtle Caughill's home. The landscape had changed, and he was confused, until he heard trickling water. The source was the remains of a 16-inch galvanized pipe that ran under the road. In Mickey's youth it had emptied into a ditch that split the driveway to the Caughill home. The water trickled out of the pipe and flowed past a few daffodils that Jes had obtained from nearby farms long since abandoned by coal industry operations in the 1920s.

Mickey looked at the old drainpipe for a few moments and then looked up at the coal haul road. His grandparents' home had disappeared under hundreds of tons of dirt and rock. A few yellow daffodils and a rusty drainpipe were all that remained, and the scene at the nearby Atlee homeplace was not much better.

Mickey made his way with great difficulty through the weeds, briars, honeysuckle, and countless green sassafras until he stumbled onto the old house where he was born. It had caved in and was not visible beyond twenty feet.

The heavy brush that Mickey had battled made him think of the twenty miles of growth Daniel Boone and his companions were forced to negotiate along the Rockcastle River in 1775. Mickey lamented that, unlike Boone, he forgot to bring an axe. The Atlee farm had once been a part of the Kentucky wilderness and had been converted to agriculture. In the 1920s it had been used by the Morrison Coal Company, abandoned, and once again grown up with brush. In the 1940s Mickey's father, utilizing a horse, road wagon, single man crosscut saw, and a double-bladed chopping axe, once again cleared the property for agriculture. The task must have been a formidable one for the small, wiry Ralph Atlee, whose son 30 years later would have difficulty just making his way across similar terrain. Once again, the land was reverting to its original state as nature reclaimed what man had put aside.

The old house was a pile of useless rubble but sticking out from the debris was a snowball bush that Mickey's father had rescued from the same abandoned farms that provided so many flowers on Jes Caughill's place. The bush was flourishing outside the bedroom window when Mickey was born. Mickey had found a board, dug a sizeable portion of the root, and taken it home, where the ancient shrub could occupy a prominent place in his front yard as an heirloom carried forth by another generation.

Those images cleared from Mickey's head, and he drove on down the Chandle Loop. In the distance he could see huge chicken houses near the old farm. A bulldozer, several years after Mickey's last visit, had effortlessly cleared the farm for a modern agribusiness pursuit. Jes and Myrtle Caughill's home could not be salvaged. It was gone forever. The coal haul road had permanently taken the domain, and no one would ever build a house and live out a life there again.

When Mickey exited the Chandle Loop, the sound of tires upon gravel gave way to the smooth hum of the truck's wheels on the blacktop of Highway 85. The truck moved smoothly through the gears as he accelerated. In the distance he picked up the image of three black buggies behind the house of a long deceased maternal relative. An Amish family had recently purchased the small farm located a short distance from the city limits of Centertown.

A neat garden greeted Mickey as he slowed down to survey the property. Leaning against a fence facing the road, three teenage boys dressed in hats, light blue long-sleeved shirts, and black trousers held up by suspenders waved as Mickey enthusiastically returned the greeting.

A hundred yards behind the youngsters a team of magnificent Belgian horses effortlessly pulled a hay wagon. A boy of no more than six years of age, dressed like his older brothers, was skillfully driving the team. Mickey laughed out loud as he imagined the chuckles of approval his father, uncles, and Grandfather Jes Caughill would utter if they could see once again a sight that was so common in their youth.

A mile apart in distance but a century in more abstract terms, an Amish family farm contrasted with a modern chicken production. The poultry operation was a business, but the Amish farm was more than a livelihood; it was a way of life. In fact, modern agribusiness pursuits reject the empirical nature of agriculture in favor of the more generic title of "producer." The frugal nature of the Amish farmer meant they could have it both ways. They enjoyed the way of life and made money.

Mickey pulled into the gravel parking lot of a tiny, modern day "Mom and Pop" grocery store in Centertown. The store was one of only two in the community and, along with a branch bank and a garage, the only businesses in town. Centertown once had been home to several stores selling groceries, hardware, feed, and dry goods. The town also had a livery stable, drugstore, barber shop, school, and a train station providing freight and passenger service. Centertown, a community of never more than 300 or 400 people, was located a few miles from Walton's Creek and had been a major shopping hub for country folks until recent years. In turn, farm families sold chickens, eggs, goose feathers, and other items to Centertown merchants.

Today the two stores in Centertown were missing the coal burning stoves, oiled wood floors, and meat cases. They served the town as little more than convenience facilities selling gas, soft drinks, coffee, cigarettes, sandwiches, and lottery tickets. The high prices and limited selection made them impractical as a primary shopping source. True grocery shopping by local residents was done in nearby Hartford and Beaver Dam, where a major portion of goods was sold in the Super Walmart store. The largest communities in the county had also fallen prey to the dwindling retail landscape. Many stores were unable to compete with Walmart and most hardware and farm implement business had shifted to the larger cities of Bowling Green and Owensboro.

Centertown seemed to exist only because it was too much trouble to go away. It was a place to live and nothing more. The proprietary rural economy that for so many years fed the retail businesses of the town had all but disappeared. All residents were forced to go elsewhere for part, or all, of their employment, plus goods and services.

When Mickey entered the store, a young female clerk had her eyes glued to a small television where Vanna White was turning the letters on *Wheel of Fortune*. Mickey suspected he could carry off half the store before she noticed. He wandered around for a few moments before selecting a bag of potato chips and a large bottle of spring water. A list of sandwiches on the wall caught his eye. Cold cuts were still made from rolls of ham, bologna, etc. Country stores had been selling sandwiches this way for many generations, and Mickey was delighted.

Mickey plopped his purchases down on the counter, but the young woman was still engrossed with Pat Sajak and Vanna and appeared not to notice. He waited a few moments before saying, ". . . Miss, I would like a sandwich of your Kentucky Gold barbecue ham with some mustard." The young clerk remained fixated on the television for a few seconds and then started walking slowly backwards to the sandwich area. Mickey was amazed that she was able to do everything without taking her eyes off the television, even for an instant.

The clerk plopped Mickey's sandwich down on the counter on top of a piece of wax paper. Mickey folded the paper around the sandwich before a fly could land upon it. He pulled out his wallet and watched with utter astonishment as the girl rang up his purchases without so much as a glance at either what he bought or the cash register keys.

"That'll be five dollars and eighty-nine cents."

"OH, Miss, I would like to buy one of your Styrofoam bowls. I need to give my dog a drink."

"Sorry, ain't got none."

"No, no, I see a big stack right back there. You sell chili and soup in them."

"NOPE, been sold out fer a week."

Mickey let out a sigh and handed the girl six dollars. She took the money and placed it in the cash drawer. Vanna White and Pat Sajak were waving bye-bye to the audience, and the girl was watching them like they were her own family members about to embark on a trip to Mars. She had either forgotten or ignored the fact that she owed Mickey eleven cents.

"Miss, I believe you owe me eleven cents."

"Thank you, sir."

Mickey dropped his head and laughed softly as he picked up his purchases and headed for the door.

"OH, by the way, Miss, the rats are eating your Twinkies."

"Thank you, sir. Come back."

Mickey was still chuckling to himself as he opened the truck door. He placed the sandwich and potato chips on top of a small cooler that rested on the front seat. Lostie immediately sprang up and started smelling the food.

"HEY, keep yere doggie paws off my lunch. I fed you before we left. Besides, I paid enough money for that stuff to retire the national debt. Now get on down here. I got you a drink of water."

Lostie bolted out of the truck cab and wagged her tail as Mickey unscrewed the cap from the bottle of spring water. He knelt down and slowly poured the water into his cupped left hand. The dog was thirsty and drank a quart before stopping. The remainder of the water was used to wash Mickey's hands, which he dried with paper towels stored behind the seat.

Mickey drove around the streets of Centertown, where he encountered only two or three other vehicles. Very few new homes had been built in the community in the last fifty years. The Ray Sawyer and Glenn Haddox store buildings had been demolished for years, along with other downtown buildings. The Centertown School had long been the pride of the community, but it was no more. The school had been converted to an apartment building for migrant workers, and the grounds were strewn with trash and old cars. Like the one-room school at Walton's Creek in another era, the school had been eliminated by consolidation.

Mickey pulled the truck to the side of the road next to the baseball field and in clear view of the school. The bleachers appeared to be in poor repair, but the concession stands and playing field were in good condition. Mickey then remembered the American Legion owned the ball field, so it was being better cared for than the old school.

The playground across the road from the front of the school building had been retained by the town and was in fine shape. A ball field for youngsters had been added in recent years. Mickey was amazed that no children were playing at the playground or at the baseball field. Unlike members of his generation, modern youngsters generally took part only in organized games. The days of pick-up softball, baseball, and tag football had all but vanished. Computers and video games occupied so much of a young person's life that the sight of children playing in the yard was starting to disappear.

The playground brought back a flood of memories for Mickey. He recalled the day when he and his recess buddy Marvin burned down the fourth graders' clubhouse. It was a highlight of his early school days. They would never forget the sight of flames licking through a roof made of tobacco stalks and straw. The boys had sworn to never "fess up" to the crime or tell their parents what they had done. Three fourth-grade boys took the blame, and Mickey was grown before he told anyone about his role.

Mickey placed the ham sandwich on his lap and the potato chips between his legs. With his right hand he searched the half-melted ice in the drink chest. He pulled a can of Mountain Dew from the cooler and looked at it with disgust before tossing it into a nearby refuse barrel. The only drink left was a can of Dr. Pepper; this was more to his liking. Mickey devoured the sandwich and shared the potato chips with Lostie. He tried to find something on the truck radio but was dismayed when all he could locate were country music stations. Finally, the weak signal of a bullfrog calling to John Fogerty and CCR tried to break through. The song and the station soon faded, and Mickey turned the radio off.

In his rearview mirror Mickey observed a Sheriff's patrol car approaching as he swallowed the last drop of the Dr. Pepper. The deputy waved when he drove by, and Mickey returned the greeting. The cruiser turned and was soon out of sight. It was a beautiful day, but few citizens were out taking advantage of it. In Mickey's youth, nearly every home in town had a garden. Today, however, there were none in sight. The revving of a car engine could be heard in the immediate neighborhood, followed by the pecking and knocking sound of the same motor still trying to run after it was switched off. The car's owner tried unsuccessfully to start the engine again and finally gave up. There was a squeaking of the car door a moment before it slammed and then total silence. A crow landed in the road, grabbed a scrap of white bread, and after looking around for competitors, flew away.

"Well, Lostie, I guess you had better pee again. We have a long ride home."

The dog scrambled out of the truck, squatted, and darted back into the cab. She curled up in the floorboard, and Mickey knew she would not budge until they got home. The spent flowers from the cemetery, a Hardee's sack from earlier in the day—the refuse from his lunch—Mickey deposited it all in the trash barrel. It was time to go home.

Despite all the fond memories, Mickey knew he would never live at Walton's Creek or Centertown again. The trips back to the old communities had grown fewer in recent years and each one felt like the final farewell. It was comforting to know that Walton's Creek Cemetery would be his final resting place, where he would be reunited with his family. The communities would always hold a special place in his heart, but only for the people and the culture that nurtured him in his early years. In recent times strip mining had revisited the area, and despite careful reclamation, the old landmarks were gone forever. The terrain was ripe for the memories of a new generation but at the expense of all that preceded it. Sometimes Mickey felt that living with the memories and values of the past in a modern world was like existing across the abyss.

When Mickey drove past the courthouse in Hartford, one solitary elderly man occupied the steps and retaining wall that encased the county's seat of power. The old man was looking around as if perplexed. His old cronies were gone forever, and the current generations of loafers were frequenting the coffeehouses, not the Courthouse Square.

Mickey only vaguely remembered paying the toll on the William Natcher Parkway at Hartford. Traffic was light and his mind started to wander. His trips back to Walton's Creek had become symbolic in recent years, but the fond recollections embedded in his mind were becoming heirlooms to be treasured for a lifetime. The trip always stimulated a replaying of family stories; and if he never returned to Walton's Creek, he could always revisit the tiny community whenever he liked by recalling a century of oral traditions. The quiet hum of the truck engine was the appropriate background as Mickey's memory went back to the time when he was a skinny little kid with a rifle and a canteen exploring the woods and fields with his beagle hound. He relived an anthology of Christmas stories, tobacco, hog killing, Possum Hunters, weddings, death, laughter, and sorrow. For Mickey, they were more than just stories, they were a treasured inheritance built upon a century of rural traditions and values.

The long truck ride back home was about to become a river of dreams. Mickey could hardly wait.

Book Two

SWEAT, TEARS AND ENDEARMENT

Grandfather and Grandmother Atlee (1913-1917)

GRANDFATHER AND GRANDMOTHER ATLEE
(1913-1917)

*M*ICKEY WAS NO *more than three years old the first time he climbed the creaky stairs to the attic in the old farmhouse. He relished the musty smelling books, clothes, and toys that were scattered about. The item that interested him most, however, was a pair of ancient saddlebags. His mom cautioned him to never touch them, explaining that they belonged to his Grandfather Atlee, who had died many years before.*

Mickey was grown before he saw a picture of his grandfather, but by that time he already felt he knew the man well. Over the years he had heard numerous stories about Marv Atlee—his father's father, a farmer and country veterinarian with a flair for artwork. Mickey learned about his grandfather only when his own father was not present. Ralph Atlee was sensitive about his dad's mental illness and always left the house when his name was mentioned. That was why the saddlebags remained in the attic.

As a child, Mickey had wanted to explore the saddlebags and learn more about his grandfather. He tried to envision Marv Atlee making his rounds on horseback, treating cows and horses in the Walton's Creek community. As an adult, he regretted not sneaking a peek inside the plain western style bags. He knew Grandfather Atlee kept a journal filled with sketches, essays, and poetry he compiled over the years. The journal was lost, however, and Mickey always wondered if it was not tucked inside the badly dry-rotted saddlebags. The Atlee family had left the farm in the late 1950s; the bags undoubtedly perished as the house succumbed to age and neglect.

Mickey searched the deep recesses of his mind for the stories that helped him imagine the lives of his paternal grandparents. He found the memory he desired.

Marv Atlee wiped his hands on a rag and methodically placed the veterinarian supplies back in his saddlebags. Like many rural vets of his time, Marv was merely a horse doctor, a self-educated man with little knowledge or training. He ordered vet books from a mail order company and applied the content of the books, living and farming in Western Kentucky to become an animal doctor. America was well into the 20th Century; but to be a veterinarian all that was required was desire, a few mail order books, and remedies.

The saddlebags that Marv carried were bulging with remedies from Dr. E.J. Smith Company, Sears Roebuck, and Dr. J.G. Lesure. Marv had a reputation with horses. An intestinal ailment in horses called "colic" had responded well to Dr. Smith's "Spavin Cure" and Smith's "Cough and Distemper Remedy." In 1895 the W.T. Rawleigh Company introduced "Stock Tonic Supplement." Marv believed many stock ailments could be prevented if the tonic was given regularly.

Marvin had purchased a variety of vet instruments over the years from the Sears Roebuck catalog—a rubber horse syringe, hoof knife, drenching horn, and the "Cattle Trocar and Canula" that was indispensable to lance and drain an abscess. Most of his supplies were readily available to the public, but it was not practical for farmers to maintain a full inventory of medicines and tools they had limited resources to buy and less knowledge to use.

The loss of one cow or horse could deal a serious blow to farm families. Many Kentucky farms of the era had only one horse or mule for farming and transportation—and a single milk cow. Marv Atlee represented hope to his friends and neighbors. Like the country doctors of his day, Marv's successes earned him high praise, and failures were generally excused as "God's will" or "he'd done his best."

Marv collected some money for his services but was often paid in hams, chickens, sweet potatoes, honey, sorghum, and other items. He never kept a record of his services, and if he wasn't paid, the oversight was soon forgotten. A deeply religious man, Marv felt that pressing a man for a debt he could not pay was oppression of the poor.

"Mista Marv, I'ze shore glad has yo come down hea' t'day. I han't got but jist dis one ol' milk cow and de younguns' 'til growin'."

"That is quite all right, Charlie. I have only one milk cow, three growin' boys, and a little gal to boot."

"Mista Marv, yo han't no pore ol' darkie tryin' scat out a livin' on dis ol' farm."

"Every man has his troubles, Charlie, and we just have to work and trust God to see us through."

Marv stood up and draped the saddlebags over his right shoulder. Charlie's old milk cow limped away and resumed her grazing.

"Well now, this old cow doesn't have the Blackleg. We seldom see cows over two years get that, and besides, you say she has been limping for a week. If she had Blackleg, she would have stopped grazing, swelled up, and fell over dead long before now. I lanced and drained that place and put this Wire Cut Remedy on the wound. I would say she probably cut it on a piece of barbed wire, but the salve you put on should have worked unless it has lost its strength or all that pus in there was holding it back. Keep the rest of this until she gets well."

"Thank ye, Misa Marv. How much owes ye?"

"How about a gallon of sorghum or whatever you can spare."

"Yassuh, Misa Marv. Dist wudn't do, ol' lady wants yo du stay suppa' dis night."

"WELL, that the best invite I've had all day. Sounds mighty fine, especially if ol' Sally is cooking up a pan of her fried chicken."

"Sho nuf. Knows dat yore favrit. Has me rung two ol' hens dis very afernoon."

Marv Atlee had visited the Charlie Smith farm many times over the years. Most people called him "Ol' Nigger Charlie Smith." Charlie lived on a small farm nearby Green River in Ohio County and only a few miles from Marv Atlee. Charlie's family was one of few blacks in that part of the county, and there had been some speculation about how Charlie obtained the 12-acre farm. It had been rumored that a white man purchased the property for him. It was also speculated that the white man was the son of a tobacco farmer who owned Charlie's people during slavery. The Smith family lived apart from a community of slave descendants residing in a bend of the nearby Green River. In Kentucky, many descendants of slave owners often "watched" after the descendants of former slaves and viewed it as a moral responsibility. The loyalty was often reciprocal. Occasionally descendants of former slaves aided the heirs of their former masters. Charlie never talked about how he got his farm, and no one knew anything for sure.

Marv and Charlie washed their hands in one of two pans of water on the back porch. Marv knew the pan offered for his use had been placed there in anticipation of his visit. Charlie Smith would never dream of asking a white guest to use the same pan and soap the Smiths used. Marv washed with a fresh bar of lye soap and dried on a clean towel.

"Miss Sally, that was the finest fried chicken I have ever eaten. I said that the last time I was here, but I believe you just keep getting better. Liz makes mighty fine fried chicken, too, but I think you have her beat as well. If Liz ever finds out how much I like your chicken … well, she might get jealous."

Marv finished his compliment with a smile. Charlie was beaming with pride, but Sally was laughing uncontrollably. She weighed nearly 400 pounds and shook all over when she laughed. Her mouth had very few teeth remaining, and one eye was clouded over. Her chair squeaked and groaned under her gyrations until Marv worried that it was going to collapse.

"Misa Marz. Yo knows Miz Lizbut han't gona be jealus' uv no big fat nigga 'ike me."

Marv tried to hide his amusement with a huge mug of coffee. He always knew what to say to please Sally. She admired Marv as much as Charlie and valued every compliment. Few white people of the time viewed black folks as equals, and Marv Atlee was not unaware of those prejudices. He was fond of telling his wife Liz, "… in the eyes of God we are all equals." For Charlie and Sally Smith, however, Marv Atlee was the finest white man alive. Despite Charlie's reputation in the community for honesty and hard work, many still said, "… nigga is still a nigga." Charlie was well aware of the feelings and addressed most white men only when spoken to and then with utmost courtesy. Marv was one of few white men with whom he carried on a conversation.

"Misa Marv, it lookin' 'ike rain. Yo got three mile on du hoss t' git home. Yo stay du night. Haf' brefast 'fore headin' fo du house."

"Mercy sakes, Charlie. I didn't see that thunderhead rolling in. I must have been too busy eating chicken. I hate to put you out any, but I don't relish riding home in the rain either."

"Hoss in du barn a'ready. Get sad'l off in a jiffy fust shows ye du room."

Marv followed Charlie upstairs to their guest room. He had spent many nights at Charlie's farm and was well acquainted with the upstairs guest room for white visitors. He always acted like he had never seen the room before, and Charlie never grew tired of showing it off. He unlocked the door and gestured for Marv to enter.

"Misa Marv, dis here fo du white folk. No nigga head ever tech that pillow or sleep in dat dere bed."

The room was precisely as Marv remembered it. A four-poster bed made up with a badly faded "Crazy Quilt" that appeared to be fashioned from wornout garments. A small rug crocheted from rags adorned the wide plank floor, and the sole window had a pair of white, heavily starched curtains. No other window in the house contained curtains. A small dresser and a chair completed the room's decorations.

"Go feed du hoss now, Misa Marv. Misa Marv, dis ol' darkie shore proud haf sech a fine Chrishun man sleep un'er my roof."

Charlie turned to leave, and Marv had just placed his saddlebags down next to the cane bottom chair when Charlie came back in the room.

"Misa Marv, did yo know me pappy an' granpappy wuz slave?"

Marv was stunned by Charlie's question. Slavery was a topic Charlie and Marv never discussed.

"Uh, well, no. No, Charlie, but I assumed as much I suppose."

"Yes, suh, but thee git free. Big backer fermer down C'lumbus make um free. Said wuz best darkies he own. Ol' Mahsuh south 'em ifin' dem bad. He done it. Pappy an' granpappy wuk on du riva. Go Noo Orlens many time. Big sto'm one night dey wuz washed. Hands tries saf um but ol' boat mate holler, '... lets um go free niggas wuth nothin' nobody.' Jist go of lets um die. Wuz no slavery ... nary none twenty year. Ol' mammy cry 'til she die. Jist awful thang."

Charlie had tears streaming down his face as he closed the door. Marv was horrified and speechless as he stared at the closed door. He could not believe that anyone could allow another human being to drown no matter what his or her race. He was equally dumbstruck as to why Charlie had suddenly brought up the story. The rain was getting hard outside, and the thunder and lightning were strong as well. Perhaps the storm reminded Charlie of the event, like Civil War soldiers Marv had known who were reminded of artillery during storms.

Marv quietly reflected upon the lives of his host and hostess. Charlie and Sal Smith lived virtually isolated in a white man's world. They were hardworking, honest, and God-fearing people. Ostracized by their race, illiteracy added to the misery of an apartheid existence. Marv's eldest son once asked why he was so nice to Charlie.

"Pa, old Charlie can't half talk where you can understand what he says. He can't even sign his name."

Marv answered young Alvin quietly but firmly.

"Alvin, Charlie and his family are God's children. They descended from slaves. They have had few of the opportunities enjoyed by people like us. They are two of the finest people I have ever known. You will address him as Mr. Smith..." Before Marv could finish his sentence, younger son Ralph did it for him.

"... like a Philadelphia lawyer, Al. Somethin' you ain't never gonna be."

Marvin smiled at his younger son. "Remember Al, Mister Fritz, the Watkins man, talks funny, too. That's because he is German. You like him because he gives all of you children a stick of candy when he comes by to sell your mother vanilla extract. Poor old Charlie cannot go into the stores in Centertown to buy candy for his own children. No matter how we look or talk, God made us all." Marvin finished his remarks by gripping the Bible firmly with both hands.

Marvin Atlee pulled a Bible from his saddlebags and looked affectionately at the leather cover. He remembered the Charlie Smith family owned a similar Bible but could not read a word. Charlie had asked Marvin to teach his two young boys to read so they could read the Bible to the entire family. Marvin realized that he needed to get busy fulfilling that promise. His own family, the farm, church, and vet work kept him very busy, but a promise was a promise. He knew that Sunday was the best time to work with the youngsters, but he had been praying for guidance on the matter. He was not certain if that was laboring on the Sabbath.

Marvin dropped his head and thanked God for his many blessings. He realized his family was the most important thing in his life and how thankful they all should be of their social standing, so different from the Charlie Smith family.

The inscription page of the Bible was always the first thing Marv read.

"Given this day by Ralph Atlee to his son Marvin and wife Elizabeth this day March 16, 1893. On occasion of their wedding. May God bless and keep you."

After losing their first child in childbirth, Marv and Liz's family had grown to include three boys and one girl in sixteen years. Liz had recorded each birth carefully in the Bible.

Sallie Marie, Born April 5, 1902.

Alvin David, Born July 6, 1904.

Ralph Linwood, Born October 16, 1907.

Timothy Roland, Born November 11, 1908.

Marv Atlee's home was a beautiful two-story white farmhouse nestled in the shade of several oak trees on a hillside less than a mile from the Walton's Creek Church, graveyard, and school. His ninety-seven-acre farm, plus ground that he rented in the Rough Creek bottoms, sustained the family. Planting and harvesting in the river bottoms was always a family affair. Marv built a small shack just out of reach of backwater where the family batched until the work was done.

The Atlee sons were introduced to farm work at a very early age. Marvin believed work and honesty were virtues that God valued above all others. In later years Alvin, the eldest son, recalled, "... din't get no britches 'til we was six. Wore long shirts and my pappy had me gatherin' eggs and gettin' in firewood 'fore I shed that shirt. Remember settin' terbacker in it, too."

Marv Atlee was working in the fields when he was six years old and expected no less from his sons. Liz Atlee also demanded that her sons grow up knowing how to do anything that needed to be done in the house. She lectured them of the importance of knowing what most folks called "women's work." She explained that the lady of the house sometimes got sick or in a family way and needed help. The only girl in the family, Sally Marie, was also expected to know something about "men's work." Sally often helped chop out corn, hoe and strip tobacco, and hitch up and drive a team just like the boys. Marv and Liz, however, did not believe a woman should have to shoulder the bulk of the farm duties unless it was absolutely necessary. Rural Kentuckians of the time who failed to fulfill their traditional male or female roles were labeled "... triflin' and no count."

The division of labor in Marv and Liz Atlee's home had less to do with tradition and more about pragmatism. The women could cook, can, raise the garden, and do general housework while providing care for infants. The family functioned as a team with tasks assigned based upon age and ability to best accomplish the work. Most families—with very few exceptions—were patriarchal in this age when women could not vote.

The Atlee children attended the Walton's Creek School except when farm work and bad weather intervened. They were expected to perform their chores, do their schoolwork, go to bed, and get up in the morning without being reminded. Hunting and fishing were the only recreation Marv felt was appropriate for young boys. Their excursions, however, came with a price; they were expected to net the next family meal. Failure always meant a supper of cold biscuits or cornbread for everyone.

Marv and Liz were strict parents but chose to raise their children minus corporal punishment or with stern lectures. They believed leading by example and giving children responsibility, love, respect, and a solid religious foundation at an early age were all that were required. The family attended church at Walton's Creek every Sunday, and Marv led the family in Bible readings after Sunday dinner.

The one-room school at Walton's Creek was one of the foundations of the community and also an important part of the area's social life. Everyone enjoyed pie suppers, and the Christmas tree provided an opportunity for the school kids to exchange gifts and to enjoy hot cider and cookies. Marv and Liz felt the Christmas tree was a little extravagant but did not object to the children's participation.

Marv and Liz were passionate about reading and learning new things. Marv had limited schooling but had read extensively and was widely regarded as an intelligent, well-educated man. Farm animals were Marv's passion, but he was equally fascinated with crops and farming. He spent most of his idle hours practicing penmanship, reading, and sketching horses.

The Atlee children were not as enthusiastic as their parents about school and reading. Alvin was very good at arithmetic but grew up believing that all it was good for was to figure the number of board feet of lumber needed to build a barn or the amount of seed needed to plant a crop. Ralph and Timmie hated school and dreamed of the day when they could quit and farm full time. Sally Marie, like her father, always enjoyed reading.

Unlike the Atlees, Charlie Smith and his family could not participate in any activities at the Walton's Creek Church or School. Black children could attend school in the county seat of Hartford or Beaver Dam, but these were too far away. Charlie and Sally did not read or write, and the boys would grow up the same way if Marv did not teach them. Educational opportunities in the county were limited for white children, but even fewer for black youth.

Kentucky farm life in 1913 was one of isolation, but more confining for the Charlie Smith family. On rare occasions Charlie ventured into Centertown. He always drove his road wagon to the rear of a store, where he knocked politely. He conducted his business without stepping inside and quickly left town. It was widely known that Centertown did not welcome Negroes. It was often said, "... the sun will never set on a nigger's head in Centertown." The coming of the Madisonville, Hartford, and Eastern Railroad in 1909 was long anticipated, but the town refused to allow black workers from the work crew building the track to enter the community.

Charlie Smith got along well with his white neighbors, but he knew all too well what happened to black folk who did not know their place. Sally Smith used the Sears Roebuck catalog for a lot of their needs. She marked what she wanted, and Charlie took it to Liz Atlee, who completed the order for her. Many drummers traversing the countryside ignored the Smith farm, except the backpack salesmen who often traded goods for a meal and a night in Charlie's white guest room. Liz Atlee, however, generally knew what Sally needed and purchased for her. One of Sally's favorites was the Watkins man, whose household items were a staple of all farm families. Farm wives loved Watkins vanilla, black pepper, and cinnamon. The men liked the liniment after a hard day in the fields, and the entire family used Petro-Carbo salve on cuts and bruises.

Ironically, the Sears Roebuck and other catalogs like Montgomery Ward, that served so many rural black families in the South, were the object of false accusations. Sears Roebuck introduced their catalog in 1891. This angered rural merchants who did not welcome the competition, and soon rumors circulated that it was owned and operated by Negroes. The gossip persisted for decades, despite attempts by the companies to dispel the myth.

The thunderstorm ended around midnight, and Marv slept soundly until he was aroused at 5:00 AM by the smell of fresh coffee and the aroma of bacon frying. He knew Sally had baked big fluffy biscuits the size of a man's fist. A wonderful breakfast that also included thick n' gravy and scrambled eggs awaited him.

Marv jumped out of the bed and started to dress, but his head started to spin and he fell backwards upon the bed. His hands were tingling, and his tongue felt so thick he was almost gagging on it. The sensation was like nothing he had ever felt before. After a few minutes the room stopped spinning, and the other sensations started to subside. He concluded that he had gotten up too quickly, and the blood had rushed to his stomach.

After breakfast, Marv stood by the back door while Charlie saddled his horse, feeling a little uneasy under the stares of Charlie's sons. Finally, Marv took a piece of paper from his saddlebags and methodically sharpened a pencil with his pocketknife.

"Do you boys know the Lord's Prayer? Well, I will read it to you some day, but right now I want you to watch closely. I have drawn a circle around this dime on this piece of white paper. I'm going to start writing inside that circle starting at the outer edge and I'm going to write in a spiral fashion, and the last letter of the last word will be right smackie dab in the middle."

Marv used his saddlebags as a desk, and while Charlie's little boys watched with fascination, he wrote the "Lord's Prayer."

"Now, you boys hang on to this and remember that God will always be your shepherd."

"We names 'em Cain and Abel, Misa Marv. Ye know that?"

"Yes, I did."

"Names um from du book. Chrisun names."

"Charlie, I have always wanted to ask you a question. Do you and Sally know the story of Cain and Abel?"

"NO, Misa Marv, but in du book. Ye teach du boys to read, and du boys read 'bout Cain 'n' Abel to ol' Sal 'n' me."

"Well, I have put off teaching the boys long enough. I may ask Liz to help me if that's all right with you."

Marv took the reins from Charlie and mounted his horse for the ride home. The dirt road had turned to mud overnight, and Marv tried to stay on the grassy side as he made his way home. The air felt clean and invigorating after the thunderstorm, and the birds were celebrating a bright sunny day in May.

The clumping of the horse's hoofs echoed against the rushing of water in the ditch alongside the road. Marv was feeling energized as he contemplated the upcoming farming season. The weather had been mild, and the burning and sowing of the plant beds had gone smoothly. Beans and corn were already popping through the ground in the garden, and the field corn in the bottoms was starting to emerge as well. His eldest son Al was already a big help with the chores, and the little ones, Ralph and Timmie, wanted to do more than was advisable for their age. This year Al had broke the tobacco patch and the garden, and Ralph disked the ground. Five-year-old Timmie, sporting his first pair of britches, stood and cried when he could not help.

The farming education of his three sons had taken on paramount importance. A family of six required a lot of food, and Marv still owed on the farm and the bottomland. The boys could play a vital role in the farm's success. Marv had learned farming in the same manner from his father, and so it had been for generations. The tradition of farming was about nurturing and respecting the land, but also about carrying on to another generation. Marv did not currently own enough land to provide three sons each with farms of their own. The Atlee sons were learning to cultivate crops and their own birthright. Marv hoped he could give each son a hundred acres when they were grown.

Marv rode along, his mind racing about the new farming season and the plans he had made for the future. He quietly prayed to God for the strength and guidance to persevere. His whispered Amen had barely escaped his lips when the peculiar sensation he had felt early that morning raced through his body like fire. He felt the horse was rearing up, and all he could see was the sky spinning in front of his eyes, then all was black.

"What are you looking at, you flea-bitten hound?" Marv heard his own voice like it was many miles away. He could see a reddish brown dog a few yards down the road, looking at him and whining. The animal was wagging his tail slowly as he turned his head from side to side.

"Get on down the road for home, dog. My horse doesn't like strange dogs. Get on now."

The dog turned and trotted down the shoulder of the road, glancing back at Marv a couple of times. Marv watched the dog until he trotted past a riderless horse that was standing at the edge of the ditch quietly grazing.

"Mercy sakes alive. I wonder where that horse came from? A fine animal and no rider in sight. Get up there, boy, we need to see who that animal belongs to. Come on, get up, I SAID get up."

Marv was trying to urge his horse forward but remained motionless. Suddenly he became aware that he was not astride his horse but standing almost waist deep in the muddy water of the ditch.

"Now how in blazes did I get in here? OH, my head hurts. The horse must have thrown me. OH dear me, that's my horse down yonder. Here, boy, come on back here. OH DEAR LORD, what's happening to me?"

Marv staggered from the ditch and failed several times to mount his horse. His head was splitting, and his arms and legs were numb and tingling. The thick tongue of that morning had not returned, but his mouth felt like he had been eating alum. The puckery taste and tingling sensation was disgusting as he tried to spit it away.

The ride home for Marv seemed to take forever as the beautiful, peaceful morning turned into a nightmare. He thought several times that he might fall from the horse and die. The thought of dying and leaving his family without a father and husband was frightening. Marv had always known that life was fragile but had never felt it more keenly than when facing death at such an early age.

When Marv tried to dismount by the back porch, he fell and the horse nearly stepped on him. He could hear Liz in the kitchen and prayed that God would let him live long enough to say goodbye to the family.

"Marvin Atlee, it's about time you got home. I was beginning to think that the darkies had kidnapped you this time for sure. OH LORD, Marvin. What on earth is wrong with you? You're soaking wet and dripping muddy water all over my kitchen. You're white as a sheet."

"Horse threw me, I guess. My head hurts. Liz, I'm not well."

"Marv, the horse that can throw you hasn't been born. You must have hit your head. Come on, and let's get you into some dry clothes."

Liz Atlee was a calm, deliberate woman, but the sight of her husband standing wet and bewildered in the kitchen was unnerving. Marv had never been sick, and he was the rock that she had leaned on since they got married. She examined his head closely, but there was no sign of injury. His head was hurting, and the look out of his eyes was the most frightening of all.

Marv refused to eat dinner and spent the remainder of the day sitting motionless in the porch swing. Liz carried him cup after cup of chamomile tea, and Sally Marie kept warm washcloths on his forehead. Liz sensed that a crisis was about to start. She had no way of knowing that her husband's illness was going to both threaten and strengthen the Atlee family. Marv wanted his children to learn farming as they built for their own future. The Atlee boys were going to learn what it was like to be men long before they ceased to be children.

In a few days Marv Atlee started to improve. The headaches went away, and gradually he was able to return to his farm and vet work, but Liz was still worried. Some days he was almost his old self, but this was frequently followed by days when he was glassy-eyed and distant. The mysterious illness, however, had not affected his ability to farm and doctor stock. Liz knew the children were upset by recent events but rarely had the opportunity to speak to them about it without Marv overhearing.

"PUT THE FOOD BACK IN THE BOWLS. We didn't pray." Marv's sudden outburst at the supper table startled the entire family. He jumped from his chair and began raking the food from his plate back in the bowls.

Liz was trembling, but she forced herself to appear calm as she addressed Marv. "Marvin, you said grace when we sat down to eat. You know that we always say grace. Besides, God will probably forgive us if we forget once in a while. He knows that we are eternally grateful."

Marv looked at Liz for a moment before retaking his seat. He looked at everyone at the table somberly before finally refilling his plate. The children did not resume their meals until Marv had taken his first bites. Sally Marie was trembling so hard that she dropped her fork. When Marv was not himself, mealtime was always a stressful event.

The fall harvest season was drawing near in 1913, and the farm work on the Atlee farm had suffered all summer. Marv was not well long enough at a time to tend to business, and the boys were still too young to shoulder the responsibility. The corn crop in the creek bottoms would need to be gathered soon, and they could not afford to lose it.

Marv asked Liz to join him on the front porch one evening after supper. He had been acting almost normal for three days, but he had also been frowning and Liz knew he was worried.

"Elizabeth, I'm not a well man. I thought that the fall from the horse was the source of my trouble at first, but now I'm concerned that I may be losing my mind." Marv finished his comment with his head down. Neither of them spoke for several long minutes. The only noise was the squeak of the swing as they quietly moved it back and forth with their feet.

"Marvin Atlee, you are the kindest and gentlest and the smartest man I know. YOU are not going crazy." Liz's voice started to crack as the final words seemed to grab in her throat. This was the first time the possibility that her husband might be insane had crossed her mind. She had convinced herself that it was an injury to his head and nothing more. She had hoped and prayed that it would go away, but now the prospect of an incurable condition was terrifying. Liz had known few people who lost their minds, but she knew how cruel people could be to them and their families. In the early 1900s, insanity was viewed as a weakness, and it left loved ones feeling ashamed.

Sally Marie was busy clearing away the table and washing the dishes from the evening meal; the boys were milking, feeding the stock, and bringing in wood and water. Marv and Liz continued to swing on the front porch. Liz sensed that Marv had more to say but appeared reluctant to bring it up.

"Liz, you know that young fella Jes Caughill. Got married to that Smith girl. Myrtle Smith. He has been working in the mines with his daddy, but he got laid off a while back and needs a job. I hired him yesterday to help on the farm. I'm giving him fifty cents a day for six days a week and a hog to kill this fall."

"Marvin Atlee, you know we can't afford a hired hand. Fifty cents a day is mighty little for him but a fortune to us."

"It can't be helped. I'm not well enough to get things done, and we have to get in the crops. He can go with me to treat stock. He can do the talking when I'm not myself. People won't know I'm not myself if I don't talk. He starts tomorrow."

Marvin got up from the swing and headed for the barn. Liz remained in the porch swing for a few minutes. The financial strain of paying a farm hand was upsetting, but she knew Marv was right. They had to do something, and Jes Caughill was young, strong, and a good worker.

Liz Atlee knew they would not be able to carry on much longer without help. The boys were still too small to assume all the responsibility of farming. Liz was a strong, religious woman and far more outspoken than most women in 1913; but the prospect of raising four children and working the farm without her husband worried her. She was becoming increasingly afraid that Marvin would turn violent. She continued to pray that his erratic behavior was the result of falling off the horse and that he would get better.

Young Jes Caughill proved to be what Liz had hoped for. He was a strong young man, very respectful, and he approached the farm work like it was his own. He genuinely liked Marv Atlee, and to Liz's relief, appeared not to notice his behavior.

Liz Atlee's fears that Marvin might turn violent were confirmed one day when she heard Alvin screaming from the back porch. There she found Marvin holding the boy by the throat with his feet dangling six inches off the porch.

"YOU LITTLE HEATHEN. You're gonna rot in HELL."

"MARVIN, you put that child down right this instant."

Marvin was startled by Liz's voice and released Alvin immediately. Liz hugged her son close as the boy sobbed and shook. Marvin appeared bewildered, and Liz suspected he was unaware of what he had done. After a few tense moments, Marv went to the barn.

A year had passed since Marvin returned from the Charlie Smith farm, and his behavior was growing more erratic. His belligerence toward Alvin was getting worse, and Liz was concerned that he might become violent toward the entire family. She knew that the neighbors were talking, and Marvin had ceased attending church and reading the Bible. Jes went with him on all his vet business and did most of the talking, while Marvin doctored the stock. Jes did his best to distract attention from his employer's condition, but everyone knew what he was doing. Before they left on a call, Marvin would always tell Jes, "... I'm not myself today, Jes. You do the talking and no one will be the wiser."

Myrtle Caughill had heard the stories about Marvin Atlee, but for many months Jes would not talk about it. Finally, he confided in Myrtle.

"Myrtle, Marv Atlee is the finest man I ever knowed, but I swear he's crazier than hell. I'm awful afraid he's gonna hurt Liz and them kids. The other day we come to the house fer dinner. We was a settin' under a tree in the yard and gettin' ready to go back to work when Liz tol' the girl she wanted her to shave the back of her neck. Well, don't ye know, ol' Marv jumped up and said he was gonna do it. Run in the house and come back with a pan of water and his straight razor. Scared me to death. Liz said fer him and me to go on back to the fields and let Sally do it. Well, he weren't a havin' no part of it and done it hisself. I was scared stiff and so was Liz, but he was as easy as ye please. I jest knowed he was gonna cut her throat, and I know she did, too. I think he knowed what we was a thinkin'."

"Now, Jes, don't ye turn yere back on the man. I know you two get along fine, but a crazy man don't always know what he's doin'. Jes, ye just gotta get 'nother job with me expectin' and all. Gotta get a better job."

"I know and the mines orta be a startin' back purty soon. I just hate to leave that woman and them kids. Heerd some talk over at Centertown that Liz was gonna have the law send 'im to the asylum. I don't know if that's true, but she just may have to do it. Awful shame a fine man like that get in sech a shape."

"It sure is, Jes. But right now we gotta think 'bout us. War over 'cross the seas is brewin' and gonna drag us in it sooner or later, and ye may have to go. Liz Atlee may not be the only woman to lose a husband 'round here if the Democrats gets their way."

Liz Atlee had tried to prepare herself for anything involving Marvin, but one thing she had not anticipated. The day Jes Caughill walked into her kitchen without knocking was one she would never forget.

"Jes, I know you weren't born in a barn. Close that screen door and wipe your feet. NO man comes in my house without wiping his feet."

Jes acted as if he did not hear a word Liz said. He stood with his head down, breathing hard and fidgeting with his hat. Liz dropped the spoon she had been using to stir the beans cooking on top of the stove. Her mind raced through all the possibilities. Had Marvin hurt one of the children? Did he hurt someone else?

"JES, good Lord, what did he do?"

"Miz Atlee, I shore hate to be the one to tell ye this and all. Mister Marv jest tried to hang hisself. Come to hisself jest in the nick of time. I, I uh need some white rags to put 'round his neck. He got rope burns. Too ashamed to come to the house, I reckon."

Sally Marie, who had been listening from another room, rushed in crying and handed her mother some strips of white cloth. The child ran back into the house sobbing as Liz nervously handed the rags to Jes. He took the rags and struggled to say something or even look up at Liz, but he could do neither. He swallowed hard, turned, and left.

Jes rushed back to the barn wondering if he would find Marvin hanging from a rafter. He swore at himself for not taking the rope when he went to the house. This was the first traumatic event in Jes's young life; and despite all the trouble he would see in the next five decades, the day Marv Atlee tried to hang himself would stand out as one of the worst.

"I came to myself just in time, Jes. If I had kicked that milk stool out of the way ... well, I don't know."

"Marvin, what made ye do sech a thing? Got sech a fine family and nice farm and all?"

"SIN, JES, sin and corruption in the world."

"Here, Marvin, let me put the rags 'round yere neck. Ye wanna have me put some salve on first?"

"NO, Jes, please go to the well and get some cool water. The rags soaked in some cool water will make my neck feel better."

Jes patted Marv on the shoulder and turned to go to the well. He stopped dead in his tracks when he saw Ralph Atlee halfway down the ladder to the barn loft. The boy was pale and looked terribly frightened. In the excitement Jes had not noticed him and had no idea how long he had been there. He wondered if he had seen everything. Jes felt sorry for him, but in moments of crisis he never knew what to say. He dropped his gaze and rushed out of the barn for the well. When he returned, Marv was still seated on the milk stool and little Ralph was gone.

Liz did not tell Jes why she was going to Hartford, and he did not ask. He suspected it might have something to do with rumors he had been hearing. The Atlees did most of their shopping in Centertown, and rarely went to the county seat. Nine miles one way in a road wagon over a dirt road meant a long day, and in bad weather the trip was almost impossible. In recent years the train had arrived in Centertown and this made the excursion faster and more comfortable.

"Now, Miz Atlee, I don't mind a drivin' this here team on to Hartford. I know the train is lots faster, but 20 cents a ridin' backards and forwards is mighty steep."

"Thank you, Jes, but I want to ride the train today. It will give me some time by myself to think. Marvin and I have always loved trains. When we got married, we talked about going by train all the way to California. Of course, we never did. We were just young and foolish and had no money."

"Yes'm, I reckon the train is 'bout as nice as the ol' river boats ever been and go lots more places too."

"Jes, we waited a good many years to get a train. Hartford did too. Marvin has always said he could not understand how a country that could build a railroad all the way to California just after the Civil War could not build one to little towns like Hartford and Centertown. It took almost 50 years more before we finally got one. The Madisonville, Hartford, and Eastern Railroad sure answered our prayers."

"Yes ma'am. They say that eventually this ol' railroad gonna connect out of state and make Hartford and Madisonville big shot railroad towns. Gonna help Centertown too."

"Jes, Marvin says that is not going to happen. He believes that the L&N Railroad started those rumors just to make sure this railroad had the money to get built. Now they own it."

"Miz Atlee, did you and Marvin come to town when the first train rolled in?"

"Yes, we did. We brought the children and rode in this very wagon. We came to see the Booster Train that came in from Madisonville, too. Did you and Myrtle come to town?"

"We shore did. Not married back then, though. Rode the train to Hartford all reared back and took the Transfer to Beaver Dam. Myrtle had seen in the paper some store up there was gonna give away biscuits cooked in this here Majestic wood cookstove. Yes sir, we ate a big ol' biscuit sopped in butter and honey right there in the store. I reckon that was the fall of '09. We got married in 1912. Now Myrtle says to me that if I expects her to marry me I gonna have to buy her one of them stoves. Workin' in the mines then at night, and I got me a day job in the sawmill and saved up the money. I went to Beaver Dam and bought that stove with cash money. They hauled it to Hartford and put it on the train fer Centertown, and Pap and me hauled it to his house. I got all shinnied up and headed to her house and asked her when we was gonna set the date, and she said that I still hadn't bought that stove. That's when I tol' her, and she said she reckoned now she had run out of excuses."

Liz Atlee laughed at Jes's story. It was the first time she had laughed at anything in over a year.

"Myrtle drove quite a hard bargain, Jes. Was that the only trip you took her on before you got hitched?"

"NO, back 'fore the train, like lots of folks, I would rent a horse and buggy from the livery here in town, and we'd go on a picnic over at Airdrie in Muhlenberg County. Right there on the Green River and right pretty with some bridges and all where that ol' furnace used to be. A spring of cold water there and some metal cups hangin' on a bush next to it fer anybody to use. Lord a mercy it was alum and mineral water and near knock a bull down. Then on we brung a jug of drinkin' water. After we got hitched, we took the train to Mammoth Cave. Only travelin' we ever done. Train or no train, travelin's not fer poor people."

Jes helped Liz down from the wagon. The train was puffing steam at the Centertown Depot as it waited for passengers and freight to be loaded and unloaded. Mixed trains carrying both passengers and freight served the town. The communities of Madisonville and Hartford had high expectations that the railroad would eventually become a part of an interstate rail system and make both towns thriving railroad cities. A few people, like Marvin Atlee, knew it would never happen. Madisonville was excited about getting shoppers and business investments and sent Booster Trains to towns along the route to promote business. Prior to the Booster Trains, the biggest event in Centertown had been the street fairs. After many years of isolation, Centertown, Walton's Creek, and the surrounding area finally had a route to the outside world.

The automobile had started to make its presence known in the county as well. Unfortunately, dirt roads were difficult to travel during the winter and early spring. Nearby Owensboro was a serious competitor with Madisonville for county business. The Hartford newspaper carried ads from the Daviess County, Ohio River city in late spring and early summer that read "... now that the roads have dried out, come to Owensboro and spend the day shopping ... you will enjoy yourself."

"Jes, I want you to hurry on back to the farm. I should have had Alvin drive me to the train. Marvin should not be left alone with the children. I'm just not thinking straight. Send Alvin to meet the train, and if Marvin puts up an argument, tell him I said so. If he starts to get angry, send all of the children to the train station. Oh Jes, I pray that I'm doing the right thing. I think you know what I mean about going to Hartford."

Jes was heading back to the farm when the train pulled out for Hartford. Liz had not said why she was going, but Jes was convinced that she had decided to ask the court to send Marvin to the asylum. He had been nervous during the trip to the train and had chatted away in an attempt to hide his own apprehension and to relieve the tension for Liz Atlee. Jes marveled at her composure.

The train trip to Hartford was only a few miles, but Liz enjoyed watching the trees zip by, and the scream of the steam whistle always gave her goose bumps. She sat alone and tried not to look at the other passengers; many of them were friends and neighbors. Liz knew some had glanced in her direction, and she wondered if they knew why she was going to Hartford. At the depot the men had tipped their hats politely, and the women smiled but no one had spoken a word. They had to know.

A large crowd met the train at Hartford. The usual rush of passengers and freight ensued, while a crowd of young boys and adults stood and watched. The arrival and departure of the train was a source of excitement, the likes of which had not been seen since the heyday of river traffic to the town.

Liz walked slowly from the Hartford Depot toward the courthouse in downtown. A dozen or more fellow train passengers accompanied her, but she had never felt more alone in her life. The short walk to the house of justice was pure agony. Liz had been taught that two of the worst things a person can do are commit adultery or get a divorce. No one had ever told her what it would feel like to have your husband committed to an insane asylum.

The train whistle was screaming and the locomotive puffed steam as the train left the depot at Hartford for Dundee. Liz was entering the back door of the courthouse and barely heard the train depart. Her mind was numb as she summoned the courage to do what had to be done. This was a trying day in her life, but there would be many more to follow.

Liz was relieved that Marvin did not ask her why she went to Hartford. The following day Jes and Marvin went on a farm call, and Liz summoned the children together to tell them what was going to happen. Sally Marie and Alvin cried, but Timmie and Ralph just looked stunned. Liz suspected the younger children were confused. They had never heard of an asylum and did not know what it really meant.

The following day Marv worked in the field all morning and was just finishing his dinner. Jes was working in the bottoms, and Liz had kept the boys busy close to the house. She no longer allowed them to spend unsupervised time with their father.

Liz and Sally Marie had just started to clear away the table when Alvin's voice carried through the screen door from the back porch.

"Pa, Pa, there's a man here to see ye with a horse."

Over the years it had become customary for men to come by with a sick horse or mule. Since Marv's illness, however, the numbers had declined significantly. Marv quickly got up from the table and went outside.

"Yessir, got a sick horse, have you? The one you are riding is a mighty fine animal. Doesn't look sick. This other horse looks pretty fair, too. I appreciate a man who takes good care of his animals."

A burly man wearing a suit and sporting a mustache sat quietly on his horse and did not comment. He did not appear to be in a hurry, nor was he anxious to strike up a conversation. Marv looked at him curiously for a moment.

"Now, if you have a sick horse, I need to know what's wrong. You may have heard of this new symptom that horses have been getting in recent years. The disease resembles laryngitis or catarrhal disease. It generally starts with a chill, and a yellow mucous is present in the nasal membrane. The horse next has a fever and loses his appetite. The horse refuses food and water. Now this horse doesn't appear to have any of those symptoms. Pray tell, sir, what is wrong with this animal?"

"Mr. Atlee, I need for you to ride this here horse."

Marvin looked stunned. He swallowed hard and said, "... I know you. You're the High Sheriff."

"Yes sir, I am." The man pulled back his suit coat as he spoke to reveal a black gun belt and a badge. The lawman still sat in the saddle looking quietly at Marv. Liz and the children stood on the porch terrified at what was going to happen next. The Sheriff seemed to be making a serious attempt to keep Marv calm as the gravity of the situation sank in.

Liz finally walked to the edge of the porch and placed her hand on Marv's shoulder. He jerked away and turned toward her, his arm extended as he pointed a shaking finger in her direction. The children flinched and Liz stepped back, but the Sheriff remained calm.

"YOU, YOU did this to me." Marv's voice cracked with emotion as he accused his wife. His arm dropped loosely to his side, and he glanced briefly at each of his children before dropping his head.

"Mister Atlee, if you please." The Sheriff held out the reins of the horse he was leading. "We need to drop the horses at the livery and catch the train to Hartford. Gotta get on back."

Marvin turned to the Sheriff and took the reins calmly. "Well, yes, of course, Sheriff. By all means. A law man riding a horse and leading another means business."

"Yessir, it does."

Marvin mounted the horse, and Alvin walked forward and handed his father a carpetbag containing his clothes, Bible, and other essentials. Alvin could not bear to look at his father, something he would regret for the rest of his life.

"Would you like for me to lead the way, Sheriff?"

"Yessir, if you don't mind."

Liz Atlee and her children stood and watched Marv Atlee and the sheriff ride away. Marv did not look back or call goodbye, and they would never see him alive again.

The day Marv Atlee left home was a memory that haunted the family as long as they lived. The children, however, were equipped to deal with adversity. They possessed the grit and courage of their mother and the compassion and sensitivity of their father. Those inherent traits would serve them well in the years to come.

Ralph Atlee had the greatest difficulty dealing with his father's fate. Liz thought it was because of his youth and sensitive nature, but Jes Caughill knew the real reason. The day Marv Atlee tried to hang himself was the day a bond developed between Ralph and Jes, and both men went to their graves without telling anyone that Ralph had been present. In fact, they never mentioned the event to one another. Jes Caughill had no way of knowing that one day Ralph would become his son-in-law, but by then Jes already thought of him as a son.

Liz Atlee knew that each member of the family would have to deal with Marv's fate in his own way. For years Ralph always left the house when his father's name was mentioned. Liz told the other children, "... just leave Ralph alone. That's just his way. Everybody has to grieve in their own way."

Liz was relieved at the way the Sheriff handled the situation. The lawman had a reputation for being as tough as the situation demanded. He was fond of saying that when he went to bring in a prisoner, the man was coming in or I "... ain't comin' back." The day he came for Marv Atlee, however, he demonstrated great patience and understanding. Liz wrote the Sheriff a letter and thanked him for his consideration. In reply, she received a brief letter in which he offered his services if she should require them and told her that he and his wife were praying for the Atlee family and for Marvin.

Jes Caughill stayed on to help Liz Atlee with the farm. The family slowly adjusted to Marv's absence as they went about the business of farm and family life. Marv sent Liz letters, but most were rambling and totally devoid of his wonderful penmanship. A doctor had written Liz to inform her that he believed something was pressuring Marv's brain and he might never recover. Liz did not share the doctor's letter with the children, as she kept the more disturbing contents of their father's letters from them as well.

Liz knew something was wrong when she saw Ralph walking across the field from the Walton's Creek School an hour early. He had his hands jammed down in his pockets, as he always did when he was upset. Liz left the front door and returned to the kitchen before Ralph arrived home. She heard him enter the front door and run upstairs. When he came back down, he had changed into his old clothes and was headed for the back door.

"Ralph, mind telling me why you're home early from school?"

"Got work to do, Ma. Gonna get thrown out anyhow."

"You had better not get thrown out of school. Go on and do your chores. After supper I want the whole family in the front room. We have some things to discuss, and not the least will be why you're in trouble at school."

The evening meal was a quiet affair. Liz knew that everyone was aware of what had happened at school except her. Al and Sally Marie exchanged amused glances while Timmie kept looking at Ralph. Ralph ate with his head down and never said a word. Liz Atlee was patient; she knew she would get the truth momentarily.

"Now, children, this evening I want to talk to you about our future. What we decide to do tonight is going to be very important. As you know, I got a letter the other day from your father, and he sounded like his old self. He said he was almost well and hoped to come home very soon so that we could get on with our lives. I was so excited; I was ready to buy a train ticket to Hopkinsville right that instant. However, today I received another letter, and this time the news was not encouraging. I could hardly read it, and none of it made any sense. Children, I am afraid we have lost your father forever."

Liz stopped talking and looked around the room. Sally Marie was seated right next to her as she always was; Al was seated to her right in the only ladder-back chair in the tiny room. Timmie was seated Indian style in the floor, and the always-timid Ralph was leaning against the door frame leading to the hallway. He always took such a position in case he wanted to leave quickly.

The silence in the room was nerve-wracking. Sally Marie sniffled quietly, and Ralph rubbed the toe of his shoe back and forth across the wood floor.

It suddenly occurred to Liz that she was now the head of the family. In the past she had always deferred to Marv, but now all the responsibility fell upon her. She prayed that she was up to the task.

"Now, children, this farm has a mortgage, and if we don't pay it off, we lose the farm and our home. We are in a pickle. Jes has a job and is going back to the mines. He's gonna help us out as much as he can, but the coal mines come first. Your Uncle Jeb is going to help out, too, but we are going to have to do the rest. Alvin is old enough to take on a lot of responsibility, but Timmie and Ralph are still awfully young. Like it or not, we have to do it. I thought about selling the farm and moving to Centertown, but there won't be much left after the note is paid off, and I don't know how we would live. I will do whatever you children decide."

"Ma, we ain't gonna lose this ol' farm. I'm the oldest, and Pa would want me to take the lead. I'll soon be 10, and that's plenty old 'nough. Jes went to the mines when he was twelve."

"Alvin, we need to have a talk about your grammar. You would not be talking like that if your father was . . ."

"Mother, I'm the oldest, not Al. I can help in the fields. I'll help the boys."

"Sally Marie, you will have all you can do to help me with everything else that needs doing. We will help the boys together when we can. I can strip tobacco with anybody."

"Ma, I can plow and disk and cut hay and all that as good as Pa could. Timmie and Ralph is a catchin' on real good. Maybe, not with no 'Walkin' Plow' yet. We can all hoe terbacker, chop out corn, sucker terbacker, and the like."

"Ye can't plow as good as Pa."

"Plow circles 'round ye, little Ralphie."

"Enough, enough. That reminds me. Why did Ralph leave school early today?"

The children started to laugh, and the tension of the moment was momentarily lifted. Ralph's faced turned a deep red as his head fell down to his chest. Ralph always amused Liz when he was embarrassed. She held her finger to her lips to quieten the other children.

"Ma, ol' Ralph busted Joey Thom in the nose," Al announced proudly.

Liz's mouth dropped open in astonishment. "Ralph Atlee, Joey is two years older and a lot bigger than you. What on earth got into you?"

"Ma, Joey said that Pa was in the looney bin, and ol' Ralph just socked 'im a good one. Blood flew ever'where, and Joey screamed like a chicken."

"All right, Alvin, I get the point. Ralph, I will not have any more of this. I'm going to school with you tomorrow, and you will apologize to your teacher and to Joey. You are not going to do things like that just because your own aunt is the teacher. Aunt Jane and I will come up with some appropriate punishment for you. You should be ashamed. Your father would be disappointed."

Liz stood, folded her arms, and pushed her chin forward. Her glasses were always right on the tip of her nose. The Atlee children carried that image of their mother throughout their lives. Al called it the "Ma means business look." The technique worked since Liz never had to shout or threaten her children about anything.

The Atlee children knew the meeting was over and it was time to get busy. Their mother was through talking for the night. Now it was time for them to get busy, and so they did. Sally Marie headed for the kitchen to clean up from the supper meal. Al jumped from his chair and started issuing orders.

"I'll slop the hogs. Timmie, you feed the chickens and bring in some water. Ralph, you do the milkin' and throw hay down for the horses." Timmie and Ralph were headed for the back door before Al finished his comments. Liz smiled to herself. The Atlee family had a big job ahead of them; but if they failed, it would not be because her children did not give it their best effort.

By the time Jes returned to work in the mines, he had developed a genuine fondness for the Atlee children. For Jes, work was one of the most important things a man could do. He felt it was not only an economic necessity, but a measure of a man's character as well. Little boys trying to work like men certainly earned his respect.

"Don't look now, boys, but I think I see ol' Doc Ivey a comin' down the road. Yessir, that's 'im."

Al, Timmie, and Ralph shaded their eyes to get a better look at the portly middle-aged man riding toward them on a mule. A grass sack served him as a saddle, and the mule's bridle was made of rope. Jes and the boys had been repairing fencing since sunup and had stopped for a drink and short rest.

Al snorted. "Pa always said we is to show them Iveys respect. Don't know why we should. Don't even believe in God. Pa said it was 'cause they're our elders."

"Al, I purt near twenty-four-year-old, and I call 'im Mister Ivey." Jes placed his finger to his lips to quieten the youngsters before adding, "... yere a bit short in the seat yet, and if yere daddy wuz here, he'd say show respect."

Doc Ivey rode his mule right up to the barbed wire fence and surveyed the group with a sarcastic grin. He spat a stream of amber at a fence post and said, "... well, if it ain't the Atlee younguns lolly gaggin' in the shade. Jes, can't ye get no work outta them little tramps?"

Jes's face burned with anger as he came to the boys' defense. "Mister Ivey, I reckon I do. The boys and me get a lotta work done."

"Well, bust my britches, ye couda fooled me. Looks like they could run off and go fishin' to me. Jest like ol' Marv Atlee, lazy and no count. Marv a laid up down yonder in the loonie-tic assloom drinkin' lemonade and a thinkin' he got Jes Caughill and the boys a doin' his work fer 'im. I always said anybody that believes the rot in that book he reads is a simple-minded fool. The Bible this and the Bible that is all he can talk 'bout. No wonder he went crazy. 'nough to make my mule puke. Younguns big 'nough to stand up and bawl fer buttermilk. Whatcha little ruffians gonna do when Jes goes back to the mines full time? Ye done worked 'im to death. Gotta get a coal minin' job so he can get some rest."

Jes was so angry that he couldn't look in Doc Ivey's direction. He knew what he needed was what his father called a good ol' fashioned "cussin," but he could never bring himself to talk to another man that way. Jes's breathing was labored, and his hands trembled. Doc Ivey's words were vicious and uncalled for. Before Jes could think of something to say, Doc Ivey spoke again.

"Well, little Ralphie, whatcha got yere back up 'bout? Standin' off over there with yere back turned and yere hands in yere pockets. Can't do no work with yere hands in yere pocket."

"We gets lots of work done, Mister Ivey. Us and Jes been fixin' fences all mornin' and bitin' heads off backer worms to boot."

"Ralph done said it right, Mister Ivey. Old Ralph is a backer worm bitin' fool. He'd grab a backer worm and bit its head and have 'nother in his mouth 'for the first one hits the dirt. All me and Timmie can do to keep 'im in backer worms."

Al finished his speech about Ralph's tobacco worm killing ability with a big grin. Timmie was sniggering, and Jes was finding it difficult not to laugh. Doc Ivey's mouth dropped open in utter astonishment. Tobacco amber was running down each corner of his mouth, but he did not appear to notice. He was clearly dumbfounded by Ralph and Al's ability to stand up to him.

"You, you dirty, nasty little boys. Jest plumb nasty. Eatin' terbacker worms. I ain't never heerd nothin' like it. I'm gonna ride right up to the house right now and tell yere mama."

Doc Ivey rode away but did not turn up the lane toward the house. Even Doc Ivey knew better than to cross Liz Atlee, especially when her children were involved. Al and Timmie were rolling on the ground laughing, and Jes had to steady himself against a fence post.

"Younguns, I said show 'im respect, but I reckon he got what he asked fer on that one."

When Jes finished laughing, he noticed that Ralph had walked away and was standing with his head down. Jes knew he was crying, and he walked over and placed a large, callused hand on Ralph's tiny shoulder.

"Son, don't pay no 'ttention to that ol' fool."

"Jes, he's the one orta be in the loonie bin. He don't have no right to talk like that."

"No, Ralph, he don't, but he done it anyhow. He's a dirty, lowdown ol' pup. World's full of 'em, I reckon, and ain't nothin' we can do 'bout it. Reckon ye and Al teach 'im to suck eggs. Served 'im right, but best if yere mama don't find out, or she'll skin us all. Not yere fault, boy, and not yere daddy's neither."

"Jes, have ye heerd all them tales 'bout the Iveys? Pa and me went to Centertown one time, and the men there was talkin' 'bout how ol' Doc sleeps in a pine coffin ever' night of the world. Wants to make shore it's comfortable in the afterlife. Said he wanted to have it outta pine so he could go through hell a poppin'. One ol' man swore he got it in his Will that a fella is gonna sit on his coffin when they carry him in the church a playin' on a fiddle 'Pop Goes the Weasel' and 'Turkey in the Straw.'"

Jes laughed. "Al, I don't reckon ol' Doc be caught in a mile of a church dead or alive. Now my own daddy swears the coffin is real ... he seen it."

"NOW, let's get to bitin' them terbacker worms 'fore they get scared and run off."

The boys laughed at Jes's last comment, and they went back to stringing barbed wire with renewed energy. Jes smiled to himself. He knew it would not be long until the youngsters would be able to stand on their own two feet and without help from anyone.

Liz Atlee took over the leadership of the family with grim determination. She soon learned she was good at motivating her young family. Marv had always told her the best leader was one who led by example, and he cited Moses and Jesus to illustrate his point.

A few months after Marv went to the asylum, Liz became alarmed by stories circulating in the community about formation of a vigilante group in the county called "Possum Hunters." The Tobacco War had been over for several years, but the ember had been smoldering for some time. Soon men in Ohio County would be donning masks like the Night Riders in the Black Patch conflict. The Walton's Creek School was the place for an organizational meeting, and Jes and his father had attended. They were told it was to discuss a tobacco pool, but it soon became evident that some people had other ideas. The rumors were circulating that the group would be "waitin'" on people who drank, gambled, did not work, etc. The new group was a "do-good organization."

Jes and his father refused to join, and this troubled Liz since it was known far and wide that he was working for her in addition to his mining job. For the first time since Marv left, she longed for presence of a man in the household. A woman alone with young children was a vulnerable target.

The Possum Hunters had been active for some time when Liz started sleeping with Marvin's Thomas Barker 12-gauge, double-barreled shotgun under her bed. The gun was Marv's prized possession for hunting. He paid nearly 14 dollars for the weapon from the Sears Roebuck catalog. Marv, as an avid artist, admired the silver image of a hunting dog inlaid in the stock. She knew Marv would never approve of her actions. He would never use a weapon against another man, even to protect his property.

The weather was warm, and a shower early in the evening had made sleeping a peaceful matter. The children were fast asleep when Liz suddenly sprang awake. She had been doing that a lot since the Hunters had been active. She lay, listening intently for a sound that should not be there. Her hair stood on end, and she broke out in goose bumps all over her body when the night air brought to her ears the faint snort of a horse. Her horses were in the barn with the cows. In a few moments the strange horse picked up a small stone on the lane leading to the house; the animal's rider was not on a social call.

Liz quietly slipped from her bed and peered out the upstairs bedroom window. A fog had settled around the hill since the rain, but she could see the image of a horse and rider emerging from haze near the orchard. When they got closer, she could see that the rider was a tall man wearing a long black coat and hat despite the warm weather. In addition to the hat, something appeared to be concealing his face. A gun was balanced across the saddle, and a lantern hung from the saddle horn. Fastened to one of the saddlebags was a coal oil can. He had come to burn her barn.

The rider appeared to be alone and was moving slowly and deliberately until he was right under Liz's window and continued between the well and the meathouse and on to the barn, which stood in the rear and to the right. Liz waited until he had passed the house before pulling the loaded shotgun quietly from under the bed. She had never been more frightened in her life, and the gun felt like it weighed a hundred pounds. She placed the barrel of the gun on the windowsill and then dropped to her knees. The weapon had to be aimed at an angle since the horse and rider were at the rear of the house and to one side.

The rider stopped his horse and looked at the barn for what seemed like an eternity for Liz. He appeared to be in no hurry to dismount or reach for the coal oil can. Liz steadied herself and leveled the twin barrels of the weapon at the rider's back. She was trembling so hard it was difficult to get her fingers around the triggers. Suddenly she remembered she had not cocked the hammers or what men called the "ears." With great difficulty she pulled back both hammers, and the gun was ready to fire.

The seconds dragged by as Liz continued to keep the gun trained on the man's back. Her stomach churned and sweat dripped from under her arms and down her back. The thought of killing another human being frightened her, but she was determined that no Possum Hunter hiding behind a mask was going to burn her barn. If the law wanted to send a woman with four children, a mortgaged farm, and a husband in the asylum to prison, then so be it. She would go to prison and keep her barn.

Liz could not understand what the Possum Hunter was doing. Why didn't he dismount or reach for the coal oil can? Surely he meant to burn the barn. She had decided not to fire until he made his move. She knew from previous experience that the gun had a tremendous kick and she would probably be knocked to the floor and the gun would fall to the ground below. She imagined the repercussion and could see the flash of the barrels in her mind. Liz knew the man would probably die that night. The sounds of his screams and those of his horse raced through her mind. The gun's report would echo down the hillside and all over the Walton's Creek neighborhood. The chickens would start squawking from inside the henhouse, and the children would be frightened out of their wits.

When Liz felt she could stand the suspense no longer, the rider turned his horse and started to ride back toward the house. He had passed the back porch and was on the opposite side of the house. For a moment Liz thought he might try to get in the house. She raced to another window just as he passed the house on his way back down the lane from whence he had come. At that moment she recognized the horse.

Liz placed the shotgun by her bedroom window and went back to bed. She prayed a short prayer to God for defusing the situation and preserving her barn. She lay in bed trying to calm down, but the image of the mare was burned in her mind. The rider had brought the horse to Marvin for treatment of Glanders. He did not live in the Walton's Creek neighborhood, but Liz knew some of his family. Marv asked two dollars for treating the horse, and the man said that all he had was a dollar and a half. Marv said that was fine and he could pay the rest at his convenience. Liz was certain Marv never got the money, and three years had passed.

Liz Atlee never knew everything that transpired that evening. A small group of a dozen Possum Hunters had met in the woods near the Walton's Creek Church to discuss burning barns. Marv's brother Jeb heard about the meeting and the possibility that his brother's barn might be a target. Jeb was as deeply religious as Marv and fearless. He rode his horse into the midst of the Possum Hunters and dismounted. Armed only with his Bible, he got down to business.

"Boys, I know ever last one of ye. Mask or no mask. God knows ye, too. I know ye come tonight to burn Marvin's barn. God only knows why. Marvin ain't here to defend his family, and I came in his place. You boys been usin' my barn to meet in. I got a promise in return ye wouldn't burn my barn or nobody else's 'round here or anybody here hurt or killed. I pray God will forgive me fer makin' a deal with evil. I release ye from that promise. Burn my barn if ye must, but don't burn Marvin's. Liz and the children are doin' their dead level best to get by. I know fer a fact that ever one of ye owes Marvin money fer doctorin' yere stock. He never dunned ye and never will. If any of ye had the faith God bestowed on ye over yonder in that church, ye would take off them masks and pay that woman what ye owe. After ye have done that, if ye gotta see a barn burn, go burn mine."

Jeb Atlee mounted his horse and rode slowly home. The tears streamed down his face as he rode away. When he was within a half mile of his home, he could smell smoke and could see the red ring of fire in the sky. The Possum Hunters did not burn his barn that night, but a neighbor was not as fortunate.

The Possum Hunters had been stirred by Jeb's speech. The orders to burn Marvin's barn came from higher up in the organization, and the local men did not understand why and had little stomach to hurt the family of a man they all liked and admired. The vote was 11 to 1 to bypass the Atlee farm. The lone dissenter, however, decided to undertake the mission alone. For reasons known only to him, he changed his mind. He went to his grave a few years later not knowing how close he came to dying that night at the hands of a small but determined God-fearing woman who was committed to saving her barn. Liz would also die without ever revealing what transpired that night to anyone except Sally Marie. The incident that would have been the talk of the country for years did not happen.

The Atlee children, like most neighborhood youngsters, went to school when they could, but farm work was always of prime importance. Liz was very pragmatic about their life, but she never lectured the children or bossed them about what needed to be done. Her directions came in the form of quiet suggestions or subtle questions about how things were going. Jes and Jeb were a tremendous help as the boys matured as farmers. Outwardly, Liz took the attitude that the children were merely doing what was necessary and no more. Inwardly, however, she could not have been more proud of them.

Liz Atlee's attitude toward Christmas and Thanksgiving was austere at best. She never told the children they were too poor to buy presents. She said the holidays were not a time for extravagance. She bought each of the boys a pocketknife for Christmas, and Sally Marie received a handkerchief. After they were grown and married, she bought them nothing. Deep down, Liz Atlee really did not believe in being lavish at any time. She also felt children would not realize they were receiving little at Christmas if the adults "... don't go 'round blubbering about it."

Every Thanksgiving Liz would announce, "Younguns, tomorrow is Thanksgiving ... somebody go ring a couple of old chicken's necks." Christmas dinner was even less generous than Thanksgiving. If the weather permitted on Christmas Eve, Liz would give each boy one 22-caliber rifle shell. Her speech was always the same, "... you boys want any Christmas dinner you have to go shoot some rabbits."

Ralph Atlee's first lesson in frugality came on the Christmas when he was seven. He accompanied Al and Timmie rabbit hunting, and each took a turn with the single-shot rifle. Al and Timmie killed a hare, but Ralph missed. Liz looked at the fruits of their labor and said, "... you killed them, you skin them." She ignored the fact that Ralph did not have a rabbit until the meal was almost over. What she said stuck with Ralph for the rest of his life: "... I reckon you all noticed that Christmas dinner was a little short of meat this year. That's because Ralph missed his rabbit."

It did not matter if it was a holiday or not, Liz still rationed each boy to one shell, and they were expected to provide the bulk of the family's next meal. Liz learned this bit of frugality from Marvin.

Al Atlee's strong personality and leadership skills were starting to develop. As the eldest son, he felt he should be the boss, but Ralph and Timmie resented his abrasive manner. In time Al learned from Uncle Jeb's low-key approach. Their uncle never tried to boss them on the farm but was always making suggestions or advising. Al soon learned suggesting to his brothers that "... this is probably what Pa would want us to do" worked better than barking orders.

Timmie and Ralph were two very stubborn little boys, but they eventually accepted Al as the leader, and they continued to seek his counsel as long as they lived. Timmie asked for Al's advice when he was thinking about getting married. Al exploded, ". . . HELL'S bells, Timmie, I ain't gonna tell ye who to marry." When it was Ralph's turn to get married, he told Timmie, ". . . I ain't gonna ask 'im, Tim. I already know the answer."

The Atlee boys worked hard as youngsters, but life was not drudgery. The time they spent in the creek bottoms was divided between work, swimming, fishing, and boating. The bond between them became very strong, but they fussed and teased one another without mercy.

Al, Timmie, and Ralph were saddled with adult responsibilities when they were mere children, but they still behaved like little boys. Timmie and Ralph scuffled frequently and often got up with black eyes and scratches. Liz never paid any attention. Once when they were wrestling by the back porch, she came out of the kitchen with a dishpan of water, which she tossed out in the yard as she did many times each day. She walked calmly back in the kitchen while her youngest sons wiped soapy water out of their eyes.

Ralph and Timmie were not above tormenting their older brother as well. One day they were resting after dinner, before returning to the tobacco patch. Ralph was seated on the ground with his back against a shade tree when Al walked by.

"Al, ye got the loudest damn feet in the whole country. Dig them heels in the ground like a bitin' sow a goin' to war."

"YOU don't say. I reckon then ye got feet like a little sparrow."

"I SHORE do. Got feet like a Philadelphia lawyer."

Al grabbed Ralph's foot and jerked his shoe and sock off. "Well," he said, "I always wondered if a Philly-delphie lawyer got toe jam between his toes."

Ralph kicked Al in the stomach, and the boys started rolling around in the grass until Timmie drowned them with a bucket of cold well water. Al and Ralph grabbed their hoes and chased their baby brother back to the tobacco patch. These escapades never bothered Liz. She knew it was a normal part of growing up for three rambunctious young boys.

Al was nicknamed "Ol' Man" by his younger brothers and was teased at length about being the boss. Timmie and Ralph loved their older brother, but the bond between the two of them was much stronger. The people in Walton's Creek, Matanzas, and Centertown communities never referred to them separately. It was always "Tim 'n Ralph." Jes Caughill said "... seen one ye seen the other ... always together."

The Atlee children had heard of telegrams, but they never expected to receive one. They sat quietly at the dinner table while their mother opened the message. A man from Centertown had rushed out to the farm with it, and they all knew that it had to be something important. Liz looked at the message for a long time before she folded it and placed it in her apron pocket. She went back to eating her meal as if nothing was wrong. When the meal was over Liz said, "Children, your father is coming home ... for good."

Charlie Smith's old road wagon lumbered down the road, slowing occasionally for a chug hole. The team of mules plodded ahead methodically, confident they were doing their job. Charlie held the reins loosely and allowed the mules to navigate the road as they saw fit. He was dressed in a starched white shirt and a new pair of overalls plus his black "Sunday go to meetin' hat" perched on top of his head. Seated next to Charlie was ol' Sal wearing a feed sack dress. Her tremendous girth took up most of the wagon seat and forced Charlie to drive the team from an odd angle. Cain and Abel were dressed in starched white shirts, almost new overalls, but were barefooted. The sun was warm and bright in late April, not unlike the day Marvin Atlee took sick while returning from the Smith farm. The clumping of the mules' feet echoed against the slow tolling of the bells at the Walton's Creek Church.

The preacher had just started to speak when Charlie pulled up the team.

"Brethern, we gather here at this gravesite to say farewell to Brother Marvin Atlee. The Death Angel recently visited the Atlee home and took from Elizabeth Atlee a husband and from her children—Sally Marie, Alvin, Ralph, and Timmie—a kind and loving father. The Walton's Creek Church lost a deacon and faithful servant. All present knows that Marvin was honest, industrious, benevolent, mild, and reticent; untainted by avarice and ambition, he glided along in the quiet undercurrent of life from whence the purest virtues flow. The community lost a hard-working farmer and veterinarian. Brother Marvin entered this life on July 15, 1868, and joined the church in December of 1882. We bow in humble submission to the will and act of our Heavenly Father. That we commend the life, conduct, and Christian character of Brother Marvin as one worthy of imitation by all our young men. That we extend to the loved ones of our departed brother, our loving sympathy and fellowship in their sorrow. May we bow our heads and pray."

Jes Caughill raised his head at the final amen. He thought the preacher would never stop. Brother Tom had just completed the longest prayer Jes had ever heard. Brother Tom always found it hard to stop praying, but today he had repeated some parts several times.

The Atlee boys walked stoically past Jes and did not speak. He was glad because he did not know what to say to them. The mourners left the gravesite, and Jes pulled back, creasing the brim of his hat nervously. From the corner of his eye he could see Liz Atlee walking slowly with her arm around a sobbing Sallie Marie.

When the last persons had left Marv Atlee's grave, Jes put his hat back on and adjusted the brim. He looked out across the cemetery just as Charlie Smith was turning his wagon around for the trip back home. They had come to say goodbye to an old and trusted friend, but the roadway was as close as they dared venture to a white man's world.

The doctors at the state hospital diagnosed Marvin Atlee as manic depressive, suicidal, and suffering from delusions because he thought he was rich. The physicians had never seen Marvin's farm or met his family and friends like the Charlie Smiths. Mentally, Marvin was a sick man, but he was indeed a rich man.

It took three days for Marv Atlee's body to arrive at Centertown. The train whistle was immediately met by the tolling of the bells at Walton's Creek Church. The bell tolled slowly, once for each of his 49 years; and Jes was at the cemetery with his tools by the time the tolling stopped. In later years the Atlee boys would join Jes many times as they dug the graves of friends and neighbors. An aging Jes Caughill would leave his sickbed to dig a grave for Timmie Atlee. Jes would tell Myrtle Caughill, "... it's the least I can do fer the youngun'."

On Decoration Day, Charlie Smith brought Liz Atlee a huge bouquet of red roses.

"Ol' Sal 'n me wud be proud ifin' yo wud put dim roses on Mista Marv's grave. Went on 'bout dim bloomin'. Say dim roses come from his mama's garden. Wud git cuttin' fir yo garden … neveuh does it. Miz Lizbut, life jist ain't t'same wif Mista Marv gone. By t'way. Cain and Abel 'ike fo' yo put dist wif dim roses and ol' Charlie sturb yo' no more."

Charlie handed Liz Atlee the roses in a homemade basket made from strips of tree bark with a small piece of paper attached to the handle. Liz could tell Charlie was crying as he mounted his old mule for the ride home. Liz carefully opened the paper, revealing a neat circle about the size of a dime. Inside the circle was the Lord's Prayer. The prayer was written in a spiraling fashion with the last letter of the final word ending directly in the middle, and the letters were large enough to read. The Smith family had treasured the tiny scrap of paper without ever knowing what it said; and with the death of Marvin Atlee, they never would.

Forty-six years after Grandfather Atlee's death, Mickey was walking down Main Street in the county seat of Hartford when an elderly friend hailed him. The portly gentleman, dressed in his customary overalls, was excited to see him. He grabbed Mickey's arm and escorted him several yards until they were in front of a frail, elderly man seated on the retaining wall in front of the courthouse. The old man struggled to his feet to shake hands. The next few minutes were ones that Mickey would never forget. The man quickly identified Mickey as the grandson of Marvin Atlee.

"Son," he said, "I know your grandpa died long 'fore ye was born. A fine man he was. I'm gonna tell ye a little story about him that you will treasure for the rest of yere born days."

Mickey stood spellbound as the frail old farmer recounted the story of Grandfather Atlee writing the Lord's Prayer inside a circle drawn around a dime. The man was right; he would never forget.

Mickey Atlee's mind drifted in and out of reality as he relived the countless stories that told his family saga. The story of Grandfather and Grandmother Atlee faded into the recesses of his mind as another drama took center stage.

Christmas Nearly Forgotten (1921)

CHRISTMAS NEARLY FORGOTTEN
(1921)

MICKEY HAD DIFFICULTY *imagining his father growing up in a household where Christmas and Thanksgiving were viewed almost like any other day. His mom, on the other hand, a prolific storyteller—became thoughtful during the holidays and mesmerized him with stories from her childhood. Despite meager resources, Jes and Myrtle Caughill always managed to put a great meal on the table and purchase a few gifts for Mickey's mom and uncle.*

The story Mickey enjoyed most was the time Jes and Myrtle had forgotten it was Christmas. After working half a day in the mines, Jes drudged miles across the fields and up railroad tracks to do the shopping. Meanwhile, Myrtle worked feverishly preparing a modest feast. The extraordinary efforts by Grandmother and Grandfather Caughill took on special significance for Mickey as he grew older.

Mickey felt a lump in his throat as he recalled the tale of the Christmas nearly forgotten.

Jes Caughill's work brogans crunched against the ice that was rapidly forming over the muddy ground. Sleet and freezing rain were falling on earth that had been soaked with rain for two weeks. The winter of 1921 had been generally mild but extremely wet. Jes had recently moved his family from the Walton's Creek community to a small three-room house near the Central Grove Baptist Church, located between Centertown and Hartford. He had secured a job in the Dilbert underground mines, located about a mile from the church. Two dollars per day, five or six days a week, was a modest wage for coal miners of the times, but not uncommon. Work had been scarce, and Jes was glad to have the job. He was relieved that he could move from Walton's Creek to find work knowing the Atlee boys were old enough to strip the tobacco without him.

Jes left for work after arising at 3:00 AM. The temperature was just above freezing, and Myrtle's laundry was still dripping on the clothesline. She told Jes at breakfast, ". . . if them clothes don't get dry today or pert near it, we gotta hang 'em in the house." He nodded in agreement as he wolfed down a meal of biscuits, gravy, and scrambled eggs—followed by a mug of coffee.

The dinner bucket Jes carried to work sloshed with water. Jes got heartburn if he ate any food while working in the cramped mine shaft. Water was the only thing he could consume. Many miners came to work with water-filled dinner buckets for the same reason and often because they had no food to bring. It was not uncommon for men to bring apple or potato peelings in their dinner bucket, leaving the rest home for the family. The most ordinary meal for a coal miner was a piece of cornbread or biscuit sopped with molasses.

When Jes arrived at the mines at 4:30 AM, the temperature was starting to drop, and a light mist gripped the air. A full moon helped light the way, and Jes could smell Mike Dilbert's pipe long before he arrived at the mouth of the mines.

"Mornin,' Jes. I knowed that was you a comin' long for ye got here. I hear one foot go clump and then after a bit another clump. You stride longer than no man I ever knowed. Been aimin' to ask ye 'bout a comin' over t'mor and runnin' them pumps. They stay idle fer a whole day after all this rain, and we'll get flooded fer sure."

Jes lit his carbide lamp, fastened it to his hat, and stared through the dim light at Mike Dilbert. He cleared his throat and said, "Mike, are ye a tellin' me we ain't gonna work t'mor?"

"That's right, Jes. I ain't gonna work on Christmas and I ain't a gonna ask my men to neither."

"CHRISTMAS DAY. Mike, Christmas is a week off yet."

"NO, Jes, this is Christmas Eve. Don't ye ever look at no calendar?"

"Well, I reckon we got one somers, but I ain't looked at it in a spell."

Jes started pacing around the front of the mines looking at the ground.

"Mike, I got two little 'uns at home, and we ain't got a fetch fired thing fer Christmas."

"Well, Jes, you live closer to the mines than any of the rest of us. If ye can run them pumps an hour or so t'mor, I'll let ye go home at dinner and pay ye fer the whole day."

Jes left the mines at noon that day, his clothes soaked with perspiration. The poorly ventilated mines of the day left the miners dripping with sweat. In a coal mining career that would eventually span more than three decades, Jes frequently walked or rode a horse or mule two or three miles home in bitter cold weather with wet clothing. Arriving home with frozen clothes was common for miners in the 1920s. Jes was accustomed to the elements, but he felt the cold drizzle about to freeze was the worst.

Myrtle's clothes were still on the line when Jes arrived home at noon. The sheets, towels, and clothing now glistened with a thin sheet of ice. Jes hardly gave the laundry a second glance as he burst in the kitchen door without first taking time to wipe his feet. Myrtle jumped with a gasp.

"Scare me to death, why don't ye. What ye doin' home this time of day? OH Lord, don't tell me the mines is gonna shut down."

"NO, did ye know this is Christmas Eve? Ye never tell me nothin'."

"Jes, are ye out of yere ever lovin' mind? This ain't Christmas Eve or least ways I didn't think it was. What did we do with that calendar? Lord, I ain't got nothin'. A little dab of chocolate fer a couple of pies is all. Got that drotted washin' to get dry to boot."

"Here it is a hangin' inside the pie safe. Lotta good it'll do us there. Well, I swan. It is Christmas Eve. MYRTLE, get me some water ready; I'm pullin out to Hartford right this minute."

"Better wash off some of that coal dust, or they will think yere a hobo. Jes, Centertown is closer."

"I knowed that. Gettin' late and stuff be half gone, and Hartford got lots more stores. Six one and half dozen another to walk. Hartford is more, but I can walk up the railroad track over half the way. Save me some time. If'n I don't get back by dark, the full moon will do jest fine."

"Better take yere carbide lamp anyhow. Fall and break yere fool neck, and I ain't comin' lookin' fer ye."

Jes quickly washed the coal dust from his upper body, dressed into clean clothes, grabbed a coffee sack, and started for Hartford. The road from Central Grove to the county seat was a "hog waller." The mild, rainy winter had left the road so muddy that travel was almost impossible. Jes had spent his entire life traversing fields, climbing barbed wire fences, and walking beside railroad tracks to work and to town. He would probably meet other men this day doing the same thing. In the 1920s the road from Centertown to Hartford was not considered an automobile route by the State, a fact known all too well by local residents.

Myrtle rarely had the opportunity to shop in the wintertime. She was not strong enough to make the overland trips with Jes, and she had two youngsters at home who could not make the journey either. Myrtle's shopping was restricted to warm weather when the entire family could go in the road wagon.

Hartford was busy with Christmas shoppers when Jes arrived in town. The rain had stopped, but the temperature was falling rapidly. Jes figured they would get up the next morning to snow on the ground. A white Christmas still excited Jes, and he knew the children would be ecstatic as well.

When Jes walked to town to shop, he was always aware of his limitations. Over the years he had carried 50-pound sacks of meal from the mill and even 100-pound bags of flour. Today he would fill his coffee sack with toys, food items, and gifts for Myrtle. The sack would rest upon his right shoulder, and a huge sack of oranges would dangle from his left hand.

Jes lingered for a few minutes at the drugstore in Hartford. The store had a Columbia Grafonola with records. A Brownie #2 camera caught his eye, but the $2.50 price was more than he wanted to spend. When he examined a woman's comb and brush and discovered the price was $3.50, he quickly left the store. Jes's shopping would be for more practical items like two pair of children's mittens for twenty-five cents a pair, an enamel roasting pan for a quarter, two children's caps for fifty cents each, a large Turkish towel for fifty cents, a pairs of ladie's overshoes for seventy-five cents, two cans of Pet Milk for fifteen cents each, a can of Calumet Baking Powder for a dime; a simple doll for a little girl cost a quarter. Jes rushed through the shopping as he calculated the figures in his head. When the total reached eight dollars, he stopped. There were more items that he wanted to purchase, but he felt eight dollars was more than he could afford.

Jes left Hartford by way of the railroad tracks. He thought about a widow lady who lived near Walton's Creek with a house full of children. A year before, Jes was walking home from Centertown with one 100 pounds of flour when the lady rushed out to the road and asked for his sack. She explained that her children were hungry and she was in need. Jes replied that he had children to feed as well, and they would go without if he gave her his flour. Once Jes watched the woman carry a large sack of goose feathers to town so she could purchase five pairs of shoes for her children. She carefully placed the shoes on the counter and then presented the feathers for payment. Jes could tell she did not have enough for more than four pairs, a fact discreetly overlooked by the proprietor. Jes wondered if that lady had food for her children this Christmas Eve.

The house Jes was renting at Central Grove cost three dollars per month. In addition to the tiny house, they had a chicken house, outdoor toilet, and a small barn. When Jes arrived shortly after dark, he hid the sack of gifts in the barn and carried to the house the cooking items that Myrtle had asked him to buy.

When Jes entered the warm kitchen, Myrtle was busy cooking, with laundry hanging on makeshift lines near the stove. The kitchen was steamy as laundry behind the stove gave off clouds of mist, like smoke. The cramped situation did not hamper Myrtle, however. She was accustomed to cooking under primitive conditions. She had not been idle while Jes was gone. Myrtle had baked two chocolate pies and chocolate cake and had made fudge as well. Jes was not surprised; he had married a woman whose skills in the kitchen had few equals. He always looked forward to her cakes and pies during the holidays.

Myrtle did not look in Jes's direction when he entered the house.

"Took ye long 'nough. Gone four hours. Where the blazes did ye go?"

"Stores all picked over. Went to a half dozen 'for I got ever'thing ye asked fer."

"Spill it out, Jes. I know ye forgot somethin'. Been sighin' ever since ye walked in the door."

"Myrtle, I always get Anna a doll. Got one this time, too, but it ain't there now. Been through ever'thing in the sack, and it's gone."

"Is that all ye got the child?"

"Purt near it. All that amounts to anything. I gotta go back and that's all there is to it."

"Jes, ye done 'nough fer one day, and besides, the stores in Hartford 'ill be closed by the time ye get there."

"I knowed that. Centertown is closer, and I'm goin' there."

"Jes. Stores down there 'll be closed, too."

"I reckon I know that. Mr. Chester lives right close to his store and he got a little gal like us. He'll help me out."

Jes poured a half cup of coffee into a cup and swallowed it with one gulp. After warming himself by the fire for a few moments, he raced out the door and headed for Centertown.

The snow was starting to fall as Jes raced across the fields. The full moon was bouncing off the new fallen snow, and the countryside that had looked so dark and bare that morning was beginning to take on a festive appearance. Jes had his carbide lamp in his pocket, but he would not need it. He met a man who was climbing a fence with a sack of groceries. The two men said "howdy" as they met and went on their respective routes. The voice was familiar; but Jes did not have time to socialize, as he began to see some faint lights in Centertown.

The town was dark when Jes arrived. He crossed the railroad track and raced up the small hill beside the cemetery. He passed by several homes with coal oil lamplight creeping faintly through the windows. The business section of town was deserted, as the merchants had all headed home to enjoy supper with their families. Jes Caughill was the only one on the streets.

Mister Chester got up from his evening meal to open his store for Jes.

"Jes, I been wonderin' why I ain't seen ye in town."

"We forgot all 'bout it bein' Christmas. I feel like a dad blasted fool."

"Oh, no need in that, Jes. Now, let me see. I know I have a doll or two left but ain't no tellin' where they are. I'm purty near stripped of ever'thing. Best Christmas we had in a spell. 'specially with times hard and all."

"Ain't that a doll over yonder on them nanners? Hold that lamp up a bit higher."

"That's it. Jes, this here doll is the gall durndest thing ye ever seen. Lay her down and she goes to sleep, and stand her up and she wakes up. Costs sixty-five cents, though. I know that's high, but I reckon that's all I got left. They got some fancier than this at Hartford fer a lot more money. No, I take that back, got a little twenty-five cent doll here somers. Wanna look fer it?"

"NOPE, done bought one of them and left it in Hartford. Gonna walk all the way to Centertown, I'm gonna buy this doll. Know how much coal a man gotta load fer sixty-five cents?" Jes laughed as he pulled the two quarters and three nickels from his pocket and paid Mr. Chester. After the two men wished one another a Merry Christmas, Jes retraced his steps to Central Grove. The ground was completely covered with snow when Jes got home, but he was in high spirits when he burst through the kitchen door.

Jes had put in a long day but still far easier than mining coal for twelve hours. He grinned as he showed Myrtle the doll he purchased.

"OH, Jes, Anna will fall in love with this. She orta treasure it if she knowed what ye went through to get it."

"Christmas only comes once a year. Might not be able to buy a drotted thing next year. Ye never know."

"Jes, lots of men wouldn't have done it. Now set yerself down here and eat some pintos, cornbread, and what's rest of the coffee. Don't be a lookin' at them pies, cake, and candy. That's fer Christmas. Now, in the mornin' I want ye to ring an ol' hen's neck. I got sweet potaters, canned green beans, corn, and beets. I'm gonna open a jar of blackberries and make a cobbler. We'll have cornbread dressin' and some mashed potaters with them store-bought peas I had ye get. With the stuff I already got baked, we're gonna have a good ol' dinner. Too bad we didn't have time to get the children a Christmas tree."

"You mean me get a Christmas tree. Now we best get things rounded up and get a little shuteye. Them younguns be up at the dead hour of midnight and there won't be no more sleep after that."

Jes and Myrtle had been asleep about three hours when two pair of little feet scampered into their room.

"WHOA there, younguns. Let me light a lamp so ye can see what ol' Santa brung ye last night. I thought I heerd him a rummagin' 'round here a while ago."

"Was that Santa, Jes? I thought you wuz just a stirrin' up the fire."

"NO, it was ol' St. Nick hisself. I couldn't see 'im real good but it was 'im. Who else runs 'round this time of year a wearin' a red suit?"

Jes had placed the children's gifts on the hearth by the grate. They were wrapped in plain brown paper and tied with white string. Myrtle had carefully written Anna's and Jesse's names on each parcel. Seven-year-old Jesse had doubts about Santa Claus, but five-year-old Anna was excited about Santa and Christmas.

The gifts in the Caughill household varied little year by year. Each child received a cap and a pair of gloves. Jesse had a cap gun and a small sack of firecrackers, but Anna's doll was the biggest sensation. The youngster squealed with delight when Jes showed her how to put the doll to sleep.

A large, graphically illustrated "Mother Goose" book fascinated both children. Jes did not have the patience to read stories to the kids, but Myrtle relished the opportunity. She pulled her chair close to the fire; and while Jes piled more coal on the grate, she read the book to them by the faintly flickering light from the fire and a single coal oil lamp.

Jes went outside for another bucket of coal and came back dragging the large bag of oranges that he had hidden in the kitchen.

"Well, lookie what ol' Santa left out in the kitchen. A bag of oranges. The ol' boy out-did hisself this year."

Oranges were a treat that generally happened only at Christmas. Jes handed Myrtle a knife, and she peeled the fruit for the youngsters while she read the Mother Goose book. Meanwhile, Jes brought out a stack of Western stories that he had purchased for himself. He pulled up his chair and read until Myrtle and the children had gone to sleep. The nursery rhyme dropped to the floor while Anna and Jesse snoozed on the warm hearth. Jes rescued Jesse's firecrackers that he had dropped dangerously close to the fire.

While Myrtle and the children slept, Jes placed a new apron, the enameled roaster pan, and the overshoes and Turkish towel on the kitchen table. They were the only gifts Myrtle would receive. Jes never received a present, and Myrtle never thought about buying him one. The presents that Jes bought her were always practical things. After the children were grown, Jes would come back from town, drop a pair of stockings in Myrtle's lap, and not stop walking. They viewed Christmas as a holiday for children and gave little or no thought to one another. In later years Myrtle did little cooking for the event unless company was coming.

At 5:30 AM Jes quietly woke Myrtle and slipped two large peppermint candy sticks in the children's stockings. They would have another surprise when they woke up for breakfast.

The snow crunched under Jes's feet as he went about his morning chores. Myrtle had enough wood for the cookstove. He started a fire in the stove at 4:30 AM, and it was almost hot enough to make biscuits. The smell of fresh wood smoke against the cold Christmas morning was a delight that no one who had never experienced it could understand. The aroma of wood smoke always started Jes to thinking about Myrtle's biscuits, and when he entered the kitchen door on a cold morning and was greeted by the smell of fresh coffee, he forgot about being cold.

Jes broke the ice on the small pond and refilled the horse's tub in the barn. He decided to leave the horse in the barn since there was little grass for grazing. He fed the animal some hay and headed to the henhouse. The chickens cackled and flapped their wings when he came inside and closed the door behind him. The light was dim, but it took only an instant to snatch a fat hen off a roosting pole. He walked outside and quickly wrung her neck. The remaining chickens seemed more interested in breakfast than what had happened to their companion. Jes tossed them some ground corn, and they flocked after it like they were starved. Jes placed the dead bird on the back porch and went to the well for a couple of buckets of water. He figured the tea kettle would be boiling when he got back inside, and with the aid of the water, the chicken would soon be ready for Myrtle to start cooking.

Jes took the wash down from the makeshift lines in the kitchen. Most were still damp and would be hung back up after dinner. Myrtle and Jes ate a quiet breakfast while the children slept by the fire. When the parents finished eating, Anna and Jesse woke up for their breakfast and afterward were allowed to go outside to look for reindeer tracks.

After breakfast Myrtle started cooking in earnest. Jes headed for the mines to run the pumps until it was time for dinner. Anna and Jesse played with their toys; for Jesse that meant throwing firecrackers at the chickens.

Christmas dinner in the Caughill household was always a feast. When the meal was over, Myrtle covered the food on the table with a tablecloth, but the chicken and dressing was stored in the warming compartment of the stove, along with the cornbread. They washed the dishes and retired in front of the grate where everyone was soon asleep.

The day after Christmas Jes returned to the Dilbert mines, the children returned to school in the one-room schoolhouse at Central Grove, and Myrtle resumed her duties in the home. Jes and Myrtle held the

Christmas holiday in high regard when the children were young and always saved a little money for a few extras. The gifts were modest, but the atmosphere in the home, plus the wonderful meals prepared by Myrtle, made the holiday stand out in the children's memory. The Caughills were poor country people, but the family always felt rich at Christmas.

Myrtle Caughill taught her children proper behavior during the holidays. They had to say thank you before opening a gift, and each package must be opened carefully and not ripped apart in zeal. All presents were to be viewed as an honored gift among adults, and with few exceptions this meant the item was never to be used. The wrapping paper had to be preserved for reuse and out of respect to the gift giver. When Myrtle died, Anna found numerous potholders, towels, sheets, etc., that Myrtle had saved over the years. They were yellow and dry rotted, but Myrtle Caughill honored the tradition even when she needed the items.

The gifts Jes gave Myrtle over the years were either practical or token gestures. She never said thank you and frequently criticized what he bought. In later years she was fond of saying, ". . . ain't never bought him nothin', but he eats 'nough cake and pie durin' Christmas he don't need nothin'."

Myrtle and her sister Kate enjoyed a family tradition that often became a contentious contest between the women. The person who said "Christmas Eve gift" or "Christmas gift" first was supposed to get a present from the other. The women schemed against one another for years. They made telephone calls before daylight, hid behind doors, and engaged other tricks to be the first to yell the greeting. One year Aunt Kate knocked on Myrtle's front door and then ran to the kitchen door. Myrtle opened the front door only to be startled by Kate bursting in the kitchen door screaming "CHRISTMAS GIFT" at the top of her lungs. The loser in the ritual always pretended to be angry, but that year Myrtle Caughill did not need to pretend.

The Christmas that was nearly forgotten in 1921 came and went in the Caughill home, but it lived on for many years in the stories of Christmas past that Myrtle told so eloquently. Anna and Jesse Caughill's childhood was accented by stories, and they became storytellers in their own right when they passed them on to their own children.

Mickey passed a slow-moving vehicle as his memory of the Christmas nearly forgotten faded away.

Working for Cyrus (1929-1931)

WORKING FOR CYRUS
(1929-1931)

*A*LL HIS LIFE *Mickey heard countless accounts of family hardships—none of these stories impressed him more than the vivid accounts of the Great Depression. Like most people, Mickey's father's family struggled; but the family farm was secure and provided shelter and sustenance, even if money was scarce for clothes and other necessities of life. The real struggle was in his mom's family.*

Jes Caughill was nearly 60 before he owned a modest home of his own. He worked in numerous coal mines while living in company housing, farmed, and worked in timber. Mickey's maternal grandfather never failed to provide for his family, but the early years of the Depression were the most trying in his life. That was why, to Mickey, stories about the three years the Caughills lived in a borrowed house and worked for Cyrus Lentz were the most compelling and entertaining in the oral tradition of the family.

Mickey filed away in his mind the story of the Christmas almost forgotten and moved on to the years when the Jes Caughill family worked for Cyrus Lentz.

"By jings, I want ye to move to my house t'mor. Need more help."

"Cyrus, ye got men a helpin' ye right now. Don't need more help. Besides I ain't got no money to pay no rent unless ye aim to pay cash money."

"By jings, ye don't need no money. Work fer me and there ain't no rent. Place fer a garden, chickens, and pigs. Barn fer yere horses. Use my pasture. Work off ground fer terbacker and corn, too. Need ye there t'mor. Ain't gonna wait 'round. Gotta be t'mor."

"Well, I reckon that there is a mighty fine offer. Best I've had in a spell. Mines wants us outta this here bat den in three weeks 'less we want to keep on payin' rent. Ain't got no place lined up neither. Be there first thing in the mornin'. Start at sunup."

Jes Caughill watched Cyrus Lentz turn his old mare named "Inis" around and ride away. Jes had known Cyrus most of his life. When they were teenagers, Jes and his father helped on the Lentz farm. Cyrus, as intelligent as he was eccentric, excelled as a businessman but was not given to long-winded conversations. His sentences were always brief and to the point. Along with his mother and sister, Cyrus took the family farm and made it successful.

"Jes, what did Cyrus want?"

"Wants us to move in that little house of his down from their place. Myrtle, he said I can work off the rent and fer some ground, too. I tol' 'im we'd be there t'mor mornin'. What a relief. Liz Atlee tol' me I can build a bat den outa slabs over there in here woods 'til work picks up 'round here. If it ever does. Gonna be hard times, Myrtle. Mines may not do much 'round here fer years. Mines been gettin' near four dollars a ton. Can't get over a dollar now. Mine boss says can't open a mine fer less than a dollar and a half a ton. This here depression is gonna kill poor folks like us."

"Jes, that little house of Cyrus's is perfectly cute, but I can't believe that Cyrus Lentz would let it go rent free. Been gettin' six dollars a month fer it."

"Cyrus ain't no man's fool. With hard times he knows nobody gonna have money fer rent. He knows me and knows he can go to the bank on my word. Knows we ain't gonna tear nothin' up neither. Better'n a settin' empty. That's how he got money and hires his work done. The man can figure the board foot of lumber needed to build a barn in his head faster any man on paper and the whole time eatin' like he was starved."

"Still don't see how he can give it up rent free. Not ever'body is flat broke, Jes."

"Purt near it. Myrtle, a feller come over to the mines the day we shut down. I reckon he was lookin' fer a job. He come back to Centertown with the wife and younguns and moved in with his father. Lost his job up there and got put out on the street. Carried a little woogit of stuff and walked to the depot and had jest 'nough money to catch the train to Beaver Dam. People in the city can't raise no food like country folks. Starve I reckon. Fellers like 'im is comin' back to the country and can't pay no rent here neither."

"Myrtle, we ain't got no time to be standin' 'round jawin'. You and Anna start packin' things, and Jesse and me will hitch up the wagon, pull up by the door, and get the cookstove loaded. If it ain't too hot."

"Jes, mind a tellin' me why in tarnation we gotta leave out at the crack of dawn? Cyrus ain't a gonna change his mind."

"Ye ain't never hauled no iron stove up a steep hill in a road wagon. Gonna need to make two trips to get ever'thing moved. Ain't got time to fool 'round."

"You better get them chickens corralled before dark. Them Banties 'ill fly up in the highest tree and yere gonna have a happy time a gettin' 'em down in the mornin' 'fore daylight."

"I reckon I know that. Gonna get Jesse busy with some terbacker sticks a makin' more crates. Got more hens than we had when we moved here. We got 'nough dinner left to have a dab of supper, and we can cook some eggs, coffee, and flapjacks over a fire in the mornin'."

"Jes, you ain't about to get my new coffeepot black as an ol' stove pipe. I ain't gonna have it. We can boil some coffee in a Dutch oven. If I catch ye with my new coffeepot anywhere near that fire, I'll knock you in the head. The first decent pot we've had since we got married."

"If ye aim to be the Straw Boss over breakfast, don't be a sleepin' 'til dinner. Need to be ready at the crack of dawn. No lollygaggin' 'round."

Jes and Myrtle Caughill fought and argued during the move to Cyrus Lentz's little two-story house, but they soon settled into their new home. Myrtle loved the house, and Jes was relieved that they were secure with a roof over their heads while he was unemployed.

The Caughills had lived in Cyrus's house for several weeks before he asked Jes to do some work. Jes had been to the house several times to offer, but the answer was always the same, ". . . by jings, I'll call ye when I need ye." Jes had been called back to the mines to work occasionally as a night watchman, but the pay was only $1.20 per night.

The air was crisp and chilly in early March when Cyrus finally decided he needed Jes's assistance. Jes walked up to Cyrus's house shortly after sunup. He could see the chickens running in the backyard and knew someone had come out to feed them. The soft clucking of a female voice was that of Molly Lentz, Cyrus's sister. Never married, Molly was always dressed conservatively, quiet and shy and totally devoid of Cyrus's eccentric ways. For some reason that he could not explain, Jes felt sorry for Molly. She always seemed just a little sad.

"OH, Jes, you startled me. I didn't see ye walk up."

"Sorry, Molly. Thought I was makin' 'nough noise to raise the dead."

"Got a full pot of coffee. Want some?"

"No, thanks. Done drunk half a pot at breakfast. Cyrus ready?"

"He's done gone down to the shed to collect the tools. He's been wantin' that slat-wire fence for a coon's age. Don't know what got into 'im to start today."

"Well, I reckon I'll go on down. Best get an early start if'n he wants to get done today."

Jes started down the hill toward the shed. The Lentz family had once lived in the little house Cyrus had rented to Jes. The kitchen was tiny, and Molly and Ma Lentz wanted to build a new one. Cyrus objected, but Ma and Molly had enough money of their own that they built the new house without any help from Cyrus. Upset that they had spent so much money, Cyrus would not let them move in it. The house sat empty for almost a year until Cyrus went to Hartford for Court Day. Molly hooked a horse to a sled, and they moved. When Cyrus got home, he was faced with doing his own cooking and laundry or moving as well. He moved.

Cyrus had idolized his father and wanted to keep everything as it had been when he was alive. That meant living in the same house and no marriage for Molly or for him. Cyrus was trying desperately to fill the role of protector in his father's absence, and that meant discouraging Molly's male suitors.

Jes could hear Cyrus rummaging in the toolshed for the tools they would need to build a slat-wire fence. Cyrus's collection of tools was a marvel. He had tools, many homemade that had been in the family for generations. A wooden hay rake, wooden tobacco pegs, wall hooks, sawhorse, filing horse, apple butter paddle, a handmade wood plane, corn knife, several hand sickles, a large sled, and two homemade grindstones rounded out the collection. Cyrus always kept his tool collection locked securely away.

Cyrus emerged from the shed and dropped some tools on the ground next to a roll of smooth wire. There were two froes, two mallets, two axes, and two saws. To make a slat-wire fence they would cut some saplings from a fencerow. The mallet and froe were used to split the wood along the grain. Some skill was required in the process since the froes were dull instruments and required force applied with the wooden mallets. After the slats were made, it took two men to weave two strands of wire at the top of the slats and two at the bottom to hold them in place.

Most mallets were made of beech or maple, with a short handle to allow the user to hold the froe with one hand and the mallet in the other. Cyrus, however, had obtained a very unusual mallet. It was made of hickory and had a three-foot handle. The mallet was heavy, awkward, and not appropriate for splitting saplings.

Jes inspected the tools and suspected immediately that Cyrus expected him to use the large mallet. Jes had other ideas. He cleared up his throat and said, "Cyrus, ye might as well take that dad blasted thing back in the shed unless ye aim to use it yerself. Swingin' that thing all day kill an iron man. That drotted thing is a ring maul and not a mallet. I guess a man could drive wedges and split logs with it. We come here to make a slat-wire and not no split rail fence."

Cyrus looked at Jes with his dark eyes snapping. Jes knew making Cyrus mad was not a good idea, but he was riled up at the thought of being forced to use the huge mallet. Cyrus pointed at the tool and said, "... well if ye ain't man 'nough to swing it, BY JINGS I AM."

Cyrus Lentz was a short, pudgy man who possessed considerable physical strength. Jes had seen him crush a handful of black walnuts in his bare hands like they were peanuts. Cyrus avoided work; but when it was necessary, he could outwork any man in the field, including Jes Caughill.

Jes and Cyrus were too mad to talk as they worked feverishly all morning. Jes knew Cyrus would work as hard as was required to outdo him. The huge mallet moved like a toy in Cyrus's hand, but it was not long until his clothes were soaked with sweat despite the chilly March air. Jes had an advantage with the lighter mallet, but Cyrus was producing as many slats as Jes. The pace was feverish as two stubborn men worked six straight hours as they raced to outperform one another. Finally, at noon, Cyrus threw down his tools and announced it was dinnertime.

Cyrus charged toward the house, leaving Jes far behind. Jes was glad to have a break from the work, but he dreaded the meal that awaited him.

Ma Lentz was a very slow and deliberate person, but her perseverance did not result in good cooking, and Molly was no better. Jes's father said, "... them is two of the finest women who ever drawed a breath but, Lord Gawd, they can't cook a lick."

Jes trudged to the house thinking about the days when he helped his father on the Lentz farm. One day after chopping out corn since daylight, they headed to the house for dinner. Cyrus, who was only a few years older than Jes, rushed ahead and in his haste to be seated first at the table, turned the table over and spilled the meal. Jes and his father surveyed the disaster for a moment and headed for the well and a drink of water. Jes's father pulled two cold biscuits from his pocket. When they headed back to the cornfield, he handed one to Jes with a wink. It paid to be prepared when working for the Lentz family.

Jes stopped at the wash pan on the back porch. He could hear Cyrus slurping buttermilk from his place at the dinner table. The kitchen smelled of old meat, and Jes knew immediately the reason. The previous fall he helped Cyrus kill hogs; and when it came time to salt down the meat, Cyrus wanted to use old salt. Jes made the mistake of calling his hand.

"Cyrus, that salt done been used once and orta be throwed out. Make yere meat taste old."

"By jings, Jes, we ain't 'bout to waste that salt. Perfectly good."

Cyrus had ruined his meat with old salt, but he ate it like it was freshly killed. He knew Jes would not eat a bite, and he did not care.

When Jes sat down at the table, Cyrus had already started eating a huge plate of food. He held a large spoon in his right hand and a huge dill pickle in his left. A portion of Cyrus's plate was covered with molasses, and he dipped his pickle in the thick syrup and devoured it in two bites. Jes poured molasses, jelly, and honey over most things he ate; but the sight of Cyrus dipping a dill pickle in molasses made him sick.

Molly handed Jes a bowl of pinto beans, and he saw immediately that they had not cooked long enough to melt the salt or the lard used for seasoning. The women may have forgotten to put them on the stove. Jes shook his head and said pintos gave him heartburn. There was little doubt the beans Molly offered him would do worse than that.

The meal proceeded for several minutes without conversation until Molly reminded Cyrus the preacher was coming for dinner on Sunday. Cyrus buried his head in his plate and muttered.

"By jings, ye don't hear me cuss, do ye?"

"The preacher ain't comin' 'bout that Cyrus. Wants to get ye to comin' to church."

"Don't drink, don't lie, don't cheat, don't gamble. Mind my own business. Don't need to go to church."

Cyrus Lentz did not feel that anyone who did not violate the Ten Commandments needed to go to church. Jes smiled; he thought if being a stubborn old cuss were a sin, Cyrus would need to live in church.

The meal proceeded without any further mention of the preacher. Cyrus tried to change the subject by pressing bowl after bowl on Jes, who was embarrassed by the tiny portions he was taking. He had grown up with the notion that one should never take more food than they could eat. Jes knew he could never get hungry enough to eat a lot of Ma and Molly Lentz's cooking.

"BY JINGS, dinner's over. Let's get back to work."

Cyrus startled Jes with his sudden announcement that it was time to resume work on the fence. It was a relief not to eat more of the dinner, but it was going to be a long afternoon keeping pace with Cyrus. He was beginning to wish he had kept quiet about the large mallet.

When Jes and Cyrus returned the tools to the toolshed, it was almost dark. Jes started wearily for home. He had been idle from hard work for some time, and today he had felt it. After eleven hours of work, they had completed a slat-wire fence of over 150 feet. Jes still had no idea what Cyrus was going to do with the fence, but the old boy was tickled with their accomplishment and appeared to have forgotten the dispute over the mallet.

Jes walked down the hill to home and supper with just enough light to see the road. The coal oil lamp in the kitchen reminded him that Myrtle would have a fine supper on the table. A feast compared to what he had eaten for dinner at Cyrus's place. He couldn't help thinking about the summer he and his father worked for the Lentzs. Cyrus was a lazy teenager, and Ma Lentz had asked Jes's dad to make him work. Jes laughed out loud at what his father had said:

"… Ol' Miz Lentz hired us to chop out corn and hoe terbacker and the like. Nothin' said 'bout makin' the moonshine in the daylight. Ain't gonna tell her, though."

The job of chopping out weeds in the corn crop in the creek bottoms was always a hot job, and Mr. Caughill and Jes generally started at daylight. The mosquitoes were still out in force, but the air was much cooler. Cyrus always rode down on an old mule around eight o'clock. A short fence and a closed gate blocked the road leading to the cornfield. The first day Cyrus had waited for someone to open the gate, but Jes and his father ignored him. Finally, Cyrus stretched out on the mule's back and went to sleep. He went back home for dinner and returned with lard buckets of food that he handed to Jes over the gate. He went back to sleep on the back of the mule as he had done in the morning. The ritual was repeated the following day and for most of the summer. Ma Lentz was pleased that Mr. Caughill had inspired Cyrus to work and never suspected what was really going on:

"Mister Caughill, I know now why young Jes is sech a good worker. Any man who can get Cyrus to work in the fields all day is a pure divine inspiration."

❖ ❖ ❖

Supper was on the table when Jes burst through the kitchen door. Myrtle turned and looked at him with her hands on both hips. Finally, she sent a stream of amber into a nearby coffee can-spittoon.

"Go ahead and spill it, Jes Caughill. Ye been up to sumpin'. Seen that Cheshire cat look on yere face too many times."

Jes started laughing as he told Myrtle what had transpired with Cyrus and the mallet.

"He was so mad, we finished a 150-foot fence in one day. I swear that man can outwork an iron man when he wants to. Bound and determined to show me, and he done it. Didn't have a dry thread on him by ten o'clock and it bein' a chilly day and all. I hope he don't get sick."

Jes placed his hat on a nail and eased into a chair at the table. The tiny kitchen was so crowded that two of the chairs had less than a foot of clearance from the wall.

"Anna, get yereself in here and help yere mama with this supper."

"Jes, you leave that youngun' alone. She done cooked this here meal, and don't ye be a hollerin' at her."

"Jesse—where in tarnation is that boy anyhow? Don't nobody show up fer supper on time but me?"

"Now ye know as well as I do ye tol' 'im to go from school over to Mister Tichenor to see if he needs help a burnin' plant beds. Walton's Creek School is two miles away, and I reckon that's what he done. Ain't summer yet, still gets dark early."

Jes was always irritated if any member of the family was late for a meal. Over the years his jobs in the coal mines frequently made him the latest one of all. He twisted his ladder-back chair in an attempt to see some sign of his son through the tiny kitchen window. The stomping of brogans and the splashing of water in the washpan on the back porch announced Jesse's arrival. The March weather was still cold to have the washpan out on the porch, but Myrtle was tired of having it in the tiny kitchen. She said, ". . . ain't nothin' I hate worse than a bunch of dirty ol' men a washin' up in my kitchen. Soon as the water don't freeze, back outside it goes."

Jesse burst through the door in a fashion not unlike his father's entries. He slammed the door behind him so hard that it sprang back open.

"Close that dad-blasted door. I knowed ye wasn't born in no barn. Ye gettin' set up to turn the house full of flies and musky toes this summer. Jest gettin' warmed up to it like ye done last summer."

"OH sorry, Pap. I was jest tickled 'bout sumpin'."

"Well, b'fore ye bust a gut laughin', did Mister Tichernor need any help?" Jes growled between bites.

"Shore did. Said he could use me a couple of days fer certain. Not sure if he can pay cash money but said if he got 'em, we can have four or five bushel of sweet taters, terbacker plants and 'mater plants, too. Purty fair deal I reckon, but I want some cash money."

"Jest keep on a wishin' 'cause nobody got none."

Jes started spooning navy beans, boiled potatoes, canned tomatoes, and pickled beets onto his plate along with a large slice of cornbread. Most meals were meatless in the Caughill home except for special occasions.

"Son, I reckon ye done sumpin' right fer a change. Now what got yere funny bone so riled up?" Jes hardly looked at his son as he spoke.

"Gettin' dark and I was gettin' hungry so I took me a shortcut 'cross Cyrus's pasture. Purt near too dark to see, but he was out on the back porch a throwin' out a pan of water when he got a glimpse of me. He hollered sumpin' 'bout it looked like rain. I jest kept on goin'. He hollered agin, and I still don't say nothin'. Ye know how nosy he is. Knows my voice and would have made me as soon as I opened my trap, so I didn't. Finally, he hollered real big and loud, 'BY JINGS, WHO ARE YE ANYHOW?' I still don't utter a peep, and he goes in the house and slams the door."

"WHY, ye young smart aleck. I orta take a terbacker stick to ye. We'd shore be up a creek if ol' Cyrus wasn't a lettin' us live here in this house. From here on out ye show that man proper respect." Myrtle pointed a paring knife at Jesse to further emphasize her point.

"Shoot fire, Ma, I didn't mean nothin' by it. I like ol' Cyrus."

"Young lady, don't ye be a sniggerin' neither. I seen ye out in the yard a mockin' the way ol' Miz Lentz walks; and some day she, Molly, or Cyrus is gonna catch ye, and then ye'll be sorry. I ain't gonna take up fer ye neither."

Jes was trying to keep from laughing as he took another big swallow of milk. Suddenly, he stopped and looked at the glass like he was seeing it for the first time.

"Where did that milk come from? We ain't got no cow. Wished we did."

"Molly give it to Anna and me when we went up to their place a while ago. Said they had so much they was givin' it to the hogs."

"Better not let Cyrus find out 'bout that. I can jest hear 'im hollerin' 'bout how they need it fer the hogs. Be hunky dory if it was his idée, but ye know how he is. Have 40 fits and a bad spell if he finds out."

"He ain't gonna find out less we blab 'bout it. For the life of me I don't know why that man likes ye so much. One stubborn cuss to 'nother, I guess."

"By the way, Jes, Molly said that the Walton's Creek School is gonna have a pie supper in a few weeks, and she wondered if we was gonna go. She wants to go if we do since Cyrus and Ma said they wasn't goin' a step. Funny thing that our own younguns a goin' to school there ain't uttered a peep 'bout it."

"PIE SUPPER," Jes squalled as he slammed his fork down on the table so hard that Anna jumped. "What in tarnation is folks gonna use fer money to buy them pies?"

"Cool yere horses, Jes. Folks ain't so poor they can't spare a little dab of money fer a pie once a year. Besides, the school needs the money."

"Pap, I got 30 cents from strippin' terbacker. Can I buy me a pie with some of it?"

Jes scowled at his son. "Jest a burnin' a hole in yere pocket, ain't it? Can't wait to blow it on somebody's else's pie. I can jest see it now in the paper, 'Jesse Caughill buys pie while family starves.' OH well, I guess I'm out-numbered. Might as well we all gonna be in the pore house soon 'nough."

"Jes, if yere done with yere little stump speech, reach over yonder on the stove and get that skillet of pore dough."

"Why in blazes did ye fix 'nother skillet of corn bread if ye got pore dough? Did ye put salt and pepper on it?"

"I reckon I know how to make pore dough. Had no butter but crumbled it up in the skillet with some water and seasoning and heated it in the oven like usual. I was afraid we wouldn't have 'nough bread fer supper. Besides, it ain't gonna go to waste. Too bad we ain't got no butter. Had our own cow I could churn us a dab of butter."

"If we had our own cow, I could put pore dough in my milk ever night of the world. Anna, get started on them dishes soon as ye finish eatin'. Can't stay up half the night a wastin' coal oil. Gotta save our money to buy pies at a pie supper."

"Jes, we ain't actin' like John D. Rockefeller. I got plenty here fer Anna to take a pie. Gettin' to be a right smart of a young lady. High time she went to a pie supper with a pie."

Jesse and Anna fell asleep that evening thinking about the pie supper. It had been some time since they had attended one, but this one would be different. Some young man would bid for Anna's pie and the privilege of helping her eat it. For the first time Jesse could join other teens as they strained to determine the young ladies behind the bedsheet. Pie suppers were part of the country courting ritual and had helped many young couples down the road of life together.

Jes was tired and fell asleep almost immediately. He did not hear Old Pete growling on the front porch or the raking of his toenails as he leaped off and raced into the darkness after a foe that only he could hear. Old Pete may have been exercising discretion. A dog of Jes Caughill's who growled or barked near the house during the night was well advised to leave the vicinity immediately. Jes generally started by yelling some well-chosen profanity at the animal; but if that failed, the dog could expect shoes to come flying through a window, and a brogan thrown by Jes Caughill was a formidable weapon.

Old Pete had been gone only a few minutes when Myrtle was startled awake by Molly's voice coming from the front yard. She punched Jes and told him to go see what she wanted.

"JES, it's Molly. We need ye to come and help Mister Tichenor hold Cyrus in the bed. He's a havin' one of them spells."

Myrtle laughed as Jes dressed in the dark. "Jes, is that the 40 fits and a bad spell you was talkin' 'bout?"

"Reckon so. He has them spells when he gets real mad or exerts hisself. Got high blood you know. Gonna have a stroke someday."

"I'd be a talkin' if I was you. Almost as bad yerself."

"If I have a stroke, it'll be cause I ain't got no sleep holdin' Cyrus in bed all night."

Jes rushed up the hill to Cyrus's place where he found Mister Tichenor mightily trying to hold Cyrus down. The two men wrestled with the powerful Cyrus Lentz for over two hours. Finally, he stopped and Jes collapsed into a nearby rocking chair. Mister Tichenor leaned back against the wall in a ladder-back chair and was soon asleep. Jes was so exhausted all he could do was doze the rest of the night.

Jes came out of a mild slumber at five o'clock when Cyrus's rooster started to crow. Mister Tichenor and Cyrus were still sleeping peacefully, and Jes did not move out of fear Cyrus might resume his spell. Jes still marveled at the man's strength.

Cyrus Lentz had always been very powerful, even when he was a youth. As a youngster, when Ma Lentz and Molly wanted to whip him for something that he had done, he was so strong he merely ran away. The women were determined that he was going to get his punishment, and they soon developed a plan. They put new domestic sheets on his bed and waited for him to be fast asleep. Quietly they sewed him up in the sheets and then thrashed him with a broom and a razor strap. The stitches held long enough for Cyrus to get his penance.

Myrtle was just finishing breakfast when an exhausted Jes Caughill got home. He poured a cup of coffee and collapsed at the kitchen table.

"Well, how's the ol' boy doin?"

"That's the strongest man I ever did see. Plumb wore us out a holdin' 'im. Worse than a day in the mines. He finally went to sleep and purred like a kitten. Woke up a while ago and looked at us and wanted to know what we was doin' there. Mister Tichenor tol' 'im he reckoned we got in the wrong house last night. Couldn't see in the dark. He says well it ain't dark now, and he pulled out to the privy, and we lit outta there."

Anna held on tight to her chocolate pie as the old road wagon eased down into a chug hole. When Ol' Sal and Ol' Bell hesitated in the pull, Jes called out, "get up there," and the horses responded obediently. Jes Caughill's horses, like his dogs, knew it was best to do things right the first time. Myrtle was on the seat between Jes and Molly. She turned and looked back in the wagon at Jesse and Anna. "Honey, you hold onto that pie good ... you ain't got but the one," she said.

Jesse pulled an old brown pocketbook from his overall pocket and counted out six nickels. Without looking at his sister, he said, "Pap said I could bid 25 cents on a pie ... said keep one nickel ... said I gotta learn not to spend ever cent I got at once. Yessir, I'm shore glad I got to help strip terbacker ... wouldn't have a cent."

Anna looked down at her pie and tried to ignore her brother, who had been bragging about his 30 cents and the pie supper for days. Anna was worried no one would buy her pie. Jesse was watching his sister from the corner of his eye and started laughing.

"Ain't no feller got one eye and half sense gonna buy no pie made by some skinny, ugly girl."

"SHET yere mouth or yere gonna get yere pie right now." Anna was furious that her older brother had sensed what she was thinking. No one needed to tell her she was skinny and gangly for her age.

It was four o'clock when Jes headed the wagon into the schoolyard of the Walton's Creek School. There were several buggies and wagons parked around the one-room school and even more across the road in the driveway that led to the church. Under a tree near the school was a brand new Model T Ford car. The sunlight played games on the car's black finish when the wind rustled the tree leaves. The men folks, especially the young boys, were carefully examining the vehicle. Jesse jumped off the wagon and ran to the car before Jes could get stopped. Anna could see many more people walking down the road toward the school, carrying pies. Pie suppers were always well attended by the local community.

Jes hitched the team and helped Molly and Myrtle down from the wagon. Anna, still nervous about her first pie supper entry, walked close by her mother. The carefully chaperoned event would allow several young couples to get acquainted in a way that met with adult approval, and the veil of shyness could begin to part.

Female voices and laughter greeted Myrtle, Anna, and Molly when they entered the school. Old Fannie Mollyhorn had left her pipe at home, but she was entertaining herself by telling the older women some tall tales. Myrtle had no use for "old huzzies" who smoked or chewed tobacco in public, and Fannie frequently did both. Myrtle enjoyed snuff and chewing tobacco and even an occasional cigar, but only in the privacy of her own home. She lectured Anna that a lady should never use tobacco in public and "... yere hide ain't gonna hold corn shucks if I catch ye doin' either one."

Myrtle ushered Anna over to Grace Burdett, who was in charge of the affair. "Well, Myrtle, I see yere young lady brung us a pie tonight." Grace's high-pitched voice could be heard all over the room. Jes said, "... that woman got a voice that will grate on a winder light."

"Yessir, Grace, her first un and a bit nervous 'bout it, too."

"Now, honey, don't ye be nervous one little bit. Jest put yere pie down over yonder and take this here number and put it down next to the pie." Grace next turned to Molly with a sly smile. "Well, Molly, did ye bring us a pie, too?"

Grace Burdett's sarcasm and obvious reference to Molly's maiden status caused Myrtle to give her a dirty look. Grace, who had no stomach for a confrontation with Myrtle Caughill, quickly walked away. Molly dropped her head, red-faced with embarrassment.

The women continued to chatter for some time before Grace decided to get the program started. She began by lining the girls up behind a sheet that was held vertically by a clothesline strung across the room. Female silhouettes could easily be seen after two coal oil lamps were lit behind them. A woman in the crowd went to the door and called for the men to enter the building. The rules required that no men were allowed inside until everything was ready.

The men shuffled into the building, acting somewhat awkward, as men of the time generally did when they were operating strictly under female rules. The older, married men stayed at the back of the room, and the young men and boys who were going to bid for a pie moved toward the front. Several pair of anxious eyes were fixed upon the female shadows behind the sheet. Each one was hoping they could identify the girl of his choice. A number of perplexed looks indicated that the job was more difficult than they had imagined.

Old "Bug Eye" Carter stepped up to the pie-laden table and pecked on it with his knuckles to call everyone to order. The room grew quiet except for a man by the back door who was coughing. Bug Eye was always selected to conduct the auction, and he thoroughly enjoyed the role. His eyes gave off a surprised look, but when he was the center of attention his pupils appeared to get larger and darker.

"ALL RIGHT, we got this here pie auction to take care of. Everbody knows the rules so I reckon we can get started. Now this here is the first pie, and who will start the biddin' at twenty-five cents?"

The bidding moved swiftly, and Bug Eye seemed to swell with importance as he sold pie after pie and collected the money in his upturned hat. Anna was at the far end of the line, and she thought he would never get to her pie. The least attractive girl was always placed at the end, a fact not lost on the bidders.

Beatrice Holloway was next to Anna and almost as nervous. Bug Eye had to ask for bids three times before a young boy bid twenty cents. There were no other bidders, and Beatrice's pie had gotten the lowest bid of the night. Anna's pie was next, and her skinny body was shaking with terror. She just knew that no one was going to bid on her pie.

"WELL, sir, I reckon we saved the best fer last. Looks like a mighty fine pie some little lady made to help out the school. What am I bid fer this here last pie of the night?"

The school was deathly silent, and no one said a word. A girl down the line sniggered, and this made Anna's apprehension turn to anger. She wished she hadn't come. She was going to be the laughing stock of the school and the neighborhood. No one wanted a pie baked by a skinny old girl.

"NOW, come now, gents. Shorely somebody wants to bid on this here pie. Looks like chocolate to me. This purty little thing went to lots of trouble."

"Looks like a mighty little shadder back there to me."

Bug Eye looked around the room quickly as he tried to identify the source of the comment. He glanced over at Myrtle Caughill who was standing by the wall with the other women. She was biting her lip as she agonized along with her daughter. The tension in the room had forced a silence that only added to Anna's torment. When it appeared that Bug Eye was about to give up, someone in the back of the room cleared up his throat.

"Sir, if ye please. I would like to bid on that there pie."

Bug Eye looked back in the direction of the voice. A young man of about sixteen, wearing a suit, stepped forward.

"Son, I ain't never laid eyes on ye before in my borned days. YES SIR, be my guest."

"I would like to bid fifty cents for that pie. I got the money right here."

The silence that had gripped the room for several agonizing minutes suddenly ended with a chorus of voices. Jes Caughill started to laugh, for the tension had also been tormenting him.

"SOLD FER FIFTY CENTS. The highest bid of the night. Take down the sheets so them boys can see who their shadder belongs to." Bug Eye seemed relieved to conclude the auction.

Anna was dripping with perspiration, anxiety, and excitement. She had gone from humiliation to sheer joy in a matter of seconds. Her pie got the highest bid of the night, and she could not wait to see who had bought her pie.

The older men went back outside to smoke, while the younger men paired off with the girls whose pies they had purchased. Anna took her pie and sat down in a far corner and waited for her mystery man, but he never came. The sting of embarrassment started all over again. Finally, she muttered to herself that she was going to smack him in the face with the pie when and if he came.

Myrtle Caughill stood talking to the other married women and pretended to be ignoring her daughter's predicament. Myrtle wanted to go over and hug her daughter and console her, but she knew this was not the time or place. That would only embarrass her more. The young man had simply bought a pie and walked out.

"Hey there, boy. Ain't ye the one who jest bought that girl's pie fer fifty cents?"

"Yessir, I bought some girl's pie. Don't know who."

"Ain't leavin' are ye?"

"Yessir, soon as I get this cinch fastened on my saddle."

"Boy, yere 'bout as dumb as owl doin's. Yere supposed to help that gal eat that pie after ye buy it. Now get back in there and do it."

Bug Eye shook his head in amazement as the boy walked into the school. The room fell quiet again when the women saw him enter the door. The only sound was the clump of his boots as he walked over to Anna. She kept her head down, looking at his feet.

"I reckon I bought that pie from ye."

"I reckon somebody bought it. Pull up a chair. I got two spoons. Let's get to it."

Slowly the conversation resumed among the women while Anna and the young man ate the pie without saying a word or even looking at one another. Anna was so nervous that she dropped her spoon. When she leaned over to retrieve it, the young man stood up and left. Anna allowed herself one quick glance at his back as he went out the door. The pie supper was finally over.

An hour after the young man left Anna, the school building was almost empty. Myrtle Caughill walked slowly over to her daughter and gave her a hug. Anna had tears in her eyes as she looked up at her mother. Myrtle could be gruff at times but always knew what to say and what not to say to her children when they needed their mother the most. This was one of those tender mother-daughter moments when nothing needed to be said.

It was nearly dark when Jes rounded up his family for the trip home. Ol' Sal and Ol' Bell seemed anxious to get back to the barn as well. Jes pulled out to the road and let the horses have their head. The sky was clear and bright, and the horses could easily maneuver around the chug holes.

"Jes, I reckon our little lady was quite the sensation this evenin'."

"I reckon. Gettin' fifty cents fer a pie. Make more money makin' pies than raisin' terbacker. Orta let her make the livin'."

"I wonder who that boy was."

"Nobody ever seen 'im b'fore. Some of the men figured he must be a visitin' some folks over at Centertown and rode out when he heard 'bout the pie supper. Mighty fancy suit of clothes he got on."

"Ain't too smart, though, to pay fifty cents fer a pie made by some skinny, ugly ol' girl," muttered Jesse.

"That reminds me. Jesse, how was that pie ye bought?"

"Oh, Pap, don't remind me. I don't like apple pie or Lucy Fritters neither. Jest wasted twenty-five cents, that's all."

Myrtle and Jes exchanged grins in the pale light. Pie suppers were both exciting and disappointing for youngsters. It was all part of growing up in rural Kentucky.

"Molly, ye ain't hardly said a word. Didn't ye like the pie supper?"

"OH, Myrtle, the pie supper was just fine. The best I been to in many a moon. I was jest thinkin'."

The excitement over the pie auction and the mysterious young man bidding fifty cents for Anna's pie had obscured another event. Molly had caught the eye of a man in his early 40s who entered the school building a little late. He wasn't a particularly handsome man; but when his eyes met Molly's for a brief moment, they both felt something. Embarrassed, Molly looked quickly at the floor, but the urge to look back at him was overwhelming. After a few minutes she looked again, and he was looking in her direction. The attraction was instantaneous, and Molly felt an exhilaration she had never experienced before.

The Sunday after the pie supper, the weather was nice, and the Caughills decided to leave the team and wagon at home and walk to church. A two-mile walk to church gave Myrtle a chance to get outside after a week of working indoors. Molly walked down from her house and joined them. Ma Lentz was not feeling well, and the man who did not need to go to church was asleep on the front porch. Molly had told Myrtle her little secret, but Jes and the children were still unaware.

Most of the congregation was socializing in front of the church when the Caughills and Molly arrived. Jes spoke and shook hands with the preacher, while Myrtle exchanged some pleasantries with the pastor's wife. Molly nervously scanned the crowd, and there he was. The man she had seen at the pie supper was tying his horse to a low branch on a shade tree. Her heart raced as she quickly looked away.

Molly looked at Myrtle with silent communication that women know so well. Myrtle looked around until her eyes focused on a man wearing a dark suit walking in their direction. Until that moment Myrtle had doubted Molly's story.

"Mister Caughill, my name is Tom Leslie. I got me a farm over 'round Sacramento. We talked down at the ferry a year or so back."

"Well, I reckon I recall that. Didn't recognize ye in yere Sunday go to meetin' clothes on. Jest need to get somethin' straight. Only preachers and tax collectors call me Mister Caughill. Jes is the name."

"Awright, Jes. Call me Tom."

Myrtle punched Jes in the back. He frequently needed prompting in social situations.

"Uh, Tom, this here is my missus Myrtle, boy there is Jesse, and my baby gal Anna. This here is Molly."

Tom nodded to Myrtle and Anna, shook hands with a very socially awkward Jesse, and turned his attention quickly to Molly. He smiled, spoke, and bowed slightly in her direction. She smiled and made a feeble attempt at saying hello.

Myrtle elbowed Jes again. When he turned to look at her, she was staring straight ahead.

"I reckon we all orta get inside. Ever'body else is. Tom, be proud to have ye set with us."

"Well thank you, Mister, ugh, I mean Jes."

Jes was slow to catch on; but once inside the church, he skillfully maneuvered the group so Molly was seated between Myrtle and Tom. When the singing started, Myrtle grabbed the songbook closest to Tom and handed it to Jes. He gave her a curious look since nothing on heaven or earth could make Jes Caughill sing in church. Myrtle winked at him, and he caught on. Tom and Molly were sharing a songbook as well. Myrtle sang out loudly, while Jes moved his lips harmlessly. The first time Jes sang in Myrtle's presence, she had told him if he expected to stay married to her, he had to stop that "catter wallin'"; and if he ever sang in church, she would leave him.

The congregation shook hands with the preacher and slowly moved out the front doors of the church. The members broke up into groups for conversation or headed to their wagons, cars, and buggies to start home.

"Tom, be proud to have ye eat a bean with us. Myrtle is a fine cook. We gonna have beans, taters, turnip greens, cornbread, and fried apple pies. Them pies well melt in yere mouth."

"Jes, that is mighty nice of ye, but I reckon I better get back home. Let me get my horse, though, and I'll walk ye down the road a piece."

Jesse and Anna were shocked that their father started the trek back home with his arm around Myrtle.

"Jes. Quit that. People is watching."

"Married, ain't we. Like ye always say, we is ol' married folks."

Jesse and Anna walked ahead of their parents, while Molly and Tom brought up the rear. Jes was proud of himself. He thought he had carefully arranged it so Tom and Molly would have to walk together. Myrtle just smiled and shook her head. The man she married had the tact and finesse of a bull, but sometimes he clearly surprised her.

When the Caughills turned onto the road to their house, Myrtle and Jes slowed the pace. They did not want to run off and leave Molly but wanted to give them some privacy as well.

"Miss Molly, I shore would like to walk ye to church next Sunday if that is all right."

"I would like that, too, Tom. Meet ye right here next Sunday if it ain't threatnin' weather. Eleven o'clock, I reckon."

"Yeah, I reckon."

Tom and Molly parted, and a clearly embarrassed Molly quickly caught up with Jes and Myrtle.

"Molly, we got plenty of dinner. Be glad to have ye stay."

"Oh, Myrtle, I surely can't. Ma ain't feelin' good, and I got to get dinner on the table fer Cyrus fer sure."

Myrtle and Jes stood in front of the house and watched Molly race up the dusty road for home.

"Jes. Ye hard headed ol' fool. Thought I was gonna hafta hit ye in the head back there."

"What did I do?"

"What ye didn't do. Orta knowed that man wanted to set with Molly in church and all. He shore in blazes didn't come over from McLean County to set by you in church."

"I done ferget what it's like to be courtin'."

"Tom acts a sight better than you. Hardly laid on eyes on ye when ye rode up in front of my house a wearin' yere Sunday go to meetin' clothes and jest walked up on the porch and flopped down on the swing beside me and said 'howdy.' I wanted to laugh. Fresh haircut and a shave with yere hair parted down the middle. Ain't hardly combed that mop since."

"Ye didn't run me off."

"My mistake. Ye hung 'round after that 'til I had to marry ye. Couldn't get shed of ye."

Jes sent Jesse to fetch a bucket of water while Myrtle and Anna went inside and started putting dinner on the table. Jes changed into his everyday clothes and took a seat at the table. The fried apple pies were still warm, and Jes ate one with his meal like it was bread.

"NOW, you younguns keep yere traps shut 'bout Molly and Tom. Nary a word 'round Cyrus or Miz Lentz or nobody else."

"Ma, we ain't gonna say nothin'. Don't know what Tom sees in ol' Molly. She ain't purty."

"Ain't no movie star yerself. Start blabbin' 'bout it, and I'll take yere hide to the tan yard with that there razor strap."

"Pap, I don't give a hoot what Tom and Molly does, and I ain't gonna say nothin'."

"Jes, Tom seems like a purty nice fella to me."

"Reckon he is. Had a wife but she died a havin' a baby. Lost the baby, too. Got a nice little farm over yonder. Got a good name, too. Long ride over here from McLean County. Shore took 'im a spell to get home after that pie supper. Must have been purt near midnight. Musta stayed the night somers. Gettin' that ol' coot down at the ferry to get up and take 'im 'cross ain't likely. Ol' buzzard goes to bed with the chickens. Must be struck on Molly real good. Cyrus ain't gonna roll over and play dead neither. No man gonna take his baby sister that easy."

Myrtle snorted. "He'd play hobby dob if it was me. I'd snatch 'im bald headed."

After dinner Jes took a chair to the front yard and relaxed under a tree with a cup of coffee. When Myrtle finished in the kitchen, she joined him.

"Any more of that coffee left?"

"I reckon. Yere the only one a drinkin' it."

Jes went back into the house for another cup of coffee. When he returned, Myrtle was placing a knife blade of snuff between her cheek and jaw. When she went to replace the snuff can lid, it slipped from her fingers and tobacco spilled on her apron. She stood up briefly to brush the tobacco powder away.

"Jes, I'm tickled pink fer Molly. Kinda like a sister to me. Kinda surprised, though. Molly is a tad old fashion. Wears old style clothes and all."

"Now, Myrtle, Tom knows a fine woman when he sees one. Molly ain't got no high fallutin' airs. Lots of men like that in a woman. I didn't marry no high fallutin' woman. She's an ol' fashion gal, and there ain't nothin' wrong in that. We eyed each other like two ol' stray cats fer nearly three years 'fore we got hitched. Wanted to see who could get the upper hand, I reckon. Been fussin' and fightin' ever since. They ain't gonna be that way. Love at first sight."

"OH LORD a mercy, Jes. What is gonna happen when Cyrus finds out? Gonna find out sooner or later. What are ye gonna tell 'im?"

"I ain't gonna tell 'im nothin'. Nothin' in our agreement says I gotta tattle on Molly. He knows better. Ain't gonna say nothin' to me no how. Thinks he's a doin' the right thing and protectin' her. Remember yere ol' daddy thought 'bout runnin' me off. Finally got used to it after a while. Cyrus will too."

Molly accompanied the Caughills to church the next three Sundays. Tom was waiting at the church and sat next to Molly as they shared the same songbook. Everyone in the community knew what was going on except Ma Lentz and Cyrus. Tom must have known about Molly's situation because he always said farewell to Molly when she turned down her road home.

"Tom, Jes and me would be tickled pink if Molly and you would stay fer dinner today. Gonna have fish, Jesse been runnin' a trot line and doin' real good."

"Miss Caughill, I haven't had a mess of fish in a spell. That sounds mighty good. Is that alright, Molly?"

"I love fish, too, Tom," Molly replied with a hint of excitement in her voice.

Myrtle smiled and winked at Jes as they walked up the road toward home. Jes had just looked at her and shook his head. Myrtle immediately suspected Jes knew something she did not know. This became evident when they arrived home.

"MOLLY, get yerself home. Gotta get dinner on the table."

Molly jumped at the sound of Cyrus's voice. Ma Lentz and Cyrus were watching from the front porch.

"OH, I'm sorry, but I hafta go home."

Molly was almost running up the hill, and poor Tom looked stunned. Jes and Myrtle looked at each other.

"Well, Tom, that fish is still warm. Mighty good, too."

"Jes, I reckon I need to high tail it fer home. Mighty nice of ye to invite me, though."

Tom mounted his horse and quickly rode away. Jes let out a long breath and shook his head from side to side as he started for the house.

"Cat's outta the bag now. I reckon they had to find out soon 'nough. Me and Mister Tichenor hafta stay up all night a holdin' Cyrus. Gonna bust a gut now fer sure."

"Ain't our fault, Jes. He gotta stop bein' an ol' mother hen."

"Maybe you orta start mindin' yere own business."

"You had a hand in it, too, ol' man."

The Caughills ate a scrumpuous meal of fresh fish while the sounds of an argument from the Lentz house found their way through the open kitchen window.

"Lord, I hope he don't have one of them fits. I aimed to set in the front yard all afternoon, but a man can't do that with all the catter wallin' goin' on up there. They'll be at it all day."

"Jes, you go on outside. Act like ye don't hear nothin'."

Jes and Myrtle spent much of the afternoon under a shade tree in the front yard listening to the off-and-on argument at the Lentz house. Finally, all was quiet.

"Myrtle, too quiet up there. I figured they be at it 'til dark."

"Not everbody fights like you and me. Oooh mercy, Jes. Molly jest come out the door and is headed this way."

"Come down here to tell us she knocked Cyrus in the head."

"Shut up Jes, ye ol' fool. She'll hear ye."

Molly walked into the yard smiling like nothing had happened.

"Jes, Ma and me need ye to drive us to Hartford t'mor if ye can. Ye can drive my car, and Myrtle can come, too."

"I reckon so. Got some work to do, but Jesse can handle it all right. Wanna leave out 'round daylight or so?"

"Maybe a tad later than that. We got all day."

"Molly, I still got some cannin' to do. Anna could go I guess, but I need her to help me. We gotta save what little dab of money we got fer Jes to put out crops and have a bit fer Christmas and such."

"Be there right after breakfast or so, Molly," Jes said with a nod.

Molly turned and walked back home. Jes and Myrtle looked at each other, bewildered.

"Well, in all my born days. If that don't take the cake. Myrtle, I ain't never heard nothin' like it."

"Jes, I forgot Molly got one of them Chevy 490 Tourin' cars. Never learnt to drive it though."

"Myrtle, Cyrus never got the hang of his Model T neither. Drive a team yere whole life and it takes a bit of gettin' used to. Took me a while myself. Now Jesse jumped under the wheel and took off the first time jest from a watchin' somebody else. Young folks can do that since their mind ain't fixed on another way of doin' sumpin'. Yep, young folks take to things better than ol' folks like us."

"Wonder why they don't sell them cars?"

"Each a waitin' on the other to blink, I reckon. Neither one is gonna be the first."

"Cyrus don't think women should drive anyhow. When he first got that thing, he done it to outdo Molly, who got one first. He run into trees, ditches, the barn, and such; but the real kicker was when he run down the hill here. Mister Tichenor says he was goin' down jest lickety split and yellin' 'BY JINGS, WHOA' 'til he finally got stopped down at the bottom of the hill. Got his team and pulled it to the barn and there it sets."

"Jes, we ever gonna have the money to buy us a Model T?"

"Maybe, if this here Depression ever ends. Get some better roads, and I can go off a piece to get work. Durn things ain't much good 'round here with mud roads. Might as well have a road wagon if ye gotta park it all winter and spring. Cost a right smart to keep up, too."

"Maybe I'm jest a silly ol' woman, but I would like to go to church jest one time in my own Model T car. Love to ride to the State Fair jest one time 'fore I die. Might help ye find better work too. Ye borrowed that Model T a few years back and drove to Herrin, Illinois, to work. I remember ye drove 700 hun'erd miles straight. Drove all night and got back home with a big ol' watermelon fer the kids. Wouda took a month of Sundays to come like that in a wagon. Still I'd like to go to church in my own Model T."

"We ain't gonna buy one jest fer that. Now a talkin' 'bout Cyrus and his Model T; I heerd 'bout this ol' feller up 'round Dundee that farmed fer fifty years with a team of mules. He got 'im one of them new Titan 10-20 coal oil burnin' tractors and run it through the barn door a screamin' whoa-mule, whoa, jest like Cyrus done. The next day he was out in the fields with his mules. Somebody ask 'im what happened to his tractor he said, ... "by God when I holler whoa to them mules they pay attention'."

Jes walked up to Cyrus's place shortly after breakfast. He placed a biscuit and a small apple in his pocket for a modest dinner. He didn't want to be tempted to buy anything. He knew Molly and Ma Lentz would probably eat in a Hartford café, but he would be with the car or walking around town most of the day. Jes had stopped at the well to fill a quart fruit jar with water. He could not afford to waste a nickel on a cup of coffee either.

"Cyrus, get outta my car. I ain't a gonna let ye drive. Now get outta there. I got Jes to drive, and that is all there is to it."

"By jings, Jes ain't gonna drive, I am."

Jes moaned to himself when he walked into the shed where Molly and Cyrus kept their cars. Cyrus was dressed in a new pair of overalls and was seated behind the wheel of Molly's car, both hands gripping the steering wheel and a five-pound lard bucket tied around his neck with a grass string. Cyrus was angry that Molly had asked Jes to do the driving and was about to take matters into his own hands. Jes knew the lard bucket contained his lunch.

"Mornin', Jes," Miss Lentz drawled when she saw Jes enter the barn. "The dad blasted fool aims to drive Molly's car."

Cyrus ignored Jes's presence and opened his lard bucket to inspect its contents. In Kentucky during the 1920s it was not uncommon for country people to take food in a lard bucket on trips to town. On Saturdays or Court Day, the courthouse often contained men nibbling on a biscuit covered with molasses. Jes knew Cyrus once sat on a jury with the bucket tied around his neck.

"Cyrus, I know ye got yere dinner bucket and all, but ye can't drive this here car. Come along if ye want. I need somebody to talk to anyhow. You'll kill yere fool self a tryin' to drive to Hartford."

Cyrus sat motionless for a few seconds, staring straight ahead. Finally, he jumped out of the car and headed for the house.

Hartford was eleven miles away and a bumpy ride on the old country roads. Jes would have preferred to take Ma and Molly Lentz to the train at Centertown. The trip would have been quicker and easier for all concerned, but he knew the women wanted to save the train fare. The Lentzs may have been comfortable financially, but they were not wasteful.

In 1930 Hartford, a city of about 1,000 people was like a major city for country folks. Most farm families in the Centertown vicinity shopped in that town for most of their needs. Cars still were not plentiful and the roads rough at best. Unlike Jes and his fellow coal miners, the Lentzs had been less severely affected by the Depression.

Ma and Molly Lentz shopped all day without taking the time to get something to eat or drink. They visited all the stores and carefully compared fabric and numerous other items for price and quality. The women rarely visited Hartford to shop more than two or three times a year. Jes knew he was in for a long, tiresome day unless he ran into someone he knew.

Jes parked Molly's car near the railroad depot, and the women walked to downtown Hartford. The M.H. and E. Railroad, a line wholly owned by the Louisville and Nashville Railroad, served the town; and one of their mixed trains of both passenger and freight cars had just pulled into the station. Several old men and young boys were loafing around the depot when Jes walked up. He was fascinated by trains and often wished he could work for the railroad.

The big engine hissed steam as passengers departed and more got on. Workers quickly loaded and unloaded freight as the conductor nervously checked his pocket watch. The fireman leaned out of the engine cab and yelled at two boys who had started to climb under one of the cars. The train had been servicing Hartford for nearly twenty years, but its arrival was still a source of excitement for young people.

When the train departed, Jes watched until all that remained was a trail of black coal smoke. The scream of a steam whistle and the ringing of the train's bell always gave him goose bumps. As he stood looking after the long-departed train, he smiled to himself as he recalled a time in 1897 when he saw his first train while riding in a road wagon with his father. When the whistle blew, the team went into a tizzie, and his father swore at the horses and the train equally.

Jes left the depot and walked slowly downtown. Some of his fondest memories of his youth stemmed from trips to Hartford for "Mule Day." The excursions were very infrequent and always a source of excitement. The town took on a carnival atmosphere as country folks flocked to town. Jes had been 16 years old before he had the opportunity to travel to Hartford for the County Fair. He was shocked at the size of the crowd and the excitement the event generated. Young boys ran at top speed as they tried to absorb everything at once.

The business section located directly behind the courthouse was all but deserted when Jes took a seat on an outdoor bench. Across the street, the courthouse was also devoid of the loafers who frequented the grounds on Saturdays. The home of county government was an old building built right after the Civil War; Confederate soldiers had burned the previous building near the end of the conflict. The present structure had a similar appearance from all four sides and had an air of sophistication with its bell tower and wrought-iron fence around the perimeter.

Jes sat on the bench for almost an hour before walking over to the office of the *Ohio County News*. He had observed three people stop and look at something on display in the window. When he approached the window, he saw several books piled upon a small table. A tiny sign in the window advertised the sale of a book by Harrison D. Taylor, *Ohio County, Kentucky in the Olden Days*. The sign read $2.50. Jes grunted and muttered half aloud, "... worked a whole day fer that kinda money." Jes walked away disgusted.

A few cars, trucks, road wagons and buggies made their way up and down Main Street as Jes meandered around town. Soon he found himself in front of the Highway Service Garage. The facility consisted of a long, white frame building that was divided into two parts. Half of the building was a garage, and the remainder contained a small café. The smell of coffee greeted Jes as he walked up. Instinctively, he reached into his pocket and took hold of a quarter and a nickel, the only money he brought with him. The temptation was great to go inside and spend the nickel on a cup of coffee, but he resisted.

The garage sported several signs, including one that advertised they sold tires, batteries, gas, oil, grease jobs, and road service. The business's motto was "You Call—We Hurry." Several six-ply, heavy-duty Path Finder tires were stacked out front, selling for $7.00 each. Jes wondered how people were able to buy gas, oil and tires for their cars with a Depression raging.

Jes wandered for several more minutes until he found himself in front of the Chevrolet dealership. The business was located in a two-story brick building with a showroom in front and service garage in the rear. A sign in the window read, "Why Walk When Cars Are So Cheap?" Jes cupped his hands on each side of his face as he peered through the window at a 1928 four-cyclinder Chevy Roadster. A sign on the windshield read $265.00. He immediately fell in love with the car but realized that even when the coal mines reopened, $265.00 was still a lot of money.

A truck drove by and backfired, causing Jes to jump. He turned away from the showroom window and leaned up against one of the two gas pumps in front of the car dealership. He pulled some twisted leaf tobacco from his pocket and cut off a large chew with his pocketknife. Jes and Myrtle preferred store-bought plug tobacco, but until the hard times ended, they would settle for leaf tobacco that Cyrus Lentz gave them. Jes found himself smoking and chewing more since he had been out of work. He got nervous, and this made him reach for tobacco more often.

The front door to the Chevy dealership opened and two men in suits walked outside. They ignored Jes's presence as each pulled smoking items from their pockets. One man lit a cigar while the other methodically filled his pipe from a leather pouch. The man with the pipe was wearing a nice suit and looked out of place in Hartford. The other man, Jes surmised, was not as accustomed to wearing his Sunday clothes on Monday.

The two well-dressed men quickly became engaged in a conversation. Jes knew the mannerly thing to do would be to walk away, but he figured that he got there first and if they wanted privacy, they should move on. Preachers, doctors, lawyers, and businessmen never took a seat on the courthouse square. This was a spot for blue-collar men alone. It was more dignified for professional men to talk while standing on the sidewalk, but Jes knew that as a working man he could stand on the sidewalk, too.

"Yessir, that six-cyclinder Chevy is a mighty fine automobile for $495. Be a durn shame fer a man like you to buy one any whara's else than Hartford. Fine a Chevy garage as they got anywhere in the country."

"Sir, you are absolutely right. I may come back down here and buy that car. I drove over today, but if I do, I'll take the train and drive her home. The wife's been after me to buy a new car. Now, as for the rest of it, I don't know. Hartford is a nice little town and all that."

"What in tarnation do ye mean? Listen. I'm tellin' ye this is where ye need to build that new store. The opportunity is right HERE. I know ye have one in Madisonville and one in Paducah and another in Hopkinsville, but Owensbur ain't the place for another one. That's a lot bigger town and all kinds of competition. Ohio County and Hartford is the place to be for the future. Madisonville merchants like you have been after our business ever since the railroad opened. Owensbur too. I can show ye in the county paper every spring of the year them merchants over there is runnin' ads a tryin' to get our business."

"I hear what you say about Owensbur. Now if I open a store over there, I'm gonna get Hartford folks and the Owensbur folks, too. Owensbur folks ain't a gonna come to Hartford to shop. Shipping is a sight better, too. Some of my freight weighs a lot."

"That may be true, but the fact remains that ye gonna have more competition, and ye won't be in a boomin' town. Open up here, and yere son-in-law gonna be on the ground floor. Needs to buy 'im one of them new buildin' lots out there on the edge of town. Fifty-five foot wide and two hunerd deep. Buy his materials local and save more'n 'nough money to pay fer the lot. Jest like gettin' it fer nothin'."

"Part of what ye say is true, but it ain't gonna be long until folks 'round here that been goin' to Madisonville and Owensbur to shop is gonna be stayin' home. I don't mean because of the Depression neither. Them ol' country jakes that right now ain't got a pot to piss in or a fire to throw it in if they did, gonna be in high cotton before long. Right now, half the crude produced in this state comes from right here in the county. What do ye think all them cars and trucks is gonna run on if they don't have gas and oil? Despite the hard times, more gas bein' sold ever year. Folks still buyin' cars. Farms prices and coal mines is gonna come back, and then this county gonna come back guns blazin'."

"I think you are absolutely right about the future, but it may be a few years off. If a man has money, NOW is the time to get ready for the boom times. When times are hard, some people just get richer. I'm not convinced though that little towns like Hartford have that much future. The roads, cars, and trains are just gonna make it easier for folks to shop in the bigger towns, and some will move there for good."

Jes noticed from the corner of his eye that the cigar chewing man was getting red faced, as he appeared to be losing the argument with the more distinguished gentleman, who stood quietly with his arms folded, puffing away on his pipe. When the pipe smoker stated he wasn't sure towns like Hartford had much of a future, the second man jerked his cigar out of his mouth and threw both arms straight up in the air.

"NOW LOOK. We got the train and the river down here, and we got better roads. New road to Beaver Dam over here, new road to Taffy and gravel now all the way to Owensbur. Got that new road over in Butler County gonna go from Morgantown all the way to Bowlin' Green. A while back this ol' boy here started a bus line from Hartford to Owensbur, and now he's gonna run from Bowlin' Green all the way to Owensbur. Tried that ten year ago he would have been crazy to even think 'bout sech a thing. Fer years we had nothin' from here to Owensbur but a stagecoach. Lord God what a ride that was! Thirty miles of it, too.

Now, we got two movie houses, and the one over yonder has spent the money to bring 'Vitaphone' talkies to the county. See a picture right here fer as little as fifteen cents. Gonna have a big barbecue at the County Fair for Fourth of July this time. Soft drinks and ice cream gonna be a nickel. Everybody ten year and older get in fer a dime. Gonna give away a pony. On top of that, we gonna have an airplane come in and give rides."

"First of August, American Legion team is gonna play Central City right here and gonna have the biggest crowd we ever had fer a baseball game. Gonna give away a Victrola. The high school up there got one of the best basketball teams in the state. One of the best schools, too. We got a train a runnin' ever day over at Beaver Dam, too. Get a special deal to ride from there to Louisville to basketball games."

"Now, I never said you didn't have a fine community here. A mighty fine place to live but just not the same as Owensbur. I'm afraid it never will be. Before the trains, it was mighty hard to ship in and out of here, and folks couldn't travel much either. This country is on wheels now, and I'm afraid the roads are all gonna lead out of places like this."

"I'll tell ye what we got that Owensbur ain't got. COAL. They ain't got coal. Factories need coal, and we got it in this county. This little ol' town done got telephones, water, sewer, and electricity. Gonna pave us some streets and sidewalks, too. When the Depression is over, the oil and coal is gonna make this town grow like a house a fire. GOOD opportunity here. That son-in-law of yours could end up a rich man, you too if ye ain't a'ready."

"Well, I appreciate you showing me around town, but I need to study on this a bit longer. If I don't build over here, I might see if one of the fine merchants in this town would like to sell me part interest in their business. I have a lot of buying power, and that could help both of us out a lot. We might make it a branch of an Owensbur store. Now, I see a café down the street a ways and I could sure use a good cup of coffee right now."

"My idée exactly. Come on, the least I can do is buy ye a cup of Hartford's finest coffee."

Jes was unaware that he had just overheard a futile plea by a small-town mayor for new business in his community. In the coming decades thousands of small communities would cease to beg for more and start searching desperately to hold on to what they had left. For Jes Caughill, traveling to Owensboro to shop was like going to New York City. He had spent most of his money over the years in Centertown, very little in Hartford, and none in Owensboro. Jes could not imagine the day when nearly all businesses would leave Centertown.

Jes chuckled quietly as he watched the two men walk toward the restaurant. When the men disappeared into the establishment, Jes started to cross the street. He noticed something shiny and bent down to pick up a nickel. He examined the coin for a moment before depositing it in his overall pocket along with his other nickel and quarter.

The sign over the hardware store read, "Sherwin Williams Paint Headquarters." Jes walked inside and took a seat in an old chair next to the coal stove. The proprietor was nervously showing a five-piece dining room set to a nicely dressed lady in her early 40s.

"Mam'm, this here five-piece set is goin' for $115 and solid as a rock. Made out of maple. We carry a full line of furniture these days."

"Well, it looks nice, but I need to get my husband to come down and look at it. We may just drive over to Owensbur as well."

The storeowner looked disappointed when the lady walked out the front door. Jes figured business had not been good since the Depression hit. He walked over and looked at the dining room set. It was nice, but Jes could not see spending $115 for it. He wondered what kind of work her husband did to afford such things. Obviously, he was not a farmer or a coal miner.

Jes picked up one of the chairs and examined it at eye level before turning to the storeowner. "Did ye say this here outfit is $115?" The proprietor nodded, and Jes put the chair down and walked out the door. He sighed despairingly as he looked up and down the street absent-mindedly. Out of the corner of his eye he got a glimpse of Molly and Ma Lentz going into a department store. He suddenly remembered the change in his pocket and fished out one of the nickels. His gaze turned in the direction of the Highway Service Garage. If someone could waste $115 for a solid maple dining room set with the country in a Depression, he could afford to buy a mug of coffee with another man's nickel.

The cup of coffee hit the spot, and Jes resumed his stroll in downtown Hartford. He stopped in front of a store and looked at a man's suit in the window for $9.90. He had not owned a suit since the one he bought when he was courting Myrtle. That had been twenty years ago. A lady's dress was also on display for $3.98, plus straw hats for eighty-nine cents and men's work shirts for thirty-nine cents. The item that caught his attention, however, was a pair of men's leather work shoes for $1.39. His only pair of shoes was badly worn, and he desperately needed new ones, but he was afraid to part with the money. Right next to the work brogans was another item he needed, overalls for seventy-eight cents. He turned and walked away. Myrtle and the children needed things, too, but he could not afford it.

A grocery store on Main Street was the next business to catch Jes's eye. He stood for a few moments, looking at signs advertising a twenty-four-pound bag of flour for $1.10, packaged oats for nineteen cents, a twenty-pound bag of sugar for ninety-nine cents, a two-pound bag of orange slices for thirty-five cents, and a pound jar of cherry preserves for a quarter. A bag of orange slices and perhaps an equal amount of chocolate drops would have to wait for Christmas.

The drugstore was empty when Jes walked inside. His attention was drawn immediately to a bottle of Sloan's Liniment. Myrtle's back had been hurting for weeks after she strained it emptying a large tub of wash water. They had been out of liniment for months, and he suddenly felt a pang of guilt over the restaurant coffee. Myrtle and the kids were home working, and he was loafing around Hartford, drinking coffee. The liniment was thirty cents, and he bought it.

Jes sat down hard on a bench in front of the old Commercial Hotel building. He bent over at the waist until both of his elbows were resting upon his knees as he looked at the bottle of liniment. The contents of the bottle had soothed away the aches and pains of many hard days in the mines, and now he didn't even have a job. Thirty cents was half the price of a cheap pair of work brogans at a store in Centertown, and he spent that amount on a bottle of Sloan's Liniment. Myrtle would chastise him for wasting money in that fashion and then ask him to rub some on her sore back.

With the liniment tucked away safely in his overall pocket, Jes picked up a badly worn, discarded copy of the *Ohio County News*. The paper was dated late January and contained a large ad for a "Thrift Carnival" at a local department store. The Chevy garage had an ad for the used 1928 Chevy Roadster, and a movie house was promoting a film featuring William Desmond. Another large ad sponsored by local merchants highlighted the town's virtues and invited outside investment. The Kentucky Utilities Company had a small graphic ad lauding the power of electricity on the farm. It said, "… motors are cheaper than muscle." Jes laughed at the utility ad since he did not know of a single farm with electricity. He rolled the old paper up and tossed it back on the bench as he stood up to leave.

Jes walked around the courthouse and headed back to Molly's car. It was getting close to noon, and he was starting to get hungry; after all, it had been seven hours since breakfast. He started to take a seat on the courthouse lawn to eat his biscuit and apple; but the quart jar of water was back at the car, and he could not eat a biscuit without a drink to wash it down. He told himself that he was not concerned Myrtle would find out. She frequently lectured the children about eating and drinking in public. She said, "… only a heathen, an outlaw and yere father would do sech a thing."

A dog with his ribs showing came up to the car when Jes started eating his biscuit. The poor old hound stood with his tail between his legs and begged in a pitiful manner. Jes tried to run him off, but the dog was not about to leave. Finally, he gave the animal some of the biscuit that he promptly wolfed down. The wretched animal did not leave until he was satisfied that there was no more. Jes drank about half of the water and started eating his apple, but before long a grey squirrel perched himself on the hood of the car. For a few minutes man and squirrel looked at one another eyeball to eyeball. Finally, Jes tossed his bushy-tailed friend the apple core with a generous amount of apple still attached. When the squirrel had raced back up a nearby tree, Jes's attention was drawn to a team and wagon under a nearby tree. The horses were quietly and immodestly relieving themselves. Jes headed for the sanctuary of some trees near the Baptist Church to do the same. Common decency dictated that Jes be discreet, not to mention the City Marshal if he should catch him being less than prudent.

The afternoon was going to be long and tiring. Jes had no desire to walk aimlessly around town a second time. He knew the storekeepers would be happy to have Molly and Ma Lentz's business but equally relieved to have them gone. Ma Lentz asked a million questions and scrutinized everything meticulously before making a purchase. Myrtle was fond of telling a story about Ma Lentz. During a shopping trip to Hartford, she had agonized over two dresses for over an hour. Finally, an exasperated clerk suggested that she purchase both of them. Incredulous, Ma Lentz replied, "... ain't gonna do no sech thing. If I can't decide which one, I ain't a gonna take ary one."

Over the years Jes had brought the road wagon to Hartford or walked during bad weather. He always rushed to get what he came for and headed back home. He knew women viewed shopping as serious business and often left exasperated husbands in the car or with the team while they shopped. Today Jes would gladly wait all day for Myrtle if only he had the money for her to purchase what they needed. "If I just had a job," he muttered.

Jes was napping when Molly and Ma Lentz returned to the car. They had remarkably few parcels for two women who had spent the entire day going from store to store. The ladies were chatting away as Jes headed the car toward the road to Centertown. He hardly heard what they were saying as he contemplated what he had seen and heard that day. He knew many of the stores in town had merchandise that a lot of people could no longer afford. For the first time he became aware of the higher standard of living for people in Hartford as opposed to the country. It would be another twenty years before electricity, paved roads, and telephones would make their way into most rural areas, and many more before water lines appeared and the outdoor toilet disappeared. Jes knew, however, that things would never get better until men like him had jobs.

It was nearly dark when Jes headed Molly's car into the shed. Cyrus came out with his key and locked the building, tossing the key that was attached to a block of wood far out into a sea of weeds. Jes smiled to himself, as he could see Cyrus searching high and low for the piece of wood the next time he needed to unlock the shed.

Ma Lentz had remained in the car for several minutes after they pulled in, telling one of her long-winded stories. She made no effort to get out of the car until she saw Cyrus.

"Cyrus, hol' yere horses 'til I get outa this here car. Don't be in sech a fizz."

Jes walked wearily down the hill to his house. He knew Myrtle was keeping a plate of food warm for him, and he truly hoped she had some coffee as well. Ma Lentz's slow and deliberate ways reminded him of visiting the Lentzs with his family when he was a youngster. They had gone over for supper, but Ma Lentz was in no hurry with the meal. Nearly everyone had dozed off when Ma Lentz, who had been telling tall tales with long interruptions in her cooking, started hushing everyone.

"SHHHH, I wish ye would listen to that ol' chaaacken. Must be fallin' weather."

Jes's father often told the story and said, "... fallin weather my foot, that ol' rooster was a crowin' fer midnight. One o'clock in the mornin' 'for we got a bite to eat. When that ol' critter dies, Saint Peter gonna hafta prop the Peerly Gates open 'til she gets ready to come in."

The week after the trip to Hartford was uneventful. The Caughills did not hear any more arguing at the Lentz home. The mail carrier dropped Tom Leslie's letters off at the Caughills, and Myrtle slipped them under a small log at the edge of the woods about a hundred feet from the house. Molly retrieved the letters in this fashion, and Ma and Cyrus had not found out. Myrtle was concerned the mail carrier might start wondering why Tom Leslie was writing so many letters to Jes.

Saturday afternoon arrived, and Cyrus prepared to pay his hired help for a week's work. Myrtle was watching from the kitchen window when Cyrus came out of the house tearing off pieces of paper from a large sheet of department store brown wrapping paper. Cyrus wrote checks on anything that was handy, and the local bank accepted them without question. Practicality and expedience were the guiding principles in Cyrus Lentz's character. As a young man he walked into the Centertown Bank and handed them a check for cash. He announced that he needed some spending money. The dumbfounded cashier handed Cyrus his dime.

"Jes, come over and look. I can't see who that fella is, but he and Cyrus is really a talkin'. He stood 'round after the other fellas left."

"Yep, the ol' boy is startin' to get lathered up 'bout sumpin'. I bet I know what."

Cyrus went back in the house and slammed the door. In a few minutes he came out and started down the hill and went directly to the log where Myrtle had hidden a letter from Tom that morning. He raced back to the house, and soon the arguing began.

"Somebody tol' 'im 'bout them letters. I wonder how that fella found out?"

"People a talkin' I guess, Myrtle. We ain't tol' nobody, but that Thompson fella must have seen ye puttin' them letters there."

"Weren't none of his all-fired business. What did he get outta tellin' Cyrus?"

"A suckin' up to the boss, I reckon. Now Cyrus can't do nothin' 'bout it 'cept bust a gut. Yep, I'll be up all night tonight fer sure. Bustin' a gut holdin' 'im in bed. Yep, they'll be at it the rest of the day. Reckon Molly ain't gonna slip us no milk today."

"Up to me, I'd throttle that Thompson fella fer shootin' off his mouth. I'm gonna give 'im a piece of my mind the next time I see 'im. If I was a man, I'd kick his back side up b'tween his shoulders."

The argument at the Lentz house was loud but short in duration. Cyrus went about his afternoon chores like nothing had happened. Jes and Myrtle kept an eye out the kitchen window, but they did not see

Molly or Ma Lentz come out of the house. They were perplexed as to why the argument had been so short. Ma and Molly had patched up their differences long enough to take the trip to Hartford, and now everything seemed harmonious after the discovery of the letters. The Lentz family proved to be unpredictable.

The following morning Molly called to Myrtle through the kitchen door.

"Myrtle, I need ye to come right away. Ma is awful sick. A takin' on somethin' awful."

"Anna, take care of the breakfast and get things cleaned and keep on with that cannin'. I may be gone a spell."

Myrtle took off her apron and started out the door. She put her arm around Molly, who was shaking and sobbing. Myrtle suddenly stopped and returned to the kitchen door. "Anna," she said, "On second thought, after breakfast go to Miz Tichenor and tell her. May need some help."

Jes and Myrtle were well schooled in their respective roles as friends and neighbors. Myrtle was always prepared to help when someone in the neighborhood was sick, having a baby, or passed away. Jes and Myrtle were willing to sit up with a sick neighbor. Jes never failed to help a neighbor man with the farm chores if he was sick. In the country, assisting one another was a necessity, but one's character was also judged accordingly. Failure to help a friend or neighbor meant that in the community you would be "... talked about."

Jes and Jesse took some biscuits with them to the creek bottoms, where they spent the day chopping out corn. It was too far to take the time to return home for dinner. Anna continued with the canning and watched anxiously out the window for her mother. Myrtle rushed down the hill at noon.

"Honey, Ma Lentz has had a stroke. Tryin' to get the doctor down, but it ain't a gonna do no good. She's as bad as she can be. Don't know how long I'm gonna be, but ye know what needs to be done. Keep the fires a burnin' jest like I was here. Have supper on the table when the men get home. That little dab of dinner ain't gonna hold 'em long. Me and some neighbor women gonna take turns a settin' up. She could last a spell like this. Right now, Molly needs me more than Miz Lentz."

Myrtle poured a cup of coffee and ate a cold biscuit covered with blackberry jam. She did not bother to sit down as she watched the Lentz house through the kitchen window.

"Mother, Miz Lentz is really gonna die?"

"I'm afraid so. I ain't no doctor but seen it too many times. Doctor can't fix no stroke. Does sumpin' to the brain, I guess. She can't talk half the time so ye can understand her. Paralyzed one whole side. Jest pitiful."

Cyrus was frantic about his mother's illness. Family meant everything to him, and the thought of losing his mother was almost more than he could bear. No one had seen him this upset since his father died. For four days he did not sleep, walking the floors day and night and repeatedly asking the neighbor women how she was doing.

The fifth day of Ma Lentz's illness was no better than the first. An exhausted Cyrus finally mustered the courage to visit his mother's bedside. He took her hand in a timid and awkward fashion.

"Is ye any better, Ma?"

"OH Cyrus, nobody knows how bad I feel."

Ma Lentz's reply to his question sent Cyrus into a panic. He ran through the house, yelling for Molly and repeating what Ma Lentz said over and over. He started rummaging through drawers and cabinets scattering their contents all over the floor. After Cyrus nearly knocked Myrtle down, Molly screamed at him.

"CYRUS, what in blazes are ye lookin' fer?"

"WHARAS the Vicks Salve? Ma says we don't know how bad she feels."

Cyrus finally located the salve, smeared some on a rag soaked in hot water, and placed it on his mother's head. He collapsed in the chair by her bed—a pale, frightened, and exhausted man. Molly allowed him to stay there for an hour before she urged him to go out.

"Myrtle, Cyrus's gonna have a stroke 'fore this is over. I never seen 'im like this. He ain't eat a bite in days."

The four days and nights that Myrtle spent helping Molly with her mother was nearly the most trying she had ever spent helping a sick person. Cyrus was driving everyone crazy, and his antics had caused some of the neighbor women to cut short the time they spent helping out.

The morning of the sixth day Ma Lentz slipped away in her sleep. Molly sat beside the bed holding her mother's hand and sobbing. Cyrus was seated in a chair in the front room, staring blankly at the wall. He had not been this quiet in days. Myrtle met Jes at the kitchen door.

"Jes, Cyrus jest 'bout worried us to death. I ain't never seen a man so tore up. Times I wanted to hit 'im with a fryin' pan but felt so sorry fer 'im, too. Molly, pore thing, blames herself fer all of it. Miz Lentz been faintin' fer months and the doctor said she had high blood. Molly thinks it happened 'cause of her and Tom. I reckon it didn't help matters none."

Jes listened to Myrtle with his head down.

"Reckon when they're gonna bury her?"

"I dunno. Get yere tools ready. I'd say tomorrow afternoon."

The following day Jes and Jesse loaded the tools in the wagon and started for the Walton's Creek Cemetery. The church bells were slowly tolling away the years of Mrs. Randolph Lentz's life. Cyrus had put on his Sunday suit the night before and sat in his chair all night without saying a word to anyone. When the church bells announced a death in the neighborhood, it was Cyrus' custom to mount his horse and ride around until he determined the identity of the departed. Today, however, he sat quietly in despair at losing another precious member of his immediate family.

When the grave was completed, Jes left Jesse at the gravesite with two other men. They would remain until after the funeral to fill the grave. Jes rushed home and quickly changed his clothes and raced to Cyrus's shed. The door was unlocked, but Cyrus was not in sight. Jes started Molly's car and drove to the front of the house. He helped Molly into the car and looked back toward the house.

"Cyrus done gone ahead, Jes. Said he'd rather walk. Left a half hour ago."

"HE done WHAT? I didn't see 'im on the road. I bet he cut 'cross the fields, and he'll have mud all over 'im by the time he gets there."

Myrtle and Anna hugged Molly as Jes drove around the mud holes in the road. Jes was frustrated with Cyrus. He could have ridden to the church like the rest of them. Molly must have sensed Jes's mood. She reached over and touched his sleeve.

"Don't be hard on Cyrus. We gotta be understandin'. He's hurtin' awful bad."

"Myrtle, I done wrote Tom a letter and tol' 'im I ain't gonna marry 'im. I can't help but think that Ma was hurried off by me and Tom."

"Molly, no sense in ye talkin' like that. Yere mama had the high blood and the faintin' spells long 'fore Tom come along. Miz Lentz and Cyrus would have come to love that man to death. He and Cyrus be like brothers. Still could be."

"Our father taught us what it means to be a family. It means ever'thing. When he knowed he was gonna die, he called us together and said fer us to always stay together and take care each other. Cyrus took it all to heart. We all did. If I marry Tom, that will leave Cyrus all alone and he may have one of them spells and die. Then I will have dishonored my father and my brother. Cyrus would die fer me, and I ain't gonna do 'im that way."

Myrtle pointed her finger at Molly. "Molly, ye listen to me. Cyrus Lentz is as capable as any man on earth to look after hisself. Got money to hire housework done if he wants to. GET 'im a woman, too, if he wants. Lots of widder women out there jump at the chance."

"Cyrus ain't a gonna get married. Don't matter with men. Bein' an old bachelor don't matter none at all. I know folks make fun and call me an old maid. Think it's awful a woman don't get married. Tom was my last chance. I ain't a gonna look back. Cyrus and me will spend out our time together."

Myrtle and Molly embraced at the kitchen door. Molly was crying, and Anna saw some very rare tears running down her mother's cheeks as well.

"Myrtle, the time you and Jes have lived here by us is some of the happiest of my life. I know ye and Jes wanna buy this house. Cyrus don't wanna sell since it was Daddy's house, but I will do my best to get 'im to sell it. He owns it, not me, or I'd let ye have it today."

"Jes and me have never had a place of our own and may never. Been a dream of mine fer a long time. I love this place, 'specially with you a livin' jest up the road."

Jes and Myrtle spent three long and agonizing years living in Cyrus Lentz's house. Jes and Jesse stayed busy working off the rent on the house and ground for crops. The first year Jes planted corn in the bottoms and lost it all to drought. That summer was so hot and dry they slept outside most of the summer on pallets. Precious money had to be spent to buy cornmeal that winter. Their meager savings were dwindling fast with money being spent on coffee, sugar, cornmeal, and flour. Jes had heard he could expect fifty cents a bushel for his corn. That would have brought in $120 of much needed cash. Unfortunately, they salvaged only enough to feed the chickens.

The second year Jes tried a second corn crop, but a late backwater ruined that endeavor. Myrtle could see the strain was starting to take its toll. They rode down to the bottoms in the road wagon to check on the crop. Jes's voice started to crack as he looked out across the field with only a few stalks sticking up above the water. His hands were shaking so badly that Jesse had to drive the team back home. The mines and sawmills were either shut down or barely operating, and Jes had little prospect of getting work. He stopped going to church and spent much of his time brooding.

The third summer at Cyrus's, Jesse talked his father into planting a tobacco crop. Jesse took the lead with the tobacco. Jes worked, but the old fire was almost gone. Myrtle was afraid he was about to give up. She kept telling him they weren't the only ones having trouble. She reminded him that the Depression was all over the world, and some people were starving.

"Pap, terbacker shore looks purty. Mister Tichenor says ours and his is the best he ever seen. Think it'll make us some money?"

"I shore hope so, son. Can't hold out much longer with no money a comin' in. Had a hunerd dollars when the work stopped. Only a little dab left. Two year of livin' in a borrowed house and a livin' off what we raise. Little dab groceries and a smidgin' fer Christmas. If it don't bring some money, I don't know what we gonna do. My shoes wore out. Anna needs a new coat. This Depression gonna be the death of poor people."

After the tobacco was stripped, Jes loaded it on the wagon and drove to Owensboro. He refused to sell to a "Pen Hooker" or anyone else. He was convinced that if he went straight to a warehouse in Owensboro, he would get more money. The trip took all day in the wagon, and he spent his last fifty cents for a room. The tobacco was on the floor and now he had to wait.

"Jes. I wish to the Lord ye would set down. Been pacin' the floor fer days and makin' me nervous as an old cat."

"The feller said I orta get a good price fer that terbacker. Best crop I ever seen. The check orta be here by now. WAIT, that's the mail buggy a comin' now."

Jes raced out the front door and took the mail from the carrier. Myrtle watched anxiously as Jes frantically ripped open an envelope. He stared at the contents for a long time, his head and shoulders shrunk and Myrtle's heart along with them. A lump came into her throat and she wanted to cry. It was bad news. They desperately needed the money, and Jes needed a victory; but his body language indicated they had received neither.

Myrtle stood by the door and waited for Jes. He started walking slowly back to the house but was unsteady on his feet. He nearly fell twice before he got to the front steps. The color had drained out of his face, and his hands were trembling. Myrtle stood aside as he staggered in the house and went straight to the kitchen. He was breathing hard when he collapsed in a ladder-back chair next to the table. His head fell into his hands, with one mashing the crumpled letter against the side of his head.

The children stood in the kitchen door shocked and frightened at their father's appearance. Myrtle walked over and carefully took the envelope from his hand. She looked at it for a moment and then pulled up a chair and sat down next to Jes. She took a few moments to compose herself before saying anything.

"Jes, ye done yere best. No man could have tried any harder. We still got a roof over our heads and food to eat. We'll make out somehow. We always have. Ain't nobody a blamin' ye, Jes. God willin', we'll pick up and go on."

"God didn't stop that son-of-a-bitch from stealin' our terbacker. A BILL, mind ye, fer 10 cents. Not 'nough to pay the floor bill. Be a cold day in HELL when I raise 'nother crop of terbacker. Be a colder day in HELL when that bastard gets his ten cents. Stole my terbacker … jest plumb stole it."

The next few weeks in the Caughill house were tension filled. Myrtle feared Jes had suffered a nervous breakdown. He was pale and shaky and exploded over the slightest noise. The children were afraid to be around him. He slept sparingly during the day and paced the floors all night. Old Pete got in his way, and Jes kicked him so hard the dog left and never returned. He was so weak and unsteady that it was impossible for him to bring in firewood or a bucket of water.

Myrtle suddenly found herself the head of the household, and she was uncomfortable with the new role. There weren't many decisions to be made, but Myrtle was keenly aware of the new responsibility. For twenty years of married life the family leadership and bread-winning burden had been Jes's alone. She had a new respect for his role in their lives.

Jesse was more than capable of meeting the work responsibilities that paid the rent. In addition, he cut the wood, slopped the hog, fed the horses, and carried in water. Anna helped with the household chores that included firing the wash kettle for washing clothes, gathering eggs, and cooking. For the first time the children were looking to their mother for leadership.

The Caughill home became a living hell during Jes Caughill's illness. The slightest provocation sent him into a rage. Myrtle cautioned the children about noise or comments that would agitate their father. Myrtle knew the situation could not continue indefinitely, but she was at a loss for a solution. It did not seem possible, but the hard times had just gotten harder.

The day Cyrus sent Jesse to Centertown with the team to bring back a load of feed was the day Jes Caughill nearly went completely over the edge. Myrtle did not tell Jes that Jesse was going to town, but when he drove by the house in the wagon, the secret was out. The roads were mud and snow covered and Myrtle knew Jesse was too inexperienced with Cyrus's team to make the trip in bad weather. Jes had paced the floor, watching out the window in anticipation of Jesse's return.

"LORD GOD. OH NO. Myrtle, the youngun done got Cyrus's team mired down halfway up the hill. They's gonna get pulled all the way back down the hill and kill 'em all. The wagon is too heavy. OH LORD. What are we gonna do? Cyrus is gonna have a fit. THROW us outa this house. OH GOD."

"JES, JES, calm down. Set down here and drink this cup of coffee. Jesse can handle that team as good as you. He ain't gonna get hurt. LOOK, I see Cyrus a comin' down the hill now with the mule. He's gonna help the youngun. He orta knowed it was too muddy and slick to pull that hill with the wagon loaded down. That ol' mule can pull like the devil. Said so yereself. Pull that wagon right on up the hill. Now just take it easy."

"I can't do nothin', ain't good fer nothin'. Lose a crop to drought, lose a crop to back water, and then let some son-of-a-bitch steal our terbacker. Now my boy done mired down Cyrus's team. Sooner be dead than live like this."

Myrtle worried about Jes's comments about dying. She could not help but think about the day Marv Atlee tried to hang himself. Surely, Jes would not go that far. The frustration was so great at times that she wanted to slap him and tell him to snap out of it. The thought that Jes might never be better terrified her.

Jesse and Cyrus finally pulled the wagon up the hill, but it took Myrtle the rest of the day to calm Jes down. Jesse whispered to his mother that Cyrus was mad, but he figured he would get over it by the next day. Myrtle put her fingers to her lips and shook her head at her son. Jesse understood and acted as if nothing had happened.

Myrtle buried her head in a pillow and cried herself to sleep every night. She prayed harder than she had ever prayed and kept telling herself he was going to be all right in the spring, that the warm weather would bring Jes out of his depression.

Jesse Caughill had been a rock for the family during the years they lived in Cyrus Lentz's house. He helped his father with everything and worked for neighbors as well. In the summertime he kept Myrtle and Anna busy frying fish that he caught on his trotlines. He trapped rabbits, shot squirrels with a slingshot, and raided bee trees for the honey. Anna picked blackberries, wild greens, and scoured the woods for walnuts and hickory nuts. The Caughill children were earning their keep.

Jes Caughill never liked hunting or fishing and did not like to keep a gun in the house. Jesse, on the other hand, was born to the outdoors. The only complaint Myrtle had was that he liked hunting and fishing more than work. She never complained, however, about the food that he supplied the table. In later years she said, ". . . never worried 'bout that boy runnin' off to no city. He'd rather live in the woods or on a creek bank."

When spring finally arrived, Myrtle sensed something was going to happen. The weather had turned mild except for the thunderstorms that upset Jes. The weather warmed early, daffodils were blooming, and the sunshine strengthened everyone's spirits; and Jes was showing some improvement. He spent most days resting in the front yard, and one day he went with Myrtle and Anna to pick a big mess of wild greens. The color slowly returned to his face, and the trembling in his hands was nearly gone. Occasionally he would participate in a conversation, as long as the subject was not serious.

Jesse wanted to put out another crop, but Myrtle would not allow him to discuss it with his father. Jesse would have to work off some tobacco plants and seed corn with a neighbor. Cyrus told him he could work off a two-acre field of high ground to raise enough corn for meal and feed.

"Son, ye gotta take the bull by the horns this year. I know ye always wanna ask Pap this or that, but not this year. He ain't never gonna touch another terbacker plant. Get seed corn if ye can, get terbacker plants and work it out with Cyrus fer the ground. Yere purt near grown anyhow. Might as well start actin' like it." Myrtle smiled as her words made her son beam with pride.

Myrtle was starting to relax some now that Jes was showing signs of improvement. She was not prepared, however, for what happened in early April. She dropped her rolling pin in the floor when she heard Jes screaming from the front yard. The thought that he had finally lost total control flashed through her mind.

"MYRTLE, WHERE IN BLAZES DID YE GET?"

Jes ran through the house screaming at the top of his lungs. Myrtle was trembling all over as she opened her mouth, but nothing came out. She was both speechless and terrified.

"DID ye see that feller drive up jest now?"

"UH, Jes, I didn't hear no car drive up. What are ye talkin' 'bout?"

"THE FELLER mine open up day afer t'mor. I GOT A JOB. Need a good powder man."

"Jes, I don't think yere well 'nough to go back in the mines."

"Well, HELL. Gonna make maybe four dollars a day. Good Lord, woman, we ain't got a dime to our name. GOTTA go back. Three years and no money. Myrtle, don't ye see. I GOTTA job."

Jes was still shaky and pale, but the life had returned. He walked the floors nervously, but now it was excitement. Myrtle knew he had no business going back in the mines, but she also knew nothing was going to stop him. His manhood had been restored, and once again he could fulfill his responsibilities as the breadwinner of the family. When Jesse came in for dinner, Jes talked to him about the tobacco crop and other issues like the old Jes Caughill.

"Son, I'm proud of what yere doin' with the terbacker. Walk back over with ye after dinner and look at it. NO, sir, I ain't raisin' 'nother crop for some jackass to steal from me. This here is yere crop. Jest as long as ye don't start din dongin' me to go to work in the mines. Purt near all I know, but ye don't have to get started. Ye don't work fer the mines, they own ye."

Before dinner was over, Jes turned his attention to Anna, who was so astounded by her father's improvement she had barely touched her food.

"Little lady, I want ye to get ready to pick blackberries this summer. Looks like a good crop. Get ten cents a gallon fer 'em at Centertown or Hartford fer sure. Anybody a payin' a penny or two a quart fer pickin' strawberries, ye can do that, too. Make a little dab. Maybe material fer a dress or two fer school. Better'n nothin'."

Jes spent the following day preparing to return to the mines. His carbide lamp had not been used in three years and needed cleaning. His work brogans were worn out, but it was the only pair of shoes he had to his name. Some patchwork made them almost serviceable for work in the mines. There were many rough edges to Jes Caughill, but he was at his best when he could work and provide for his family.

Myrtle stood by the kitchen door at 4:00 AM when Jes left for the Feller mines. She stood watching long after he disappeared into the darkness. Despite his newfound vigor, she was still apprehensive about his return to the mines. Jes was one of the best around at the job of shooting down coal with black powder or dynamite. Myrtle knew all too well what happened to powder men who got careless, and she hoped he would remember to be cautious.

Jes's first day back at the mines was fretful for Myrtle. She tried to stay busy, but she became more apprehensive as the day wore on. She had almost forgotten what it was like to see her man leave for the mines early in the morning, not knowing if he would come back. Myrtle wondered what would happen to her and the children if Jes was seriously hurt or killed in the mines. This worry plagued the wives of all coal miners. The sound of an explosion, a screaming whistle at the mines, or the sudden clanging of church bells was the sound that sent family members into a panic. A wagon stopping in front of the house in the middle of the day often meant a miner was coming home seriously hurt or worse.

Jesse and Anna were in school, and Myrtle had the house to herself. The only sound other than what she made with pots and pans was the ticking of the old mantel clock. When the clock struck 12 noon, she jumped. That was the final straw. She stopped, placed her hands on her hips, and announced out loud, ". . . get a hold of yerself, ol' woman. Ye ain't the only woman with a man in the mines. Keep on and be as crazy as he is. Get this house cleaned up and get supper ready. RIGHT now."

For the next two hours Myrtle worked feverishly to get the housework done. Pinto beans were slowly simmering on the stove. The potatoes were ready to put on to cook, but it was too early. She had two-quart jars of tomatoes and another of apples to open, and the cornbread would be the last thing to prepare.

"HALLO, the house. BY JINGS, anybody home?"

Cyrus Lentz's voice startled Myrtle. He was sitting astride of his old mare in the front yard when Myrtle opened the door.

"Cyrus, Jes went to work in the mines this mornin'. Thought ye knowed that."

"By jings, I knowed that. Done thought it over. Ain't gonna sell. Gonna keep it in the family. Jes got a job. Don't need 'im to work no more. He can pay rent. Six dollars a month."

Cyrus stated his business and rode away without another word. Myrtle was flabbergasted. She had convinced herself that Cyrus would work out a way for Jes to buy the place. Jes had warned her that Cyrus viewed rent as a better arrangement. Rent for Cyrus was like collecting a house payment while maintaining ownership. "Besides," Jes said, "Cyrus's daddy's little house, and he ain't gonna sell to nobody."

Myrtle walked back into the kitchen and after stirring the beans, she collapsed at the kitchen table, crying. Alone where no one could hear, years of frustration and torment boiled out. Thirty minutes went by before she finally regained control. She had to stiffen her resolve and not let Jes and the children see that she was upset. She looked at herself in Jes's tiny shaving mirror hanging on the kitchen wall, shook her finger at the image staring back at her and said, "... stop yere blubberin', ol' woman, and get back to work."

Before supper Jesse carried in several armloads of wood for the kitchen stove while Anna brought in two buckets of water and fed and put the chickens up for the night. Myrtle held supper until nearly seven o'clock, but Jes was still not home. Anna fixed a large plate of food for her father and covered it with a dishtowel. Myrtle insisted on washing the dishes since this gave her a clear view of Jes's route home, and she could watch for him without alarming the children. He would return home by a shortcut across Cyrus's pasture, but this was an hour later than usual, and she was worried.

Cyrus Lentz locked his barn door and slopped the pigs as the sun started to fade.

Myrtle occasionally glanced at Anna and Jesse to make certain they had not detected her concern. So far she had been successful, but she was not certain how long she could keep it up.

A commotion at Cyrus's place caught Myrtle's attention. The sun was starting to slip away as she peered out the window to see what had Cyrus's chickens in an uproar. The old gander was chasing them again. "BY JINGS, leave them chickens alone ... DO ye hear me?" Cyrus raced toward the henhouse waving his arms and screaming.

Cyrus hated the gander, especially when he chased chickens. A drummer had sold Cyrus the goose for ten dollars after telling him he was a fighting grey goose from Germany. Supposedly, he was a prizewinner when it came to fighting other ganders, but terrorizing the chickens is all he had been good for since Cyrus bought him.

Myrtle watched as Cyrus grabbed the clothesline pole and started after the gander. The goose was accustomed to the chases and fled just out of Cyrus's reach. The pursuit entered the pasture, and Cyrus swung the pole with determination but always missed the goose by a couple of feet. Molly came to the kitchen door and pleaded with her brother to forget about the goose and come to supper. He ignored his sister and continued thrashing at the bird. Myrtle could see only a faint outline of Cyrus against the sunset as he chased the bird to the far end of the pasture.

The goose versus Cyrus drama would end by Thanksgiving. Jes and Myrtle would join them for Thanksgiving dinner consisting of a huge turkey and a goose. They did not dare ask Cyrus why he was having two birds for dinner.

The children went to bed at eight-thirty, while Myrtle waited for Jes at the kitchen table. She heard Cyrus's back door slam and figured he had either given up on catching the goose or the bird was dead. She tried in vain to read a book by the light of a coal oil lamp. It was no use; she was too worried. Her mind raced back to the day five years before when a man came to their door to tell Jes that his father had been hurt in the Centertown mine. Jes cut across the field to his father's house, but neither he nor Myrtle suspected the seriousness of the injury. A few hours later Jes returned, and his drooping shoulders told the whole story. He walked in the door, let out a sigh and said, "... I tol' 'im that mine's not safe."

When the clock struck nine o'clock, Myrtle's stomach was tied in knots. She started to blame herself for letting him go back to work so soon. It was too dark to watch for him through the kitchen window, so she sat listening for his brogans stomping on the back porch. He was coming home; she was sure of it. It was only a matter of time until he would burst through the kitchen door, and drop his carbide lamp and lunch bucket by the door. His clothes would be covered with coal dust and soaked with perspiration, and the putrid odor of sweat and dirt would fill the kitchen. He would holler, "MYRTLE, ye got supper ready?"

Gettin' Married (1937)

GETTIN' MARRIED
(1937)

*M*ICKEY ALWAYS SMILED *recalling stories about the hot Fourth of July weekend in 1937 when his mom and dad walked to the preacher to get married. Two stubborn and fiercely independent people were about to start a life together in one tiny upstairs room provided by a generous neighbor. The sight of Anna Caughill striding down an old dusty road, lugging a wood-frame suitcase, was as vivid in Mickey's mind as if he had been present. He knew by Depression standards, work in a sawmill at three dollars per day, six days a week was good employment. Ralph Atlee's first car, a Model T Ford that he shared with his brother Tim, was rusting away behind Liz Atlee's barn. The old Tin Lizzie would have to wait for the Depression to end before precious funds could be spent on repairs. For Anna and Ralph this was not important; their love was too strong.*

The image of his mom's family, working for Cyrus Lentz faded from his mind and refocused on the day his parents walked to the preacher and got married.

"I'll show THEM a thing or two ... get married if I WANT to ... I ain't gonna be no ol' maid ... I'm 21 years old; I'LL get married if I WANT TO."

Anna Caughill's long legs carried her down the dusty road: her wooden suitcase—a heavy-grain black fiber stretched over a wood frame with metal reinforced lid—slapped against her leg. The suitcase, Anna's only piece of luggage, had been ordered in the spring from the Sears Roebuck catalog for ninety-five cents. In addition to the modest travel case, Anna had purchased for a dollar what the catalog called a "Cool and Dainty Dotted Swiss Dress" with slimming lines, fancy pockets, buttons, pleated short sleeves, and a pleated yoke. The previous summer Anna had picked and sold blackberries for a dime a gallon; she had saved enough money to purchase the suitcase, the dress, and a few other items for her wedding day. Her father, who must have suspected what she was doing, growled, "... whatcha buy them fer? Ye ain't gonna go no wheras."

Ralph Atlee and Anna Caughill had been talking about getting married for over a year. Anna's parents, Jes and Myrtle, were set against it. They liked Ralph but had no "hankerin'" to give up their baby girl.

"I ain't got nothin' agin' Ralph. Knowed 'im most of his life. Like one of my own younguns. Worked fer their daddy on the farm when me and ye momma got married. Ralph is a fine feller, but that won't put beans and taters on the table. Times is hard ... rather see ye dead than married durin' hard times."

"Daddy, I can't believe ye would say that to yere own daughter."

"'cause a Depression is a goin' on. Ain't been over five years when we went three year and not made a cent. I reckon ye forgot that. Livin' in a borrowed house and livin' off what we growed. Had our backs to the wall and NO money a comin' in."

"Honey, yere daddy's right. Need to wait fer better times. We seen hard times, and we know what we're a talkin' 'bout. Another dad-burn war a brewin' 'cross the sea, or I'm two foot high. Bad time fer young folks to think 'bout gettin' married. Ralph go off to war and leave ye with a youngun, and then what?"

"Ralph ain't got no car and hardly anybody got money fer gas and tires anyhow. That ol' Model T of his and Tim's is a settin' up behind Liz Atlee's barn right this instant a growed up in weeds. I'd sell mine if I could find some fool wantin' to buy it. Ralph ain't even got a road wagon and a team."

Jes and Myrtle had not raised a shrinking violet. Anna stood toe to toe with her parents as the argument raged for hours. Jes's old dogs left the porch and headed out across the fields, and they would not return until the argument was over. Myrtle stood with her hands on her hips, making points when Jes and Anna gave her an opening. Jes paced the floor, waving his arms and making other animated gestures.

The long years of doing without during the Great Depression had instilled a foreboding about the economic future that would last Jes and Myrtle the rest of their lives. Jes had nearly been crushed by the Depression once, and he would never forget it. Anna Caughill, though, was now a grown woman and felt only the excitement of starting a marriage to a man she loved dearly. She might lose the argument to her parents, but she was determined to have the final word.

"Daddy, Ralph got a job over at the mill. Three dollars a day fer five or six days a week. 'Less they got WPA, lots of folks don't have that. Gonna put some crops out over on his mama's place, too. This is 1937, I'm 21 years old, and I ain't gonna be no old maid like Molly Lentz, a livin' with her parents."

"Ol' Roosevelt. I wish he had the WPA a stuck up his you know what. MEN need real jobs ... sumpin' he ain't never had. If that good fer nothin' ol' pup ever gets elected agin', I'm gonna take his possum grinnin' face to the back house and wipe on it," Myrtle growled.

"I don't like Roosevelt neither, but lots of folks be starvin' without WPA, Mother. Things is gonna get better."

"I love my mother and daddy, but I'm a gettin' married this afternoon, and they ain't invited ... ain't none of their business anyhow. Daddy's out choppin' wood, and Mother fell asleep sewin', and I jest walked right out that door and never looked back. Ralph got the Fourth of July weekend off, and we're gonna have Preacher Smith marry us."

Anna was hardly aware that she was talking to herself as she walked down the dusty road on a hot July day. Her heart was pounding with excitement, as a new chapter in her life was about to begin. Her white dress and white shoes were tucked away in the suitcase. She would put them on at the preacher's house and marry a man she had known her entire life. Ralph was nearly ten years older, but Anna had known she was going to marry him since she was ten years old.

Anna did not mind walking a mile and a half to her own wedding. She told Ralph it would be best if she slipped off to avoid a scene with her parents.

Ralph nervously paced the front porch at Preacher Smith's while he waited for Anna. He was somewhat apprehensive that Jes and Myrtle had talked her out of getting married. Ralph fidgeted with his new suit of clothes from Sears Roebuck. The suit was blue wool serge with a two-button lapel, and it cost him twelve dollars and seventy-five cents. He could have been measured for a new suit at a store in Centertown, but the catalog description was too enticing, even if it did cost him better than a week's wages.

"Hey, Ralph. Looks like Anna a comin' down the road right now. Want me to run down and get her in the car?"

"NAW, never mind, Tommy. With them long legs she'll be here 'fore ye get turned 'round."

"Never said why you and Anna waited so long to get hitched."

"Had to wait fer her to grow up, Tommy. Ol' Jes wouda shot me if I tried to rob the cradle."

"Here he's 'bout to shoot both of ye right now."

"NAW, ol' Jes is a bunch of hot air. Fine fella and knowed him since I was knee high to a grasshopper. Taught me, Al, and Tim how to raise terbacker, kill hogs. He'll get over it."

Preacher Smith's wife ran out the front door when Anna walked up on the front porch. She was crying and hugged the young bride like she had been her own daughter.

"OOOH, honey, come on in and get freshed up and get that new dress on. You men stay outside 'til I call ye. Ralph, ye ain't supposed to see the bride no how."

Ralph, Tommy, and Preacher Smith grinned at one another. Dodie Smith always made over the brides in this fashion. Myrtle Caughill said, "... that woman is a 'Nervous Nellie' and she gets on my nerves 'til I could scream, but she shore is a fine woman."

The uncomfortable menfolk leaned against the side of Tommy's Model T while the women got ready inside the house.

"Ralph, been aimin' to ask ye, but where you all aim on livin'? Reckon yere ma got room?"

"Preacher, Mister Chester tol' us we can have that upstairs room of his. Tommy gonna run us over right after the I do's. Nobody but 'im in that big ol' house. Rent free since he says he owed Pa money for doc-torin' stock. Good way to pay a debt. Gotta get my own coal, but he said put out a garden and have all the eggs we want. Now we all know ol' Chester bends that elbow a mite, and that worried Anna. I tol' her he's as harmless as a fly."

"Ralph, that room ain't got no kitchen."

"No, it don't, but it has a big old coal stove, and we can cook on that. Jest as soon have fried cornbread as baked anyhow. We can make out 'til we find somethin' bigger."

Finally, Dodie Smith called the men into the house, and the wedding was underway. Dodie tried to play "Here Comes the Bride" on a poorly tuned piano, and the whole affair was over in less than fifteen minutes. Preacher Smith held open the front door for the newlyweds, while Dodie sprinkled them with a few grains of rice. Tommy ran ahead, opened the car door, and started blasting on his uncle's old trumpet from the Spanish-American War. His Uncle Ben claimed to have been Teddy Roosevelt's bugler, but no one ever asked him why he had a trumpet instead of a bugle as a souvenir of the war.

"Tommy, stop honkin' on that dad blasted horn and let's get goin'," Ralph laughed as he helped Anna into the car. The wedding had been a very casual affair with no family members from either side. Liz Atlee told Ralph she did not want hard feelings with Jes and Myrtle and suggested no one stand up with the couple in their wedding. Tim and Al Atlee wanted to participate in the big event in their brother's life, but they never questioned their mother or went against her wishes. Liz did not think it was right for them to attend when Anna's own parents were not invited.

Thirty minutes after the wedding was over, Ralph and Anna were at Mister Chester's house. The old two-story farmhouse was beginning to show some neglect after sheltering three generations of Chesters. Mister Chester was a widower with no children, and with age his interest in keeping up the property had declined. Ralph had warned Anna, "... the old coot will be drunker than a hoot owl when we get there but nothin' to worry 'bout. Sometimes though he falls down and can't get up."

"WELL, them newlyweds are right here on my front porch. Well, don't just stand there. Ralph, grab up that little woman and run up them stairs like the dogs is after ye."

Ralph picked up his bride, who was clearly two inches taller, and raced up the steps two at a time.

"Chester, the dad blasted door is locked. Got a key?"

"OH, damn it to hell. I tol' yere mama yesterday not to lock that door. Now where in tarnation is that damn key?"

Ralph and Anna stood by the door laughing as Mister Chester searched and swore for nearly ten minutes looking for the door key.

"THAR ye are, ye damn rusty coffin nail. Ain't been used in forty years."

Mister Chester started up the stairs with the door key gripped firmly in his right hand. He was so drunk that he stumbled and nearly fell twice before he reached the top of the stairs. He was reeling from side to side as he tried unsuccessfully to place the key in the lock. Ralph gently took the key from him and opened the door. Ralph gathered Anna in his arms, crossed the threshold, and closed the door with his foot. Mister Chester went back down the stairs with almost as much difficulty as he had climbing them.

Anna gasped when she saw the room. She ran about looking at everything. A large coal stove rested about three feet from one wall, a small table and two chairs painted white would serve as a breakfast set, a kitchen sideboard, wardrobe, large four-poster bed, a bedside table for a wash basin, and two rocking chairs made up the furniture. Liz Atlee had brought over some sheer curtains and three braided rugs for the floor. The old sideboard would serve as a kitchen in their tiny abode.

"Ralph, this is the cutest place I ever seen. I wasn't expectin' anything this nice."

"Ma and me worked on it a bit. I painted the floors and Ma helped me put up new wallpaper. Ma painted the table and chairs, too. She brung over some bedclothes, curtains, and a few cookin' things. I gotta cured ham, flour, bag pinto beans, and some navy beans, a fifty-pound sack of taters, and twenty pound of cornmeal. Two quarts of buttermilk a hangin' down Chester's well, and he said his hens is layin' up a storm and we can have all we want. If ye want it ain't too late to plant a little dab of late garden. Take Chester's mule and order one up in two shakes of a lamb's tail."

"Ralph, all yere mama and not mine. Mine didn't do nothin'."

"Yere mama didn't know nothin' 'bout it. Didn't know we was gettin' hitched neither."

"Ralph, I want ye to change yere clothes and hitch up Chester's mule. We got plenty of daylight left, and we can plant garden. OUR very first garden. OH shoot, we ain't got no seeds."

"Ma figured on that, too. Got bean seed, squash, Detroit Red beets, cukes, and I reckon that's 'bout all we can expect to raise in a late garden.

Got mustard and turnip seed fer fall plantin'. Honey, we ain't gonna starve. I got a big crop of sweet taters over at Ma's farm, and Chester's got a root cellar out back yonder for taters and turnips if we raise a good crop."

"Real romantic honeymoon, Ralph. Got married, moved into an old farmhouse with an old drunk, and now gonna spend our honeymoon a plantin' garden."

"Take ye back home if it don't suit ye."

"NO, I married ye 'cause I love ye, Ralph. If ye want to spend our honeymoon on the creek bank, a fishin', that's fine with me. Plantin' garden is fine with me. Let's get to it."

"Well, let me go down and bring up yere suitcase."

Before Ralph could open the door, they heard a loud commotion on the front porch. They knew Chester had fallen, and they listened for a moment to see if he had hurt himself.

"DAMN IT TO HELL. Who put that dad blasted suitcase on my front porch?" Ralph and Anna fell across the bed laughing. Living in the same house with Mister Chester would be an experience they would never forget.

Monday morning Ralph returned to work in the sawmill. Anna got up at four o'clock to prepare his breakfast and to see him off to work for the first time. They had planted a small late garden on Saturday afternoon, walked to services at Walton's Creek Church on Sunday, and spent the afternoon strolling in the woods behind Chester's house. Anna was beaming, but Ralph knew she would never be totally content until she made peace with her parents.

"Anna, Jes and Myrtle ain't really mad. Stubborn ol' coots and don't want to be the first to give in. You're the daughter, and they expect ye to do that. Gonna hafta jest take a deep wind and go see 'em. They ain't gonna run ye off." Ralph gently pressed his new bride to resolve the strain with her parents.

"Ralph, I know that, but they ain't yere mama and daddy. Yere mama don't whoop and holler when she gets mad. Mine do. Course that's jest their way. I know they love me and want what's best for me."

"That's right, jest their way. Knowed yere daddy since I was a little toad. Been kinda like a daddy to me all these years. I ain't afraid of 'im. Course I don't want Jes mad at me neither."

"I gotta have an excuse to go back home. I'll think of somethin'. I don't know what, but sumpin'."

The weeks flew by as Anna and Ralph settled into their new marriage. Ralph worked hard at a sawmill that was powered by a twenty horsepower Advance Rumely steam engine. He came home each evening drenched with sweat and anxious to eat Anna's simple meals prepared on top of the old coal stove. A large oak tree outside their bedroom window protected the house during the day and helped keep the heat to a minimum as they slept.

It was during the third month of their marriage that Ralph did not come home from work with a big grin on his face. He acted sheepish and withdrawn and did not say a word during supper. Anna had known Ralph for many years, and she knew something was bothering him. He wasn't angry, but his feelings were hurt or something was troubling him.

"Ralph, ye been actin' worse than a little whipped pup ever since ye got home. What's eatin' at ye?"

"Don't wanna talk 'bout it jest yet. Later on, I guess. Embarassin' to talk 'bout, but it shore has stuck in my craw. Thirty years old and never heard tell of sech a thing. Wish I never had. Seen Al today and he said he had heard of sech and figured I had, too. Jest makes me sick."

"Ralph, stop beatin' 'round the bush and spit it out. The suspense is killin' me."

"Well, this fella over at the mill was a talkin' while we ate our dinner. Talkin' 'bout these two women over at Sacramento who live together. Two old maids."

"What's wrong with that?"

"If that was all, I guess nothin'. He says they live jest like they're married. Like you and me. You know. Says they sleep in the same bed and don't wear nothin' either. I don't know how he knows that."

"GOOD LORD! I never in my borned days heard sech nonsense. That fella is a windbag."

"NO, he ain't. Hardly ever says a thing. Fred said he had heard 'bout that some, too. Not 'round here, mind ye, but up in Louisville. He worked up there a spell and says they got men up there doin' it, too. They call 'em queers up there. Cities got lots of it, I reckon. I got so upset a listenin' to it, my hands jest shook. I shook all over."

"Ralph. Even stock don't act like that. We had a dog once, come to think of it, but Daddy run 'im off. When my daddy run a dog off, he don't come back."

"I felt like a durn fool a settin' there with men my own age and not knowin' 'bout sech carryin' on."

"Makes my skin crawl. DON'T ye ever come home and tell trash like that, or I will go back home and stay."

"I don't blame ye. Anna, livin' here at Walton's Creek is what Atlees been doin' fer a 120 years. They come to Kentucky fer a better life and found it right here. Times get hard sometimes, but I don't wanna live nowhere else. Least ways 'round here men don't sleep with men and women with women. May hafta go to the city to work sometime, but this is always gonna be home."

Anna was so upset over Ralph's story she knew a conversation with her mother was the only thing that would put her mind at ease. Myrtle Caughill was a very wise lady and understood people and what made them behave as they did. Anna had always depended upon her mother for advice and understanding. She missed that and was determined to see Myrtle, even if she was still mad.

Myrtle Caughill started to cry when her daughter walked through the front door. The two women embraced and Anna started to cry. Myrtle was the first to regain her composure as she ushered Anna to a rocking chair. Anna knew she should have come sooner, and the guilt was crushing.

"Honey, now hush that cryin'. Get an ol' woman started to blubberin'. Yere daddy and me has been two pig- headed ol' fools. Shouda come to see ye long 'fore now. Didn't even get to see ye get married. Course our parents didn't see us neither. Jest feel bad that you felt like ye had to slip off. We had no right to interfere, but Jes and me was jest concerned 'bout ye. Ain't none of our business. How's Ralph?"

"He's fine, Mother. He loves you all."

"He's a fine man. I'm proud fer both of ye. Times may be hard, but young folks got to marry. Wait fer the good times and they may never come. Times always been hard fer me and yere daddy."

Myrtle and Anna talked for hours. The tension was gone, and the old mother-daughter bond had reemerged. They talked about cooking, sewing, gardening, and a novel that Anna had been reading; but Anna discreetly avoided the topic she had discussed with Ralph the day before.

"Honey, you got sumpin' on yere mind?"

"No, nothin' special."

"Don't go to fibbin' to me. I know when somethin' is botherin' ye. Ever'thing ok with Ralph?"

"OH yes, Mother. Well, Ralph did hear somethin' at work yesterday that has got both of us upset. I don't know how to talk 'bout it. I'm too ashamed."

Myrtle opened a cigar box, removed a plug of chewing tobacco, cut off a piece with an ancient paring knife, and put the tobacco in her mouth. She looked at her daughter curiously as she placed the cigar box back on a lamp table. Anna always got uncomfortable under her mother's silent gazes. Myrtle frequently did this as she attempted to gauge the situation. The technique worked like a magnet on Anna, who generally responded by opening up.

When Anna started talking, her voice sounded like it belonged to someone else. She related what Ralph had told her as quickly and discreetly as she knew how. When she finished, the look or her mother's face was one of astonishment. Myrtle sat perfectly still and looked at her daughter in pained disbelief. Anna started to suspect her mother was learning of this behavior for the first time as well. The long and awkward silence was finally broken when Myrtle leaned over and sent a stream of amber into a coffee can. She wiped the corners of her mouth with her apron and motioned toward the lamp table.

"Honey, reach over yonder and hand me my Bible."

Anna did as her mother instructed and sat quietly as Myrtle thumbed carefully through the family Bible. She always handled the pages like they were the delicate petals on a flower. When she found the passage she wanted, she handed the Bible to Anna.

"Take the Bible and read that passage out loud and tell me what it means."

Anna read half aloud, ". . . and if a man also lie with mankind, as he lieth with a woman, both of them have committed an abomination; they shall surely be put to death; their blood shall be upon them."

"Now wait a minute. Give me that back. Ye jest read from Leviticus in the Old Testament. Now read this passage and don't mumble this time."

Once again Anna took the Bible and read. ". . . But before they lay down, the men of the city, even the men of Sodom, compassed the house round, both old and young, all the people from every quarter. And they called unto Lot and said into him, where are the men which came in to thee this night? Bring them unto us, that we may know them. And Lot went out the door unto them, and shut the door after him. And said, I pray you, brethren, do not so wickedly. Behold, now I have two daughters which have not known man; I pray you, bring them unto you, and do ye to them as is good in your eyes; and only unto these men do nothing."

Anna closed the Bible and handed it back to Myrtle, who carefully placed it back on the lamp table. She spat once again into the coffee can before resuming the conversation.

"Men a sleepin' with men and women with women is why God destroyed Sodom and Gomorrah. Ye jest read from Genesis in the Old Testament. Been goin' on a long time I reckon. Don't feel bad. Jes and me had been married a spell before we heard 'bout it. We went to a tent revival one time, and this preacher come through and he preached on it. He talked like it was goin' on ever'where. Everbody got upset, and they made him leave after the first night and got somebody else to finish the revival. Honey, 'fore ye leave this world, yere gonna find out that folks can do lots of awful things. Ever'body 'round here sees what folks is doin'; but when they get in them big cities, some jest do ever'thing imaginable. They think nobody gonna know ... BUT God knows."

"I don't feel so bad now. Ralph was really embarrassed, and so was I."

"Folks orta be embarrassed. People doin' stuff like that is an awful shame."

"Mother, up until now I thought the worst thing was to run off and get married."

"Speakin' of such. Is an ol' pig-headed woman invited to see how her little girl is livin'? Ain't too old to walk a couple of miles, do me some good."

Myrtle and Anna walked along the dusty old road to Mister Chester's house, laughing like two schoolgirls.

"Mother, I miss havin' these little talks with ye."

"That's what happens when ye become an ol' married woman. Ain't always gonna have yere mama 'round to talk to. I still miss talkin' to my old mama. She was a wise ol' bird."

When the women arrived, Mister Chester was asleep in the porch swing. They eased open the screen door and went inside. Anna was anxious for her mother's approval of their modest living quarters.

"Well, bust my britches. This little old place is down right cute. Been in this house b'fore but never upstairs. Not real big, but Jes and me have lived in a lot less. If ye had a kitchen, it wouldn't be bad at all."

"Well, this here is what we call home fer now. Miz Atlee helped us get it ship shape. Now Ralph got his eye on that ol' farm over on the Billy Goat Road. You know the one, and it ain't far from his mama's place and close to Centertown, too. Don't know when we can buy it, but that someday will be our little farm. Ralph has always wanted a little farm of his own right here in the Walton's Creek community. The Atlees been here a spell, and Ralph wants to raise our younguns right here."

"Well, I'm shore glad you younguns is doin' all right. I'm gonna gather up some things and have yere daddy bring 'em over. The only way he'll come, I reckon. Yere daddy is still a stubborn ol' cuss. Aunt Kate got a weddin' gift fer ye. She bought a new eggbeater and sent ye her old one. Never occurred to the old critter to send the new one, but that's just Kate."

Anna sat down on the edge of the bed while Myrtle rocked in one of the rocking chairs. Myrtle had just announced that she needed to get home and fix some supper for Jes when a terrific explosion shook the house. The windows rattled, Chester's chickens were running and cackling, and dogs were howling for miles around. Anna and Myrtle looked at one another with stunned expressions. The color drained out of Myrtle's face. She had been a coal miner's wife too long not to live in dread of an explosion from underground mines. The noise was too close to be the mine where Jes Caughill was working, but the same horrible thought raced through Anna and Myrtle's minds.

The women hurried down the steps and onto the front porch. Mister Chester had been startled awake and had fallen from the porch swing. He was still trying to get to his feet when Anna and Myrtle ran to the road. The bells at the Walton's Creek Church were clanging an alarm, and in a few minutes cars, men on horseback, and some walking were headed down the road toward the Deiss mine. A large cloud of dust was boiling into the air.

"Mother, where is Daddy?"

"He ain't down there. Been helpin' Tom Berry in that little one-horse mine he got. OH them pore men down there. I wonder what happened?"

"Men done gone by now or least ways most of 'em. Jim and a couple of boys orta be shootin' down the coal fer t'mor. Sumpin' musta gone awful wrong." Mister Chester answered Myrtle's question as he hobbled up behind the women.

Myrtle, Anna, and Mister Chester went back to the front porch to wait for news.

"Honey, I ain't goin' home now. Jes will head straight fer the Deiss mine to help out. No tellin' how many men got hurt, and us women may be needed to help with the hurt. Ol' woman and I ain't never had to help with a bunch of men butchered up in the mines. Hoped I never would."

The dust and smoke hovering over the Deiss mine cleared away, and the parade of men headed in that direction had dwindled. The tension was unnerving as Anna and her mother sat on the porch, their eyes glued in the direction of the Deiss mine.

"Mother, reckon we orta walk down there to see if they need help?"

"I was just a thinkin' the same thing. I reckon that's what we orta done from the start. Ain't doin' nobody any good a settin' here. Let's go."

The women walked out to the road just as Jesse Caughill's Model T Ford came around the bend in the road.

"That's yere daddy and yere brother now. I reckon they jest come from there."

"I mighta knowed I'd find ye over here," Jes muttered as he climbed out of Jesse Caughill's car.

"Walked over here and stayed after the explosion. Thought I might be needed. Jes, what happened?"

Jes stood with his hand on his lower back as he stared at the ground. He had not looked in Anna's direction.

"I knowed this was gonna happen. Jim and three other fellers was a shootin' down coal after everbody else done gone home fer the day. Shet down awful early fer some reason. Still had the mules back in the mine."

"I tol' Jim a hunerd times that he's too stingy with his powder and he was gonna get hurt. Ye drill back in the coal with yere auger and pack it with pellet powder and then blow her down. Use pellet black powder when ye ain't gotta lotta gas. Got lotta gas, ye use dynamite. If ye don't use 'nough powder and the coal don't blow down, well, the force of the explosion shoots back at ye like a cannon. Reckon that's what happened."

"Ye see the right way to do it is to fix the drill hole, and then take yere copper tampin' bar and push the powder charge back into the hole. I usually wrap the charge in some ol' newspaper. Now ye lay this here needle alongside the tampin' bar when ye push the charge in. Next ye pull out the tampin' bar and leave the needle wire in there. Then ye tamp it full of dirt. When ye get the hole full, ye start a wigglin' the needle wire 'til ye got this nice little hole all the way back to the charge. Then ye put in the fuse, we call 'em a squib, yell fire 'n the hole three times, light the fuse, and run like the dogs is after ye. Do it right, and everthing is hunkie dorie. They did sumpin' wrong, and it blowed them and ever tool plumb outta the mine. One feller got a broken leg, two skinned up pretty good, and Jim hurt sumpin' awful. Found that boy with the busted leg a hunered foot outside the mine and Jim right at the entry with most his head blowed off. Men got there quick, and we got 'em all taken care of. Doctor comin' to set the boy's leg, but he ain't gonna be able to help Jim, I'm afraid. He ain't gonna make it."

"Jes, did it kill them mules?"

"Nope. Scared hell outa them though. They was back in this room and didn't get hurt."

"Pap, I can't see fer the life of me how a little dab of powder can do that much damage. The whole damn mine blowed up."

"That's 'cause ye ain't no coal miner or shot down coal. The more pressure ye got, the more power it got. I betcha they tamped that hole full of coal dust 'stead of dirt and it blew up, too. The mine is dusty and that blowed up, too, and all together ye got a big bang. I tol' Jim the mine was too dusty fer me and I wouldn't work fer 'im. Ralph said the same, that's why he went to the mill. A team of wild horses couldn't get me in there. Lot of fellers will 'cause they need the money. Can't make a livin' if ye get blowed up. I play it safe."

Anna gasped at the sound of her busband's name. "Jesse, where is Ralph? Did he go over to the mines? He orta be home by now."

"We left 'im at the mines. Wanted to stay in case somethin' else needed to be done. I aimed to tell ye. He orta be along any minute. He and the boys over at the mill run down there when they heard the explosion. Still some men went down there in cars. He can catch a ride up here in a bit."

Jes walked over to Jesse's car and looked at the right front tire. He still had not looked at his daughter. Anna could not take the tension any longer and quickly embraced her father. Jes reacted awkwardly for a moment before placing his hand briefly on her shoulder, then pulled away and opened the car door for Myrtle.

Anna stood beside the road, crying softly as she watched her parents drive away with Jesse. She could hear Myrtle's voice over the sound of the car's engine.

"Jes, I want Jesse to take me down to see 'bout Jim Deiss."

"Ain't no sense in it. Ain't gonna live. Be dead by mornin' anyhow. Doctor done seen 'im."

"Goin' anyway. Greta be there if it was you hurt."

Anna wiped away tears as she walked back to the house. Mister Chester had gone inside to eat his supper. Suddenly, she realized her husband was on his way home and she had not prepared anything for the evening meal. She raced around behind the house and searched the hens' nests until she found seven eggs. She had two biscuits left from breakfast and a half-gallon jug of tea, and that would have to be supper.

The Walton's Creek neighborhood pulled together in the coming days. The man with the broken leg would be laid up for some time, but the neighbors were helping out. Jim Deiss died from his injury, and the crowd at Walton's Creek Church for the funeral was too large for the sanctuary. Coal miners from all over the county came to pay their respects. After the service Jes Caughill said, ". . . cut one coal miner and we all bleed. Nobody who ain't mined coal don't understand what it's like. Jim made a mistake and paid with his life. Next time it could be me. That's jest the way it is."

Jim Deiss had been buried nearly a week when Ralph and Anna heard Mister Chester talking to someone on the front porch. They had just finished eating supper when the screen door squeaked, and heavy footsteps could be heard on the stairs.

"HALLO THE HOUSE. You all got supper ready?"

Jes Caughill's voice carried through the door. Ralph grinned as he rushed to open the door. There stood Jes with a big toothless grin and a bulging grass sack on his shoulder. He stepped in the door and shoved the sack into Ralph's chest with such force it sent him staggering backwards. Still grinning, Jes took off his hat, looked at Anna and said, "WELL, YOUNGUN, learnt how to be an ol' married woman yet?"

The Ol' Homeplace (1947)

THE OL' HOMEPLACE
(1947)

TEARS WELLED UP in Mickey's eyes as he recalled his parents plunge into matrimony. It was a beautiful story. It was time, however, to move on to another chapter in the life of his family.

Mickey never grew tired of family stories about how his parents cleared their farm on the Billy Goat Road and made it their home. It was only a few short miles from Mister Chester's place but ten long years of living in rental property. Mickey visualized Ralph Atlee as he cleared saplings and brush from the old farm. A plow horse, axe, and a road wagon were his only tools. He knew well the story behind every shrub and rosebush that had been salvaged from nearby abandoned farms. It was a primitive beginning by modern standards, but a far cry from the hardships endured by early Kentucky pioneers. For Ralph and Anna Atlee, however, it was a labor of love, and they would not have traded it for a mansion. For their son, the stories were worth a fortune. Mickey felt sorry for modern families who lacked an old homestead and the nostalgia that one nurtures. The Depression and World War II delayed Ralph and Anna's quest for a homeplace.

The bells of Walton's Creek Church joined thousands of church and courthouse bells all over the United States in celebrating the end of World War II. Dozens of young men from Ohio County had died in a war that left Europe in ruins, the Japanese Empire defeated, and America poised to be the world's most powerful country. The awesome manufacturing capability of the nation had churned out the weapons the Allies needed to defeat the Axis powers. For the first time, American women had gone to work in large numbers in the factories that built the weapons of war, and many Ohio County women had worked in the Ken Rad defense plant in Owensboro. The country had sacrificed gasoline, tires, sugar, coffee, and other products for four years in support of the war effort.

Many young men returned to Walton's Creek and countless similar communities after the war and picked up their lives where they had left off, unlike the returning Civil War soldiers who had found their farms in disarray. Others smelled the winds of change that were beginning to blow and left for jobs in Louisville and cities in the North, where indoor plumbing and electricity were the norm. Prior to the war, the Atlees and much of rural America and Kentucky had neither. A smaller number went to college on the GI Bill and embarked upon professional careers. The experience of war had conditioned them for the striking changes they would see at home. America's post-war transition would be dramatic, but nowhere more profound than in rural Kentucky communities like Walton's Creek. World War II had changed the Atlees' lives. For decades rural people had been moving to the cities, but the post-war era in Kentucky would see an accelerated migration, plus a total upheaval of the rural culture. Customs, traditions, and a way of life would disappear so rapidly and so profoundly that their passing often went more or less unnoticed. Many towns lost train service and, once the depots and tracks were removed, soon forgot it had ever existed. Coal was still an important part of Kentucky's economy, but a more modern method of mining, called strip mining, permanently altered the landscape and a way of life.

Ralph Atlee had received a deferment from military service by working in underground mines. This was considered defense work, and he also worked on the WPA construction crew that built the county's new courthouse.

Anna Atlee had been listening to their battery-powered radio on December 7, 1941, when the Japanese attacked Pearl Harbor. She had started screaming at Ralph, who was asleep on his mother's old davenport.

"RALPH, them ol' Japs have done bombed Pearl Harbor."

Startled, Ralph had sprung up as the radio announcer excitedly made the announcement. "Anna, where in the dickens is Pearl Harbor?"

"Radio says it's the home of our navy in the Pacific. Hawaii, I reckon."

"That's where William's ship is. I hope he's ok. Nothin' but a kid."

The following days and weeks had been agony for the families of service members stationed at Pearl Harbor. Four weeks had gone by before Ralph learned that his third cousin William had gone down with the West Virginia. The war that had been raging in so many parts of the world had come home to Walton's Creek, and now its sons would be joining the war.

The newspapers had carried detailed accounts of the war, but the medium of radio brought the war ever closer. President Roosevelt's *Fireside Chats* had reassured Americans during the trying days of the Depression, and the nation had listened spellbound as he addressed Congress and asked for a declaration of war. The fiery rhetoric of Adolf Hitler had helped spur the German people to war, and the calm, determined oratory of Winston Churchill and FDR had rallied British and American citizens to stop them.

Anna Atlee had started a scrapbook of newspaper clippings about friends and relatives serving in the military. Most returned home safe, but some did not. Several young men hung their caps on nails in the Centertown Garage when they left for service, vowing to return for them. Each cap had been observed reverently until the war ended and its rightful owner reclaimed every cap.

When the war began, Ralph Atlee had been working in underground mines. Since this was considered defense work, he had received deferment from military service. Tim Atlee was farming full time, and this was also classified as vital to the nation's war effort, and he had not served in the military. Al Atlee had volunteered for a government-sponsored course in electricity in Owensboro. Ralph had warned him that the completion of the course would result in him being drafted. Al had laughed and said, "... Ralph, I'm past forty. They ain't gonna take no ol' fart like me." Ralph had been right, and soon Al had found himself in Basic Training with men less than half his age. After the war, he laughed about his experiences.

"Never went no closer to the war than England. Now a growin' up on the farm was good trainin' fer the army. Them young city squirts named me 'Pappy' and told me they was gonna look out fer me since I was too old to be doin' that kinda stuff. Marchin' and gettin' lots of exercise is what I done all my life. Nothin' new, but I tol' them I appreciated it jest the same."

"One day we was gonna go on this twelve-mile road march with pack, helmet, and rifle. This young kid said, 'now, Pappy, gonna get tired today, and when ye do, jest let me know and I'll carry yere pack.' I said that was nice of 'im, but I could manage. We marched about eight mile or so 'til we come to this big ol' gully. Jest straight up and down on each side. I run up and dwn spoil banks my whole life, and I knowed how it was done. I run down one side and without callin' a halt went right on up the other side. The key is not to slow down. A mile or so down the road I realized that kid wasn't behind me no more. I asked the sergeant what happened to 'im, and he said, "He went down one side of the gully and never come out the other side." The ambulance got 'im, and we never seen 'im again. God help us when we hafta fight wars with jest city boys. Ol' country jakes didn't have no problem. Shootin' rifles easy, too. Growin' up huntin' rabbits with jest one shell helped a bunch. Got Ma to thank fer that."

Ralph and Anna had always expected to spend the rest of their lives at Walton's Creek. The war, however, brought stories of the good money to be made in the defense plants. They had decided to try their luck in Owensboro. Unfortunately for the Atlees, a lot of other people had the same idea. Finding a place to live was difficult; and although Ken Rad had quickly hired Anna, Ralph had been forced to take a job firing a boiler at a distillery on the night shift. Ralph was accustomed to hard work, but the job soon proved too difficult.

Anna had to walk to work at 4:00 AM. During the early morning hours, she walked with dozens of black people going to work as well. She had been around few Negroes in her life, and she found the experience unnerving. They acted as if she did not exist, but she had never walked faster in her life.

The Ken Rad plant had been considered an important defense facility and security was tight. The number of men walking around carrying guns had alarmed Anna. They viewed everyone with suspicion, and after a month Anna was a nervous wreck. The final straw came when a guard slipped up behind her. She turned around and came face to face with a Thompson submachine gun. She screamed so loud the guard jumped and beat a hasty retreat. The next day, armed with their final paychecks, Ralph and Anna rode the Fuqua bus to Hartford and caught the train to Centertown. They carried their bags and walked from the depot to Walton's Creek—the little community had never looked so good.

Several buses had run each day from Bowling Green to Owensboro, ferrying workers along the route to work at Ken Rad. Many had made the trip twice daily from Bowling Green, standing up on the packed coaches. Country folks were fleeing to town in search of work, but Ralph and Anna may have been the only passengers of the war who fled in the opposite direction.

Jes Caughill had spent much of the war building wooden barracks at Fort Knox, but his days of performing backbreaking labor in the mines and sawmills were coming to a close. Work was all that Jes had ever known, and as his strength began to fail him, he started to brood.

Liz Atlee's health had detoriated throughout the war, and by 1945 she was too ill to live by herself. She moved in with her daughter Sally Marie and died of a stroke two years later. She had wanted to die at home, in the house and on the farm that had been part of the Atlee family for so long. Now the children who had worked so hard to save it from foreclosure would have to decide its fate. The Atlee children had shared a lot of good times and some bad on the old farm, and selling was heart wrenching.

The family stories about much of Mickey's parents' life from 1937 until they had a place of their own raced through his brain. How they purchased an old rundown farm, however, that would be the scene of his birth was one of the most poignant. His mind focused on that memory.

"RALPH, another copperhead. Get over here and kill this thing."

Ralph Atlee walked quickly toward the big copperhead snake and soon decapitated him with one swing of his axe. He reversed the axe and used the handle to pick the creature up.

"Well, I wish ye would look. Bigger than the last one ... must be over four foot. I seen bigger though."

"Ralph, when are we gonna be shed of them things? Scare me to death. I can kill chicken snakes and the like, but rattlesnakes and copperheads is where I draw the line. We can't move over here 'til we get shed of them things."

"Keep yere shirt on, woman. I gotta get this farm cleared off first. They'll skedaddle when the brush and saplings is cleared out. Once I get some fencin' up, I'll bring ol' Dick over from Ma's place, and he can help me pull out some of the stumps. Get us a little backer base, and we can start earnin' a little dab of money."

"Yere granddaddy used to make sorghum. I've been thinkin' that maybe we could do that. Do ye know how?"

"Reckon so. Ain't a whole lot to it. Plant yere sorghum a tad later than corn since it comes in quicker. When it's ready, ye strip the leaves and cut off the tops where it stands. Next ye cut and bundle it and take it to the press. Run a few of them stalks at a time through yere press, and the juice runs out into this here trough; then run it through some feed sacks to strain it out in a barrel. Run yere pipe outa yere barrel downhill into a metal vat. Now ye need a shed 'round the vat. That's what they call the 'Cookin' Shed.' Gotta build a rock firebox to heat the vat. All told it'll take 'bout four hours. Gotta keep it stirred with some wood paddles and the foam skimmed off. If it ain't cooked 'long 'nough, the syrup is cloudy, and cooked too long it has a burnt taste. Either way, it ain't fit to eat. Need to trim a little stick outa wood and dip it in the syrup and when it comes out in a long stream that's when she's done. Nothin' to it."

"Good, let's do it."

"Ain't got the equipment but that ain't a bad idée though. Granpap used to make three and sometimes four-hunerd gallon a year. Make a little money in a good year. If we done that, raise a little backer and some pigs, we might do fair. Raise us a big garden, chickens, ducks, geese. Bring Ma's ol' milk cow over. Got her churn, too. We'll do fair."

"Ralph, ye know where we talked 'bout a puttin' the meathouse? Well, I want ye to dig a cellar under that meathouse. Gotta have a place fer all our canned stuff, potaters and the like."

"Woman, ye got a lot of good idees for ME to do. Root cellar needs to be lined with field rock, and I reckon I can find plenty of that."

"Ye sure Carl don't mind us a stayin' at yere mama's 'til we get this place goin'?"

"What he said. He ain't gonna live over there no ways. Said take our time 'bout movin'. This ol' house needs new winder lights and it ain't been painted since Noah's Ark. Gonna seal it first with aluminum paint and then paint her white. Do some work on the inside, and she'll be home sweet home."

"How deep is that well? Water is so full of salts we ain't gonna be able to use much of it fer drinkin' water."

"That well goes to China. 'Til I get the pond cleaned out, ol' Dick and the cow and the chickens can drink from the well. Plenty of water. Drinkin' water is gonna be a problem, but I think we got us a freshwater spring over yonder at the bottom of that hill. Gonna dig out a little spot and see if it fills up. Gonna be plenty of water fer washin' and the like from that well."

"Ralph, are ye sure Carl didn't want to sell yere mama's house and the ground around it? Much nicer place up there."

"I asked 'im. He said he didn't wanna divide the place. We thought 'bout dividin' it when ma died, but once it goes four ways, ye ain't got much left and only one house. The way the place is laid out kinda hard to divide anyhow. That's the way it is with a handin' a farm down to the kids. Alright if ye only have one youngun, and then that youngun has kids, and there ain't nothin' left to divide."

Ralph tossed the carcass of the snake into some weeds. He grinned at his wife as she took the lid off a gallon glass fruit jar filled with water and took a long drink.

"This place ain't a gonna be bad, 'specially with yere mama a livin' right down the road from ye."

"My mama lives over a mile away, ye ninny."

"Not fer long. I sold Jes an acre of that flat piece down by the creek. Gonna build a house there, a startin' first of the week. Jesse gonna dig him a cistern, too."

"HOW come I didn't know anything 'bout that? How much did ye charge 'im?"

"I tol' ol' Jes I wouldn't take less than a dollar fer it, and he paid it. Lord a mercy, I done sold a piece of ground so that white-headed ol' she-devil, Myrtle Caughill, can move right down the road from me."

"Well, I'm glad. They ain't never had a place of their own, and Mother is sick of movin' round, livin' in coal mine housin' and the like. NOW, if she heerd ye callin' her an ol' she-devil, she'd snatch ye bald headed."

"Jes is gonna buy some stuff from the mines to build with. Jesse gonna haul a little buildin' from over at the mines fer 'im. Gonna use it as a meathouse. Got a winder in it and a flue. Jes bought 'im a big tent from the Sears Roebuck, and they'll live in that this summer while Jes builds the house."

"Ralph, ye gotta help 'im. He can't work at the mines and do that, too."

"Yere daddy done quit the mines. Said his coal minin' days is over. Not up to it no more. Tim done tol' 'im he can help us kill hogs and make sausage. Got jest a mile down the road to the slaughterhouse. Gonna raise 'im a garden and maybe smoke a few hams. Gonna retire and draw his little pension and Social Security."

"Ralph, Mother and Daddy wanted that little house of Cyrus Lentz, but he was too contrary to sell. One time, I guess back in the '20s, Aunt Kate come over with a page outta the Sears Roebuck. It was an ad for one of them 'Honor Bilt' already cut homes. It cost $1,200.00 and ye could pay $18 a month. It had a livin' room, dinin' room, two bedrooms, and a kitchen. Catalog said it was twenty-seven foot wide. Musta been tiny, but Mother fell in love with it. Daddy got mad as usual. Tol' her to forget it … couldn't afford it. Well, she tol' 'im that dreams don't cost nothin', and she hung it on a nail over the door. The next mornin' Daddy used it to start a fire in the cookstove. That was one of the first times I ever saw my mother cry."

"Anna, I'm gonna get some of them flowers, rose bushes, and sech from up on the old Hacker and Royal places. I'll get Jes to go with me, and he can get Myrtle some, too. All kinds of stuff up there and been there fer years. All growed up and the coal people don't care. Shame to let 'em go to waste."

"That's a good idée. Nice to have them right down the hill a piece. Daddy is too old for coal mines and sawmills, and they're both too old to be movin' from pillar to post. I guess a runnin' the tipple over at the mines is the easiest job he ever had, but he don't have no business a doin' it anymore. SAY, ye never did tell me why this has been sech a big secret."

"Well, Myrtle asked me not to. Said she wanted to surprise ye. I guess I let the cat outta the bag, though. Think she wanted to tell ye herself. GOT another little thing she'll brain me fer tellin'. Myrtle says that with them a livin' right close by, maybe she will get to see a little grandson runnin' down to her place before she dies."

"YOU don't mean it. My mother said that. Well, I guess I'm a gettin' a little old to be havin' a kid. You better hurry up and get this place cleaned up so we can move in."

"Jest give me time. Rome weren't built in a day, and Jes gonna need a little help, too. Now ye know ol' Jes gettin' to retire is due to two men that ol' Myrtle hates more than anybody. Jes gonna have Social Security 'cause of old FDR and the miner's pension 'cause of John L. Lewis. If ye ever tell her I said that, make sure I ain't in a mile of the place. Yessir, 'cause of them pensions, ol' Jes and Myrtle can settle down in their old days. Sumpin' I ain't ever gonna be able to do. Be workin' on this place 'til I croak."

In 1947 Jes Caughill finished a little house on the edge of Ralph Atlee's farm. The home was modest, but Myrtle finally had a place she could call her own. Jes seemed content, too, but he tried not to show it. The Atlee farm was still a work in progress, but in the same year Ralph had the house livable, and they moved in. Ralph always wanted a farm of his own where he could make a living and raise a family.

The month of December 1949 was cold and snowy, and Dr. Alvin had told Anna she could expect to deliver her baby sometime around Christmas. She worried about the youngster getting chilled in the drafty old house that was fired only by coal grates. Ralph told her not to worry since babies had been born in old farmhouses for years.

"RALPH, go get my mother. The baby is comin'. I know it."

"ALL RIGHT, but I gotta go over to Carl's and call the doctor. Gotta go out to the highway and meet 'im. His car ain't gonna get in over this snow."

"RALPH, quit talkin' 'bout it and GET goin'."

Ralph's heart was pounding with excitement as he rushed to his truck. The wind was bitterly cold as it swept the six-inch snow that had fallen. He was also concerned about the lack of warmth in the old house. He had to get a Warm Morning coal stove and get rid of the grates where much of the heat was lost up the chimney.

Ralph Atlee never expected to become a father at age 42, but he was already planning how life was going to be. He teased his wife that if it was a girl, he was going to have her behind a plow before she shed her diapers. Anna had informed him that no daughter of hers was going to work in the fields like an old "Clod Hopper." Ralph was somewhat stunned when Anna told him, ". . . if I have a boy, he ain't gonna be no tobacco farmer or coal miner; and if she's a girl, she ain't gonna marry one neither."

"Is that so? Jest maybe you and me ain't gonna have nothin' to say 'bout it. Seems to me I remember a few years back about this stubborn, long-legged ol' gal who packed her suitcase and walked to the preacher to get married. Her parents didn't know nothin' 'bout it. Ol' Jes snorted and reared but ye done it anyway. They didn't have nothin' to say 'bout it."

"Well, that was different. Times was different, and you and me was different."

Ralph and Anna were going to have a child after twelve years of marriage. For Ralph it was like a dream. His mind was racing as his truck fish-tailed down the Billy Goat Road to Jes and Myrtle's house. No one had been over that stretch of road since the snow, and the chug holes that could mire him down were hidden; but Ralph was able to detect their location by the landscape.

Myrtle Caughill rushed out the door, pulling her coat on as she went. Ralph had never seen his mother-in-law move so fast. She was almost as excited as he was. When they arrived back at the house, Myrtle leaped from the truck and headed for the door.

"WHOA, slow down ol' woman. Ain't a gonna do us no good if ye fall and break yere neck."

"I'll ring yore neck like a chicken if ye don't go call that doctor," Myrtle yelled back over her shoulder as she plowed through the drifting snow.

Ralph and Jes had a bond of respect and admiration between them, but Ralph's relationship with Myrtle was one of affection. They joked, laughed, and teased one another without mercy. No man had ever been able to talk to Myrtle Caughill the way he did. The first time Ralph and Anna came together for a visit after their marriage had sealed their relationship, Myrtle had opened the front door and stood with her hands on her hips.

"WELL, I reckon it's 'bout time ye come fer a visit. What took ye?"

"Myrtle, this ain't no visit. I brung her back. Ye didn't tell me she couldn't make thick n' gravy."

Myrtle Caughill never grew tired of telling the story. She said, ". . . knowed the boy all his life, but didn't know he could make a dog laugh. Yep, Ralph is a purty good fella even if his mama and daddy was Democrats."

Ralph slid, spun wheels, and skillfully managed to avoid more snow-covered chug holes and picked up Dr. Alvin at the slaughterhouse by the highway. The portly physician at seventy-five years of age had delivered thousands of babies at home in a career that spanned five decades. He had traversed the county day and night over the years, delivering children and tending the sick and injured. He frequently went home with his car laden down with hams, eggs, garden vegetables, molasses, and other items that he had received for his fee. The old doctor never sent anyone a bill and always considered whatever he received as payment in full. The country preachers were a vital part of the rural community, but the doctors were essential.

"Doctor Alvin, this youngun is skinny as a little rat."

"AHHH, don't worry 'bout that Myrtle. I seen many a little fella, and this one is healthy and gonna do just fine."

"You saved me from nearly dyin' twice, and I guess if anybody knows, it's you."

Myrtle and Doctor Alvin were busy with the baby when they heard Anna's weak voice calling the doctor from the next room. Doctor Alvin knew immediately what was wrong and raced to her bedside. He threw back the covers and grabbed Anna's abdomen with both hands. He squeezed as hard as he could and slowly eased his body down on the edge of the bed. Anna was pale and faint as the doctor continued to apply pressure for the next thirty minutes. Finally, Anna's head cleared, the bleeding had stopped, and she was going to live to see her baby, a little man-child they named Mickey Lynn born two days after Christmas 1949.

The two weeks following the birth of her baby, Anna Atlee spent most of her time in bed, regaining her strength. Jes Caughill and Ralph stayed busy slaughtering hogs and making sausage at the slaughterhouse. Myrtle Caughill came over each day to help out with the baby and the housework. The new baby had been named Mickey from a character in a radio program.

The quaint old Walton's Creek Church burned on Sunday, Christmas Day, before Mickey's birth on Tuesday. Anna broke down and cried when Ralph told her the news.

"We done lost the school and now the church. I reckon that beautiful old bell is ruined."

"Reckon so. They jest rolled it off to the side. Tim says the county is gonna give us the old courthouse bell. Didn't make room fer a bell in the new courthouse, and they ain't got no use fer it."

"Ralph, what are we gonna do fer a church?"

"Oh, we're gonna have a new church if my brother Tim got anything to say 'bout it or has to build it hisself. He says he got 'nough timber down on his place to build a new one and he's gonna cut it as soon as the weather lets up. That boy is shore upset 'bout that church. Tried everthing in his power to stop them from closin' the school, ye remember."

"Ralph, a new church will be nice, but it ain't gonna be the same. That old church was so pretty. New stuff ain't always as good as the old."

Anna and Ralph now had their own home and a baby. The old farm was a relic of better times, but it was their homeplace. Ralph had big plans for the farm, not the least of which involved buying a tractor to replace Old Dick, who had died before Mickey was born. The Farmall tractor was introduced in 1924, and it had been said that this was the year the Industrial Revolution hit the American farm. Ralph fell in love with the next-to-smallest tractor in the series, the Model A. Unlike a horse, he would not need hay or pasture.

The Model A was considered a Godsend for small farmers in both size and design. The "A" configuration was called "Culti Vision." The new design featured the engine offset to the left and the seat and steering wheel positioned to the right, and the rear axle was longer on the left than on the right. This gave the driver a clear view of the crops being cultivated. The wide front design was broad enough and adequate to clear most crops, like Anna's huge garden and Ralph's tobacco patch.

The magazine advertisements for the Model A with its bright red paint job made Ralph forget he had grown up farming successfully with horses and mules. In 1952 he spent all the money he had saved to buy a used 1941 Model A plus plow, disk, and cultivators. The equipment was in poor condition, but Ralph hoped the new tools would help him develop the profitable family farm that he always dreamed of owning.

Before he shed his diapers, Ralph's young son Mickey could draw a perfect image of a John Deere or Farmall tractor. He squealed with delight every time he heard the distinct popping sound of a "Poppin' Johnny," a name commonly used for the John Deere.

The tiny Farmall Cub, introduced in 1947, was destined for more production years than any other tractor in the world. The Cub was a scaled-down version of the Model A and sold new for $545. Al Atlee bought one to tend his tobacco patch and garden. The Cub was perfect for men like Al, who did not have enough land to support a horse or mule. "Yessir," Al said. "The little Cub don't need no hay or pasture. Sets there and waits 'til I get ready to use 'er."

The family milk cow had gone dry, so Ralph sold her and did not buy another. Ralph said, "Anna, little dab of milk and butter we use, a cow ain't worth the effort. Buy it in the store."

"Yes, Ralph, but now we ain't got no horse and we ain't got no cow and no manure to put on the fields. Didn't have 'nough as it was. 'cept fer a little dab of chicken manure we ain't got nothin'. Rather have my own cream and my own butter."

"Gonna hafta buy fertilize for the fields. Everybody else is. They say that's the only way a man can farm these days. Big shots say manure ain't no good. Fertilize is better."

"Ralph, them big shots a tellin' ye that are tryin' to sell ye fertilize. You men like them tractors 'cause ye feel like a big shot a ridin' 'round up there on it. Don't look big 'nough to be behind an ol' plow horse. Plow horse don't cost as much and don't need gas and oil neither."

"No sir, but a plow horse needs pasture and hay, and that takes ground, and we ain't got much ground. Al bought that little Farmall Cub 'cause he only got an acre and can't take care no horse on that little dab of ground. Got him a tractor fer the garden and backer crop. Tractor jest sets there and waits 'til he's ready. Gotta take care of a horse."

"Now, Ralph, Al paid $545.00 dollars for that tractor brand new. How many crops of terbacker is he gonna have to raise to pay fer the blame thing?"

"I didn't pay that much fer ours."

"No, ye didn't, and that's why it don't run half the time. Work yerself to death a workin' on it. Ol' Dick jest needed to have harness put on, and he was ready to go. A little slower maybe, but he done a good job. I miss that ol' horse. He was jest like a member of the family, and that ol' tractor don't come and eat cornbread outta yere hand."

The Atlees tried a variety of things on their small farm, but nothing proved profitable. They raised cucumbers and tomatoes for a cannery; but when the crop was really starting to produce, the company stopped buying. The chickens ate cucumbers and tomatoes for the remainder of the summer. The following year they tried an acre of bell peppers with another company—with the same results. Another year Ralph came home with a flyer from a cannery that wanted farmers to grow green beans. The company offered to provide the seed and fertilizer. The offer was too tempting, and the following year they raised an acre and a half of green beans. When the beans were ready to pick, a company representative came to inspect and announced that the company did not want them. Ralph and Anna stood and watched the green bean company field man drive away.

"Did he say why he didn't want them beans?"

"Nope, jest took a quick look see and walked off. Finest beans we ever growed, and they don't want 'em. Frost gonna be on the beard of ol' man time when I do that agin. From now on we gonna raise chickens, garden, and backer."

After four years of failure raising vegetable crops, Anna was ready to try raising pheasants. When the flock was finally large enough to start selling, the number of people who wanted one for Thanksgiving was amazing. In one week, Anna sold 500 dollars' worth of pheasant. Unfortunately, when she tallied up her expenses, they had actually lost money. The wild birds consumed huge quantities of feed, and the Atlees were faced with growing large amounts of grain to feed the birds. The pheasant idea soon went the way of the vegetable crops.

Despite the failures with crops and poultry, Ralph and Anna were still in love with their homeplace. They raised most of what they ate, but modern conveniences forced Ralph to be away from the farm working at public work. When Mickey was three, they had the house wired for electricity, and this meant a monthly electric bill. Two years later they added a telephone bill to their expenses. A television, electric stove, and refrigerator also cost money to operate. Modernization of the farm and the house taxed their resources, and the farm was unable to provide the income to pay for it. To remain on the farm, Ralph Atlee became a weekend farmer.

When Ralph became a part-time farmer, after his horse died and the cow went dry, he never had the time to erect proper fencing, fix the barn, or clean out the pond. Every attempt he made to modernize forced him deeper into a hole from which there was no quick way out.

Jes and Myrtle Caughill lived quietly in their little retirement home. Like Ralph and Anna, they added modern conveniences. Jes's modest retirement was adequate to meet the added cost, but the old coal miner fretted that if hard times returned, they would regret their decision. Myrtle Caughill insisted they were getting too old to live the old way. "Besides," she said. "We been circlin' 'round fer years like a couple ol' buzzards a lookin' fer a place like this to settle down. Glad we finally found it 'for we died, and I aim to enjoy it as much as I can. We finally got our own homeplace. Ain't much, but it's ours."

Country life was all the Caughills and the Atlees had ever known or wanted. Kinship with the land and the sense of individualism that farm life provided were sufficient motivation for the Atlees to hang on desperately to that way of life. The clouds of forboding were starting to gather, however; and one day soon those hopes and dreams they cherished would be shattered.

Book Three

A VERY COMMON PLACE

Little DeVonda (1952)

LITTLE DeVONDA
(1952)

*A*N SUV PASSED *Mickey on the Parkway. A little curly-haired girl stuck out her tongue, then grinned and waved. The precocious little girl reminded him of a child who entered his childhood many years before. A three-year old girl, the daughter of a migrant worker, had touched everyone's heart; Mickey had seen his dad and Grandfather Caughill cry, along with his mother and grandmother when "Little DeVonda" left their lives for good. Mickey had taken sanctuary behind the meathouse in an attempt to hide his own emotions. He often wondered what had happened to her.*

"Jes, I got a bowl of beans, some potaters, half a skillet of cornbread, quart of buttermilk, and a gallon jug of drinkin' water. I even put a banana in there—the only one we had—fer that little thing."

Myrtle Caughill had prepared a meal for a man and his little girl from what remained from their own supper. Jes sat stoically at the dinner table, looking at a half empty glass of buttermilk. He slowly got up from his chair, walked to the sideboard where, with his hands resting upon the small of his back, he surveyed the meal. He let out a long sigh, walked to the back door, took his hat down from a nail, and went outside.

A red sunset was starting to burn in the west as Jes walked to his toolshed. He stopped for a moment as he examined an old screen door that leaned against the front of the building and just to the right of the door. The shed door was made of eight-inch planks, and the steel hinges that held it to the structure squeaked when he opened the door. A small garter snake darted between his legs when he stepped inside. Jes selected a handful of nails and a claw hammer from atop a small workbench made of upturned sawmill slabs anchored to vertical railroad ties cut in lengths less than four feet.

Jes's wheelbarrow was always at the ready at one side of the shed. He placed the nails in his pocket, dropped the hammer in the wheelbarrow, and rolled his single-wheeled cart to the back porch. He left the kitchen door open as he loaded the food into the wheelbarrow. An old towel and washcloth were used to secure the quart jar of buttermilk and the jug of water. An old grass sack in the bottom of the wheelbarrow helped cushion the ride for the bowls of food. When Jes was finished, he stood looking at his cargo for a moment. Myrtle walked out on the porch as Jes was leaving.

"Jes, hug and kiss that sweet little thing for me," Myrtle called tearfully after Jes as he walked away.

The screen door was carefully placed upon the wheelbarrow handlebars and tied in place with a piece of copper wire slipped through an eye hook that served as the anchor for the door hook. If Jes was careful, the door would ride to its destination without slipping loose.

The steel wheel on the wheelbarrow made a singing sound when it rolled over the fine gravel on Jes's driveway as he made his way from the shed, past the coal house, and to where the driveway crossed a bridge made of railroad ties over Walton's Creek. The driveway became a road that wandered off into a wooded area to the side of a hill and bordered the creek on Jes's right. The rush of water grew louder when Jes made his way down the road that was now made up mostly of finely packed coal slack as he approached the old coal tipple. Every day the headwaters of the creek received a plentiful dose of polluted coperace water that drained from two abandoned strip-mine pits about a half-mile away.

The slack-covered roadway and the absence of vehicle traffic made rolling the wheelbarrow a smooth matter, and the screen door and the bowls of food and jars of liquid rode along nicely. Jes had gone about a hundred yards when the road opened up to a clearing. On his left were the remains of a wooden coal tipple from a long-abandoned tunnel mine that had been dug into the side of the hill. The structure was rickety, the timbers were weather beaten, and some had fallen to the ground. To Jes's right was a mine toolshed that rested about twenty-five feet from the creek. The building was constructed on skids and measured 8 feet by 12 feet, with one doorway and a tiny window of pane glass. The skids were resting upon four large sandstones and in most rainstorms protected the structure from rising creek waters. The building was identical to one Jes was using as a meathouse and like dozens that he built for coal mines over the years.

Behind the coal mine shed the water from the strip pits was rushing through a 16-inch galvanized pipe, into a pool, where the water collected in a pond about a foot deep before overflowing into the tiny creek that drained into the much larger Rough Creek a few miles away. Near the pool of water, a slender, black-haired man about thirty years of age was busy washing the arms and face of a beautiful blonde-headed girl no more than three years of age. The youngster's naturally curly hair bounced as she turned her head toward Jes, smiled, and waved. The child's smile was electric; it reminded Jes and Myrtle of Shirley Temple.

"Sam, ortan be washin' a child in that ol' coperace water. Ain't good fer 'er. I fetched ye some fresh drinkin' water anyhow." Jes had to raise his voice to be heard over the roar of the running water. He parked the wheelbarrow next to the building and started to unravel the wire holding the screen door to the vehicle's handle.

"Mighty fine of ye, Mister Caughill. I see we got a little dinner in there, too. I ain't got nothin' fer the child to eat but a can of pork n' beans and a Baby Ruth bar. Thinkin' bout comin' down to bum some water off ye. Youngun been a settin' in my brother's car all day whilst we worked. Hated to drag her and walk two and half miles to town to the store. Probably been closed time we got there anyhow. Seems like jest been askin' ye fer sumpin' all the time. Hard when a man got a child by hisself and gotta work, too."

"Sam, ye think her mama ever come back?"

"Nope, likes her fun too much fer that. Don't want her back no how."

"Awful shame fer any self-respectin' woman go off and leave a sweet little child like DeVonda. Never had no use fer a MAN that done that. In ALL my borned days I never knowed a woman to pull sech a rusty. WELL, Myrtle sent a little tad to eat. Got some pinto beans, taters, cornbread, buttermilk, and a banana. Plenty there for both of ye. I dug out this here screen door. Ain't in the best of shape but ain't got nary a hole. Sleepin' in there with no screens ain't healthy with a little tyke. Musky toes carry ye off, and a snake or possum liable to crawl in and make hisself at home. Come back and get it t'mor. Still leavin' out in the mornin'?"

"Yep, my brother is comin' by right 'round daylight. Gotta head out fer 'nother job. Maybe we can find a place to stay this time. Told my brother we orta get us a tent. Beats sleepin' in the car or a shack like this. Don't know what I'll do when she starts to school. Try to settle down somers I guess. Batchin' all right for a couple of men, but not a little girl. No sech problem if the old woman hadn't run off."

Jes was busy talking to Sam but was acutely aware the darling little girl was holding on to his leg with her arms wrapped around them. He tried not to look at DeVonda and once again feel the surge of emotion that he and Myrtle had both felt the first time they saw the child only a few days ago. Finally, DeVonda slapped her little hand against Jes's leg, and he glanced down at her face. She smiled up at him, and Jes felt his stomach turn to jelly.

"Mister Cock Hill, I love you." Little DeVonda's voice had a melodic quality that broke into a slight giggle when she got excited. Jes looked down at the child, smiled, and patted the curls on top of her head. He wanted to pick her up in his arms, but instead he gently pushed her over to her father.

"Well, I guess I better get this here door hung. Skeeters be boilin' outa that there creek in a bit. Some been out and about all day but come heavin' outta there once it gets dark."

While Jes fixed the door, Sam prepared a small bowl of food for DeVonda. The child sat on an overturned metal water bucket and ate her supper of beans, potatoes, and cornbread; but she never took her eyes off Jes Caughill.

"Mister Caughill, leave them bowls on top yere cistern in the morning when we lite outta here."

"NAW, leave them bowls and jugs right here, gotta come after the screendoor anyhow."

"NO SIR, I ain't gonna do it. Some squirrel get in here and get 'em broke. Leave me that hammer, and I'll bring the screen door back, too."

"Ye ain't gonna do no sech thing. No sense in it. Come up here all the time anyhow."

"Much obliged to you and Miss Myrtle. We ain't met no nicer folks in a long time." Sam held out his hand to Jes.

"WELL, I reckon this is so long. Sam, take good care of this little lady. Feel like we knowed ye fer years 'stead of jest a week. Get back in this neck of the woods, stop by and say howdy."

"Sure 'nough, do jest that."

"Sam, if something should happen and ye hafta …" Jes's voice started to crack, and he could not finish the sentence. Sam's eyes dropped to the ground as Jes grabbed the handles of his wheelbarrow and headed for home.

"Bye, bye, Mister Cock Hill, I love you." Little DeVonda stood beside her father and waved as Jes pushed the wheelbarrow as fast as he could. The sound of the little girl's voice only encouraged him to walk faster. He knew he could not turn around and see DeVonda's beaming little face. The voice echoed in his ears as tears filled his eyes. If only he and Myrtle were a few years younger, and Sam would agree to give up the child … Jes knew he and Myrtle would never live another fifteen years and thinking about raising a child late in life was out of the question.

Myrtle was tidying up the kitchen when Jes walked in and hung his hat on the nail by the door.

"Still leavin' in the mornin', I reckon?" Myrtle's voice was emotional, and her eyes were starting to fill with tears. Jes did not answer as he filled his cup with coffee from the old speckled-ware pot on the back of the stove. He walked through the house and took a seat on the front porch. Myrtle fastened the inside hook on the kitchen screen door and joined Jes outside. They rocked slowly in the porch rockers until the mosquitoes started biting. The lightning bugs were out in force, and night was settling in quickly when they went inside. Jes lit a coal oil lamp, and Myrtle turned back both beds for the night.

Myrtle said a silent prayer for DeVonda and then lay on her back waiting for the sleep that seemed so far, far away. She could tell by the sound of Jes's breathing that he was still awake as well. A little three-year-old girl they had kept for a few days during the week had pounded their emotions like nothing they had experienced in years. She had captivated Anna and Ralph as well, but they still had a child to raise. Jes had roared and laughed, like he had not done in years, when little DeVonda climbed into his lap and called him "Mister Cock Hill."

Jes and Myrtle had slaved to raise their children and always felt they would be content when the task was complete. There had been something lacking in their later years, but they did not realize what it was until DeVonda entered their lives. Much of their married life had been devoted to maintaining a modest home and raising a boy and a girl.

Times had been hard, and all of their energy had been devoted to the task at hand. The opportunity to fully enjoy their children had been limited. The child needed a home; but for Jes and Myrtle, little DeVonda was a reminder of the pleasure they still desired.

"Jes, ye 'sleep?" Myrtle asked quietly. "Do ye reckon we really are too old to raise 'nother child?" Jes did not answer except for a loud sigh. He did not need to respond since they both knew the answer.

Myrtle dozed off about 10:00 o'clock, but her sleep was fitful. She dreamed that little DeVonda and Anna were little girls together and she dressed them in identical dresses, only to have Sam come and take DeVonda away. In her dreams she ran after Sam as little DeVonda cried and held out her arms.

It was shortly before daylight when Myrtle awoke from her dream, breathing hard and perspiring. In a few moments she heard the rumbling of a car muffler coming up the driveway from the direction of the coalhouse. The car stopped in the vicinity of the cistern, and a car door squeak told her Sam was probably dropping off the dishes. She continued to listen as the car rumbled slowly past the house and eased over the bridge. The driver slipped carefully across the bridge, keeping the rattling of the boards to a minimum at such an early hour. In the dim light she could see Jes rise up and look out the window by his bed. Myrtle got a faint glimpse of the car's taillights as they disappeared down the Billy Goat Road.

"That them, Jes?" Myrtle asked quietly, but Jes did not answer. She sobbed for a moment, and a slight sniffle indicated Jes was battling similar emotions. Sam had left with little DeVonda, and they would never see her again.

Jes did not get up at the usual hour and remained in bed until after Myrtle had built a fire in the kitchen stove and started breakfast. Myrtle was rolling out biscuit dough when Jes walked through, carrying the slop jar to be emptied in the toilet. When he returned, he was carrying the dishes and jugs that Sam had left on the cistern.

Jes and Myrtle ate breakfast without uttering a word. They had done this many times in their long marriage. Conversation was often lacking when they were angry, worried, or sad; and in a marriage that had reached back over four decades, there had been plenty opportunities to remain silent.

After breakfast, Myrtle filled the dishpan with scalding water from the teakettle and cooled it down with some water dipped from a water bucket. Jes took his hat down from the nail, picked up his claw hammer, which he had placed by the back door, and went outside. Myrtle watched him until he had crossed the tie bridge over the creek and disappeared down the road to the old coal tipple. He returned in about twenty minutes, carrying the screen door he had loaned Sam the evening before. Myrtle had halfway hoped she would see Jes return leading DeVonda by the hand; but when he walked back across the bridge, he carried the hammer in his left hand and the screen door in his right. She continued to watch as he placed the door and the hammer by the shed and walked to the house.

Jes walked in the kitchen door, placed his hat on the nail, picked up a clean cup from the sideboard, and poured some coffee from the old pot on the back of the stove. "They're gone." The two words Myrtle had dreaded to hear fell on a silent room. Jes stood still for a moment, looking into his cup of coffee. Myrtle quietly started to wash a dirty breakfast plate. In a few moments, Jes walked through the house to his chair on the front porch. Little DeVonda, a sweet child who needed Jes and Myrtle more than they needed her, was gone forever. There was nothing left to say.

Ol' Slickum (1953)

OL' SLICKUM
(1953)

*P*OLITICS WAS ALWAYS *the object of heated discussion in Mickey's childhood. He knew Grandmother Caughill hated FDR and Harry Truman. His mother also disliked Franklin Roosevelt but had similar feelings for Dwight Eisenhower. Mickey's grandmother disliked all politicians with a "D" after their name and revered those with the letter "R." Anna Atlee had to keep her dislike for Republican Dwight Eisenhower a secret from her mother.*

Grandfather Caughill and Ralph Atlee kept their political opinions to themselves. Mickey's dad said, "... in this family you live longer that way." Consequently, Mickey never knew their political beliefs.

When it was time for a local election, Mickey listened to the adults berate every local or state politician that the family viewed as a scroundrel. There never seemed to be a shortage of "dirty low-down" politicians to lambaste. Mickey particularly enjoyed hearing about Pete "Ol Slickum" Corning. No trip back in time for him was worthwhile without remembering a tale or two about "Ol'" Slickum.

It was early November when Ralph and Jes left the Atlee Brothers Slaughterhouse to make deliveries of country sausage. The time to start the route was 5:00 AM since the meat was delivered from the back end of Ralph's pickup truck without the benefit of refrigeration. The cool weather meant the meat would be secure in grocery store meat cases long before it could be contaminated. Stores in Ohio, Butler, McLean, Grayson, and Muhlenberg counties sold the Atlee Brothers sausage. Today Jes and Ralph would deliver to stores in Hartford, Centertown, Beaver Dam, McHenry, Rockport, and Dundee. The stores in Centertown, the first town on their route, were closed when they drove through. Ralph had told Jes when they got in the truck, "Glenn and the boys ain't open yet. Get them last on the way back."

Ralph usually made the deliveries alone, but the weekend was coming up, and no more hogs would be killed until Monday. Most stores ordered two twenty-pound tubs of sausage once or twice a week. Wax paper was pressed tightly over the meat, providing its only protection during delivery. Today Ralph was in a hurry since it was looking like rain and he had forgotten his tarpaulin.

Glenn Haddox's grocery in Centertown was the last stop. The delivery had been timed perfectly, as a few drops of rain were starting to fall. Ralph carried in the last tub of hot sausage, and Jes followed with the sole container of mild.

Glenn took Ralph's ticket and speared it on a nail in the wall behind the counter. The ticket was at home with other cash-out deliveries from milk suppliers and bread companies. The store did not have a cash register or an adding machine. All transactions were conducted from a cash drawer, and lengthy additions of customer purchases were done with a pencil and a scrap piece of butcher paper. Most customers bought the same thing each week, and Glenn had the totals memorized. Today he knew he owed Ralph four dollars, and he pulled it from the drawer without looking at the ticket. Ralph took the three one-dollar bills and four quarters and placed them in his cash bag without so much as a glance. The contents of the bag would not be counted until it was taken to the bank.

"Ralph, I been aimin' to ask ye 'bout some buckets of lard. I know most folks run by the slaughterhouse and buy it, but we got some widder women here in town who can't get out there."

"I gotta come to town t'mor to buy a little dab of groceries and I'll run some by if we got any left. Not much money in lard and lots of stores get it from the meat packers. Ye can, too."

"OH, I know that, but folks 'round here rather have yours. Wish ye boys was big 'nough to keep me in bacon, pork chops, and the like. Them big outfits is all right, I reckon, but ain't like dealin' with hometown boys."

"Gotta head fer the barn, Glenn. Run by in the mornin' with that lard."

"OH NO, look out, boys, but look what the cats jest drug in. That's 'Ol' Slickum' Pete Cornin', or I ain't standin' here. Ain't seen that scoundrel in purt near a year."

Jes and Ralph stopped a few feet from the door as Pete Corning burst through the door with a big Certified Bond cigar in his mouth. Most

men smoked the five-cent King Edward cigars; Corning, however, preferred the much stronger fifteen cent Certified Bond.

"WATCH out, boys, I'm in a hell of a hurry. WELL, bust my britches.
Al Atlee, how the hell are ye?"

"I ain't Al."

"Dammit, I'm sorry, Tim. Orta know ye anywhere."

"I ain't Tim neither. Lost Tim a few months back. Heart attack."

"Oh, sorry. Didn't know 'bout Tim. Damn fine feller. Well, if ye ain't
Al and ye ain't Tim, who the HELL are ye?"

"I'm their brother Ralph."

"The HELL ye are."

"Now, this feller must be uh ... DON'T tell me, I don't ever forget
nobody. Jes Brown."

"Jes Caughill; Ralph is my son-in-law."

"OH HELL, I knowed that."

Pete Corning was a wheeler-dealer in county Republican politics.
His nickname, 'Ol' Slickum', was given him by the many people in the
county, especially Democrats, who disliked him. He had held very few
real jobs in his lifetime but had served as Constable, Deputy Sheriff,
Deputy County Clerk, and Magistrate. In addition to politics, he had
a strong passion for hard liquor and women. Corning, who had won
nearly every election, was well known as a skilled politician.

Pete Corning may have been an unsavory person, but he was a quick
judge of any situation. He could see the look of irritation on Jes and
Ralph's faces. They were potential votes in the next election, and he
needed to remedy the situation.

"DAMN, I'm hungry. Why don't ye boys join me in a bite? I'M BUYIN'."

"Ralph, you all still makin' that damn fine sasage down yonder?"

"Yep, still stickin' them hogs and grindin' 'em up."

"Glenn, ye got any of them boys' sasage? I could eat a pound right
now. Wrap me up a pound of the mild and one of the hot. Fix us three
bologna and cheese on crackers while yere at it. BOYS, grab ye a Co-cola
outa the box and get me one, too. Ralph, grab us all a Moon Pie, and
let's grab a seat over here by the stove. DAMN, Glenn. Chilly in here.
Done let the fire go out."

The handle of a coal bucket by the stove provided a good place for
Corning to anchor his cigar. Jes and Ralph joined him around the stove.

Pete sat down in a badly worn ladder-back chair with a seat woven of grass string. Jes and Ralph took a seat on two old wooden dynamite boxes that had been in the store for years. Pete jumped up when Glenn brought their food out to the front counter. After handing the bologna and cheese to Jes and Ralph, he pulled some change out of his pocket.

"Now let me see here. Sasage twenty cent a pound, Co-colas a nickel each, pies a nickel, and sandwiches a dime. BY GOD that's an even dollar ain't it?"

Corning slapped four quarters down on the counter and resumed his seat. Glenn looked at the money with disgust and walked away.

Corning devoured his lunch like a ravenous animal. He talked feverishly between bites of bologna and cheese. Jes and Ralph were not half finished when Corning swallowed his last bite. He relit his cigar and started sipping his drink. Pete was quiet for several moments as he studied Ralph's face. This made Ralph uncomfortable, and he looked down at the floor.

"Ralph, how is that sasage business anyhow?"

Surprised by the question, Ralph answered, ". . . always be better, I reckon."

"HELL, yere a makin' money ain't ye?"

"Keep body and soul together, I reckon. The business belongs to Al anyhow. I jest help out when I can. Been doin' it since back in the '20s."

Corning nodded at Ralph's answer as he shifted the cigar from side to side in his mouth. "That's what I mean," he said.

"Gonna get better. Gonna get lots better. Ol' Jes there done spent his life in the mines a makin' ten, fifteen, twenty cent a ton a loadin' coal. Done a little farmin', too, I reckon. Ain't that right, Jes?"

"Thirty-two years and raised two kids. Done it six days a week, fourteen hours a day."

"Yep, back in the '20s, two and three dollars a day was common in the mines. Some parts of the country miners a beggin' to work fer a dollar a day. These young fellers comin' 'long today is gonna have it a whole lots better. I know what yere a thinkin' with this here mines down here closin' down and all. Now mines is gonna close and mines is gonna open. That's jest a fact. You boys ain't a gonna be able to make 'nough sasage. By God it ain't gonna be long 'til we all is gonna be in high cotton. That's right, that's right, I know what I'm a talkin' 'bout.

Coal in this here county fer who laid the rail and them coal companies know it, and they're a comin' after it. Be diggin' shaft mines ha'fway to China to get that coal."

Ralph and Jes exchanged glances and resumed eating. This did not go unnoticed by Corning, who quickly recognized skepticism. They did not believe a word he was saying.

"BOYS, I'm a tellin' it like it is. You wait and see. Peabody Coal and Sinclair is a gonna merge, or I'll eat my cigar. The future is in strip minin', and Peabody knows it. They ain't a gonna get rid of underground all together. Some coal gotta be mined that way. Peabody gonna get Sinclair to get into surface minin' and then look out. HELL, Jes look at them ol' mines. Fer years ye left ha'f the coal, or ye couldn't pillar up and keep the ceilin' from a fallin' down. Worried 'bout gas and 'Black Damp', and they still do. Thirty odd men died in that Wickliffe mine over in Muhlenberg County. Back in 1910 wuzn't it Jes? Don't have none of that in strip minin'."

Pete Corning rolled his cigar between his thumb and index finger for a few moments as he sized up his audience. He knew Ralph was a Deomcrat and Jes a Republican; and he sensed strongly that neither man had any use for him, but they did take him up on a free lunch offer. Pete was fond of saying, "... if a man takes yere seegar, ye got his vote."

"Boys, gonna be union jobs. Them mine bosses tell me someday gonna be payin' twenty to thirty dollars a day plus health insurance and retirement. Them companies ain't happy 'bout them big paydays; but it's all gonna be UMWA, and they know that'll be the cost of doin' business fer a while. Gonna be a big payday fer them, too. NOW I ain't agin' a man tryin' to make a livin' farmin', but HELL's bells, we got folks 'round here gonna make more in one day a sellin' them little farms out to the coal company. More than they could make in ten lifetimes. YOU may be one of 'em, Ralph. NOW, don't misunderstand me, I hate to say it, I hate like HELL to say it, but the little man is 'bout done. Ever'thing gotta be big time. Government wants it that way. Ain't gonna make no livin' a farmin' forty odd acres with a little ol' tractor or a mule. GOTTA BE BIG, have a million acres and be in debt up to yere ass."

Jes Caughill pointed his half empty drink bottle at Pete Corning and asked, "What's a gonna happen to poor people? Answer me that.

Everbody can't be a big shot. Lots of folks is born poor and die poor. Ain't got no say in the matter. Scratched a livin' my whole life."

Corning suspected he had lost the argument with Jes, so he decided to address Ralph directly and with a different approach.

"Ralph, how ye boys make that sasage so damn good?"

"Ain't no secret. Tim started makin' it in Ma's meathouse back in the '20s. She showed us how. Take a twenty pound of ground hog and add a pint of shaller salt, 2/3 cup ground sage, 1/2 cup black pepper, 1/4 cup red pepper, and a cup of brown sugar. Back in them days we growed our own red pepper and sage there on the farm. Ma said the sage we growed been there since 'fore the Civil War, and it was good. Al buys store-bought now. What Ma had finally died out, and it was lots of trouble a pickin' and dryin' it. The store-bought ain't as good, but most folks don't know no better since they never had any of the old stuff. Al says we gotta change with the times."

"BY GOD, that's jest what I been sayin'. Gotta change with the times. Now the Atlee boys run that slaughterhouse down there, and ye ain't got no refrigeration, no runnin' water or nothin' like that. Ye deliver the sasage outa the back end of that ol' pickup. Now tell me how much longer ye think the government is gonna let ye do that. Say yere gonna make somebody sick and shet ye down. They'll make ye spend money ye ain't got to modernize or give up."

"NOW see here, we been makin' sausage purt near thirty years, and we ain't made nobody sick yet. Country folks been livin' without electricity and refrigerators for many a moon. Only a fool kills hisself or gets sick eatin' spiled meat. Keep the flies out and use yere nose to smell fer bad meat. Hung sausage and milk in a well or a spring my whole life and ain't NEVER been sick. Only feller I ever knowed got food poison was one who got it from a can he bought in a store. The government had better worry 'bout what them big companies is a puttin' in stuff and not us. We eat what we make. Think them fellas at Campbell Soup eat that stuff?"

Pete Corning's face was beet red as he clamped down hard on his cigar. He rocked back and forth in his chair, as he grew increasingly frustrated with his inability to score points in the argument with Jes and Ralph.

"Ralph, I don't disagree with ye. Not fer one cotton pickin' minute. BUT it don't matter. Them big packin' houses gonna get tired of ye one day, and they'll pay off some boys in Frankfort, and the State will shet ye down. Hell, someday them packin' outfits may come in here and tell Glenn if he aims to keep on buyin from them, he's a gonna hafta stop buyin' Atlee sasage. What choice he gonna have? That's it, boys. Work in the mines or move to the city and work in a factory or steel mill. Ain't gonna be all bad. Farmin' was a good life and the way God intended fer man to live fer a long time. Simple way is gone. Now a man can raise a terbacker crop fer a little dab of extra money and work the mines. Terbacker ain't a bad deal. Make a little extra money when the mines is shet down."

Jes glanced over at Glenn, who was leaning across the counter listening to what Corning had to say. His face had turned red when Corning mentioned the packing companies forcing him to stop buying Atlee sausage. The thought had never occurred to Glenn Haddox, but he knew that was a battle his little store and the Atlee boys could never win. Except for Atlee sausage, he bought all of his meat from the companies.

"YESSIR, the good ol' days may be gone, but the good times are a comin'. Ye can't stop it. Day is comin' when the boys 'round here gonna be buildin' new houses and drivin' new pickup trucks. Tall cotton. The REAL tall cotton."

Corning paused to relight his cigar while Ralph and Jes finished their Colas thoughtfully. Despite their disdain for Corning, they suspected he was probably right. They hated both the message and the messenger. Jes cleared up his throat and cocked one eye at Corning while the index finger of his rough calloused hand pointed out from the Coke bottle in his hand and directly at Corning.

"How do ye know all this?"

Corning seemed startled by the question. He looked at Jes for a few seconds until he was painfully reminded that he was still holding a lighted match in his fingers.

"DAMNATION," Corning snarled as he dropped the match and shook his fingers. He looked at Jes as if he thought he was responsible for his little accident.

"My business to know, Jes. I talk to them minin' people and the big shots from outa state who bankroll 'em. They say Kentucky got 'nough coal to last a thousand years. Country needs coal. Since the war, England and France ain't shit compared to the ol' U.S. of A. This country is the biggest and meanest bird in the henhouse, and it's only gonna get better. The future 'round here is strip minin'. Peabody gonna buy Sinclair, and then they gonna buy out all the little two-bit operations. Two-bit farmin' and minin' is over. It ain't a gonna quit, jest gonna get bigger. Little guy ain't gonna hold out much longer."

Corning stood up, stretched, and yawned. He figured he had said all he could to Jes and Ralph. He knew they did not need to like him to vote for him, and he hoped his little speech had done just that.

"Glenn, boys, I gotta get on down the road. Got people to see and things to do, and the ol' woman gonna have a chicken fit if I don't get in by dark. You boys remember that County Judge race when it rolls 'round next time. I ain't sayin' I'll be in it, but I ain't sayin' I won't neither."

Corning picked up his two pounds of sausage and, with a trail of smoke circling back over his shoulder, raced out the door, jumped into his car, and sped away. Ralph looked at the bottom of his drink bottle to see where it had been bottled.

"Mine was bottled at Central City. What 'bout your's, Jes?"

"Eyes ain't good 'nough to see."

"Lemma see. Central City, too. Tastes better from over there I think."

Glenn Haddox scraped the coins Corning left into the cash drawer and started laughing.

"Boys, I get mad ever time that windbag comes in here, but ye hafta hand to 'im. He shore can spin a big yarn. Reckon that's what it takes to be a politician. Helps to be a crook, too. Ye heard 'im say how he talks to the mine people and the big high rollers, but the only time he talks to the little man is when he wants a vote. He ain't got mine. Never has, never will."

"Glenn, politicians like Corning suppose to look out fer us; but if the State tried to shut us down, he wouldn't lift a finger. Tell 'em to go right ahead."

"Yere right there, Ralph. Ol' Pete got that nickname 'Slickum' fair and square. One time a few years back Pete and the Republicans was a tad short of money, and they knowed the Democrats was gonna hit Hayti in Hartford and Beaver Dam to buy the colored vote. They didn't have 'nough money, so Corning got this here idea to load all the darkies up he could get in a big truck and take 'em to McLean County and give 'em some moonshine. Got 'em all drunk as skunks and brought 'em back after the polls closed. Yessir, sent 'nother truck 'round courthouse square to pick up all the drinkin' and gamblin' white boys and hauled them to Grayson County. Made the difference and the Republicans won. He strutted like a big ol' bird fer a time after that."

"I remember that. That's when Pete got in as Magistrate, I think."

"Ralph, I don't remember. What I do remember is that the next time the Republicans rubbed salt in the wounds by stuffin' the ballot box and won by a landslide."

"I think that's right, Glenn. I recall after that the next election I was deliverin' sausage up at Hartford, and everybody was a talkin' 'bout it. Turned off cold early that year, and we started killin' hogs early. They said ol' Pete showed up fer the election drunk as a hoot owl, and nobody was payin' 'im any mind. He asked that the ballot boxes be moved out behind city hall. The Democrats didn't object and didn't suspect a thing, even when fellers was holdin' their ballot over their right shoulder 'fore they dropped it in the box. They said Corning had a man on the top floor of the city hall with a telescope a checkin' ballots, and he was yellin' downstairs to the moneyman who handed out five-dollar bills to the ones who voted right. Got jest 'nough votes that way to sweep the Democrats. Some of them boys took the Democrats' money, too."

"Ralph, do ye remember the time they counterfeited some Republican ballots over at Beaver Dam? I seen some of that goin' on. The Democrats started payin' three dollars fer ever Republican ballot somebody brought 'em. Ol' Slickum got 'im a blank ballot and run over to the newspaper and had 'em run him off a bunch. 'fore long the Democrats was a buyin' them no-count ballots 'til they run outta money."

"Well, Glenn, I reckon that vote buyin' is 'bout to be a thing of the past. Used to lots of folks sold their vote 'cause they needed the money and didn't think nothin' of it. Course there was always somebody like Ol' Slickum Pete a tellin' them it was the American way. The funniest one I ever heard on Pete was the time he took that ol' colored woman a new dress. Jes, ye know that's how they used to buy a woman's vote. Guess some still do. This ol' gal they say dressed out around 350 pounds. Say she throwed that dress down and stomped it; and when Pete bent over to pick it up, she lit into 'im with a broom. Chased 'im all the way to his car a screamin' how she weren't gonna sell her vote to no white man."

Jes and Glenn roared with laughter. It was several minutes before the three men could regain their composure. Glenn laughed until he strangled and had to go outside to spit. When he came back inside, he was wiping tears from his eyes with a handkerchief.

"Boys, I'd a give a day's pay to seen that ol' gal lit into Pete. Funnier than a bunch a dogs a fightin' over a bone," laughed Jes.

"Jes, Ralph and me wouda paid off that day's pay, too. I wonder if he lost his seegar?"

"Glenn, mighta been funnier if Pete had made the mistake of offerin' that dress to Myrtle Caughill. She wouda hit 'im with a fryin' pan. No broom to it. No matter if he was a Republican. Aint't that right, Jes?"

"Boys, politics shore has changed. Pete come in one time a blowin' off that folks take it too seriously. Jest a game is all it is. Said he got drunk a many a time after an election with the Democrats, and they would chide each other 'bout what they was gonna do to 'em the next election. Cuss and snort at each other fer weeks, then go get drunk with 'em." Glenn pulled a Lucky Strike from beind his left ear and lit it as he finished his remark.

"Glenn, my daddy used to say that the church was God's business and politics was the people's business. Jest like the sausage business. Ain't gonna be funny if I beat ye outta ten pound of sausage."

"Ralph, yere right, but them politicians don't always see it that way. Wheelin' and dealin' and back room deals. Politicians don't know the difference in right and wrong or tellin' the truth. You boys run that slaughterhouse like that and go outta business or go to jail."

Jes Caughill cleared his throat. "Both ye boys is old 'nough to know that most folks only vote one way, the way his daddy voted. Folks in this here county who always voted Republican 'til ol' Roozevelt come along and they switched. He done somethin' fer 'em, don't ye see?"

"Right as rain there, Jes; but when ol' Harry Truman come along a bunch of 'em switched back to Republican," laughed Glenn. "WHOA, hold on there a minute, Glenn. I never been in a union, but Jes has. 'Fore the unions them straw bosses was a tellin' the men to vote Republican 'cause the company wanted it that way. Then the unions come along and tol' 'em to vote Democrat fer their own good. Some men voted to keep their job."

"Ralph, I know that and so does Jes, but when a man buys only one kinda chewin' terbacker 'cause that's what his daddy bought ... well I rest my case."

Ralph started grinning and winked at Glenn. "Glenn, ain't been that long since the women got the vote, and some of them is like that, too. I know a white-headed ol' woman who never voted any way but Republican 'cept once since the women been votin'."

"Jes, Ralph ain't a funnin' me, is he?"

"I ain't a sayin' nothin'. Know where my nest is made."

"Jes knows, Glenn. Now that one time come after ol' Myrtle went to Hartford to be a character witness fer some woman. This old lawyer got up and started lambastin' women fer ever'thing. Said none of 'em was any good 'cept his wife and daughter. Made ol' Myrtle mad as a wet hen, and she swore she'd walk to Centertown to vote fer any Democrat who run agin' 'im no matter who he was. Said he orta be run outa the Republican Party."

"Come on, Jes. Ralph's a pullin' my leg ain't he?"

"NO, he ain't," Jes answered as he pushed his hat toward the back of his head. "That election I brung a road wagon into town to vote, and she walked purt near three miles. Tol' me if that worthless ol' pup ever run fer anything she would walk to Centertown to vote agin' 'im, and she done it. Rode in the wagon back home, though, and said she was gonna peel my onion if I ever tol'. SHE done tol' ever'body she knowed inside a week. Then blamed me fer ever'body a findin' out. Figured ye heard it. What made her even madder was the ol' lawyer won the election. Think that was the year the Republicans got the votin' moved out behind city hall up at Hartford."

Ralph and Jes waved goodbye to Glenn and started for the slaughterhouse. They were still chuckling when they climbed into the truck but soon fell silent as Pete Corning's predictions echoed in their heads. Jes's life was nearly over, and he was somewhat bitter that a man could work himself to death over a long career and have very little to show for it. At age forty-six, Ralph knew it was no longer possible to make a good living without working in the mines or leaving Walton's Creek.

The drive from Glenn's store in Centertown to the slaughterhouse took only a few minutes. Ralph pulled his truck up close to the hog pen, his front bumper almost touching one wooden post. Ralph pushed himself up in the truck seat and quickly counted the hogs in the pen.

"Looks like we got six or eight new hogs, Jes. Harold musta brung them over I bought off 'im the other day. Al been jumpin' up and down that we needed them hogs. Harold don't ever get in no hurry. Hope Al done rendered out all that lard. I'm ready to go to the house. Gonna take me a couple sacks of them cracklins today. Anna gonna make us a batch of cracklin' bread. Need one of them sacks to get past the dogs. They ain't a gonna let me in the house if I don't. Dump one sack and then run fer the door with the other. They'll fight fer an hour over them things."

"Put a brogan in their backside, and ye won't have that problem," growled Jes. "'Sides, a man ortan wake up all his dogs if he ain't got but one bone. Heerd that my whole life."

"Jes, I ain't got a size 13 shoe like you. Might as well grab ye a big sack fer yere dogs and have Myrtle make you all a mess of bread, too. Do it while ye got a ride to the house."

"Walked to town and hauled groceries back on my back most of my life. I reckon I can walk a mile or so with a little dab of cracklins. SOONER walk anyhow. Besides, the cloud done blowed over. It in't a gonna rain nary 'nother drop."

Ralph was silent for a moment before he turned toward Jes, grinning. "Jes, didn't ye hear what Ol' Slickum' said back there? Can't do that no more, GOTTA change with the times."

'SLICKUM, my foot. Makes my back end wanna chew terbacker," snorted Jes.

The Trip Back Home (1953)

THE TRIP BACK HOME
(1953)

*M*ICKEY'S DAD OFTEN *worked on power line rights-of-way, and the jobs meant traveling to the far corners of the state. In 1953 the entire family was in Sparta, Kentucky, when a broken axle on the family truck almost left them stranded during the Fourth of July weekend.*

Anna Atlee insisted that they return home to Walton's Creek if they had to walk. They begged a ride to Carrollton, Kentucky, where they met the Greyhound at the Gypsy Grill. Mickey experienced air conditioning for the first time on the Greyhound but became ill from the heat when they switched to an ancient, unairconditioned Kentucky Bus in Louisville for the final leg of their journey home.

Mickey would never forget the trip's bizarre twists and turns. In addition to a cool ride, he saw his first city and realized how members of another race were treated under Jim Crow laws and customs. At the end of the adventure the Atlees were back home in Walton's Creek, where they still lived with coal oil lamps and a battery radio.

The trip back home was one of Mickey's earliest memories.

"Now, Ralph Atlee, I don't care if the axle is busted on that ol' truck. I'm goin' back to Walton's Creek this weekend if I hafta walk. Been cooped up in this ol' farmhouse fer months a cookin' fer a bunch of roughneck men 'til I could scream. Ain't hardly talked to 'nother woman in weeks. I'm tired, and that's all there is to it, and I wanna go see my mama."

Ralph Atlee calmly ate his breakfast while his wife vented her frustrations. He had learned after nearly sixteen years of marriage that it was best to let her wind down before saying anything.

"I know ye wanna go home. So do I. Hard on a woman a bein' up here day in and day out like this. Us men don't give a hoot. Now Tom and Jim went over to Carrollton the other night and ate some apple pie at a place called the Gypsy Grill. Jest so happens the Greyhound stops there. Jim had this woman check the schedule to ride the bus back to Ohio County. Said we could catch the Greyhound there and go to Louisville and then take the Kentucky Bus to Beaver Dam. Take best part of a day, I reckon, but takes a spell in the truck, too. Jim knowed ye wanted to go home fer the Fourth of July since we got a four-day weekend and all. With all the boys a ridin' back two to a cab, no room fer us to ride with nobody. Awful nice of 'im to ask."

"Ralph, I been after ye to check the train schedule fer a week. The L&N goes right here from Sparta to Louisville. I love to ride a train. I watch them passenger cars rollin' by here ever' day of the world, and I can jest see us a settin' up there a ridin' along."

"Hold yere taters a minute. I got a right-away to cut, and I ain't got no time with us workin' 12-hour days and six days a week, to be traipsin' 'round a lookin' fer train schedules. Had that kinda time I'd fix the truck. You ain't got no time neither. Jim says he thinks we can catch the Greyhound over at Warsaw, too, and that's closer. But he done got the schedule fer Carrollton, and that's how we aim to go. Bus probably costs less than the train and hafta get a cab from train station over to the bus station anyhow. This way is better."

Ralph Atlee had started working for the Lamb Forestry Service in the late 1940s. His work crews kept power lines clear of limbs and cut new rights-of-ways as the more remote areas of Kentucky ushered in electricity and the household products associated with it. Refrigerators, electric stoves, and televisions were changing the rural culture of the state like nothing since the Model T Ford. Anna Atlee was tired of keeping milk cold by hanging it in the well and listening to the battery radio by coal oil lamps. She was saving her money as a cook for the work crew to wire their house.

The old ramshackle farmhouse at Sparta was typical of the places Ralph rented to house the workers. Ralph, Anna and three-year-old Mickey lived in a small travel trailer while the workers stayed in the dingy, hot farmhouse. The work had paid better than anything he could find back home at Walton's Creek, and the money would allow them to purchase more modern conveniences.

Eagle Creek at Sparta bordered the Atlee's temporary home on one side and the railroad track on the other. Sparta in 1953 was a tiny community of about 500 people. The town had a post office, a few tiny grocery stores, and one hotel.

The summer heat had been brutal for Ralph and the workers, but the heat in Anna's kitchen was stifling. She was preparing the meals on a wood cookstove in a house without the protection of a single shade tree. Ralph was so concerned he purchased a small Westinghouse oscillating fan for her to use. The cost of the fan was 40 dollars, but it was offering some comfort to Anna in the kitchen by day and for the entire family by night in the trailer.

The Sparta job was not the only one where the Atlees had endured discomfort. The summer before, Anna's parents, Jes and Myrtle Caughill, had accompanied them to Vine Grove, Kentucky. Jes and Ralph were the only workers as they trimmed trees away from power lines. The company would not provide housing for a two-man crew, so Jes and Ralph obtained permission to build a cabin back in the woods. They hauled slabs from a nearby sawmill and erected a very modest one-room dwelling. The floor was covered with straw, and sheets of burlap were tacked down over it.

The little cabin was stifling hot day and night. The heat was intensified by the use of a tiny wood stove they used for cooking. Anna and Myrtle fixed breakfast long before daylight and saw the men off to work. During the day they sat outside with two-year-old Mickey in old ladder-back chairs. A small creek ran through the woods and served as a source of water and a place to keep milk cool. For his daily bath, Anna placed Mickey in a small spot in the creek where the water pooled. He squealed and slapped at the water with delight. Heat rash and mosquitoes bothered the youngster, but Anna bathed him carefully each day and applied Calamine lotion.

In spite of the discomforts, Anna enjoyed spending time with her mother. She knew, however, that this would be their last job together. Jes was struggling with the heat and would not ask Ralph to hire him again, and Myrtle was not well and could not endure another blistering hot summer under these conditions.

Despite the hardships, Anna and Myrtle had viewed the experience as an adventure. Myrtle had kept Anna entertained with stories about things that had happened in the past. Two or three times a week Myrtle would announce, "... I got this here dime jest a burnin' a hole in my pocket." This was the signal for a sojourn out of the woods and down the road to an out-of-the-way country store. With Mickey riding on Anna's hip, they walked almost a mile to the store where they enjoyed two bottles of Orange Nehi. The storeowner was a chatty fellow, and they passed some time with him before starting back to the cabin.

Big Jim Waters headed his pickup out Highway 35 toward Warsaw. The town of Warsaw was nine miles from Sparta, and Big Jim would switch there to Highway 42 for the final leg of the eighteen-mile trip to Carrollton. The cab was crowded with three adults and one child, but the trip passed quickly.

"Jim, don't ferget when ye get to Centertown to run by Blade's and have 'im meet us at the bus in Beaver Dam. I figure you'll get there an hour or so 'fore we do."

"I ain't gonna ferget. If Blade ain't home, I'll hotfoot it on back up there and get ye myself."

"Ye ain't doin' nothin' of the kind. I'll call Al from the café there and get 'im up there. NOPE, ye done a plenty a runnin' us over here."

"Anna, I was tellin' Ralph that the woman up here at the Gypsy Grill was a sayin' that them Greyhound buses a comin' in there these days is all brand new and got air conditionin'. Wish I wuz a ridin' with ye. This ol' truck gonna het up a mite 'fore I hit Centertown. Only air conditionin' I ever been 'round is the drugstores up at Hartford. Be a sight better than cookin' fer a bunch of roughnecks like us."

"Anythin' is better than cookin' in that ol' house. Hottest place I ever been in my whole born days. I hope I don't get bus sick. Only rode one once. I get carsick, but mind ye I don't get truck sick. Don't know what the difference is. Mickey gets sick in the truck, though. We both may get sick today, air conditionin' or no air conditionin'. Get sick as dogs."

"Honey, you and the youngun' gonna get sick as Greyhounds."

Ralph laughed at his silly joke, but Anna just gave him a disgusted look and slapped his arm. Big Jim just shook his head. He had to endure Ralph's feeble attempts at being funny all day in the hot sun where nothing was amusing.

Big Jim's truck entered Carrollton, and they made their way to the Gypsy Grill. In 1953 Carrollton was a sleepy little river town whose streets were lined with trees and dotted with numerous old homes. Anna fell in love with the community right away and was reminded of the images she carried in her mind of Tom Sawyer_and Huckleberry Finn. Incorporated in 1794, Carrollton had a long history. The town was originally called Port William and renamed in 1838 in honor of Charles Carroll, a signer of the Declaration of Independence.

The Gypsy Grill was an important spot in Carrollton. The café was famous for great food and also doubled as the town's bus station. The sign advertising the Gypsy Grill cafeteria swung from a metal pole that stretched from its anchor point on the front of the brick building and across the sidewalk. Slightly above the cafeteria sign and anchored close to the building was the Greyhound sign. A green canopy completed the décor of the building's front.

The Gypsy Grill and bus stop was typical of small towns across America at the height of intercity bus transportation. Countless small communities depended upon Greyhound's passenger service and freight deliveries for local businesses. Carrollton was fortunate to be located between Louisville and Cincinnati. Greyhounds traveling north and south passed through the Gypsy Grill day and night.

A Greyhound bus sat idling at the side of the Gypsy Grill when the Atlees arrived. Ralph rushed inside to purchase the tickets, while Anna and Mickey waited by the bus. When Ralph returned, Mickey was pointing to the running dog painted on the side of the bus. He giggled and said, "... doggie, doggie, I see a doggie."

When Ralph returned with the tickets, he tickled his son's ribs. Mickey started giggling.

"Son, can ye say H-O-U-N-D dog?"

"'Ound dog, 'ound dog, Daddy."

"Ralph, what's the holdup?"

"Nothin'. The driver is a takin' a coffee break. Be 'long in a minute. Lady says not to worry since be 'nother one right behind this one in a little bit. Got 'em comin' and goin' day and night."

"Ralph, this is a big pain in the rear. Wish we couda took the truck."

"Truck ain't got air conditionin'. Gonna rear back and ride in style." Ralph grinned, clasped his fingers behind his head and leaned backwards to illustrate his point. Anna punched him with her elbow and frowned at him.

Passengers lined up on the sidewalk behind Ralph, Anna, and Mickey. A few were already in line when they arrived. In a few minutes the driver, a man in his early 50s, came out of the Gypsy Grill. He stood by the door and took tickets without even looking at the passenger. Ralph handed him their tickets and with a grin said, "gonna be 'nother scorcher." The driver took the tickets and ignored him completely. The driver acted annoyed by the lady behind them who wanted to check her suitcase. He opened the cargo bin and threw it in with a bang.

Ralph motioned for Anna to take the front seat opposite the driver. He took the first seat immediately behind the driver.

"Honey, that ol' boy don't act all that friendly."

Anna whispered back, "I hear all Greyhound drivers is like that. Think their doins' don't stink."

When all the passengers had boarded, the driver walked up the steps and started counting his passengers. He made some notations on a piece of paper and started to crawl under the wheel when a voice called to him from outside the bus.

"Suh, cans we come 'board now?"

The driver turned around and with a disgusted look on his face said, "... yeah, I reckon."

Three-year-old Mickey's eyes grew as large as saucers when two young Negro men boarded the bus. He had never seen a black person up close before. He watched spellbound as the driver abruptly took their tickets. The two men started walking slowly toward the back of the bus. The first man paused and looked at the two empty seats behind Ralph, but the second man pushed him slightly and said, "keep it movin'."

Ralph caught Anna's attention and motioned with his eyes to a sign in the front of the bus directing Negroes to the back four rows of seats. Anna nodded as she looked up at the sign.

Ralph and Anna knew bus terminals, like courthouses and other public places, had separate restrooms and drinking fountains for blacks; but Greyhound officials were somewhat ambivalent about the seating requirements on the buses. The enforcement was generally tempered with local customs and at the driver's discretion. Negroes who broke the rule were occasionally asked to move or get off the bus, and sometimes police were called.

Living near Walton's Creek and Centertown all of their lives did not give the Atlees much of an opportunity to see segregation up close. A storekeeper in Sparta had given Ralph a lesson on how it worked in that community. He told Ralph that Sparta once had a white hotel and a black hotel. The black establishment burned in the 1940s, but for years the two hotels served the large number of farmers who came to town on weekends for livestock auctions. If the white hotel was full, the black hotel could rent rooms to whites, but the reverse was not true. The black hotel was famous for fried fish, and the white inn served a great meal for fifty cents. Ralph thought it was odd to have segregated facilities but then allow whites to stay in the black hotel.

The Greyhound bus was relatively new; the seats smelled fresh and clean, but the cool air made the coach heavenly. Ralph leaned across the aisle and whispered, "Now don't this take the cake. Beats a burnin' alive in that ol' truck fer three or four hours, don't it? Orta have this at home."

Anna whispered back, "I'd settle fer electric lights at home and gonna have it too, jest as soon as this here job is done. Gonna have me jest 'nough money."

The Greyhound driver did not pull away from the Gypsy Grill until he was certain that the two black men were seated in the rear. Periodically he glanced back at them in his mirror to make sure that they had not moved.

Mickey looked out the bus window spellbound. Carrollton was a community of about 3,400 hundred people but was the largest place that he had been in his short life. The first time he saw black people up front and his first experience with air conditioning were things about the trip would always stand out in his mind.

The Gypsy Grill would still be in business fifteen years later when Mickey and five other soldiers, fresh from Basic Training at Fort Dix, New Jersey, would enter the café for Cokes and candy bars. The young soldiers were unaware that they were patronizing a facility that had served the Carrollton community and thousands of soldiers twenty-four hours a day from the 1940s until the 1960s. Two years after Mickey and his fellow soldiers, dressed in their summer brown khaki uniforms, got back on the Greyhound in route to Fort Knox, the Gypsy Grill would lock its doors for good. Like the taverns and inns that serviced the stagecoach era of the early 19th Century, the Gypsy Grill's time came to a close.

Ralph, Anna, and Mickey were settled in their seats as the Greyhound left Carrollton and rolled along highway forty-two. For a short distance the road was in sight of the Ohio River. Ten miles from Carrollton at the base of Bedford Hill, on the right, was a large colonial style building called the Colonial Inn, and the community of Bedford rested at the top of the hill. The quaint colonial style courthouse at Bedford had been gutted by fire in the 1940s, and the community would lose their present courthouse in 1954. Bedford, a community of fewer than 1,000 people, had two bus stops. Trailways operated service over the same route as Greyhound in anticipation of Greyhound giving up the route. The Trailways stopped at the Tic Toc Restaurant, but eventually with limited freight and passenger business, Trailways abandoned the route.

The Greyhound double-parked in front of the Sweet Shop restaurant, a short distance from the Tic Toc. The Sweet Shop was located in a two-story building on Main Street with sleeping rooms available on the top level. The driver unloaded several pieces of freight while one passenger departed and another got on.

A couple of miles from Bedford, the Greyhound passed Bray Fruit Market, and a few miles further the bus entered the community of Sligo. The driver started to slow down as they headed past a garage, a cemetery, and a Baptist Church. The bus pulled into the White Cottage Inn, which stood at the intersection of Highway 153 and Highway 42. The driver stood up and made an announcement.

"This here is Sligo. No rest stop here, but I'm runnin' a tad ahead. Be here ten minutes. Wanna stretch your legs, that's ok, but be ready to go when I am."

"Ralph, that's a pretty place. Let's go inside. May not get to stretch agin' 'til we get to Louisville."

Ralph carried Mickey as he and Anna followed the driver into the café portion of the structure. A filling station occupied the remainder of the building. The aroma of food met them as soon as they entered the door. Anna immediately sniffed the air. She would not eat in any restaurant that smelled of old grease, but the air smelled only of fresh coffee, roast beef and cornbread, and fried fish.

"Ralph, this here is a nice place. Need to stop by here sometime and eat dinner."

"Now done got ye spoiled. Ride in an air-conditionin' bus, and ye wanna eat somebody else's food."

"Jest once I'd like to eat in a restaurant when we eat sumpin' other than hamburgers, french fries, and a Coke."

"Eat whatever ye want, but me and Mickey gonna have hamburgers, french fries, and a Coke. Ain't that right, Son? Like hambuggers, don't ye?"

The Greyhound driver walked up the counter and bellowed, "HEY, MISS KETTLE, I need a cup of mud and some jam cake."

A parrot occupying a perch by a huge fireplace answered, "hound dog, hound dog."

The driver laughed, "Miss Kettle, are ye ever gonna teach that bird to say Greyhound?

"Sam, I don't teach that bird nothin'. Picks it up from patrons, I guess. SAY, the missus and you a comin' to the wing-ding this weekend? This is our big Fourth of July fish fry and potluck. Gonna be right out back here, and gonna have music and dancin'."

"Lordy mercy, Miss Kettle. When I get to Nashville, I have to take a charter to New Orleans. Won't see me before the end of next week. Maybe not then. We sure had a big time last year."

The Atlees walked around the restaurant while the Greyhound driver drank his coffee and ate jam cake while standing. Several men were drinking coffee, and the sound of a pinball machine echoed from the back room. The breakfast customers were gone, and it was too early for the noon meal crowd.

When the driver swallowed the last of his coffee, Ralph nodded for Anna to start for the door. The driver glanced at his watch and bellowed out, "GREYHOUND FOR LOOIEVILLE, ooh say, Miss Kettle, is Miss Sally goin' to play the ponies today?"

"Sam, ye know she won't ride with none of the other drivers. Probably standin' by the bus a waitin' on ye."

When the Atlees got back to the bus, an elderly woman was waiting for the driver.

"Miss Sally, you done had me worried. Thought ye weren't gonna play the ponies today."

"Sam, ye know better than that. Gotta play my ponies come what may."

The driver was in a jovial mood with his new passenger. Mickey dozed off with his head resting on his father's shoulder, while his parents relaxed and enjoyed the scenery. After a few minutes they were startled by the conversation going on in front of them.

"OH, SAM, I done forgot all 'bout that. YESSIR, they done that and lots worse when they was little. Beatin' 'est boys I ever seen."

"I would have skinned that grandson of yours if I had known what he pulled. It was several years back, and I was snowed in back there at Sligo for two days. Them boys ice-skated down the road there from Bedford that mornin'. My settin' down place was worn out, and I got a call from my boss who said to get that thing to Cincy come hell or high water. I had a bunch of wore out passengers, too. I got me some old cable from the garage and made me some chains for the wheels and got going. Couldn't make more than ten or fifteen mile an hour, but better than a settin' still. Them boys, without me a knowin' it, hung on the back end all the way to Bedford. One of them cables comes loose, it could'a' cut one of 'em in two. Well, maybe not. Wasn't going fast enough, I don't reckon."

Ralph grinned and leaned across the aisle and whispered to Anna, "Sounds like sumpin' me, Tim, and Al wouda pulled when we was younguns."

The Greyhound stopped at the Goshen Inn and closer to Louisville, the Melrose Inn. Along the route they passed through several tiny communities like Goshen, Skylight, and Prospect, where another elderly lady flagged down the bus. The driver laughed when he saw her.

"Miss Sally, I reckon Miss Thompson is headed to Louisville to do a bit of shopping."

The bus came to a stop, and the lady slowly climbed aboard. The driver watched her with some apprehension.

"Easy does it, Miss Thompson. Don't need ye fallin' on me again."

"I'm a tough ol' bird, Sam. Fell out the front door the other day and landed on my feet."

The lady handed the driver a quarter and took a seat next to Miss Sally. The two women immediately engaged in an intense conversation about shopping and horse racing. The bus stopped again and picked up a young man who took his time pulling the money from his pocket. The driver was irritated and waved the man to a seat. "I ain't got all day," he growled. "Count out twenty-five cents if ye can, and I'll get it at the bus station."

The driver's face was red as he methodically shifted the bus through the gears. He seemed to have little patience with anyone except Miss Kettle, Miss Thompson, and Miss Sally. Anna leaned across the aisle and whispered to Ralph, "...parrot got his number."

When the Greyhound entered the city of Louisville, the conversation among the passengers ceased as everyone looked at the sights. The bus engine alternated between a roaring sound with acceleration and a whine as the driver quickly slowed down in the ever-growing traffic. The final stretch to the Greyhound station was slowed by the cars and occasionally stopped completely by a traffic light. The sidewalks of Kentucky's largest city were crowded with people, and the line of buildings seemed to go on forever.

Mickey woke up from his nap and stared out the window at more buildings and people than he had ever seen. One building looked like a huge mountain glaring down at them like they were so many ants.

Ralph whispered to Anna, "Couldn't hire me to live in this God forsaken place."

"Me neither," she replied. "More sin than Sodom and Gomorrah. Jest get me back to Walton's Creek."

When the Atlees got off the bus at the Greyhound station in Louisville, the scene was abuzz with activity. Numerous bus engines were idling with a groaning cadence that hampered normal conversation. Passengers were unloading from some buses while other coaches were filling up. The public address system was announcing the arrivals and departures while several scruffy looking men, both black and white, roughly loaded and unloaded luggage and freight from the bus cargo bins.

Mickey started to tremble as he tightly hugged his father's neck.

"Ralph, I need to use the restroom, and I'm sure Mickey does too. I'm afraid to go here. SO many people."

"Hold on 'til we get over to the Kentucky Bus station. Jim said he thought it was between Jefferson and Liberty Street and jest west of Second Street. Jim says there ain't as many people over there. I'll ask that cop over there to make sure where we're goin'. Only got an hour 'fore the Kentucky Bus leaves, and we gotta step on it."

The Atlees raced from the Greyhound station to the Kentucky Bus depot as Mickey hugged his father's neck for balance while they walked. He looked over his father's shoulder at the large Greyhound building. The structure had a large Greyhound sign mounted horizontally across the front and topped by a second sign anchored vertically. The building had rounded corners, indicative of cars, planes, trains, and busses of the era and similar to Greyhound depots across the country.

The Kentucky Bus station was much quieter. Anna took Mickey and went to the restroom while Ralph purchased the tickets.

"Man says we got 'bout half an hour 'fore the bus gets here."

"Ralph, we orta drink us a Coke while we wait. Still a long way to go 'fore we get to Beaver Dam."

"NAW, jest make ye wanna pee, 'specially this youngun' here. Be there in no time, and we can get us a hamburger and a Coke while we wait on Jesse. Chances are he won't be a waitin' on us."

"Now, Ralph, I put some ice in this pint fruit jar to wipe this youngun's face 'case he gets sick. Been a spell since he had his breakfast. That Kentucky Bus may not be air conditioned. If it ain't, we're gonna parch."

"We can hold out."

When the Kentucky Bus pulled into the station, Anna jumped as the ticket agent sang out his call on the public address system.

"Folks, the Kentucky Bus for Paducah is a loadin' right outside for E-Town, Clarkson, Caneyville, Leitchfield, Beaver Dam, Central City, Greenville, and Paducah. Get yere tickets ready. All aboard."

The Kentucky Bus was a silver and red 1941 model Flxible Clipper with seating for twenty-five passengers. Flxible claimed to be the first manufacturer to have air conditioning, but on this day the Atlees would not be riding one of those. The twelve-year-old vehicle showed it had been wrecked, and several windows were cracked. The KBL was a small company that operated predominantly commuter lines in the Louisville area, plus the cross-state route to Paducah. The company seldom had more than a dozen buses in its fleet, and none that compared favorably to the coaches operated by Greyhound and Trailways.

Ralph picked Mickey up in his arms and followed Anna aboard the bus. They were followed by a dozen more passengers, who handed their tickets to a portly driver standing at the top of the steps. The heat on the vehicle was stifling, as Anna quickly took a seat by an open window.

"Gonna set here. May be the only window that'll open. Yessir, wait 'til Beaver Dam to get a Coke. The Greyhounds is all air-conditioned ... ride in style. Sooner cook in that hot kitchen. Least ways I could drink a Coke or get a drink of water." Anna fussed as she took her seat.

"Now, when we get started, the air is gonna roll in here, and it won't be that bad. No worse than the truck."

"Hot 'nough to roast a hoot owl in here. This baby is gonna get sick as a dog and me too. All yere fault."

"Yere the one wanted to go home for the Fourth of July. Yessir, one ride on an air-conditioned Greyhound and got ye spoiled rotten."

The KBL driver's uniform was soaked with perspiration as he counted his tickets and sorted them by destination. He fastened them to a clipboard and went inside the terminal. The Flxible's engine was idling roughly, causing the bus to rock slightly from side to side. The cargo handler was busy tossing suitcases and freight roughly into the cargo bin.

"The ticket man said this the second bus goin' to Paducah. First one left full, everybody goin' to Paducah. Called up this one as a backup. Holiday and all. Looks of this thing it must be a spare."

"The first one was probably air-conditioned. Did ye get us a cut rate fer ridin' this junker?"

"Ye ain't gonna let up are ye? Honey, where did that driver go to? Like to get this show on the road."

The KBL driver emerged from the station drinking a Coke. When the Coke was gone, he placed the empty bottle in a 24 slotted wooden drink case leaning against the side of the building. The man did not appear pleased about something as he nervously checked his watch.

"Ralph, is that buzzard gonna stand there all day drinkin' Cokes? Don't he know this thing is hot as a firecracker?"

"Some kinda holdup I guess. OH, there comes yere answer. Look."

Three Negro men emerged from the KBL depot and handed their tickets to the driver, who took them without even an upward glance. The men were young and dressed in work overalls. They walked slowly toward the bus and acted bewildered when they came aboard. The driver followed them aboard and watched as they walked slowly down the aisle.

"You boys, keep goin' all the way to the back of the bus. NO where else."

The driver's voice clearly revealed his disgust for the young Negroes. He shook his head, frowned, and climbed under the wheel. The bus resisted being shifted into reverse and then slowly backed away from the depot. When the driver shifted into first gear, he glanced once again into his rearview mirror.

"HEY, did ye hear what I said? NOW get back there."

Ralph and Anna looked back toward the rear of the bus and saw one of the Negroes seated halfway. He got up, glared at the driver, and joined the others in the rear of the vehicle.

The Kentucky Bus made its way down Highway 61 and traveled through the communities of Okolona, Mount Washington, and Shepherdsville in Bullitt County. For bus travelers in the early 1950s, like the Atlees, Shepherdsville was a quiet agricultural community that showed no evidence of the salt production boom that highlighted the area during its early years or the mineral spa named Paroquet Springs, an important resort in the years preceding the Civil War. KBL did not have an official stop in Sheperdsville, but a man and woman flagged the bus down from a street corner.

The bus went from Shepherdsville to Lebanon Junction, another lazy town that had seen a heyday as a refueling depot for the Louisville and Nashville Railroad come and go. Two passengers departed at Lebanon Junction. The town did not have an official bus stop, but two men got on alongside the road.

From Lebanon Junction the KBL went to Boston in Nelson County. Kentucky Highway 61 joined at Boston on Lick Creek with U.S. Highway 62. The bus would transfer to Highway 62 and proceed to the next official bus stop in Elizabethtown.

When the bus entered Elizabethtown, Ralph started looking for the Greyhound station.

"Anna, looks like the Greyhound depot a comin' up ahead."

"GOOD, ye run in there and get us all a Coke. This child is hot and white as a sheet."

The E-town depot was located on South Mulberry and Helm Streets. A two-foot by four-foot Greyhound sign adorned the front of the plain concrete block building. The large windows in front exposed a 1600 square foot building equipped with a ticket desk and a waiting room. In the 1930s the downtown Joplin Hotel was the bus station. During World War II when thousands of soldiers flocked to nearby Fort Knox, the number of buses to accommodate them overwhelmed that facility; and the depot was moved to the Mulberry and Helm location to allow several buses to pull off the city street.

Ralph was raking through his change when the bus came to a stop. The driver climbed out of his seat and made an announcement.

"Folks, this here is E-town. Ain't gonna be here no more than five minutes or so. Don't wander off no wheras. Next rest stop is Leitchfield."

"Honey, I see a Coke machine in there. Won't take me a jiffy."

Ralph raced off the bus behind the driver and went into the station. Anna's heart stopped when he came back out almost immediately empty handed. He walked back to the bus, stood by the door looking around for a minute before coming aboard.

"DON'T tell me."

"NOPE, machine as empty as a gun barrel. Guess we gotta wait 'til Leitchfield. We orta brought that thermos jug of mine. Put some ice water in it and we'd be fine."

"Been fine if we had bought a Coke in Louisville. But no. Half this water done gone and Mickey looks like a cholera chicken. I feel like death warmed over myself."

"Honey, Leitchfield ain't that far, and we gonna get us a Coke there. Been through E-town many a time but never looked at much. Right cute little place. Gotta Kroger grocery over on that corner, hardware store over yonder, school over there, and the bus depot right here. Had a church close-by and have everthing a man' needs in life right nearby."

"NO, Ralph. THEY ain't got no cold water or cold Cokes."

"Honey, we ain't got no real cold water at home and no cold Cokes neither. Least ways not 'til we get lights."

"Well water is as cool as ye please. Cold 'nough. When we get lights, I'm gonna get me a refrigerator or bust in the attempt."

"Well, lost a couple folks and got a few more. Throwed off a few boxes and put on a couple more. I think he's ready to go. I can jest barely hear that ticket man a callin' it off. Listen, listen. I LOVE to hear 'em do that." Despite the heat, Ralph was thoroughly enjoying the trip.

The KBL bus left E-town and again picked up Highway 62. Despite its importance in the lives of Kentuckians like the Atlees, few travelers knew the road's importance to the rest of the country. Originating in

Buffalo, New York, Highway 62 entered Kentucky near Maysville in the east, crossed the state, and said farewell at the western border of the Commonwealth at Wickliffe. The highway crossed the Mississippi in pursuit of its final destination at Carlsbad, New Mexico. The road was a favorite of travelers in the 1950s, taking thousands to Kentucky Lake and points west. Author John Steinbeck called the great east-west highway Route 66 the "Mother Road," but in 1953 Highway 62 could easily have been called the "Big Sister."

Hot air poured through the windows of the Kentucky Bus as it traveled through the tiny communities of Summit and Big Clifty before the next official stop at Clarkson. Three passengers got off at Clarkson, and two more got on. After unloading a few small pieces of freight, the bus was back on the road for Leitchfield and the biggest stop on the first leg of the journey.

The temperature inside the bus and the swaying of the vehicle as it meandered down the highway were making Mickey sicker. Anna continued to wipe his face with the water from the small fruit jar, but the container was almost empty. She had been embarrassed to bring a quart jar, but now she wished that she had. Ralph's thermos jug would have been preferable.

The bus stopped in front of a Texaco filling station and restaurant in Leitchfield. The building sported a façade of white tile trimmed with green. Two garage bays were complemented by a tiny café with ten stools for customers. The café was a popular establishment in the county seat of Grayson County. Leitchfield was very proud of the Texaco garage, bus stop, and restaurant when it opened for business in 1942. The Chaudoin Bus Line operated the Louisville to Paducah route in those days and moved their bus stop from the downtown Alexander Hotel to the new facility.

Located on the corner of North Main and West Chestnut Street, the café opened at 4:00 AM for breakfast and closed at midnight. The garage and café closed only for Christmas Day. In addition to the three Kentucky buses daily, the station also served three Trailways coaches daily from Nashville. Café patrons dined on bacon, eggs, toast, and coffee for breakfast plus honey buns, cheeseburgers, and tuna and chicken salad sandwiches for lunch and dinner. Meal times were generally very hectic in the cramped café as employees rushed to serve meals, sell bus tickets, and look up travel information for patrons. Meanwhile, the garage pumped gas, stored bus freight, installed car batteries, changed oil, and tuned up cars.

"Folks, this here is Leitchfield. Gonna be here ten minutes. Be ready to go when I am. Gonna blow the horn, and ye better come runnin'."

Ralph laughed as they followed other passengers off the bus.

"I think that ol' boy was born in a hurry."

"Ralph, listen to me. That little ol' café ain't gonna hold us all. I see a Coke machine right over at the side of the building. Go get us a Coke over there."

Ralph handed Mickey to Anna and started counting his change.

"Ralph, I wish ye would look. Them Cokes is a DIME. Still a nickel over home. Mercy, that's high."

"Reckon they gotta charge that. People take 'em on the bus, and they don't get the bottles back. Well, we need us a drink. Thirty cents ain't a gonna break me this one time."

Ralph found three dimes, transferred them to his left hand, and returned the remaining change and his pocketknife to his right front pocket. He felt a finger punch him in the back and a voice whisper over his shoulder.

"I wish ye would look at that. They got that drink machine blocked. They don't aim to let nobody get to it."

Ralph turned around and faced a large older man who had been seated behind him on the bus.

"Now, gonna take more than a couple of darkies to keep me from gettin' my wife and youngun' a Coke."

"No, Ralph. They mean business. We can hold out fer Beaver Dam."

"Naw, they ain't gonna do nothin'. Jest a standin' there."

Despite Anna's protest, Ralph headed for the drink machine. The three Negro men had formed a half circle in front of the machine with their backs to anyone approaching. An elderly man tried to get between two of the men but was successfully blocked. Ralph walked deliberately and without slowing down slipped his wiry body between the same men before they could react.

"HOWDY, BOYS, hot ain't it? Been spittin' sawdust since E-town."

Ralph never stopped talking or grinning as he went about the business of purchasing three Cokes. He dropped a dime in the machine and pulled a drink out and transferred it to his right hand. He held the narrow vertical door of the machine open with his knee, dropped in the remaining dimes, and extracted the Cokes. When he was done, he was holding one drink in his left hand and the other two held tightly to his body by his arm. The men quietly closed ranks. He knew they were going to try to prevent him from leaving, but Ralph was small and quick. Without warning, he stepped sideways and tried to squeeze between two of the men. They anticipated his move and held fast. For a moment he thought he was in trouble until something about the largest Negro caught his attention.

"WELL, I'll be giggered. Yere ol' Charlie Smith's boy. I orta knowed. Yessir, I remember when ye used to ride that ol' mule with yere daddy up to the house. We wuz jest little shavers. My daddy used to doctor yere daddy's stock."

The look of contempt and defiance on the face of the largest of the three men quickly evaporated. He looked stunned as he stared at Ralph. After a few long moments, without saying a word, he stepped aside.

"Ralph Atlee, that was a foolish thing to do. OH LORD ye forgot to open them things. Wait, I got a bottle opener right here in my purse."

"Plumb forgot to open the durn things. Thought my cake was dough fer a minute. Ye ain't gonna believe it, but one of them men is ol' Charlie Smith's boy. Ain't seen 'im since his mama and pappy died. You remember them. Jest looked at me kinda funny and stepped aside. Other two looked like they wanted to kill me. Reckon they didn't have no money fer a Coke and wuzn't gonna let nobody else have none neither. Can't really blame 'im. Can't even get a drink of water. That little café probably wudn't allow them in the door. Jest mad. They ain't gonna bother nobody."

"Here, ye hold Mickey, my arm is about to break. Make 'im drink that kinda slow, or he'll have hot water a runnin' out his nose."

"Honey, didn't one of them ol' Smith boys go to the pen?"

"Daddy said one did. Sold that place after Charlie and the ol' woman died and went to Owensbur. Heard they got in with some mean people and one cut a white man with a knife and went to the pen. What was their names, Cain and Abel?"

"That's it. Never knowed which was which, but Ma and Pa thought the world and all of Charlie and his ol' woman. Real good people. Worked like dogs. Break their heart to know how them boys turned out. Always wondered why they didn't stay on down there in the Point. Farm awful small, though. Hard to make a livin'. Pa always said he was gonna teach them younguns to read and write but never got 'round to it. If he had, they mighta turned out better. Hard ol' world if ye ain't white."

"Ralph, it ain't jest colored folks who turn bad in the city. Ye remember that preacher's boy from over at McHenry? He went to Chicago and jest went right to the dogs. Found 'im dead under a bridge up there. The city does that to people. Ain't a fit place to live for nobody. My Mama told me once that folks jest act better in places like Walton's Creek and Centertown."

"Reckon so. That's why I hope we don't ever hafta move to no city."

When the bus horn sounded, Ralph rushed to place the empty Coke bottles in one of two drink cases leaning up in front of the building. He raced back, took Mickey in his arms, and they reboarded the bus. They felt better after drinking a Coke; but the afternoon sun was overhead, and the bus was hotter than ever as they left Leitchfield for Caneyville, the second largest community in Grayson County.

"Anna, Big Jim was a tellin' me we orta come up here some time when we ain't cuttin' trees somers. They come up here on Sundays after church to a place called Pine Knob. Lots of shade trees and a spring with water a runnin' outa the side of this hill. Water cold as ice. Good place to get outta the heat."

"Ralph, if they got cold water, we orta go right now."

"There ye go agin'. Risk life and limb to get ye a Coke, and that's the thanks I get."

Ralph leaned back in his seat, laughing. The bus ride had not been difficult for him. He had spent long, hot summers cutting and trimming trees in the heat and had grown accustomed to it. In fact, he had rather enjoyed the little trip.

"You know much 'bout Leitchfield?"

Ralph turned to the elderly man seated next to him, who had gotten on the bus at Leitchfield.

"NO, sir, been through here a bunch is all."

"Well, sir, my name is H.B. Smith. My great-granddaddy was Mordecai Lincoln, ol' Abe's first cousin. Yes sir ol' Mordecai lived right back yonder in Leitchfield. Born here myself. Now ol' Mordecai was no Abe by a long shot. Spent most of his life in court. Plumb near run outta town one time. Had a still in his backyard and some neighbor's hogs got loose, tore down the fence, and got in that brew. Several drunkin' hogs a runnin' all over town. Mordecai was a shoemaker and a born hell raiser. My daddy always said ol' Abe liked his shine a bit, too. Heerd of ol' Cole Younger, I guess? He was my daddy's double first cousin."

Anna looked at Ralph and smiled. Ralph was trapped in a conversation that he neither wanted nor had the power to end. He glanced at the old man occasionally and nodded politely. Fortunately, the old man grew tired of listening to his own voice and nodded off.

The engine and transmission made a rhythmic grinding and humming sound as the Kentucky Bus swayed along the twisting Highway 62. The Atlees knew the trip would soon be over when they passed through Horse Branch in Ohio County. Suddenly the bus started to slow, and they suspected the driver was preparing to pick up another passenger along the side of the road. The driver was laughing.

"WELL, wish ye would look. Ol' Sam gotta load fer Looieville and a headin' in the wrong direction."

When the bus halted, the driver opened the door and hollered, "Get on in here, Sam, ye old scoundrel. Ain't seen ye in so long I figured the buzzards done got ye."

An elderly man wearing an ancient suit coat and faded filthy overhauls and a crumpled black hat struggled aboard, dragging a decrepit suitcase held together by two leather belts. He handed the driver some change and made no attempt to find a seat. The bus started up, and the old man obviously intended to stand next to the driver.

"Sam, are ye still makin' that pond water?"

"YESSIR, that little dab of Ruvavelt pension needs a little help now and agin'. So I run me off a little pond water."

"Ain't never picked ye up a headin' in this direction before. Ain't lost are ye, Sam?"

"NO SIR, I ain't lost. Last time I went to Looisville, and this ol' cop took all my money and poured out my pond water. I tol' 'im I'd been sellin' pond water on them streets 'fore he was borned. Gonna try Padukee this time."

"Knowed ye purt near twenty years now, Sam. Are ye ever gonna get shed of that ol' suitcase? Looks like the rats nested in it."

"Now, ye jest tend to drivin' this here bus and leave my suitcase alone. Over fifty-year-old and them belts almost as old. Folks see this here suitcase; they know it means ginny-wine pond water. If'n it was a tad bigger, I'd be buried in it. This ol' suitcase and me could tell many a story, and most of 'em true."

"OK, Sam, yere kinda a legend, I guess. Ever made that stuff outta anything but pond water?"

"Nope, pond water is the best. I tried all the others, but it ain't the same. Big Revenoo man tol' me one time that moonshine would be legal if it all made from pond water. I tol' 'im I wouldn't know since I didn't make moonshine jest pond water. He plumb near died laughin'. Got 'im good one time. Sold 'im a jar of pond water, and he had me hafway to Owensbur 'fore he found out it really was pond water. Dad blasted Revenoor. Aimed to make a fool outta 'im in court."

"How much money ye get fer that pond water these days, Sam?"

"Well, not as much as I used to. Back durin' the first world war got fifteen dollar a gallon a sellin' it up at Camp Taylor or Knox. Nothin' like that now. Probition best thing ever fer pond water sellin'. Tell folks they can't have it, and ever'body wants it. Lots of folks still do."

Ralph grinned and chuckled as he listened to the conversation between the driver and the old moonshiner. A glance in Anna's direction, however, clearly revealed that she was not impressed. In fact, she looked disgusted.

The bus started to slow as they neared the intersection of Highways 62 and 231. Sheffield's restaurant was located at the intersection, and like the Leitchfield bus stop, was both a garage and a restaurant. The business's location was a strategic one for travelers. Highway 62 temporarily ended there and resumed three blocks away in downtown Beaver Dam. The restaurant, noted for good southern food, catered to travelers in the 1950s and 1960s. As country folk, the Atlees, however, felt more comfortable dining in the downtown café.

The Beaver Dam Cafe in downtown Beaver Dam was the depot for the Kentucky Bus Line. The café had been in business since the 1920s serving travelers, shoppers, and business people.

The bus circled the block behind the restaurant and double-parked directly in front of the café. The elderly man with the ancient suitcase was still chatting away with the driver when the bus stopped. Anna, Ralph, Mickey, and two other passengers got off, and two more got on.

"Anna, I see Blade's truck over yonder."

"Well, if ye would use yere eyes, you'd see 'im a standin' right there."

Blade Caughill was leaning against a light pole with his cap characteristically pushed back on his head. He was chuckling when the Atlees walked up.

"Well, if the three of ye don't look like a bunch of cholera chickens. Them ol' busses get hot, don't they?"

"Jesse, we rode like the Queen of England on that nice cool Greyhound and then roasted on that hot box. Worse of all we had this ol' drunk get on up near Horse Branch with a load of moonshine in a suitcase. Ol' coot smelled worse than a polecat. Overalls hadn't been washed in twenty years."

"You don't mean it. Some ol' geezer with a suitcase full of moonshine. I thought that ol' codger was dead."

Ralph shifted Mickey from his left arm to the right so he could turn and face Blade Caughill.

"Blade, we ain't had a bite since sunup. Somebody forgot to bring 'long any peanut butter and crackers. Can ye wait while we get a hamburger?"

"Fine with me if ye can buy me a cup of coffee."

The Beaver Dam Café was still packed, despite the fact that it was well past noon, and the only available seats were at the counter. Anna always insisted on eating at the counter since she believed the tables were for big shots. Ralph argued that the restaurants don't care where people ate, but Anna held firm that "… clodhoppers ain't welcome at the tables."

Ralph had just finished placing an order for three hamburgers, three bottle Cokes, and a cup of coffee when the Kentucky Bus pulled away to continue along Highway 62 to Central City and Greenville in Muhlenberg County and ultimately to Paducah. Passengers could make connections with other buses in Paducah. The Greyhound and Southern Limited served the Ohio River city, and the Brooks line made several trips weekly to Detroit; but for the Atlee family, the day's travel was over.

Mickey took his hamburger in both hands and started devouring it. Between bites he said, "Hambugger Daddy, hambugger." Blade laughed as he watched the youngster attack the burger.

"Ralph, that youngun' acts like he never seen nothin' to eat."

"Always acts that way with hamburgers. Put some vegetables on his plate, and he pretends to be sick. Like them hambuggers, son?"

"Ralph, when we get home, I want ye to go over to Daddy's and get some eggs fer supper and breakfast in the mornin'. Need a bucket of drinkin' water, too, while yere over there."

"Ralph, ye better take a wheelbarrow for them eggs," laughed Blade. "Pap been gatherin' them twice a day fer ye. Layin' fer who laid the rail. They been eatin' them three meals a day, and they give us five dozen the other day. Don't know what on earth yere a feedin' 'em, but it's workin."

"Now, one more thing 'fore I forget it. Remind me to take back my three-bladed cabbage cutter. Sick and tired of makin' slaw by cuttin' cabbage usin' a cut-off can heated on the stove. Works all right but I burn my fingers. Don't cut good 'less it's red hot."

When Anna Atlee finished giving Ralph instructions, Blade drained his coffee cup and leaned back on the stool and stretched.

"Ralph, job a comin' 'long all right?"

"Fair, I guess. Been awful hot and that's got ol' Pappy down. Don't look fer 'im back next week. He must be seventy and fat as a hog to boot. Done worked the baby fat off that Whitley kid. Real good worker. Big Jim treated 'im bad at first. One night after supper, Jim picked 'im up and tossed 'im into a rose bush, and he didn't have no shirt on. Youn-gun' went out back and come back with a big ol' tree limb. Jim wanted to know what he was gonna do with that, and he tol' 'im he had to go to sleep sometime. Wouldn't get shed of it 'til Jim said he was sorry."

"Ol' Jim is a good feller, but he can be ornery sometimes. Big 'nough to get away with it. Say now, if Pappy don't come back is that gonna leave ye short handed?"

"Yep, could use 'nother man anyway, but boss won't let me hire any-more. You ain't outta work, are ye?"

"Not completely, but things been mighty slow."

"Tell ye what. We get up there, and Pappy don't show, I'll call the Centertown garage and leave word. Get ye a cot, yere tools, and high tail it to Sparta. It ain't hard to find and no bigger than Centertown. When ye get there, ask fer the ol' Taylor place. Shore use yere help to put a new axle in the truck. Got all my tools in it, and we need it on the job."

"Hate to work off a ways, but I reckon a few months won't matter. When ye gonna get done?"

"Hope the first of November. Gotta help Al and Tim kill hogs this winter."

Ralph handed the waitress a dollar bill, and she gave him fifteen cents back. He glanced at the money for a moment and laid it on the counter next to his plate. He picked Mickey up in his arms and started for the door.

"Well, younguns, best get on home. Had 'nough excitement fer one day. Blade ain't a gonna wait on us no longer."

When Blade Caughill and the Atlees walked out of the Beaver Dam Café, a Fitzjohn passenger bus from Fuqua bus line drove by.

"Blade, reckon where that bus is headed?"

"Runs from Bowlin' Green to Owensbur'. Ye orta know that. Been runnin since late '20s I guess. A bunch of 'em a runnin' through here durin' the war a haulin' folks to work over at Ken Rad."

"Yeah, that's the one Anna and me rode back from Owensbur' when we tried our hand a workin' over there. Had to stand up comin' back. Lots of ol' country jakes headed to Owensbur' to work and us headed the other way."

"Oh yeah, Blade, I plumb forgot. A colored boy on the bus was ol' Charlie Smith's kid. Ye remember 'im?"

"Never was 'round 'em much, but Pap always liked Charlie. Said he was a good fella and knowed his place." "Sis, if ye think that ol' moon-shiner smelled bad, ye orta rode that ol' Fuqua bus a few years back when this ol' man come on with his pet hog. Brought 'im right on the bus 'til people started complainin' and they made 'im stop."

"OH, yere makin' that up."

"I ain't done it. Tell her, Ralph."

"Now ye leave me outta this. I don't know nothin' bout no hog 'less it's one we stick and grind up fer sausage."

"Well, this ol' truck is a holy fright but crawl in if ye can."

"Blade, the back end is where I haul my tools. Ye got 'em right up here in the cab and a settin' on 'em."

"Ralph, I ain't got no fancy little house on the back of mine like some folks I know. Besides, nobody ever rides in here but me." Jesse laughed as he started his truck.

"Now, Blade, get ye some two by fours and some tarp and make ye one like I done. Jest the berries to carry tools 'round and not get wet."

Blade Caughill pulled his 1949 Ford pickup away from the curb and drove north from downtown Beaver Dam.

"Ralph, a talkin' 'bout that Fuqua bus a minute ago. I worked on that new WPA bridge over the river there at Hartford fer a while. They went up river there a ways and pulled a couple of old wooden ferries together and tied 'em to the bank to make a temporary bridge. Cut the bank down on the south side of the river but still steep as all billy get out. Ever day that ol' boy would come through a drivin' an ol' Packard, and on top he had 15 or 20 cases of milk fer the CC camp there at Hartford. Ever day I bet this ol' boy I worked with he wouldn't make it, but he would cross them old rickety ferries and gun that thing and up that bank he would go. Never failed."

"Blade, yere ol' pappy knowed the fella that started that, and he tol' me one time he got into that when he heard they was gonna gravel the road from Hartford to Owensbur'.'"

"I guess that's right. When they built the road from Morgantown to Bowlin' Green, they seen a chance to run from there all the way to Owensbur'. 'For' that if ye didn't catch the train outa here in the winter time ye didn't go no where much. Morgantown up there had the river, and that was 'bout the only way to get terbacker or anything to Bowlin' Green."

"Musta been real bad fer folks back 'for' the trains and decent roads. Folks wuz jest stuck here and hard to get stuff in and out, too. You know, Blade, ol' man tol' me one time back when the fort was here at Hartford, ye had to walk through the woods and all to get from the Ohi' River over where Owensbur is now. Then a man had to stand off a ways and holler to folks to get permission to come in. Folks stand out there with a rifle trained on ye."

"Ralph, I don't doubt that one particle. We seen a world of change since we been alive. Gonna see lots more. No tellin' what my boy and that youngun' of yours is gonna see. Pap was a great big kid fore he got to come to Hartford."

In 1953 a person could still catch the L&N train at Centertown and ride to Hartford for a dime. The Illinois Central railroad still serviced Beaver Dam, but in a few short years all passenger service would end in the county. In 1941 the L&N removed the track from Hartford to Ellmitch, thus severely limiting train service to the county seat. The trains the county had fought so hard to obtain were starting to fade as roads were improved and cars became more plentiful. Anna Atlee's dream of traveling back home from Sparta by train would remain just that.

In the 1830s travelers could take the stagecoach from Louisville to Nashville, a two-day trip of more than one hundred and eighty miles for a twelve-dollar fare. The Atlees had finished a somewhat shorter trip, absent the overnight stays and the possibility of bandits along the route. Their trip had been faster and more comfortable, but the adventure of the trip and the quaint communities and bus stops along the way made the excursion memorable.

The conversation ceased as Ralph, Anna, and Mickey snuggled together in the cab of Blade Caughill's 1949 pickup. Ralph had to move his leg when Blade shifted gears, and the open windows sucked hot air like those on the Kentucky Bus, along with an occasional horsefly. The trucks of the time were not built for style, comfort, or transportation; but for the Atlees, all this truck needed to do was get them from Beaver Dam to Walton's Creek for the Fourth of July weekend.

The weekend that Anna Atlee wanted so desperately was uneventful. She spent three hours visiting her mother on Saturday afternoon. Jes Caughill and Ralph caught a mess of bluegill in Morrison's Pond, and they all enjoyed a fish supper. Mickey had the opportunity to renew his friendship with the family dog, and on Sunday they all squeezed back in Blade Caughill's truck for the ride to Beaver Dam. The Kentucky Bus was just as hot during the ride back to Louisville, but this time Anna Atlee held a gallon canning jar of ice water on her lap. She wasn't happy the Beaver Dam Café charged her a nickel for the ice, and most of it would be gone before they arrived back at the Gypsy Grill.

The Possum Hunters (1954)

THE POSSUM HUNTERS
(1954)

*F*ROM THE TIME *he was a small child, Mickey had been fascinated by the stories adults told about a vigilante group known as the Possum Hunters. He knew they terrorized much of Western Kentucky some years after the Kentucky Tobacco War. He had heard tales about people who were beaten, local men who belonged, and the way Hunters gripped the community with fear for two years. He was equally perplexed that well-meaning people thought they did a lot of good by punishing criminals and lazy people while others chastised them for allowing unsavory types to use the organization for personal gain. That degree of fear and the division in the community had not been seen since the Civil War days.*

Mickey squirmed around to get a more comfortable position in the truck seat as his mind prepared to relive the tale of the Possum Hunters.

It was a hot July day in 1954 when sixty-four-year-old Jes Caughill walked out the back door of the Hartford courthouse. His long, lanky frame was bent from over thirty years in underground country coal mines. He pulled a can of Velvet Smoking Tobacco from his pocket and quickly but awkwardly rolled a cigarette. Despite a lifetime of practice, rolling cigarettes was an art Jes had never perfected. The cigarette dangled from his lips like it would fall at any moment. He had lost his teeth many years ago but could never be persuaded to get false teeth. His face was now sunken, and his lips seemed to be hiding inside his mouth.

Jes had just finished testifying as a character witness in court for a man that he hardly knew. He looked up and down the street from under the brim of his old hat. After tossing the cigarette, he pulled his Ingersoll Radiolite pocket watch out by a metal fob embossed with the image of a Caterpillar bulldozer. It was after 1:00 PM, and he had eaten breakfast at 5:00 AM. He had rushed out the door and forgotten to put some sausage and biscuits in his pocket. The Car Barn Restaurant on Main Street was a familiar sight, and he headed that way.

The Car Barn was located across the street from the front door of the courthouse and was a popular eating establishment. The café was nearly full when Jes walked through the door. Police officers, lawyers in suits, business people, and shoppers jammed the facility. Saturday was Hartford's busiest shopping day as country folks flocked to town to purchase grocery items, hardware, and dry goods.

Jes did not bother to see if the Car Barn crowd included anyone he knew. He spotted a stool at the counter and straddled it without a glance around the room. A waitress walked over with a glass of water and a menu. Jes shook his head and waved off the menu. He ordered coffee, a hamburger, and French fries. The food was soon devoured, and he asked for a second cup of coffee and a piece of pie. Jes seldom ate in a restaurant, but the food was good and a welcome change from the usual fare of beans, potatoes, hominy, and cornbread he had at home.

The waitress placed Jes's ticket face down on the counter as he was eating the last bite of pie. She did not appear inclined to pour a third cup of coffee, and he was not about to ask. He turned the ticket over and looked with disgust at what he saw: coffee ten cents, hamburger fifteen cents, fries ten cents, and apple pie fifteen cents. He fished two quarters out of his pocket and slapped them down hard on the counter muttering to himself, " … nickel worth of food fer fifty cents … damn money-makin' racket." Jes walked out the door of the Car Barn café fuming about the free enterprise system and how it was out to take advantage of poor people.

Jes retraced his steps back across Main Street to the courthouse. The rock retaining wall around the center of justice was filled with men who frequented the area either on a daily basis or on Saturday afternoons when weather permitted. The area was a meeting place for retired coal miners, farmers, and timber workers who told stories about their glory days and criticized the younger generation for being lazy and shiftless. Younger men congregated there less frequently. Women avoided the area like it was diseased, and many defied their husbands to be caught anywhere near what they viewed as a den of lies, profanity, amber, knife dropping, and occasionally a bottle of whiskey.

A bench under a shade tree on the backside of the courthouse was whimsically referred to as the "Liars' Bench." Most women looked upon the rickety old bench as the center of unregenerate behavior. A brief stint on the retaining wall could be tolerated, but any husband who ventured to the infamous Liars' Bench could expect a harsh lecture, while others occasionally found themselves bodily pulled off the bench by their spouse. Jes recalled a woman's response to her husband when he asked how she knew he was sitting on the Liars' Bench. She clasped her hands together, looked up at the sky, and said, "the LORD told me."

Jes walked past about twenty or thirty men seated on the wall. Still angry, he did not look in their direction. His nose, however, detected a cornucopia of aromas. Many men who lived in the country came to town not only for a haircut at one of the local barbershops, but for a shave as well. Some did not own a razor and frequented the barbershops on Saturdays for a shave. Most workingmen of the era never shaved more than once a week unless it was a special occasion. The fragrance of bay rum mingled with that of cigarette, cigar and pipe tobacco, amber, lye soap, body odor, plus the unmistakable smell of whiskey.

Other male members of the community also shunned the patriarchal crowd around the courthouse. Lawyers, doctors, merchants, and above all ministers looked upon the scene with almost as much disdain as the women. Politicians, however, were frequently seen mingling with the crowd, as was the Sheriff when he needed to seat a jury.

Jes found the Liars' Bench unoccupied, and this suited him as he continued to fume over the fifty cent lunch. He crossed his legs and pulled a plug of Apple chewing tobacco from his pocket. The small blade on his pocketknife was well worn from many years of cutting tobacco and dipping snuff. Jes felt a knife blade, like a good hoe, wasn't any good until it was half worn out.

The minutes ticked by, and Jes spit out the remains of his chew of tobacco. A man sat down hard next to him, but he paid the man no mind as he pulled out his Velvet Tobacco can and rolled a cigarette. Once the cigarette was gone, Jes once again peeled off a piece of chewing tobacco. He was daydreaming and only barely conscious of what he was doing. Suddenly, he was snapped back to reality when the man next to him called his name. Jes jumped slightly as he turned to face the man who intruded upon his solitude.

"Mind if I chaw with ye a spell, Jes?"

The speaker was a few years older than Jes, dressed in badly faded overhauls with a cloudy eye that gazed off to one side and a small number of badly tobacco stained teeth. Jes recognized him as a fellow worker from his mining days.

"Mike Stewart, I didn't see ye come up there."

"Been a settin' here ten minutes. Thought I was gonna need to hit ye with a rock. Jes, it's been a long time. What brings ye to Hartford?"

Jes seemed unaware of Mike's question as he looked at him. "Mike, been five year ago that we worked over at the Baker mines. Ain't that right?"

"Sound 'bout right to me. Course I don't remember so good no more. Doc says I got high blood, and I must be gettin' close to seventy. Don't rightly know. Don't really give a damn. Workin' any wheras these days?"

"Naw. Help the Atlee boys with a little hog killin' is all. Taught them boys how to kill hogs when they wuz jest little shavers. Too little then to do it by theirselves and now they think they can't do it without me. Raise a little dab of garden, cut firewood, and set on my ass the rest of the time. Don't feel like doin' any more. Wish I did."

The conversation stopped for a few minutes as Jes and Mike peppered the dusty ground in front of the bench with amber. Mike spit the remainder of his twist tobacco out into his hand and tossed it on to the sidewalk. A small dog trotted over, gave it a quick sniff, and walked away.

"Jes, I reckon ye remember them Possum Hunters back in '14 and '15?"

"I reckon so but sooner not. Them was troublin' times."

OH, hell, Jes. Them Possum Hunters done a lot of good 'round here. Put some folks right with God and the law."

"Ain't so, Mike. They hurt a lot of good people who never done nothin' to nobody. Know what I'm talkin' 'bout. They burned barns and whipped people and even killed that ol' darkie over at McHenry, and don't reckon anybody ever paid fer that."

"Jes, I reckon yere right 'bout them hurtin' some good people."

Jes was angry, and Mike Stewart knew when Jes Caughill got mad it was best to leave him alone until he cooled down. The days when vigilantes terrorized the county was one topic where Jes Caughill held very strong views.

"Jes, did ye know there ain't been but two hangins' or so in this county since they built the fort here at Hartford? Fer years the thieves, whores, and no counts have had the run of the place. Possum Hunters put the fear of God in some of 'em. Now understand I wuzn't one of 'em, but I knowed many a one in my day, and they say it did good with folks the law wouldn't touch."

Jes seemed to ignore Mike's comments as he stared straight ahead. Finally, he cleared his throat and, without looking at Mike, said, "HEERD from many a feller ye wuz one of 'em. Deny it all ye want. Orta be ashamed."

"Jes, ye knowed me thirty years, and I swear I never whipped a man in my life or burned a man's barn. Never even whipped my own kids. GOD knows they needed it."

"Mike, Pap and me went to a meetin' over at Walton's Creek School when they got that up. Thought it was gonna be a meetin' over a tobacco pool. Get more money fer terbacker. All they could talk 'bout was all the meanness goin' on and doin' sumpin' 'bout it. We never went back. If a man sins, that's 'tween 'im and God. Breaks the law it's 'tween 'im and the Sheriff. Ain't none of my business if he ain't doin' nothin' to me."

"Jes, I never rode the goat back then, and I'm too old now. I'm a tellin' ye it's high time the Possum Hunters rode out again. Been some talk over at McHenry and Beaver Dam, too. Some of the old Possum Hunters is a talkin' it up. Tryin' to get 'nough boys interested so they can have a meetin' over at the ol' gamblin' house later on in the fall."

"Mike, you and me is ol' men, and most of the Possum Hunters is older. Bunch of tommy rot."

"I know that, but they aim to get some of these young bucks in to do the heavy work. Old timers aim to be the leaders."

The conversation stalled again as Jes thought back to the troubling times when he was a young man with a wife and baby. Farming was a sideline for him as he spent most of his years in the coal mines; but many of the Possum Hunters came from the ranks of the coal miners, and this troubled Jes. A miner had to be able to trust a fellow miner, and the secrecy and treachery of the vigilantes threatened that bond.

Mike Stewart sat patiently and waited for an opportunity to start the conversation again. Meanwhile, Jes and Mike observed Haygood Hensley walking down the street. Hensley was the city police chief, a title often scoffed at by old timers who preferred the title of Town Marshal. Hensley was a new breed of lawman who, unlike the marshals of another time, wore a uniform and drove a police car equipped with a radio, red lights, and siren. Many parts of rural Kentucky were not yet acquainted with the modern tools of law enforcement. Nearby Beaver Dam once had a city marshal who did not own a car or a gun. He enforced the law with a very powerful fist and transported prisoners to jail in a taxicab. Hensley had learned to be patient with people who had yet to learn that a police car with lights and siren was a signal to stop.

Hensley came on the scene in Hartford the same year that Kentucky introduced a statewide law enforcement agency. Frankfort had argued that with so many cars there was a need for a police agency whose jurisdiction transcended county lines. Many local officials feared it was an attempt by the state capital to drain off local power and control. Federal agents were the principal agents in pursuit of moonshine stills, and they had soon learned some sheriffs and state police could be trusted to assist and some could not. For many officers in Kentucky, the laws that needed enforcing were still a matter of opinion.

Jes and Mike could tell by Hensley's demeanor that this was not one of his periodic strolls to keep alcohol use to a minimum. They watched him walk past the Liars' Bench and in the direction of Main Street. Suddenly, a man rolled off the retaining wall and sprawled on the sidewalk. No one went to his aid, and it was obvious he wasn't sick. Hensley, a powerfully built man, reached down and pulled the man to his feet with one hand. He held on to the back of his overhauls and gave him a boot in the seat of the pants with his knee. The man bolted upright and with some encouragement from Hensley was soon walking toward the county jail. After a few yards his will began to decline, and once again Hensley applied some friendly persuasion. The knee-boot routine was repeated several times before they reached the jail.

Jes and Mike joined a chorus of chuckles that accompanied the Chief and his prisoner as they made their way around the courthouse en route to the jail. Hensley tempered law enforcement with a degree of common sense. Drunks who had not committed any other crime and did not resist arrest seldom went to court. Hensley frequently told the jailer to release them after they sobered up. Many drunks who preferred jail to the tongue-lashing that awaited them at home frequently went to the police station to turn themselves in and occasionally woke Hensley up at night or got him away from the supper table.

The men around the courthouse square enjoyed the arrest of the drunk. Hensley used such occasions to send a message. He could easily have driven his car to the scene and transported the man with less effort. Hensley did not make a lot of arrests, and he was fond of saying, "… walkin' them lasts longer and everbody gets a good look."

The tension between Mike and Jes had evaporated, as Jes was clearly amused by the scene with the drunk. The conversation about the Possum Hunters resumed. Three more men joined them on the bench, including an elderly man who leaned forward heavily on his cane. After a few minutes the old man bolted upright and looked at Mike Stewart.

"WHAT was that ye said?" The old man's voice echoed obvious irritation.

"I said we wuz a talkin' 'bout them Possum Hunters." Mike Stewart's reply revealed his annoyance at being interrupted.

"POSSUM Hunters. Them damned sons of bitches." The frail elderly man struggled to his feet muttering under his breath. He made his way to the edge of the retaining wall and nearly fell as he got down to the sidewalk, stomped the concrete with his cane, and walked away.

"Jes, did ye know that ol' feller?"

"Don't reckon I do, Mike."

"NOW, if I ain't mistakin', he's the one with a brother who had a big farm up 'round Cromwell. Some big shot in the Possum Hunters, I ain't a sayin' who, wanted that farm but the ol' boy wudn't sell. Give 'im the chance a time or two and then laid a bundle of switches on his porch and a warnin'. Stubborn cuss and still wudn't sell. Took 'im out one night and beat hell outta his hide. Sold then and left the country. His brother blowed off a lot 'bout what happened, and they sent 'im a warning that he was next. He sent word back that he'd be a waitin' on the front porch with a pound of lead. They let 'im alone after that. NO, NO, I got that wrong. 'Fore that they burned his barn and killed two of his horses. That's when he said come on."

"Jest what I was a sayin', Mike. Good folks got hurt."

"Jes, I agree with ye. Wuzn't always good. Now, I swear to God I had nothin' to do with any of that. Jest heerd plenty."

The two remaining men who had joined Jes and Mike on the Liars' Bench had been listening intently to the conversation. One man, a farmer from near Olaton, signaled that he wanted to speak by clearing his throat.

"Boys, them was bad times. I was workin' in the mines over at Echols back then. They said they was a 'Do Good Organization,' and that's what started the shootin' down there. You boys probably remember the coal company store down yonder back then. Possum Hunters got the idée that the fellas a runnin' the store was laid up there with a couple of women and doin' some drinkin' and gamblin' and the like. Possum Hunters aimed to get 'em, but somebody tipped 'em off. The night they come fer 'em, they was barricaded in there with a bunch of guns and bullets. They knowed they was gonna hit 'em after one of 'em went out to get the mailbag the train dropped. About 11:00 o'clock at night. They run up the back steps and tried to bust door down with a crosstie. All hell broke loose. Musta been a hundred shots fired, and a bunch of them Possum Hunters got hit, but none killed. They dropped that ol' crosstie and high tailed it. Them ol' boys in the store was plenty scared, too, and they got on some horses and lit out of there for Central City."

"I remember that. Jes probably does, too."

"Mike, what I recall is that the ol' Possum Hunter doctor or least ways they tol' it, run 'round all the next day a treatin' the worse outbreak of pneumonia in years." Jes finished his remark as he scratched at a spot of dandruff on the back of his head.

"What I aimed to tell ye boys, too, is that they say the Possum Hunters come back after them ol' boys lit outta there and shot the place up to make it look like a bigger fight than it was." The Olaton farmer finished his story, looked at his watch, and said, "... been good talkin' to ye fellas."

"Jes, didn't wanna said nothin' while that feller wuz here, but he got part of that story of the Echols shootin' all wrong. I heerd that one of them storekeepers was a Possum Hunter. He wuz supposed to hide the guns when his partner went to get the mail. Double-crossed 'em, don't ye see. He wuz the bookkeepin' man, I think. Ever Possum Hunter I ever knowed said one thing fer sure, the guns wuzn't hid and more than one man a shootin.' Some figured them women wuz shootin', too, but I don't think they wuz there. Ol' boys rode off by theirselves. Also heerd the ol' storekeeper seen this hand get inside the door when they was a bustin' on it with that crosstie, and he jest aimed where he figured that feller's belly wuz and fired. Got 'im in the gut. Good thing it wuz jest buckshot. Rifles and pistols, and a bunch of 'em mighta died that night. As it was, none hurt too serious."

"Mike, ye shore know lots 'bout somethin' ye didn't have nothin' to do with."

"Well, Jes, I learned lots of it a settin' on this here bench."

The last man on the bench with Jes and Mike then decided to speak.

"I was jest a boy a livin' over at McHenry back in them days and actually heard the shot that killed that colored fella'. My daddy knowed that ol' colored man and the man who shot 'im. Can't remember the old darkie's name to save my life, but he was from Beaver Dam and left when he and his ol' woman started havin' trouble. Moved in with the biggest bootlegger in the county. Ever'body knowed the Possum Hunters was gonna wait on 'im sooner or later. Done warned 'im to stop sellin' whiskey.

"Way my daddy told it, the night they went out to get that ol' boy, they took the old colored man 'long to keep 'im from givin' the alarm. Had no intention of layin' a hand on 'im. I reckon a bunch of white men a wearin' hoods, overcoats, and carryin' guns at night gonna scare hell outta any darkie ...would me. They say he wuz so scared he broke and run, and one of them Hunters drew his pistol and shot 'im dead. Didn't get fifty feet and shot in the back. Bunch of Possum Hunters was plenty riled 'bout that. Said there was no excuse fer what he did, especially shootin' a man in the back. Some fella went to the pen over it, but others say he wuzn't the one. Don't rightly know."

The story of a man dying at the hands of the Possum Hunters sobered the group for a few minutes. Jes's hands trembled as he rolled another cigarette. Mike Stewart twisted uncomfortably on the bench. Jes thought he was acting like a man with a guilty conscience.

Mike Stewart finally broke the silence. He spat a long stream of amber and turned to the storyteller.

"Who wuz the fella that went to the pen? The one who done it or the one they say done it?"

"Well, I think he's dead. Been dead a long time, and anyhow he still got livin' kin 'round. I ain't gonna say no more than that. All that was no more than a half mile from our house, and the shot woke me up. Next mornin' at the breakfast table Pap told us all 'bout it."

The man got to his feet, stretched, and yawned. "Well, fellers," he said. "Gotta get goin' or the ol' lady gonna peel my onion."

Mike and Jes were left alone on the Liar's Bench. Jes finished his cigarette and thumped it at a squirrel observing them from a few feet away. The animal obviously knew it was not a scrap of food and ignored it.

"Mike, since ye know so much 'bout Possum Hunters, tell me, is it true they wuz much worse over in Muhlenberg County? Always heerd they wuz."

"I reckon so, Jes. Now, here comes a man down the street that can tell ye more 'bout that than I can."

Jes observed a portly, bald-headed man walking down the sidewalk and eyeing the Liars' Bench with a frown on his face. Mike Stewart started laughing and slapping his leg.

"E.P., get yereself up here and tell us some lies."

The man struggled to climb the wall and walk up the slight incline to the bench. He plopped down, breathing hard and perspiring like a man who had been running a long distance. He pulled a red handkerchief from his pocket and mopped the sweat from his face and bald head.

"E.P., this here is Jes Caughill. Jes is from down 'round Centertown and Walton's Creek. A coal miner like us."

"Yere youngun' married one of them Atlee boys down there. Is that right?"

"One and the same."

"Glad to meet ye, Jes. How ye been, Mike?"

"Fair to middlin', I guess. E.P., me and Jes and some of the boys wuz jest talkin' bout them Possum Hunters back in '14 and '15. Ye worked mines in Central City back then."

"Shore did and damn lucky to still be alive to talk 'bout it. Bad over here but worse over there. I wudn't join 'em, and that didn't suit. Ol' lady said she would leave me if I did. One of 'em was a friend of mine, and he kept sayin' I had to join. Straw boss at the mines put me on nights, and that saved my bacon fer a year or so. Can't go on a raid if yere workin'. Ye see they wanted lots of folks along on raid. Safety in numbers. Finally, they said I had to go on a raid even if I didn't join. One night they took a big bunch of non-members on a raid over here in Ohio County."

"What was the idée of that, E.P.?"

"Jes, them lawyers was gettin' State's evidence and the like, and they was gettin' scared up. Got Ohio County boys to come to Muhlenberg County to whip folks, and the Possum Hunters over there come over here. Thought it would throw the law off. 'Bout thirty of us non-members come over here that night when they whipped this fella up 'round Horton. Him and his wife. Now the non-members didn't do nothin'. A hun'erd yards away at the time, but they got an awful beatin'. Ol' boy wrote a poem later and printed it on a broadside with their picture. Possum Hunters said we had to keep quiet since we was as guilty as they was."

"E.P., didn't they shoot out the man's winder lights?"

"Jest one shot to get 'im to come out. Man was pleadin' fer mercy and askin' why they was doin' it. Pleaded fer his wife, too, but it done no good. Beat the livin' daylights outta both of 'em."

"Jes, did ye ever see that poem the fella wrote?"

"Mike, I don't reckon so but heerd 'bout it. Dead now, ain't they?"

"I reckon. Never knowed 'em. Never knowed why they got whipped but said friends and relatives wuz in the mob. Sumpin' personal, I guess."

E.P. mopped his face, neck, and head a second time. The blood looked as if it would burst through his skin. He acted as if he was not comfortable talking about the Possum Hunters as he looked down at the ground for a moment and shook his head.

"I never went on any more raids. Things was gettin' hot on 'em 'bout that time. The law was plenty fed up and lots of folks was. Folks got real scared when they found ol' Mack Shoals a hangin' to that tree. Ever'body knowed he was the Muhlenberg County leader of the Possum Hunters. Nobody had any idée who hung 'im. Possum Hunters swore they was gonna get even, but I think they was spooked, too."

"Friend of mine was there when they cut 'im down, and he swore right then he was dead when they hung 'im. Saw a hangin' once when a fella killed hisself. Said his eyes was near popped outa his head. Ol' Mack wasn't like that. Look like he jest went to sleep. Neck not broke neither."

"OH HELL, E.P., the law hung ol' Shoals."

"Ain't so, Mike. I always figured they knowed 'bout it and didn't give a damn. Never tried to find out who done it. Now, over the years I found out what happened. A bunch of anti-Possum Hunters got together. They decided to grab ol' Mac and make 'im tell all there was to know about the group. Called 'im outta the house in his gown tail and throwed a sack over his head, put 'im in a car, and drove down to the mines. He wudn't talk so they shocked 'im with a generator and that shore got his attention. Begged 'em to stop, but when they did, he clammed up agin'. Shocked 'im agin' but forgot and let a charge build up and killed 'im deader than hell. Stumped then. Didn't have any idee what to do next, so they jest took 'im out and hung 'im to that tree. Didn't aim to do it."

"E.P., that's quite a story. Seems like we heerd a little 'bout that down at Centertown, but we heerd so much back then. Did ye know any of the fellas that hung that fella?"

"EVER damn one of 'em, Jes, and by God I'll take their names to my grave. They done the right thing. Took guts to do what they done, and they didn't aim to kill nobody. Shoals was a cold blooded son-of-a-bitch from all I heard. Everbody said so."

"E.P., them lawyers was a gettin' them indictments up 'bout that time."

"Mike, yere right, and that's why they needed information outta Mack Shoals. He swore that nobody was gonna go to jail. Set out to scare any man who might set on a jury. Workin', too. Ol' Mack and some Possum Hunters a wearin' masks rode their horses right into Greenville and paraded 'round the courthouse. Had a big ol' flag with the picture of a possum on it. Never said a word but folks got the message. Still scared after he got killed. Governor offered two-hun'erd dollar reward fer who done it, and the Possum Hunters said they was gonna kill who done it. Scary times they was."

"E.P., I know the law called a big meetin' over there and said to everybody all was gonna be alright. Tried to calm folks down."

"I went to that meetin', Mike. Now some folks, and ye can include me in that, thinks that some of the Possum Hunters wanted to end it as well. Men like Shoals was scarin' the hell outta ever'body. Some wasn't agin' killin' people. Some of us think that some of the more peaceful Possum Hunters helped the law put an end to it. The law shore was startin' to find out a lot from somewhere."

E.P. struggled down from the top of the wall and left Jes and Mike alone on the Liar's Bench. Both men remained quiet for a few minutes until Mike Stewart tried to restart the conversation about the Possum Hunters. Jes seemed lost in thought and almost oblivious to Mike's presence.

"Jes, I heerd when they had them trials over at Greenville, lawyer said that a way one Possum Hunter knowed 'nother was by a safety pin under his lapel. Said after they tol' that in court the floor was plumb full of safety pins."

Jes did not act as if he heard anything Mike had said. For a few minutes Mike sat on the bench, obviously uncomfortable, before getting to his feet and saying, "... been good a talkin' to ye, Jes."

The afternoon wore on and Jes sat alone on the bench. A car horn startled him back to reality. He stood up, stretched, and raced into the back door of the courthouse to relieve himself. When he left the building, the jailer was locking the doors, and Jes knew he had let the time slip away. A quick check of his pocketwatch revealed that he had ten minutes to meet the mail carrier behind the post office. He walked quickly to Main Street, looked both ways, and crossed the street. The post office was about a hundred feet down Peach Tree Alley, with a narrow passage between it and the only other building on that side of the street. Jes ducked down the well-worn path and emerged at the loading dock for the post office.

Jes had just arrived at the rear of the post office when he saw Frank Hendley's 1950 Ford pickup turn off Washington Street and enter the parking lot. For a moment the gears protested being shifted into reverse before Hendley backed his truck to within a foot of the loading platform. The large doors at the rear of the building opened with a loud thumping noise as the Hartford postmaster came out dragging two large bags of mail. Hendley tossed four bags of mail out of his truck onto the dock, and the postmaster deposited his bags into the back of the truck. Hendley had built a wooden frame on the back of his truck and had covered it with a tarpaulin. This protected the mail as well as an occasional passenger from the elements.

Hendley was a private contractor who carried the mail from Cromwell to Beaver Dam to Hartford and on to Centertown twice daily. Truck deliveries were starting to replace trains on shorter routes. Different trains served Hartford and Beaver Dam, but Hartford could still ship mail to Centertown by the L&N.

"Jes, got Miz Sadie in the front. Mind ridin' back here?"

Without a word, Jes crawled in the back of the truck, took a seat on a mailbag, and draped his elbow over the side of the tailgate to steady his ride. He swore at himself at nearly missing a ride home, especially since he thought the train had already run for the day.

The nine-mile trip from Hartford to Centertown took about ten minutes. Jes always enjoyed looking out the back end of a moving vehicle. "Least ways," he said, "ye know nobody is a chasin' ye." Hendley slowed nearly to a stop to allow a log truck to cross the iron bridge that spanned Muddy Creek about two miles out of Hartford. Jes looked carefully at the corn crops growing in the creek bottoms that flanked the road the first few miles of the route. The road to Centertown was winding and twisting, but Jes could still remember traveling the old dirt road in a Model T or a road wagon.

Hendley pulled up in front of the Centertown Post Office, and Jes handed him the mailbags marked for Centertown before climbing out of the vehicle. He dropped a dime into Hendley's shirt pocket and hollered "much obliged" as he walked away.

Jes walked quickly down the street to Haddox's Grocery. When he walked through the door, the bell jingled. The store was warm, and the air filled with the smell of bananas, potatoes, and other items in the small grocery. The aroma of work clothes and gumboots was also detectable from a side room. Glenn Haddox was standing behind the counter, swatting at flies with a nearly worn-out flyswat.

"Jes, didn't know if ye wanted me to run yere stuff on out to the house or not. Ye didn't say. I got the milk and sausage back in the meat box a waitin' on ye. Jesse a comin' after ye?"

Haddox handed Jes his milk and sausage. Jes made room for them in the cardboard box that contained the remainder of the week's groceries he had purchased earlier in the day. Jes acted as if Haddox had not spoken a word as he walked to the front of the store and looked out the window. He had forgotten to have the groceries delivered, and he was too old to walk two miles while carrying them—a task he had performed many times over the years. His old Model T was sold right after World War II when he decided he could no longer see well enough to drive. His dime store glasses were barely adequate for reading the newspaper, and all he could do now was wait patiently for his son and hope Jesse had not forgotten.

After a few minutes a large truck pulled up in front of the store, stirring up a cloud of dust and rattling the windows when it stopped. The engine cadence was loud, and the vehicle appeared not to have any sign of a tailpipe. The black smoke curling around the vehicle made it look like it was on fire. The engine died and the driver's door squawked a protest when Jesse Caughill pushed it open. Jesse's long slender frame strode toward the front door with his signature engineer cap cocked on the back of his head. His face and arms were browned by the sun and helped highlight the black hair, tinged slightly with grey, which stood out around his cap.

The smell of gasoline and fumes rushed through the screen on the front door. Glenn Haddox made a face and shook his head as he looked out at the wreck that passed for a truck.

"Lord a mercy, Jesse. Where did ye get that thing?" Glenn Haddox laughed.

"Junkyard, Glenn."

"Can ye get 'em to take it back?"

Jesse did not seem to see the humor in Glenn's question as he scooped up Jes's groceries and headed out the door. Two concrete blocks helped anchor the box of groceries on the flat wooden bed of the old truck. The truck bed had no sides, and it appeared that some time in its life the vehicle had been used to haul logs.

Jes pulled open the passenger door and climbed into the cab. The seat consisted of springs covered with grass sacks. The windshield, which had a large crack, was so dirty it was difficult to see through. The door did not want to close, and Jes had wired it shut with a coat hanger that, from its rusty appearance, had been performing that task for some time. The floorboard on the driver's side contained a huge hole that required the driver to make a careful entry into the cab.

When Jesse stepped on the starter, the old truck violently resisted. He jumped out, and after some adjustments under the hood, the engine sputtered to life. The smell of gasoline and fumes in the cab was all but overwhelming. Jes was glad he did not have far to go.

Jesse pulled away from the store by gunning the engine. He slammed the gears hard as the old truck roared, rattling the window lights of every store and house along the route out of town. Jesse Caughill was known far and wide as an expert mechanic and operator of heavy equipment. However, no one who ever rode with him could say that he drove with finesse. Quick turns and gear jamming were his style.

When the old truck reached fourth gear, it settled down to a moderate roar. Yelling above the racket Jes asked, "Where did ye get this hunk of junk?"

"Traded that ol' Case tractor fer it this mornin'. Gonna burn her out behind yere coal house in the mornin'. Sell her fer junk. Need a little dab of extra money these days."

"Gonna burn that wood bed, too?" Jes was thinking the truck bed could be used for firing the wash kettle.

"Yep, 'bout rotted out anyhow."

The engine noise made conversation difficult, but Jes knew what Jesse had in mind. The junkyards wanted all non-metal removed from the vehicle before purchasing it. Jesse remedied that situation by soaking the vehicle with gasoline and burning it.

When Jesse turned suddenly off the highway onto the Chandle Loop, Jes held to the seat springs and the dash. The rickety door anchored only with a rusty coat hanger was too risky to trust with one's life. The gears screamed when Jesse shifted down to second gear. Jes thought the entire transmission was going to fall out, but his son did not seem concerned. The old truck did not have much time left on earth, and Jesse saw no need to pamper it.

"Son, what kinda truck is this thing anyhow?"

"A Reo I think, Pap. Motor ain't the same. The cab is 'bout all that's a Reo."

"When ye turn onto the Billy Goat up here, stop so I can get my mail."

Jesse made the turn onto the Billy Goat Road and stopped long enough for Jes to retrieve his mail from the mailbox. He climbed back in the cab and made a futile attempt to wire the door closed with the coat hanger. The wire broke, and Jes held the door closed by holding on with his right arm and leaning toward the center of the cab. The old truck fussed and growled furiously as they maneuvered through numerous chug holes in the road.

"Pap, jest let the door go. If a tree limb knocks it off, it ain't a gonna matter none."

"Matter plenty if I fall out this contraption and break my neck. Knowed this I wuda walked home. Probably bounced out ha'f them groceries by now."

"Keep yere shirt on, Pap, purt near home now."

Jes Caughill's chickens were squawking and running in every direction when Jesse drove up in the old Reo. The air was filled with black smoke, plus the troublesome odor of a considerable quantity of gasoline.

"Be glad to be shed of this thing. Nothin' but a death trap. Catch fire and burn down haf the country," Jes growled as he climbed out of the truck coughing from the fumes. "Ten times worse than worse coal mine I ever saw."

Jesse picked up a can of hominy, a two-pound bag of pinto beans, and a box of baking powder that had bounced from the grocery box and landed on the truck bed. He pulled the box off and headed for the back door. The door opened as he approached, and Myrtle Caughill stood aside as he entered the kitchen.

"Son, ye scared them chickens so bad when ye drove up they ain't a gonna lay fer a month of Sundays."

"Ma, don't start that. I done been laid out to cool by Pap. The old junker headin' fer the junkyard t'morrow."

"I smell gas. Is the gas tank a leakin' on that thing?"

"Ma, ain't nothin' that ain't leakin' on that thing. Ain't got much gas in it, though."

"Don't like it a settin' there so close to the house. Catch a fire."

"I ain't a gonna be here long."

Jesse went to the sideboard and picked up one of Myrtle's gold coffee cups. She was proud of her little cups that had been packed in boxes of Quaker Oatmeal. The coffeepot had been on the back of the wood cookstove since early that morning; but Jesse Caughill, like his father, had never found any cup of coffee too strong. He poured about a half cup and sipped it as he walked around the kitchen.

Jes started unpacking the grocery box while Myrtle looked through the mail. She found an envelope that looked interesting, and quietly slipped it into her apron pocket.

"Thought ye was gonna have Glenn bring this stuff on out. I hope to the Lord this milk ain't been a settin' out all day."

Jes ignored Myrtle as he roughly put away the groceries. When the task was complete, he opened the kitchen door and tossed the box as far as he could into the backyard. The chickens had just started to calm down from the loud truck noise when Jes nearly hit the old rooster with the box. The Rhode Island Red ran a few feet and then started crowing. The hens cackled and then slipped over to inspect the cardboard missile.

Jesse closed the door and leaned up against the facing. Jes poured a cup of coffee and started pacing the room like a caged animal. Jesse knew something was wrong when his father acted like this. Myrtle Caughill took the lid off a Dutch oven and stirred some pinto beans.

"Son, ye gonna stay fer supper?"

"No, gotta get home. Gotta get back over here early in the mornin' to burn out that ol' truck. Pap, are ye gonna help me?"

"If it'll get shed of that pile of junk any sooner."

"Jes, quit pacin' 'round and get ready fer supper. Wash yere hands and try usin' a little water fer a change."

"Water is 'bout all we gonna have with groceries as high as they are. The pore house ain't far off."

Jesse sensed it was a good time to leave since Jes and Myrtle were well known for their vitriolic arguments. Before dark the chickens might have more frightful moments. He placed his empty coffee cup down on the table and slipped outside.

The old truck refused to start and after several minutes of coaxing, Jesse gave up and headed back to the kitchen door.

"Pap, I mighta knowed I couldn't shet that thing down. Gonna walk home. Gotta bring the International over here t'morrow to haul it off anyhow."

"Are ye gonna leave that thing there to burn the house down tonight?"

"Ma, it ain't got 'nough fire in it to light a cigarette. Gas tank purt near empty."

Jesse headed out the road for home while Jes and Myrtle got ready to eat supper. The house was hot, and Myrtle's temper was short. She had spent most of her life cooking on woodstoves in stifling heat, but now she was an old woman, and it was taking its toll. She knew Jes had gotten upset about something in town and his nervousness would probably lead to an argument.

The supper meal passed without either Jes or Myrtle saying a word. Myrtle could not complain about her husband's strong work ethic. He had worked like a dog to provide for a young family, but in his later years he had become pugnacious over money matters.

When Jes finished eating, he slammed his plate across the table and resumed his pacing. Myrtle pretended not to notice as she pulled the envelope out of her apron pocket. She wanted to open it privately since the contents would also restart an argument that she and Jes had been having for months.

"Jes, take them jars over yonder on the cabinet and put up that milk. Better get 'em over to the well 'fore it gets dark. Good idée to put this here sausage down there, too; too hot to risk pork in this heat."

"I reckon I knowed that." Jes growled as he poured the milk from their paraffin coated cardboard containers to glass fruit jars.

When Jes left the house, Myrtle opened the envelope and immediately started to cry. She read and reread the contents before tucking it back inside her apron. The news was the best she had ever received.

Jes walked back into the house and let out a long sigh. He stood motionless in the middle of the kitchen like he was expecting Myrtle to say something.

"What wuz it? Don't try to pretend ye don't know what I'm talkin' 'bout. I seen that letter and I seen ye hide it in yere apron. I know good and well ye ain't got no boyfriend."

"I got it, Jes. Almost 600 dollars. We never had this much money since we been married. Never had this kinda money."

"Gonna need it with groceries goin' up ever day."

"Now, Jes, I see my name on this here check. I'm the one who fell down the steps at the Hartford store and got laid up with my back fer six months. I'm GONNA spend this here money the way I want. Gonna have Al Atlee wire this house and gonna get a refrigerator and an electric stove and a fan to air out this bat den. This ol' woodstove is a cookin' dream but will work ye to death a cuttin' wood and all. Been hangin' milk in the well or a creek all my life. Never thought nothin' of it when I wuz young, but now that I'm gettin' old..."

"That's it, waste all yere money with times 'bout to get hard agin'. Gonna be 'nother Depression sooner or later. How we gonna pay the light bill?"

"Ralph and Anna pay their light bill all right. Eight dollars a month. We can handle that."

"The bad times is comin'. Possum Hunters a ridin' agin'. Bad times right 'round the corner."

"POSSUM HUNTERS. Jes, the Possum Hunters stopped forty years ago. Where on earth did ye get that fool notion?"

"The talk all over Hartford. Talkin' it up in Beaver Dam too."

"Jes, ye been talkin' to Mike Stewart. Don't deny it. I cannot understand why ye listen to that drunken ol' fool. He jest talks to hear his head rattle. He was a Possum Hunter hisself. Only thing he ever done to make hisself feel like a big shot. That Liars' Bench at Hartford orta be busted up and used for kindlin'. Nothin' but a place fer a bunch of ol' fools to sit, tell lies, and fret 'bout things."

"What the HELL do ye know 'bout it? I'm the one had to go in the mines day in and out. I'm the one had to worry 'bout havin' the hell beat outta me 'cause I wudn't join 'em. Wudn't help with their meaness. Bad times back then. Men a runnin' 'round with masks over their faces and scarin' hell outta law 'bidin' people. Always somebody wantin' to do that. Dirty, lowdown bastards."

"LIFE ain't been no picnic fer me neither. Ain't my fault that women ain't strong 'nough to work the mines. I HAVE worked like a dog. Worked as hard as I was able to do, and I had two babies. How many did ye have?"

Jes was angry. As usual, Myrtle was winning the argument. He grabbed his hat and stormed out the back door. He raced across the backyard, and with a well-placed kick sent the cardboard box flying. The chickens had already occupied the roosting posts in the chicken house. Jes counted them and after being satisfied that all were present, he closed the door.

Jes's homemade gasoline-powered saw sat next to a pile of kindling. He pumped the kickstand on the two-cycle engine until it sputtered to life. Sawing wood was one of the ways Jes used to cool down when he was angry. The wood cookstove had a ravenous appetite and required an endless supply of wood. Jes would not admit it, but he was sick and tired of cutting wood; and the number of trees on the wooded hillside across the creek from his home was not infinite. Jes preferred to cut smaller trees since he did not have a horse or mule to haul the wood to the house. In fact, cutting large trees was just too much. An undertaking that did not bother him when he was young now was an insurmountable task.

After fifteen minutes of sawing, the saw motor started to sputter as it sucked up the last fumes from the fuel tank. When the saw stopped, Jes slammed a piece of wood off the side of the motor and headed for the house.

Myrtle was seated on the front porch fanning with an old newspaper. Jes went straight to bed. The house was brutally hot but no hotter than houses Jes had lived in for nearly seven decades. Many times in their married life Jes and Myrtle had slept in the yard to escape the heat. Jes thought about going outside, but he knew that— with the coming darkness—mosquitoes would be swarming out of the nearby creek, woods, and large rain barrels located at every corner of the house; and the pesky little blood suckers would be worse than the heat. He wondered if a fan would make that much difference and could they afford to run it. Soon his body was dripping with perspiration.

Myrtle went in the house when the lightning bugs took over the front yard and it was too dark see the creek. She carefully made her way into the kitchen and lit the coal oil lamp. She walked back to the bedroom amd moved softly past Jes's bed. His breathing indicated he had drifted off to sleep. She marveled at his ability to sleep in such heat. The many years he had spent in the underground coal mines had conditioned him. Myrtle placed the lamp on a table by her bed and pulled back the covers.

The bed covers burned against Myrtle's back. She took a deep breath and thought about her insurance check. The money would make life easier for them, but she knew Jes had to be resentful of the money. She had taken a fall and earned more money than Jes had earned in most years of his work career.

Myrtle was too excited to sleep without the heat. She lay awake for hours thinking about the last forty years. The country had been terrified when the Possum Hunters were raging. She had known Jes was in danger, but for reasons they had never understood, he was not threatened. Jes and Myrtle had seen some very hard times, but one way or the other they had put food on the table three meals a day without fail. They had survived the Depression, two world wars, drought, floods, and sickness—and the Possum Hunters. As the years piled up, it had become difficult for them to look forward, and Jes lived in constant fear of the bad times returning.

Sometime after 10:00 o'clock the sky started to light up with dry weather lightning. A cool breeze started to blow, and a few drops of rain tap danced on the tin roof. Myrtle heard a dog or perhaps a fox splash through the creek. The house was starting to cool down slightly, and she drifted off to sleep, comforted by the thought of getting some things that would make life easier.

During the era of the Possum Hunters, Myrtle had looked out her kitchen window each morning right after dawn to see a neighbor man riding his horse down the road. He had been out all night and had a lantern and long, dark overcoat draped across his saddle. Jes met him most mornings going to the mines, and both men spoke when they met. It was common knowledge that the man was one of the ringleaders of the Possum Hunters.

Myrtle's night sleep was not restful. She dreamed that the neighbor man with his lantern and long, dark coat was riding down the road by her house. In the dream he stopped and rode his horse around and around the house and then tried to ride the animal through the door. Despite Myrtle's attempts to block all entrances, he kept pushing the doors partly open. The man was well known to her, but in the nightmare she could not see his face. Like many dreams, it seemed to go on for hours until she finally sprang awake in a heavy sweat and breathing hard.

She could hear Jes's breathing and knew he was resting comfortably. A hoot owl landed on the roof and hooted to all who listened. Myrtle jumped with fright and then grew furious with herself for being alarmed by a sound she had heard all of her life. She was no longer angry with Jes for being upset at reports that the Possum Hunters were reorganizing. She knew the stories were nonsense, but they had stirred something inside her. Jes and Myrtle Caughill were not the only ones haunted by demons from the past. The rumors about the Possum Hunters organizing were spreading, and people who should have known better were concerned as well.

"WELL, well, come in here and sit down, my old friend. Jim, what brings you to Greenville? Can't get enough lawyering in Hartford these days?"

"OH, I get enough to keep an old man going I guess. My daughter drove over here this morning to see about a school teaching job, and I rode along in hopes of catching you out of court. I don't get around much anymore. Quit driving when my old Model T wore out. Didn't mind the Model T at all, but these new-fangled cars is nothing but an aggravation. The world has done gone off and left me. I won't fly in an airplane either."

"Jim, did you ever ride the riverboats?"

"Indeed, I did. I rode them many a time over the years."

"Now, that's the way man was meant to travel. I once rode the Evansville all the way to Bowling Green. She was the last of the Green River packets. I got on at Ceralvo and rode the way God intended, slow and peaceful. A man could stand on the deck and watch the world go by, have a chew of tobacco and a drink if he wanted to. The best show on earth was when The Rousters broke into a coonjine. Only a bunch of darkies could make loading and unloading freight a show worth watching. There was always a story behind the little ditties, and you had to listen careful to catch it. Do you remember when the Captains would play a tune with that whistle?"

"I remember one of them used to play *My Old Kentucky Home*."

"OOOH, that used to bring tears to my eyes. It did bring tears to my eyes when I heard that the Evansville had burned."

"Jim, it sounds like you're getting old and starting to talk about the good old days."

"Maybe so, Bill. Maybe so but if a man can't reminiscence a little, what can he do? By the way, Bill, how's the law business for you?"

"Not bad. You know the coal companies are a Godsend for an old country lawyer like us."

"Bill, that might be true for you but not much for me. They throw me a little dab and other lawyers in Hartford poke the piddlin' stuff off on me, and that's about it. I'm not a store-bought lawyer like you. No sir, I can't claim to be a Philadelphia lawyer. I was on my own when I was ten years old. I slept in a man's barn and did chores for one meal a day. I grew up the hard way and read law to become a lawyer."

"Jim, Jim, Jim, I grew up poor, too. If you weren't so durn ornery, you might have more law business. I bet you have a gun and a bottle of whiskey in your pocket right now."

"Now Bill, I haven't left home in forty years without a gun and a bottle of good whiskey. I'm going to be buried with the bottle but not the gun. A man told me one time you can't shoot your way into heaven, but I bet old St. Peter can be had with a good bottle of Kentucky Tavern."

"Speaking of guns—Jim, we keep hearing reports from over around Hartford that some folks are trying to reorganize the Possum Hunters. The Sheriff over here has heard it being talked around the courthouse. If it's true, we can't figure out for the life of us why. Any truth to it?"

"Yes, if you want to count some old drunks like Mike Stewart. The real answer is no. Just a bunch of old farts talking to hear their head rattle. You remember Mike Stewart. The biggest damn liar that ever drew a breath. The only thing he ever did in his life that he thinks was important."

"I remember him. I did my dead level best to send him to the pen, but he is slippery. He was a master at diversion. He would go out and do something and then spend the next week planting cover stories all over the country. The next thing I knew I had folks swearing he was twenty miles away when it happened."

"Bill, the Possum Hunters have ridden out for the last time."

"Well, I hope so. Most of them are old or dead, but some that I sent to the pen are still alive and not sending me any Christmas cards."

"If any had planned on getting even, it would have happened by now. Besides, the old timers would need to enlist some young bucks to get anything done. Now, I had one who held a grudge against me for years; but we settled it and he's dead now, too."

"Jim, who was that?"

"Well, Bill, he has some living kin that I would not want mad at me, but if I just call him old 'You Know Who,' I betcha you can figure out who I'm talking about."

"SAY no more. I don't want to hear his name. That was one of them that we worried about for a long time. They hung the meanest one over here, but he was the worst in your neck of the woods. It gives me cold chills to even think about him. Now, I don't understand why he hated you."

"He hated me over a land title I worked on back before the Possum Hunters got started and tried to use that as a way to hang me."

"HANG you?"

"That's right. Well, I guess I need to tell the whole story. You see, you prosecuted the Possum Hunters, but it was some folks inside the gang and the Masons that threw the dirt on them for good. I was one of them involved down at Centertown and Ceralvo with the Masons' trials of some of those boys. The Masons were mighty upset about the whole thing for several reasons. We had Masons in it, and that was causing some talk that the Masons were behind it. You know folks have always been thinking the Masons are some kind of a dark criminal group. The Possum Hunters were using some of the Masons' rituals like 'riding the goat' and all that."

"Whoa a minute, Jim. I don't know where you aim to take this little ditty, but I may have a notion or two myself. That meeting down there around Centertown at Atlee's barn had a lot to do with us getting some of those boys in Ohio County. You remember that old Toll Gate Raiders law about confederating and banding together to injure other persons. That was the purpose of that meeting. That law was passed back in '97 and repealed in 1902, but the juicy part of Chapter 20 is still on the books. That's how the law got 'em."

"I understand that, but law or no law, a large and significant part of the community wanted it stopped and that as much as anything, maybe more. Now, before I forget it and get into the rest of my tale about how 'You Know Who' tried to have me killed, I have a piece of paper right here in my pocketbook that will tickle your funny bone. There was an old boy down around Centertown who wrote this about the Possum Hunters and named names. It is a wonder they didn't whip him over it. I won't use names in case some of them are related to you.

Come all you rounders if you want to hear
The story of the Possum Hunters far and near.
They meet in the barn and they met in the shed,
And how they all wished them four men was dead.
There was 'You Know Who,' the dirty old pup,
Run around all day and stirred the mess up . . ."

"Well, I think I'm gonna stop right there and let you read the rest of it to yourself. People coming in and out of the outer office, somebody might hear."

Bill took the paper from Jim and read it thoughtfully for a few moments. He smiled and shook his head before returning the aging document.

"Jim, that's the darndest thing I ever heard, but I believe I heard it years ago. I don't blame you for leaving out the names. Better to leave sleeping dogs asleep. Of course, I know 'You Know Who' and I remember the man with the stick. I had him on the witness stand, and he was scared to death. I asked him if he was at that meeting at Atlee's barn with a gun. He said from what he remembered it was a stick. The whole courtroom hollered and laughed. Who were the four men they wanted dead?"

"Well, one of them was me, and the others were just men who took a drink now and then. No need to name them. The main story has to do with me. One of the men there in Centertown went into the livery stable one day to take a leak, and he overheard some Possum Hunters planning this meeting where they were going to discuss hanging me. This fellow was sorta a friend of mine, and he just shows up at the meeting; and before they figure out that he doesn't belong there, he knows everything. They tried to get him to swear that he wouldn't talk, but he swore that he was going to tell the whole country. They didn't want to hurt him, so they let him go. The fact is they didn't have the stomach to kill anybody, and besides, one of them was his own brother-in-law."

"Why not just give you a good whipping?"

"I got the reason right here in my pocket. They knew I would use it. And I don't mean the bottle either."

"Did that meeting happen before or after the meeting at Atlee's barn?"

"It took place afterwards. This was a follow-up meeting. At Atlee's barn, as I understand it, it was agreed that a group would pay a visit to the automobile drivers in Centertown and around to warn them to stop hauling folks who were bringing whiskey back from Owensbur', Hartford, and Beaver Dam. Another group went to see the Mayor and Council in Centertown to advise them to hire a town marshal and to start enforcing the laws about bootlegging and drinking. The Possum Hunters were concerned because there had been a lot of talk about setting up 'Blind Tigers' in and around Centertown. They thought the talk was serious and the automobile drivers would be hauling in the booze. Really, all that was going on was men coming back with their pockets and snoots full of spirits. The automobile drivers were not responsible for that."

"Jim, are you telling me that your friend breaking into that meeting had more to do with breaking up the Possum Hunters than what we did in court?"

"Well, yes and no. Keep in mind that I'm just talking about what happened in the Centertown area. I know for a fact that anti-Possum Hunters had a lot to do with it over here in Muhlenberg County."

"Jim, I think you might be confusing people who gave State's evidence for anti-Possum Hunters. We had some who would have turned in their own mothers to stay out of the pen."

"There may have been some of that, too. Now, the meeting at Centertown revealed some of the ringleaders in that area, and that put a scare into them. There had been a lot of suspicion, but after that, everybody knew for sure. Now they had leaders around the rest of the county and over in some other counties, but down there the cat was outta the bag. Sure wasn't gonna be anymore talk of killing somebody. We heard that some of the leaders elsewhere got nervous about the ones at Centertown. They got afraid they might start talking."

The sad truth, Bill, is that the preachers sat back and did not do a thing. You know as well as I do that in the old days the churches took people to task. If you did something wrong, they called you on the carpet. They even put people out of the church. That used to mean something, but not anymore. Now, men who belong to the Masons, that still means something. None of us want to be put out of that organization. The Masons wanted the Possum Hunters gone for good, and we meant business, even if it meant throwing out some of our best members."

"Jim, you're entitled to your opinion, but the indictments is what I believe got the job done. No man wants to go to the pen, and that's worse than being tossed out of the Masons."

"Maybe that's because you are not a Mason, Bill. The law is important but does not mean a thing without the support of the people. You may bring a man to trial, but it's still a jury of twelve citizens that decides; and if you can't find twelve people who believe in what you're doing, then it's a waste of time."

"Jim, we can argue this all day, but what I really want to hear is about you and 'You Know Who.' First, clear something up for me. That meeting was at Jeb Atlee's barn. Did he have any involvement?"

"Good Lord, no. Jeb was a very religious man. He would have no truck with the Possum Hunters, and the ringleaders did not like that, or least ways the ones in the countywide organization, and they threatened to burn his barn. I heard he told them to go right ahead, God would forgive them, and he would build another barn. So, after that they threatened to burn his brother Marvin's barn. Now Marvin was in the insane asylum, and his wife and kids had their backs to the wall to hold on to their farm. Jeb finally told them he would let them use his barn for meetings if they would not burn any barns around Centertown and

Walton's Creek. Later he heard they were gonna burn Marvin's barn. They met down there by the church, and old Jeb rode right in the middle of 'em and talked them out of it."

"The Possum Hunters liked getting innocent folks like Jeb involved some way. They wanted safety in numbers. Some folks thought hard of Jeb for letting them use his barn, and others criticized him over saving his brother's barn. I guess it depends upon who you talk to. I know that he never forgave himself for letting them use that barn."

"I know you want to hear about 'You Know Who.' I told my wife back before the Possum Hunters broke up that one day, I was gonna kill him or he was gonna kill me. I wanted the family to be prepared because I truly thought it would happen. I kept this old pistol cleaned and oiled every day and right in my pocket so I could get to it. I heard from others that he was doing the same. Every time we met on the streets of Centertown or Hartford, I avoided him, or he avoided me. This went on until 1923."

"The end of it came as complete shock to me. Now, 'You Know Who' was a second cousin, I guess it was, to Jes Caughill's wife. Did you ever know old 'High Pockets' Jes Caughill? Well, it doesn't matter. Old Jes stopped me in Centertown one day and asked to speak to me privately. I thought he was acting awful nervous. His wife, Myrtle, despised old 'You Know Who,' and she and Jes never had any use for the Possum Hunter business. That may be why he sent Jes to deliver his message. Jes told me 'You Know Who' wanted to meet me on the top floor of the drugstore in Centertown. Well, I figured this was it and he aimed to kill me, or I would kill him or there was a chance that he was serious. I went to the barbershop and got a haircut and a shave, and had my suit cleaned and pressed. I rode the train down from Hartford, and on the appointed night we both showed up in our Sunday suits and he had a fresh haircut and shave, too. I reckon we wanted to save the undertaker the trouble. I could see from across the room that his coat was open, and his gun was at the ready. That was fine since my coat was unbuttoned and my old Merwin-Hulbert pocket pistol was also at the ready. I'll never forget what he said."

"Jim, I'm getting cold chills just listening to this."

"Well, he said, 'Jim, we been feudin' fer years. I think it's time to call it off. I'm twenty-five years older than you, and some day ye can kill me off like swattin' a fly. Ye got a young family, and I jest don't wanna hurt ye anymore. Can we shake on it?'"

"Now, I knew who I was dealing with and didn't trust him for a minute. We talked on for over an hour before I was satisfied that he meant it, and we shook hands. What finally convinced me was when he offered to put down that gun before he walked the thirty feet that separated us and shook my hand. I said that wasn't necessary since I was gonna need to trust him in the future with or without that gun. We stayed friendly until the day he died. If he had been a few years younger, I probably would not be here today. He was sure one mean son-of-a-bitch in his day.'"

"JIM, that is one HELL of a story. You have more nerve than I ever had. I have heard a bunch of Possum Hunter stories, but that one takes the prize. NEVER heard that before."

"Bill, I don't think he ever told it, and you and my wife are the only ones I have ever told. I didn't figure anybody would ever believe me."

"Let's get back to those rumors for a minute. I'm not worried about a bunch of old men talking around the courthouse. The young toughs are the ones that bother me. They all have guns and fast cars these days. Jim, you have to remember that we had flareups with Night Riders and some barn burning into the '20s in some parts of the state. I grant you that most of it was over, but not all."

"The Sheriffs all have cars, too, Bill, and we got the State Police now, and the Governor can send in the militia, too. Besides, the tobacco money is better and the coal mine jobs is mostly union. This day and age a man isn't trapped here. He can go somewhere else if he doesn't like it. Fifty or a hundred years ago a man with a little farm, a coal mine job, or log woods, and that was the end of his world. He couldn't see beyond that, and when it was threatened, he fought back. Not that way these days."

"Jim, the Possum Hunters wasn't about tobacco. The Night Riders and tobacco war was long over with. That meanness grew out of the tobacco war. Some folks saw it as a way to even some scores and the like. Some weren't interested in whipping criminals and deadbeats since they were the criminals and the deadbeats."

"You're right, and another thing, it wasn't as bad around here either. Down around Hickman, Eddyville, and over in Missouri things were real mean. They got after the darkies over there and dynamited their houses. Some of them lit out of there with just the clothes on their backs. We didn't have any of that around here. Bill, I have a question for you. Whatever gave folks the idea of Night Riders and Possum Hunters?"

"Well, Jim, I guess it goes back to the Klan and the Civil War and the Regulators before that. My daddy used to talk about all the meanness that went on in this state during and after the Civil War. Old Kentucky was a state of lawlessness with the Klan running wild. I would not be surprised if some of the grudges being settled didn't go back to that time. You remember some Civil War soldiers still alive then. Not many, though; but the hard feelings were still there. Many of them old Possum Hunters had a daddy or an uncle in the Civil War. Jim, some folks still think hard about that war. I have a question for you. When we started getting indictments, a bunch of the boys around here hightailed it to Herrin and Marion, Illinois. They had a lot of labor violence up there in the '20s. Did any of our Possum Hunter friends get into any of that?"

"Bill, I did some lawyer work up there in the '30s. I heard some stories you would not believe about the old Charlie Berger and the Shelton boys a fighting and scratching. Now back in '22 is when they had that strike up at Herrin and the coal company brought in the scabs. The union boys I think killed about two dozen of them. The Ku Klux was big up there, and the preachers were pushing it, too. They organized to get rid of the roadhouses and whorehouses. They even got some legal authority and were carrying out raids on the roadhouses. They made it hard on Catholics and Jews, too."

"I never heard tell of any of our preachers getting involved around here or law officials either. Some folks did complain lawmen were members, but I don't know. The law was into the Klan up there. The funny thing about that situation was that the bootleggers and some anti-Kluxers stopped it up there. It took bullets and not the law."

"Jim, you're a far better lawyer than you give yourself credit. YOU still haven't answered my question about our boys."

"I was getting to that. Our boys for the most part had quit and come back home by then, I guess. There were some boys, two brothers I think, from around here that went up there in the '20s. They came back driving a new car and wearing suits with pistols in shoulder holsters. They strutted around Hartford, bragging that they were working for Al Capone.

I always figured they were running whiskey for Charlie Berger. They unloaded a big crate there at a Hartford garage one time and left it for a year. Men sat on it and played cards and everything else. Nobody knew what was in it. One day they loaded it up and took it down in the Rough Creek bottoms and hid it."

"There was a drinking man there in town that had already figured out that it was whiskey, and he followed them. He decided that they would never know if he took a little snort once in a while. He must have taken one too many because they started missing it. They decided to lay and wait for him that Saturday night; and when he showed up, they jumped up yelling and shooting their guns in the air. They yelled, 'we got that dirty son-of-a-bitch, AL, we got 'im'.' That boy run through the thickets all the way back to Hartford and tore all his clothes off and scratched from head to toe. Scared half to death."

"OOOH Jim, I have a silver dollar that says I know who that was. I would have run, too, if I thought old Al Capone and his boys were after me."

"Well, I can't really blame that old boy. I heard that was some fine drinking whiskey brought in from the Carribean, but not worth getting shot over."

"Jim, I hope we have seen the last of that kind of thing."

"Bill, I reckon we have. The country has grown up a lot in our time. The law works like it should most of the time. Unless we have a complete breakdown of law and order or the 'Bible thumpers' and the Law try to ban whiskey again, we should be all right. I do worry about one thing. If we have trouble again in the future, it will be over the Coloreds. That has been simmering under the surface for years, and one day it is going to boil over. Riots and killings, I'm afraid. Gonna have to start treating them a lot better, or there won't be enough Sheriffs, State Police, or State Militias to put the cork back in that bottle once it gets out."

"You're probably right. Old codgers like us won't be around by then. I hate to say it, but the Possum Hunters and the Klan might come back strong if that happens. That could mean a race war. I hope I'm dead by then."

"Bill, I'll drink to that. Well, my friend, I need to meet my daughter out front in a few minutes. Good to see you again. If you get over toward Hartford, let's have a cup of coffee."

"Jim, always good to see you. I'll take you up on that cup of coffee if the Car Barn is still there. I have to go to court over there next month. I reckon I'll see you over at the courthouse."

"Car Barn is still there, and I'll be at the courthouse, Good Lord willing and the creek don't rise.

Aunt Polly's Iced Tea (1955)

AUNT POLLY'S ICED TEA
(1955)

A S A YOUNGSTER, Mickey had to endure countless lectures about proper behavior in church, stores, relatives' homes, or any other place that his mom thought he might embarrass the family and cause them to be socially ostracized by the entire human race. His dad, however, was concerned only about his young son obeying safety rules around the farm.

Trips to Uncle Al and Aunt Polly's were always the most stressful for Mickey. His mother worried that Al and Polly, who had no children of their own, would view their nephew as a "whine bag" and a "spoiled brat." To remedy this possible humiliation, Mickey had to endure countless lectures or "marching orders."

A trip to his Uncle Al's was always memorable for Mickey when he recalled a beautiful pitcher of lemon adorned iced tea on his aunt's kitchen table. Unfortunately, he had had little opportunity to sample the delightful contents.

Mickey was still many miles from home, and it was time for another memory.

"Now, my young man, gonna go over to yere Uncle Al's and Aunt Polly's today. Gonna spend the whole day. I done give ye yere marchin' orders, but I'm gonna do it ag'in. Better pay attention. Uncle Al and Aunt Polly ain't used to no snotty nosed kids a runnin' 'round the house and ding dongin' them ever fifteen minutes fer somethin' to eat or drink. Stay outta the house 'cept when I call ye fer dinner. When we set down to dinner, don't be askin' fer nothin'. I'll fill yere plate, and don't ye take a bite 'til the grownups start to eat. Mind yere manners, and don't ask fer seconds, or I'll wear ye out when we get home."

"Anna, why don't ye jest ship the youngun' off to the French Foreign Legion. Ye been brow beatin' 'im fer three days. He ain't no bad kid. Shudder to think what ye would do if he wuz."

"Ralph, younguns need remindin' and so do adults. Ye ain't combed yere hair or got yere belt on."

"I ain't done dressin' yet. Besides, we ain't goin' to see the Queen of England or King neither."

"I can't ever get ye to help me get ready fer sumpin' like this. I got a couple dozen tomatoes, cucumbers, squash, and a peck of Top Crop beans; but that corn ain't fit to take."

"I done tol' ye that Al says that they got more garden stuff than they will ever eat or put up. Been tryin' to give me some. Now ye go over there a waggin' more."

"I ain't goin' to my sister-in-law's empty handed. My husband and kid ain't gonna look like no bum, and my son ain't gonna act like some wild Indian. They'll think we jest come fer a free meal."

"Ye go over there a waggin' all that stuff, and they'll think we think they're starvin' to death. On commodities or headin' to the Poor House. Woman, ye try to do too much. Jest relax, and let's go over and spend the day and eat an ol' country dinner. Stop actin' like we got an invite to the White House."

Anna Atlee fretted all the way to Al and Polly Atlee's place. She worried that they had not brought enough food or that she had forgotten something. Ralph drove along totally unconcerned, and five-year-old Mickey sat between them, too scared to move. Visiting friends and relatives was always a trying time for the Atlees. Anna Atlee wanted everything to go smoothly, and she worked overtime to make sure it did. Ralph was uninterested in the details, and that contributed to Anna's anxiety.

"Ralph, I been runnin' myself to death getting' things ready to go over there, and ye ain't done a thing."

"That ain't so. I took a bath, shaved, combed my hair, and put on some decent clothes. I aim to eat all the dinner I can hold, I'm gonna thank Al and Polly for the invite, and then I'm gonna head to the house. Same thing Al does when they come over here. Not a drotted thing."

"Jest like a man, let me do all the worrin'."

"Shore do. Yere durn good at it. Can't improve on perfection and I ain't a gonna try."

Ralph pulled his pickup under a peach tree to the right of Al's driveway. A little red dog ran out to meet them when they got out of the truck, and Al Atlee raced out the kitchen door, slamming the screen door behind him.

"Little Red Dog, get back and don't ye be a jumpin' on 'em. They didn't take ye to raise. Dad blasted worthless pot licker. Ralph, ye wanna dog?"

"Nope, dog pore at our house now. Jest got shed of one egg sucker and don't need no more."

"EGG sucker. Twelve-gauge cure that fer good. This thing too drotted lazy to eat eggs 'less somebody cooks 'em first."

"Anna here done brought ha'f the garden to fix fer dinner."

"Lord a mercy, why did ye do that? We got stuff runnin' out our ears. WELL, well, I almost missed this big fella here. Mickey, why ye hidin' behind yere daddy's leg fer? Ralph, that youngun reminds me of his daddy at that age. Looks like two terbacker sticks a walkin' in a pair of britches."

"Not hardly, Al, we didn't get britches 'til we wuz nearly five. Run 'round in them long shirts. He don't wanna eat nothin' but maters and cukes. Kinda startin' to learn to like pinto beans and cornbread. Spoiled so that salt ain't gonna save 'im."

"Anna, why don't ye and Ralph take that stuff ye brung on in the kitchen? Yessir, Polly done made a rhubarb cobbler fer dinner. That'll put some meat on this youngun'. Go on inside. I got sumpin' to show Mickey."

Ralph took a bushelbasket nearly full of fresh garden produce and followed Anna in the kitchen door.

"Come on in if ye can get in. Anna, what did you all bring over here? I tol' Al not to let ye do that. Got stuff a runnin' out my ears now."

"Polly, ye orta know better than to tell this woman a thing like that. Ain't goin' empty handed. Went to a restaurant one time and she brung her own tomatoes."

"I did no sech thing. I jest had one in my purse in case they didn't have none fer our hamburgers."

"I rest my case. Well, I'm gonna let the womenfolks run this part of the shindig. Al and me gonna jaw a spell."

"Send Mickey in here. He ain't even said hello to his Aunt Polly."

"Anna, I was jest getting' ready to ask ye where he was."

"Al took 'im to show 'im sumpin'. I don't know what."

"OOOH, I do. Come here and I'll show ye. Look out there under that tree in the front yard. The other day he found a little trickle of water out there and he decided he found 'im a little spring. Started diggin' and it jest filled up, so he dug some more. Next thing I know he got a pick out there a tryin' to dig outta rock. He got 'im a little pool dug out and he lined it with rocks, and it holds water real good. No bigger 'round than a washtub. I asked 'im what he was doin' it fer, and he said he was diggin' it fer Mickey. Next thing I knowed he had jumped in the truck and lit out fer Hartford. Went to the dime store and bought three goldfish. To beat that, he spent a dime on a box of food. I said he could feed 'em oatmeal; but, no, he gotta spend a dime on food. Now he got Mickey down there feedin' them fish. Actin' worse than some kid. He spent a half a day workin' on it. That's when he decided we orta ask you all over fer dinner. He wanted to show Mickey that pool."

"Polly, ye know, Ralph ain't like that. He ain't in fer anything like that."

Al Atlee was down on his hands and knees with Mickey, peering into the little pool.

"No, no, that's enough. Feed them fish too much, and they'll die. Ain't that sumpin'. Need to ask yere daddy to fix ye a little fish pool like this one. Now, I got some light bread here. Let's go feed some ducks. I bet ye mama and daddy ain't got no little ducks."

"Al, what in tarnation ye doin' with that youngun'? Don't spoil 'im worse than he is already."

"Ralph, we been feedin' goldfish, and now we're gonna feed ducks. I ain't spoilin' 'im either."

After Mickey had thrown a few scraps of bread to the ducks, his Uncle Al directed his attention elsewhere. Al always doted on Mickey when he first arrived, and then all but forgot he was around.

"Al, ain't got a good look at yere 'backer patch."

"Well, let's take a little sasshay down there. Lookin' purty good."

"Well, I'll say it does, but when ye gonna hoe the weeds outta that patch?"

"WEEDS, I ain't got no weeds in my terbacker patch."

"Whada call that?"

"WELL, smarty pants if ye don't like it, I got a hoe up yonder by the shed; ye know how to use it."

"I reckon I do. Don't see no weeds in my 'backer patch. Gonna hafta get my Sunday shoes dirty a hoein' weeds fer my poor ol' brother."

"Well, ye don't say. When we get through cuttin' out all them weeds ye say is there, we can grab us a can of coal oil and go after them worms."

"COAL OIL. Whada we need with that? Seems like I remember us a tellin' ol' man Ivey that we bit their heads off back when we was kids."

"That's right, Ralph. We tol' 'im, but we didn't do it. That ol' man turned plumb green when we said that. Ye was jest a little squirt and come out with that, and I near fell off that fence. Ever time I seen 'im after that I would smack my lips, and he'd look the other way. Reckon he thought we really done it."

"Mickey, ye play 'round here in the yard while Uncle Al and me do some grownup things."

Al and Ralph made their way through the tobacco patch, laughing, joking, and chiding one another as they had done since childhood. They left Mickey alone in the yard without a thing to do. The child knew better than to enter the house, and he had been forbidden to bring any toys to play with.

Old Red Dog was sprawled under a large oak tree, licking himself where boy dogs sometimes do. Mickey went over and started rubbing his ears. The little dog enjoyed the attention, but the large number of puffy dog ticks on the dog's head was too tempting for the youngster. He had been told repeatedly to never pull off a dog tick. At first Red Dog did not object, and Mickey rapidly accumulated a huge pile of ticks.

"Been aimin' to get some powder fer them ticks on that mutt. Little buzzard run off the other day and come home loaded with ticks and fleas. YOUNGUN, don't pick 'em off if ye don't aim to kill 'em."

Mickey jumped when his uncle stomped the large pile of ticks. Al and Ralph went to the well and drew a bucket of water. Suddenly Mickey was very thirsty and wanted a drink as well.

"This well water is almost as cold as the ice box, and we won't get in the women's way. Never get in a woman's way when she cookin' dinner. Ain't good fer yere health."

"Uncle Al, I ..."

"Mickey, get back outta the way, and don't interrupt when grownups are talkin'. Yere Uncle Al and me are tryin' to talk."

Mickey stood and watched as his father and uncle drank their fill from a large bucket of cold well water. This made his thirst much worse, but he was afraid to say anything. He walked over and wrapped his arms around his father's leg. Surely, he thought, his dad would recognize that he needed a drink of water, too.

"Mickey, quit hangin' on to my coat tails. NOW, go play."

Mickey stood and watched his Uncle Al pour the remainder of the cold well water in a pan for the ducks. He turned the bucket upside down on the well, and the two men walked to the toolshed. Old Red Dog resisted any attempts at removing more ticks, and the youngster was forced to think only about his growing thirst. He tried watching the ducks and turkeys, but all they were doing was drinking water. Even Old Red Dog was lapping out of a battered water pan. He tried throwing and running after a stick, but the exercise only made his thirst grow. The morning dragged on, and his desire for water became unbearable.

The screen door was open, and Mickey was standing in his aunt's kitchen before he realized what he was doing. Marching orders or no marching orders, he needed a drink of water. His mother turned and looked at him in a very disapproving manner.

"OH, Mickey, come over here and give me a big ol' hug. I been so busy I didn't get to see ye when you all got here. Whatcha think of yere Uncle Al's fish? OH, I betcha yere dyin' fer a drink of water. Here, I'll get ye some right outta the icebox. GOOD and cold."

Mickey watched his aunt pour a cold glass of water for him with one eye, but with the other he was keeping a close watch on his mother, who was still staring at him. He took the glass and weakly said thank you. His mouth and throat were so dry he could hardly talk. He started to drink the cold water and had managed only a few swallows when he felt the glass being jerked out of his hand. His mother's hands turned him around and pushed him toward the door. Aunt Polly had come to the rescue, but his mother's marching orders had trumped the situation, and he was back outside and still thirsty.

The sound of his father and Uncle Al fussing over an old cream separator led him down to the toolshed. Maybe he could get their attention and get a drink of water. He started running in that direction, but when he got there, they headed for the barn and left him far behind. The well was full of good cold water, but he was too little to get any, and his father had strict orders about not playing around the well.

The sun was rapidly moving toward the top of the sky, and the smells coming from the kitchen indicated that dinner would soon be on the table. Mickey, however, could not wait any longer. He had to have a drink of water. He remembered the fishpond in the front yard, where the water felt cool to his touch. The three little goldfish swam to the surface and looked at him, as their tiny mouths seemed to be trying to tell him some secrets. He cupped his hand and filled it with water, and it was almost to his mouth when he heard his father's voice.

"Mickey, stop playin' in that water and get on in here. Dinner's ready."

When Mickey walked into the kitchen, his mother grabbed him, washed his hands with a washcloth, pushed him down in a chair at the dinner table, and shot him one of her famous, "don't move, I mean business" looks. The table was loaded down with green beans, potatoes, fried chicken, corn, macaroni and tomatoes, cucumbers and two large skillets of hot cornbread. Mickey, however, had his eyes fixed upon a large pitcher of iced tea garnished with lemons. The smell of the lemons overpowered every other smell in the room and only served to remind Mickey of his raging thirst.

"Now, you all go ahead and set down, I'll pour the ice tea. That pitcher is too heavy fer anybody to try a pourin' it a settin down. Ralph, you and Anna sit over here, and Al and me will sit over on this side. Al gets cranky if he has to sit in a different spot. Mickey, gonna pour ye a glass of this tea first. I bet yere thirsty."

Aunt Polly placed a big glass of tea by Mickey's plate, and he could not take his eyes off of it. He wanted to grab it and drink every drop, but his mother's snapping brown eyes had him in her radar. She acted as if she was anticipating such a move and was ready to pounce. He would have to endure Uncle Al saying grace, and that could be good or bad. If his uncle was hungry, the prayer could be short and sweet.

Once the amens were said, Anna filled Mickey's plate with a sampling of the food on the table. Again, he got a look that reminded him he could not start eating until all of the adults had begun to eat. Food, however, was not what he had on his mind. He could not keep his eyes off the big glass of iced tea. When the time came that he could start to partake of the meal, he reached with both hands for the tea glass. His fingers had hardly touched the cold wet vessel when his mother pushed his hands away. She picked up the glass of tea, and Mickey thought for a moment she wasn't going to let him have any. He was almost in tears, but his mother was merely afraid he would spill it and was picking it up for him. At last, he had it in his hands, and the wonderful beverage was flowing down his throat. It was the best-tasting drink he had ever had.

The iced tea glass was quickly jerked from his hand as soon as it was empty. Anna Atlee's stare had returned, but this time her eyes were open wide and very dark. It was not good manners to gulp down anything all at once, but it sure felt good. The meal progressed nicely, and Mickey actually enjoyed his food; but he wished his mother would stop watching every move he made. The adults all got a second glass of iced tea, but his glass remained empty. He opened his mouth to say, ". . . Aunt Polly, can I . . ." but the words never came out because his mother had already anticipated what he was about to do and was giving him another look.

"OOOH, Mickey, I didn't pour that child any more tea. I bet he's dyin' fer some more. Anna, why didn't ye say sumpin'?"

"Now, Polly, that child has had 'nough. Jest drunk 'nough to float a rain barrel."

"Well now, a tad more won't hurt 'im. Let me get that glass."

Mickey's mouth was watering with anticipation. Good old Aunt Polly had come to the rescue a second time. He was thirsty, and that was the best iced tea in the world. Aunt Polly took the glass and started to pour as she resumed her story about a new kind of beet they had ordered from Henry Fields. She stood with the pitcher poised over the glass as she told Anna all about it. Finally, she put both the glass and the pitcher down and headed for the front room. She had forgotten Mickey's iced tea. His heart sank.

"Anna, I can't remember the name of them beets to save my soul. They ain't them Detroit Reds; we been raisin' them fer a spell and they're real good. This is a new kind. Oh, Anna finish pourin' that child some more tea."

"AAAH, he don't need no more. Let me see that catalog. I ordered outta the Henry Fields this spring and don't remember seein' anything like that in there. Are ye sure it wasn't Burpee?"

Mickey sat in his chair dejected. His father and uncle had left the house after announcing they were headed into the woods in search of a bee tree. Aunt Polly and Anna discussed the beets in the Henry Fields catalog for a few minutes until Anna discovered her son still seated at the dinner table. Mickey kept hoping one of them would remember to give him another drink, but that hope was dashed when his mother pulled him up from the chair by the arm and ushered him out the kitchen door.

Mickey sat down on the concrete steps that led to the kitchen door. The air was hot, and Old Red Dog was rolling in the dust under the old oak tree. The hot sun had caused the geese to retreat inside the shed next to their pen. Anna and Aunt Polly were clearing away the table from the noon meal, and Mickey could hear Uncle Al and his father's voices echoing in the woods behind the house. Mickey just sat on the step, feeling sorry for himself. It would be hours before they would get home and he could drink all the water he wanted.

The afternoon dragged on, and Mickey kept his seat listening to his mother and aunt talking.

"Anna, them men is some bee tree hunters. Lit outta here fer the woods and didn't take no smoker, ax, or pans or nothin'."

"Polly, they ain't goin' up there to do nothin' but talk. Don't want us in a mile, and ye know why."

"Does Ralph talk 'bout losin' Tim much?"

"No, and I don't ever bring it up."

"Me, too. Sometimes I ferget and say sumpin', and Al jest gets up and leaves the house. It still hurts a lot."

"They wuz the closest brothers I ever seen. Tim and Ralph never apart a growin' up."

"I know they wuz. I think it bothers Al 'cause he's the oldest and never expected to bury his little brother."

Mickey listened intently to the conversation about his Uncle Tim. He had died suddenly, and Mickey could only vaguely remember what he looked like. His father always looked very sad when Uncle Tim's name was mentioned. Once he saw his father crying on the back porch, and Mickey had hidden behind a barrel so he would not be seen. He did not like seeing his father cry, but he sensed that his dad did not want to be seen.

The afternoon wore on, and Mickey's thirst started to take second priority. The big glass of iced tea had filtered through his system and now was demanding to exit. He did not dare ask to use Aunt Polly's bathroom. His mother would probably have had what his father called a "buck egger." The urge was getting stronger by the minute, and he knew wetting his pants was not an option either. He had to use the bathroom. He stood up from the step and turned toward the screen door only to be confronted by his mother glaring at him through the screen. She pointed her finger and mouthed softly, "you go play."

Mickey walked slowly across the backyard. He was afraid to run or walk fast. One sudden move and it was all over. He had to find a place to go and not be seen. The toolshed offered the best protection, and he headed in that direction. When he got behind the toolshed and unbuttoned his pants, he could hear his father and Uncle Al coming back out of the woods. He was about to get caught.

The urge to pee was now nothing short of torment. He had been so close to relief and now had to hold it once more as he searched for the right place. The shed next to the duck pen was the only place he could go. The building hid his view from the toolshed where Uncle Al and his father searched for the smoker. They really had found a bee tree.

The buttons to Mickey's fly always presented a problem for his small hands, and now they were being unusually stubborn. Finally, everything was ready to take care of business. When the stream started, it was like something had burst inside of him. His little body shook all over as ecstasy rushed through his entire being. When he had finished, his breathing was hard like he had been running. Uncle Al and his father's voices were disappearing back into the woods once again and Old Red Dog was asleep, and the ducks did not care what he did.

The afternoon heat was becoming unbearable, and Mickey's empty bladder was sending signals up the chain of command that it wanted some more of Aunt Polly's iced tea. The final order was received when Mickey's mouth turned to cotton. A quick glance in the kitchen door revealed a half of a pitcher of tea on the cabinet. It was only twenty feet away, but it had might as well been China. It was out of Mickey's reach.

After a few minutes Aunt Polly walked to the screen door. Mickey looked up at her with a pleading face.

"Honey, do ye want some more of Aunt Polly's iced tea?"

Mickey's hopes skyrocketed once again. Aunt Polly was going to rescue him momentarily. However, his hopes were again dashed by the sound of his mother's voice.

"Polly, where did ye get them salt-and-pepper shakers? Look like two hens a settin' on a nest."

Aunt Polly quickly forgot about the tea and headed into the living room. Mickey's aunt had a passion for collecting salt-and-pepper shakers.

She could talk about them for hours, but Mickey did not have hours; he needed a drink now.

It was nearly five o'clock when Uncle Al and Ralph Atlee returned from the woods empty handed. The bees had abandoned the tree, and the two men were arguing about who was the best at tracking down a good bee tree. They put the axe and the smoker back in the shed and headed for the house

"All right, youngun, are ye ready to go home?"

"ANNA, shake a leg in there. Gotta get to the house. Gotta bring in some water, put the chickens up fer the night, and as yere ol' daddy would say, we gotta get up in the mornin'."

Mickey only heard the part about his father bringing in some water. His mouth and throat were so dry he was almost in tears. He couldn't ask for a drink now. Aunt Polly and Uncle Al hugged him, and his mother instructed him to thank his aunt and uncle for everything. Mickey opened his mouth, but nothing came out.

"There ye go actin' like that agin'. Now, say thank you to yere Aunt Polly and Uncle Alvin."

Once again Mickey opened his mouth, but he could not say a word; however, out of the corner of his eye he could see his father was getting impatient.

"OH, come on you two and get in the truck. The child is wore out and wants to go home. Say thank ye some other time."

Ralph Atlee picked up his son and after waving to Al and Polly, headed for the truck. Anna quickly followed along behind.

"I can't believe it. Come down here and stay all day, and when we get ready to go he embarrasses me 'cause he won't say thank you."

"Leave 'im alone. Ye got the kid spooked sumpin' awful. Don't know when he can open his mouth."

"Men don't care if kids jest run wild. Leave us women to take care of everthing."

"Didn't run wild when I was a kid. Ma never yelled at us and never laid a hand on 'ary one of us kids. She would jest give us a look once in a while, and that's all we needed. BUT to change the subject a minute, did ye ever drink any better tea than that today? Them lemons really set it off. We need to get some lemons once in a while. I could drink a pitcher of that tea and not stop."

"Ralph, yere right. Yes sir, that tea was real good. I had three glasses of it. Real, real good."

Mickey sat between his parents during the painfully long ride home. He tried not to listen to them talk about iced tea, but a vision of the old water bucket at home was fixed in his brain. The iced tea was back at Uncle Al's; but the water bucket was home, and he could get a drink any time he wanted. All he had to do was get there.

When his father finally turned onto the Billy Goat Road, Mickey knew it would not be long until they would be home and he could have a drink. He was finally going to have some relief. He would pull a chair up to the table that held the water bucket, climb up and take the dipper in both hands, and scoop up a long drink of warm water. It would not be ice-cold tea garnished with lemons, but it would quench his thirst and he would not need anyone's permission.

Parents have a way, however, of derailing even the best of plans made by their children. A quarter of a mile from the house Ralph Atlee suddenly stopped the truck.

"Anna, take a gander over yonder in that fencerow and tell me that ain't a bunch of dewberries. Them kind that trails on the ground."

"I believe yere right. Don't see many of them things anymore. Wonder why we never noticed 'em 'fore now? First thing in the mornin', I'm comin' down here and pick me a bucket full. Makes the best cobblers in the world."

"Ain't 'nough fer a bucket full, but ye can get 'nough fer a couple of cobblers. If ye get 'nough, can a quart of 'em fer a Christmas cobbler."

Mickey loved blackberries and dewberries but at the moment he needed a drink of water. Tears were starting to cloud his eyes. He was in agony. "Please, Daddy," he said to himself. "Let's go home."

When the truck stopped in front of the house, Mickey could stand it no longer; he was climbing over his mother's lap as she opened the truck door, and he ran toward the house as hard as he could run.

"Ralph, I wish ye would look at yere son. Plumb run over me a gettin' outta the truck."

Mickey grabbed the quart fruit jar that he used as a beverage glass. He poured it half full from the water bucket and was drinking and choking and spilling water down his shirt when his parents came in the house.

"Well, I wish ye would look. Drinkin' water like he's starved. As if he didn't drink water and iced tea all day. Be up to pee half the night."

"Whoa there, Son, slow down yere gonna make yerself sick. Now what did ye say 'bout 'im drinkin' water all day? Saw 'im drink a glass at dinner. Is that all he had?"

"Well, I guess, come to think of it . . ."

"Did he ask fer any?"

"Well, he come one time, but I jest figured he was ding dongin'. Ye know how kids are."

"Yeah, I know. They get thirsty like grownups."

"He shouda asked."

"Ye tol' 'im not to."

"I never meant . . ."

"Yes, ye did; yes, ye did."

"I guess ye would have dropped everthing and give 'im a drink if he had asked."

"Durn tootin' I would. Me and Al was gettin' water there at the well, and he jest stood there and never opened his mouth. Wouda got 'im some if he had asked. Whoa. Wait a minute. He didn't ask 'cause ye tol' 'im not to. No, I tol' 'im not to interrupt when grownups is talkin'. That's what I tol' 'im. I bet the little bugger wanted a drink right then."

"Ralph, do ye remember how it was when we was growin' up and we had company and had to wait on the grownups to finish eatin' 'fore we could eat? Half the time not half 'nough to eat when they got done. Said I would never do my kids like that. Not gonna treat my younguns like they was stepchildren. NO, sir, not me."

"HUMPH. Honey, looks like we done done it."

The memory of Aunt Polly's iced tea reminded Mickey that he was really thirsty. He needed a drink and a short break from his recollections. A McDonald's was near the next exit, and Lostie probably needed to pee. A cold Dr. Pepper would hit the spot as they resumed their journey and Mickey went back to his memories.

THE END
Volume One

Volume Two finds Mickey back on the road, and his mind traveling memory lane. The book continues with a wealth of stories, including Mickey's journey and coming of age tale. The saga ends as Mickey leads his father's truck toward a setting sun. He has no worries; the old pickup knows the way back home to Walton's Creek.

About the Author

Rickie Zayne Ashby is retired and lives near Bowling Green, Kentucky, where much of his time is spent gardening and reading.

About the Artists

Eric Lindgren — Born in Idaho in 1962, Eric Lindgren wandered back and forth across the nation a few times before finally attending Western Kentucky University in Bowling Green, Kentucky. He and his wife of nearly thirty years are now residents in the city, and he has been producing whimsical fantasy line art that he turns into coloring books for kids and adults as well at DriveThruFiction.com under the title Meadowshire.

John Ward — National award-winning artist John L. Ward is known for his artistic talent and ability to capture on canvases the movements and expressions unique to his subject matter. A self-taught artist, John creates his art in a variety of mediums including oil, watercolor, color pencil, marker mixed media, and graphite.

John is a true Kentucky artist, living and working in the heart of the bluegrass state. John finds inspiration for his pictures from Kentucky's beautiful scenery and his life experiences. From horses, farms, wildlife, nature, and more, John's artwork features real sites and locations. John's artistic talent is vividly displayed on the front cover of this book.

Joe Vick — Born in Springfield, Missouri, Joe Vick has had a lifelong interest in art. Joe was raised by missionary parents in Ethiopia, and also lived in Norway for a period of time. He has traveled extensively throughout Europe and the United States. In 1983, at the age of 24, Joe received Christ as his personal savior. At that point, he also committed his art talent to the Lord Jesus Christ.

The art produced by Joe can be viewed at many shows throughout the Southeastern United States. He currently resides in Lyes, Tennessee, with his wife and nine children.